About the Author

Shannon Curtis has worked as a tea lady, waitress, distribution coordinator, dangerous goods handler, switch bitch, betting agent, and now runs her own creative services consultancy. She decided to write a story like those she loves to read whilst at home after the birth of her first child. Her first two books were shortlisted for Favourite Romantic Suspense by the Australian Romance Readers Association. Visit her website: shannoncurtis.com

Bewitched

Bewitched:
Seduced by the Enemy

SHANNON CURTIS

MILLS & BOON

First Published in Great Britain 2023
by Mills & Boon, an imprint of HarperCollins*Publishers* Ltd,
1 London Bridge Street, London, SE1 9GF

www.harpercollins.co.uk

HarperCollins*Publishers*
Macken House, 39/40 Mayor Street Upper,
Dublin 1, D01 C9W8, Ireland

ISBN: 978-0-263-31916-3

Printed and Bound in the UK using 100% Renewable Electricity
at CPI Group (UK) Ltd, Croydon, CR0 4YY

WARRIOR UNTAMED

Prologue

He heard the grate of a key in a lock, followed by the creak and clang as the gate at the far end of the corridor was slowly opened. He kept his eyes closed, bending and working the blazing colors in his mind like a fiery kaleidoscope. The warmth and light in his mind kept the dark chill at bay, the cold stone against his back and beneath his buttocks a sensation he'd learned to ignore.

He heard the whispers, the rough slide of regulation boots on stone floor, felt the faint stir in the air currents as one—no, two people made their way toward his cell. It was her scent, though, that caught his attention. Something light, floral…he could almost sense the innocence, the naïveté—the gullibility. He resisted the urge to smile. No sense in giving anything away.

The peephole in his cell door slid open, the noise an annoying squeal in the silence of the tomb—for this was a tomb. There was no other word for it. It was where they hoped he'd spend the rest of his lifetime, and the next.

"What's he doing?" He heard the woman whisper. He couldn't tell much from the soft sound, but her scent was now stronger, laced with a tired curiosity. Like a wilted frangipani.

"Dunno. Meditating. Plotting. Maybe just losing his sanity. He's like that all the time." He knew that voice, had become quite practiced at ignoring it, but this morning—or was it evening—he decided to give it his attention.

"He doesn't do anything else?" Her voice was raspy, as though even the question taxed her reserves. She sounded fatigued. Drained.

She didn't know the meaning of that word. *Drained.* But she would.

"Nope. Pretty easy duty, I must admit."

"Why is he locked all the way down here? There's nobody else in this block."

"The lights. There is no natural light in here, so it's fluorescent lighting."

He knew they couldn't see the clenching of his shoulder muscles beneath the rough fabric of his prison uniform, but he still tried to mask it with a deep inhalation. He needed something to relax him whenever he thought of his current circumstances, the weakness that even now leeched the energy from his limbs. He needed light. Or *something*. And he wasn't getting it down in the bowels of this prison, thanks largely to his sons.

White-hot rage welled inside him whenever he thought of their betrayal. Ryder, he could understand. That kid had always been ungrateful. But Hunter—his son's betrayal stung the most. Hunter had worked diligently by his side for years, just like a sheep, following his every command. Until that last night… The cold kiss of fury snaked down his back. He hadn't seen that betrayal coming. He'd always believed that if it came down to it, Hunter would choose his father over his brother, but his son had surprised him. Just like his mother.

He exhaled, expelling the tension. But he would have his due. The light, floral, stale scent of the prison guard teased his senses again. And soon.

"What do the lights have to do with anything?" he heard her whisper.

The rustle of fabric told him the guard was shrugging his shoulders. "Who the hell knows? We're just here to make sure he rots where he sits. He organized the murder of an Alpha Prime. He deserves everything coming his way."

There was a brief silence, and he found himself waiting for her response.

"I heard about that. He supposedly conspired with the Woodland Pack?"

"Yeah, with the Woodland Alpha Prime. But seeing as that was pack against pack, that case has been handed over to Alpine Pack under tribal jurisdiction."

"Well, it was their Alpha Prime who was murdered. But wasn't he murdered in some dentist's chair? Why is this guy here?"

He took another slow breath in. She was asking questions. Good. She had doubts. He was going to exploit that, and he was going to enjoy it.

"This guy organized the poison to be delivered. The dentist knew nothing about it. Get this—the dentist was his *son*."

His jaw muscles clenched. Well, Ryder had deserved it. Pulling away from the family like that, ignoring them. He'd ceased to be his son the day he started using his trust fund on his own practice—that would be in competition with the family's medical center. Hell. What did Ryder think would happen, that he'd actually give his blessing? He almost shook his head in disbelief, but kept himself still. What Ryder had done, well, it was to be expected. Hunter, though—that stung. That really, really stung. He thought he'd raised him better than that.

"But why is he *here*? He hasn't had a trial yet. I thought everyone was innocent until proven guilty?"

"Good grief, how long have you been working for Reform?" The male guard wheezed with laughter. "There's no such thing as innocence here."

"I just thought—"

"Don't. Don't think he can be saved, don't think he's decent and don't pity the bastard. Just look in on him once in a while, make sure he hasn't strung himself up with his bedsheets—or if he has, make sure he's good and dead before you call anyone."

There was a hesitation, then finally a sigh. "Sure. What else is there to do?"

"I'll show you the break room. It's going to be where you spend most of your time—the screen in there is awesome."

He heard the snick as the peephole was closed, then the soft shuffle of footsteps until they reached the gate at the end of the corridor. It wasn't until the gate had opened and closed, the keys had clinked as they turned in the lock and the scent had faded, that he let the sly smile lift his lips.

Arthur Armstrong opened his eyes slowly. They had no idea who they were dealing with.

Chapter 1

Melissa Carter tried to be patient. Really. But it wasn't her strongest personality trait. Actually, most would argue she didn't possess it at all. And she hadn't had a decent night's sleep in so long. "Anytime this century, Lexi."

Lexi glanced up and frowned. "If I have to wear this day in, day out, then I need to make sure it's *right*."

Melissa pursed her lips but refrained from comment as she let the young woman scan her rings for the fourth time. It was fine. She could handle this without screaming. She could prove her mother wrong and be *patient*.

"And it has to be a ring? Not a necklace?" Lexi asked wistfully, eyeing an intricately woven Celtic knot pendant on a stand behind the counter.

Melissa kept her expression neutral as she heard that same question for the third time. She shook her head. "No. You're likely to change a necklace depending on

the outfit. Or it might get snagged—or yanked. A ring
is more likely to stay on, and that's what we want for
you, Lexi. Something to stay with you." Her irritation
died as she remembered the reason for this, and she
kept the sympathy out of her eyes, out of her voice.
Lexi didn't need sympathy. There were times when she
thought Lexi needed a smack upside the head, but she'd
leave that to Lexi's older brother, Lance. For now, she
just wanted to make Lexi safe, and if Lexi had come to
her, it meant the young woman had come to the same
realization—she was out of her depth and needed help.
The fact she'd come to Melissa, well, perhaps *that* required some sympathy, but Melissa preferred action to
the warm and fuzzies.

She leaned over the tray, and scanned through the
silver jewelry. Usually she let the stones in the jewelry
speak to her clients, and attract them on their own. But
her bookstore was filling with customers, and Lexi suf-
fered a lack of confidence—hence her current situation. She still couldn't quite understand that one. Lexi
was beautiful. Blonde, petite, the kind of woman guys
wanted to do things for, like open doors and carry bags.
She sighed. She couldn't remember the last time someone offered to carry something for her. Oh, wait. Lexi's
brother, Lance, had—but he'd been carrying her supplies, and it had been his job, so that didn't really count.

"How's Lance doing?" She hadn't seen him for a few
weeks. She didn't get along with a lot of people, but
Lance was an exception. He was the only set of fangs
she allowed in her zone, with a special dispensation built
within her wards to give him access. He'd worked hard,
never complained—a trait she admired in her staff—and
had always been punctual. Not too chatty, but decent,
in a rough kind of way. She didn't make a habit of hir-

ing ex-cons, but he'd been her exception. He'd needed a job, she'd needed someone to haul supplies—and his fangs were actually the good kind. Perfect. The fact they'd formed a strong friendship surprised them both—and probably everyone who knew her, considering her personality didn't really lend itself to making a lot of friends. After what had happened with Theo, though... she blinked. Lance had gone above and beyond the duties of a friend, then.

"Haven't heard from him in a while," Lexi said, shrugging.

Melissa frowned. She knew the kind of trouble Lance chased. Admired him for it. "You're not worried?"

Lexi looked up and blinked, her eyes taking on a blank glaze. "What? No. Everything is fine," she said in a flat voice.

Melissa's eyes narrowed. Ri-ight. Lexi definitely needed to get away from the compelling effects of her current boyfriend.

"What about this one?" She tapped at a delicate ring. Its band was intertwined silver strands, and the stone was speckled with green and black. "Green snakeskin jasper. It's a protective stone, perfectly suited to what you need, and it matches your..." She flicked her gaze up to Lexi's eyes. Oh. They were a deep blue. Melissa's eyebrows dipped briefly. She'd never noticed that. Lexi's brother had worked as a stock boy—okay, stock *man*—for her a few years ago, and his eyes were the darkest green, almost black. She'd never noticed the siblings didn't share the same eye color. Her gaze drifted downward. "Scarf. They match your scarf."

Lexi wore a bottle green-and-black scarf to go with the rest of her outfit. She frowned. "But that's just today."

"And you look fantastic, so it obviously agrees with

you. With your coloring, this ring will either complement or present a tasteful contrast with any of your other outfits," Melissa lied quickly.

Lexi looked at it doubtfully. "Really?"

Melissa nodded as she plucked the ring from the tray. "Yep. Trust me. Let me go enhance it for you." She stepped into the back room behind the shop's counter— it was basically the size of a broom closet. She placed the ring on the midnight blue swath of velvet that lay on a low shelf. She closed the door and pulled on the cord. Warm light bathed the tiny space, and she stood there for a moment. Shelves lined the space, and a sporadic collection of small bottles, vials and bowls were placed in order of need around the working space. These were only her more commonly used ingredients. Her lips pursed. Not as many as there should be, thanks to the pyro jerk who had torched her hidden apothecary below her bookstore.

She was slowly renovating the space, though. It was no secret she was a witch—a witch who sold spells, incantations and laced trinkets. Those customers who wanted more than books usually stepped below stairs… but she'd learned a hard lesson five months ago. Never trust a soul—no matter how innocent and tempting he looked. She'd lost so much…it was taking a lot longer to rebuild her valuable stock, damn it.

As tiny and as bare as this space was, it was fast becoming a haven for her. There were no requests from customers, no pleading and no demands for attention in here, just her and her magic. She eyed the ring briefly. Green snakeskin jasper guarded against negativity and could act as a shield against psychic attack, protecting the wearer against harmful or destructive temptations. Lexi had a vampire boyfriend, and Melissa could sense the compulsions at work on the young woman. The fact Lexi was still wearing a scarf inside her store didn't escape her, either. It was cold outside, and dirty snow lined the gutters and sidewalks of Irondell as winter descended on the city, but inside the Better Read Than Dead Bookstore it was warm and cozy. Consciously or unconsciously, Lexi was hiding the bite marks and she needed a little help to withstand the mesmerizing coercions this man was exerting over her. If she didn't resist soon, she'd end up a vamp slave... Melissa shuddered. It was one thing she couldn't quite comprehend, those people who willingly surrendered their blood and actively sought to be bitten by the vamps, chasing one bite after another, after another. The life span of a vamp slave wasn't long, for obvious reasons. Why Lexi was with a bloodsucker in the first place, Melissa couldn't understand. But she could help.

She held both her hands over the ring, closed her eyes and drew on her magic. She could feel it rising to her fingertips like a warm bath of light, and she focused, chanting a protection spell to further imbue the natural qualities of the stone. She added in a little layer of confidence, as well. Lexi had to stop hanging out with the Mr. Wrongs, and start believing she was worthy of a Mr. Right—not that Melissa would ever have that kind of conversation with the woman. She soooo didn't do warm and fuzzies.

Melissa opened her eyes, and the stone in the ring glowed briefly as the spell anchored, and then the magical light slowly banked. Melissa lifted the ring, feeling the warmth and weight of its new power. She smiled with satisfaction. The ring was constructed of silver— she'd like to see Mr. Wrong try to take this off his little blood bag.

She left the broom closet—no, Power Room. She frowned. She had to come up with a better name for it. Maybe the Dark Well of Influence? She wrinkled her nose. She'd keep working on it.

She smiled brightly at Lexi and handed her the ring. "Here you go."

Lexi reached for it timidly, eyeing it before sliding it onto the middle finger of her right hand. She tilted her head, then her gaze flicked to Melissa across the counter.

"I don't feel anything. Are you sure it's working?"

Melissa rolled her eyes. "These things don't come with a built-in electric shock, Lexi. Give it time. It will grow on you."

Lexi sighed, then nodded. "Okay. I hope this works." She dug her wallet out of her handbag. "How much?"

Melissa named her price, and Lexi's eyebrows rose in surprise. "Oh, cool, I thought it would be more."

Normally it would, but Lexi was Lance's sister. This was the least she could do for a friend. She didn't have many friends.

Melissa met her gaze squarely. "Stay safe, Lexi."

Lexi nodded, then fidgeted with her scarf. "You do like to crank the heat up in here, don't you, Melissa?" She loosened the scarf, and Melissa could see the edge of a dark bruise, and the open, angry bite mark.

She reached beneath the counter. "Hey, try this." She handed over a small tub of lotion. Lexi tilted her head as she read the label.

"What is it?"

"An all-over body moisturizer with a new scent I've been working on. This is a sample bottle. Let me know what you think."

Lexi flipped the cap and sniffed the contents, then

smiled. "Okay, thanks." The young woman eyed her for a moment, and her brow dipped. "You look tired."

Melissa winced. "Thanks."

"No, seriously. You look tired, and you never look tired. What gives? Is your mom giving you grief?"

Melissa's smile was brittle. It was no secret her mother always gave her grief. "I'm not sleeping well," she admitted. She wasn't in the habit of confiding with Lexi—with anyone, really, but maybe it was an indication of just how tired she was that she relaxed her usual guard with the petite blonde.

Lexi raised her eyebrows. "Is something troubling you? Bad dreams?"

That was an understatement. It was as though all her awful life moments were on auto-replay whenever she closed her eyes. Especially the day her mother told her she'd never let her daughter step in as Elder Prime... And the night her father walked out... She blinked. Yeah. Those weren't dreams. They were nightmares. And she most definitely didn't want to "share" those. Not with Lexi, not with anyone.

"I'm fine. I'll just drink some chamomile tea tonight."

Lexi shrugged, then placed her items in her tote bag. "Whatever. I have to hustle. I have a hot date tonight."

Melissa smiled, mentally batting away a tiny green flame of envy that flared within her. One, she wasn't interested in any dates, hot or otherwise, and two, Lexi was dating a shadow breed, for Pete's sake. There was nothing worthy of envy there.

"Well, that moisturizer is guaranteed to make the night interesting," she murmured, and Lexi laughed as she left the store. Melissa watched her briefly in the street. The young woman eyed up and down the street, then loosened the scarf some more so it fell open. A smile twitched at Melissa's lips as Lexi strode down the street, a confident sway to her hips catching the eye of males passing by. The ring was working. Good.

She hoped Lexi would try that "moisturizer" as soon as she got home. It was a mix laced with lavender, chamomile and a heavy dose of verbena. No vampire would want to get near her if she slathered that toxic herb all over her.

Her watch beeped, and her smile fell. Great. Time to feed the pyro jerk. She beckoned Jenna, her assistant, over.

"Can you man the cash for me? I'm going to take a quick lunch break."

Jenna nodded, stepping behind the counter.

Melissa grabbed the brown paper bag and a plastic bottle of water from the bottom shelf of the counter, and strode toward the door behind a stack of books at the back of her store. When she reached that last stack, she pulled her heavy keyring from the front pocket of her jeans, and sifted through them until she found the two keys for the double-lock system she'd asked her brother, Dave, to install on the door, and then pulled on the cord that lit the stairwell. She could use her magic to open the doors, but loved to hear the click and snick of the locks. She skipped lightly down the stairs and stopped to key in the code to unlock the next intricate lock system she'd installed on the second door.

The heavy steel door swung inward and muted lighting automatically switched on, illuminating the work areas, but leaving the rest of the area in soft shadows. She stepped inside the large room. Now it bore little resemblance to the scarred and ashen remains of five months before. They'd installed fire-retardant hardwood and plastic composite to limit the possibility of a fire occurring again. Like anything below surface, this place was off the plans, off-the-record—and not insured. She'd have her apothecary back soon, and then she'd be able to do more than just bespell jewelry and mix herbs into lotions and drinking drafts. She'd be able to do some considerable damage to the damned shadow breeds. Her eyes narrowed, and she stepped farther into her secret space.

It was the door she'd cleverly painted as an intricately carved tree trunk that she now made her way over to. This one had a series of locks, but was also warded, so she waved her hand to lift the spelled lock, then opened the door. She grabbed the large torch that she hung off a hook just behind the door, flicked it on and stepped carefully down into the dark void, her sneakers squeaking softly on the steep narrow metal steps that led down into the darkness. The light emitted was blue—something she knew her prisoner couldn't draw on.

The air down here was dank and musty. She took a deep breath. Metal. Rust. Concrete. Stone. It wasn't exactly a forgiving place, all hard surfaces and cold darkness. She thought of her prisoner, and her mouth firmed. A fitting place for the pyro jerk. Goose bumps rose on her arms as she located the trapdoor. That trapdoor was about three stories below street level, and she'd never ventured beyond it. She'd opened it once, hauled it up with the help of a crowbar. She'd been curious... but when she'd crouched at the lip of the hole, she'd paused. Listened.

Something had slithered in the darkness, something that breathed, and...*waited*. She'd leaned forward, and the shuffling noise sped up, grew louder, and she just managed to replace the lid—but not before she caught the glimpse of that pale hand with the elongated gray fingernails.

Even now, she shuddered at the memory. Creepy. She'd heard tales of Old Irondell—hell, every parent seemed to enjoy bouncing their child on their knee and freaking the crap out of them with the old stories—hers included.

But that's what they were to most people—stories. Wicked, cautionary tales to make kids toe the line and not wander off.

Only, she knew they weren't *just* stories. Old Irondell may be just a pale memory that was passed down, less and less, from one generation to the next. But there were some folks who still knew of the origins of the Reformation, of the time of The Troubles, when humanity discovered the existence of the shadow breeds: the vampires, werewolves, shifters and other creatures that were just plain weird, but who seemed to be on a mission to eat, or kill, or eat *and* kill any human they encountered. It had started a war that had lasted generations, until the time of Resolution, when all breeds gathered to negotiate a truce, which led to the Reformation, the redefining of territories and laws, and society itself. The homeless, the outcasts, those who didn't "fit" into the normal, new Reform society had migrated to dwell below Irondell, away from the light. Away from Reform law. Nobody went into Old Irondell and came out unchanged.

If they ever returned. Most didn't.

She didn't need to go into Old Irondell. She had enough problems dealing with the shadow breeds above surface.

She turned back to the door, slid the peephole open and peered through the slot. There he was. Pyro jerk.

That mean, homicidal son of a—oh. Wow. She swallowed.

He was doing a handstand. Correction, he was doing push-ups in a handstand position. He was shirtless and the jeans he wore were smeared with dirt, rust and grime. His chest glistened, his muscles rippling with each dip and raise, from the corded strength of his broad shoulders down to the ridged abdomen that showed the control and power of each move. His hair was long, touching the floor when he moved, and the beard that covered his jaw gave him a wild, untamed look. She'd made a point of providing her prisoner with a bucket of water every other day so he could wash, but she'd never seen him actually bathe, or sweat—or glisten. She swallowed again.

He pushed himself up, exhaling in a gust, then slowly lowered his feet to the ground with the grace of a gymnast. He rose from his position, his back to her, and he rolled his shoulders. There wasn't an ounce of fat on him. Sure, he'd been on a prison diet for the last five months, but still, he didn't look like he was wasting away. No. He looked….healthy. Very…healthy. The chains that connected his wrists to the bolt in the wall clanked with his movements. She stared at that glorious wall of muscle, his figure an enticing V that narrowed into lean hips and a tight, tantalizing butt. He turned his head from side to side, as though stretching out some kinks, shook out those massive arms and then paused.

His head turned slowly to his right. He didn't face her, but she could see the corner of his mouth lift up in a sexy little curl.

"Why, hello, Red."

A sneaky, traitorous warmth flared inside her at his familiarity, quickly squashed by a wave of annoyance. No warmth for him, damn it.

Chapter 2

Hunter turned to face the door, refusing to let her presence bother him. She was right on time. He wasn't sure if his captor's punctuality was something he appreciated, or whether it irritated the hell out of him. It depended on his mood. He stood there for a moment, assessing his mood, and his stomach growled. Okay, so today it was appreciation. He was hungry, and she'd brought him food.

He raised his hands to his hips and tilted his head back to meet the green-eyed gaze of the witch behind the door. She stared at him for a moment, her gaze full of suspicion and wariness. He wasn't going to try anything. He'd learned that lesson. Four times. Didn't mean he wouldn't try again, he just wasn't feeling it today.

"Back up against the wall." Her voice was low, husky and, just like yesterday, and the day before, and the day before that, the sound curled inside him, and he hated it

as much as he enjoyed it. Five months he'd been trapped
in this hole in the wall. Five lonely months. He'd never
really been a social kind of guy, but after too many
months of his own company, he was beginning to look
forward to these too-brief moments of company with the
bitchy witch. Crave it, even. Resented it, but craved it.

Yeah, he was a sick bastard. He backed up against
the wall as instructed and folded his arms. If he didn't
threaten her, his cold little captor might stay longer.

The key clanked in the lock, and then the heavy
steel door swung inward. She stepped into the room,
and straightaway, he could smell her, *feel* her. Cinnamon and smoke. Lazy heat. He didn't think the smoke
could be blamed on him, though. He'd heard the sounds
from above, the drilling, banging and clanging. They'd
cleaned up that little mess he'd made. No, that scent of
smoke was entirely of her own making. He was pretty
sure his captor dabbled with fires of her own. As usual,
she carried a torch. He hid a smile. She'd done her re-
search. No candles, no flames, no access to sunlight, no
fire of any kind...and blue light. But blue light was notoriously difficult to get hold of, so his captor had used
a blue slide over the head of the torch. Sure the color
of the light was blue, and gave an interesting hue to her
skin, making her look otherworldly, but it was still light
behind the shade. He could still use the feeble light of a
torch to feed his power, if only a little. Yeah, they hadn't
put *that* little tidbit in the history books. It wasn't the
most efficient way for him to recharge—the light warriors had made sure to keep that one secret, too—but
the glow from a torch did help. Each day, she fed him,
both in food and energy.

Today she wore some sort of silky green top that
flowed about her. It didn't hug her form, but just hinted

at the willowy, lithe frame beneath. Her jeans were tucked into leather boots. Boots with heels he knew from experience that hurt like the dickens if she kicked him.

She crossed to the pulley of chains that hung against the wall, set the brown paper bag and bottle of water on the floor and started to drag down on a length of chain. His jaw tightened as the iron chafed against his skin, and he could feel the sting as the cuff burned him. He thought he'd get used to it—especially with the efforts he'd put into those chains recently, but he hadn't. Each contact of the metal with his body was like a hot poker to his skin.

Soon his right hand rose with each pull on the chain, and when she was satisfied with the position of his arm, she roped the chain around a hook on the wall. Then she started with the second chain. She did this every time, and he sighed. Damn her caution.

Of course, he'd given her good reason to exercise it whenever she was around him.

She left just enough give in the chain for him to have a limited range of movement with his left arm, then stooped to pick up the brown paper bag. He eyed the silky top as it gaped open with her movement, and he caught a glimpse of the creamy swell of her breasts, the scalloped pattern of black lace. He should be angry at himself. One, for being a pervert, and two, for spying on *her*. But, no. Five months. No sex. *Angry* wasn't the right word for what he was feeling.

She opened the bag and pulled out a sandwich wrapped in plastic. She unwrapped it, then tossed it to him.

He caught it easily, eyeing the distance between them. She was just outside of his reach. Pity. He had fantasies of her stepping too close, of him stepping up and grabbing her, of him…doing wicked things. And then he'd call himself all sorts of a pathetic idiot for thinking anything remotely lustful about his captor and would replace those secret fantasies with something harsher, like forcing her to set him free.

He stared at her for a moment. She had red hair that looked like it had a life of its own, all vibrant curls and shiny locks, and green eyes that were a vivid spark of color, the pale complexion with a faint tinge of pink high on the cheeks was smooth and clear. The woman had the face of an angel, a body built for sin…and the ferocious temperament of a saltwater crocodile at sunset.

He looked down at the sandwich. Peanut butter and jelly. He was heartily sick of that combination, but damn it, he was also hungry. At least she gave him something more substantial in the evenings. Mostly. He tried to lower his other hand to hold the sandwich properly, but the chain clanked against the wall, and he hissed softly at the sting at his wrist. He covered the noise with a tight smile.

"Come on, Red," he crooned. "How about loosening up the other one?"

She arched an eyebrow and stepped back. "You only need one hand to eat, jerk."

His lips pulled up at the corners. And there it was, her regular endearment. He gestured toward her. "What, you're not going to join me? We could swap sandwiches and bitch about our boyfriends."

She would come, feed him, and when she was sure he'd eaten, she'd fetch him the bottle of water so he could wash it down. Before she left, she'd loosen the chains enough so that he had more slack in his restraints. Enough for him to make use of the crude seat fashioned on a stone ledge across the stone room he'd called home for way too long, and to walk a little around the room.

"Just eat."

He should be thankful they were now on speaking terms. For the first two months of his captivity she'd treated him to a cold silence—and a blinding headache each time he tried to talk to her.

Or attack her.

He chewed on his peanut butter and jelly sandwich, then forced the food down his throat. "You know, one day we'll have a proper meal together, Red. I'm thinking filet mignon and a glass of fine wine."

"I'm thinking I'd rather hang myself up by hooks in my eyelids than spend one evening with you," she said, folding her arms and leaning back against the stone wall. He watched as she crossed one long, slender leg over the other. Again, something curled inside him, something he resented, but couldn't fight. Yeah. Five months, no sex. It screwed with your brain, making the most unsuitable woman seem compellingly attractive. Desirable. Sweet. He met those frosty green eyes again. Maybe not *that* sweet.

He needed to get out of here. He wanted to get back to work. Being alone with his thoughts was depressing. Too much time to think, to remember. To grieve…to regret. *Ugh*. He needed to work, otherwise he just sat here in this cold, dank little hole with only his memories and Steve to keep him company. At the thought of the rat he'd befriended, he broke off a portion of his sandwich and tucked it into his jeans pocket for later. She watched his movements, but just like every other day, didn't query him. Probably thought he was squirreling away afternoon tea. He almost laughed at the suggestion of decorum and propriety in this misery. He took another bite of the sandwich, and chewed slowly, drawing their time together out. She glanced pointedly at her watch, and he grinned.

"If this cuts into your day, Red, you could always release me," he suggested smoothly. "Just think—you wouldn't have to spend so much of your culinary talents on me, such as they are. You wouldn't have to stand and wait, watching me chew every bite...wouldn't have to watch your back every second you're down here. Set me free, Red."

She rolled her eyes. "Don't you ever get tired of this conversation?"

He shrugged. "I'm afraid I'm not much of a conversationalist after being in the dark for so many months."

Her gaze flicked around the cell. "You brought this on yourself."

His gaze dropped. Yes, well, he couldn't argue with that. "Why don't we start over?" He smiled, calling on his customary charm he knew worked so well with the ladies.

Her eyes narrowed, and she straightened from the wall. "You tried to kill me. There's no starting over."

Except for this lady.

He sighed. "How long can you hold a grudge?" he asked, tilting his head to the side. "Aren't you bored with this yet? Isn't it exhausting, keeping me fed and watered, dreaming up new tortures? All that effort..."

She smiled, but it wasn't a warm, friendly smile, and she stepped closer. "Oh, I still post hate mail to my first ex. That's since second grade."

He eyed her. He couldn't tell if she was joking or not.

"Look, I'm sorry. How many times do I have to say it?"

"If you mean it, only once." The remark was quietly

spoken, and gave him pause. Her green gaze was blazingly direct. He ate the rest of his sandwich, forcing the gooey mess down his throat. Her gaze dipped to his throat, then lower, before it flickered away. Not quick enough that he didn't notice it, though—or the faint bloom of color in her cheeks.

Interesting.

He lifted his hand to indicate the gloomy room. "Trust me, I'm sorry."

She nodded. "Yeah. You're sorry you're stuck here. That's what you're sorry for." She turned back to the door, halted, then faced him. "You tried to kill me," she said, her voice low and shaking with anger.

He held up a finger. "No, I just wanted to destroy your shop," he corrected her.

Her eyes rounded. "With me in it."

He winced. "Yeah, well, that was my bad." He did feel guilty over that. Just a little. Not that he'd let her know.

Her lips firmed, and he focused on her mouth, those full, pouty lips that were pressed together so tightly. "You torched my apothecary. Do you have any idea what you've cost me? Or my clients? I have had to turn away people in need because of you."

He snorted. "Please. You create more damage than you know with your little witchy-woo spells and potions. I spend half my time cleaning up your messes."

She tilted her head back, her vibrant red curls a blaze of color in the gloomy, torchlit cell. "Oh, that's right. You're *their* doctor."

He'd have to be blind and deaf to miss her contempt, particularly when she talked about the shadow breeds like some stinky mess she'd stepped in and needed to wipe off her shoe. He smiled dryly. "I'm getting this vibe that you're not really into the shadow breeds."

Her smile was brittle and tight, and she stepped away from the wall, strolling slowly toward him. "Were-wolves, vampires, shifters...your kind," she said, casually lifting a hand to indicate him, "you all deserve to die." She said it so matter-of-factly, he almost didn't take offense. "You consume humans, with little or no regard for our lives. You all behave as though we are of no consequence, and yet you think the problem is ours when we arm ourselves against you." She shook her head. "Hypocrite."

His eyebrows rose. "*I'm* the hypocrite? You talk as though we're the only ones capable of evil, yet you create the cruelest weapons for your precious humans to use against the breeds. Do you have any idea what your wolfsbane tisanes do to the intestines, to the stomach or throat? You think *we* are cruel, yet slipping a toxic corrosive to a living being is all in a day's work for you." As a shadow breed healer he'd seen the horrors humans had subjected the shadow breeds to, and had made it his mission to help them. "You've held me here for months, *starving* me of light. That's the cruelest torture for one of my kind, yet you stand here and spout righteous indignation when you are guilty of doing the same yourself."

"You are so deluded. You are here because you tried to *incinerate* me."

"You're fine," he retorted. He still couldn't figure out how that had happened. "I didn't even singe you."

"Only because I had defenses, not because that was your intention," she snapped, stepping closer. This close, he could see the rosy bloom of anger high on her cheeks.

"And I've been paying for it ever since. Let me go. Let me get back to my life, to my work." Hell, what had happened to his clinic in all this time? Had his brother, Ryder, stepped in? Or did it lie in ruins? Despite what everyone thought, he did care about the business, about what they did. Well, what he did. He had been surprised to discover what his father had been doing... His work was the only good thing about him. If he didn't have his work, then he really was the selfish, destructive bastard everyone claimed him to be.

He'd be just like his father.

Damn it, he'd been confined in this prison for long enough.

First there'd been the spiders, then the rats. She'd even covered the floor with snakes once. Sure, it had been an illusion, a spell, but he'd still felt trapped, and the hallucinations had been terrifying.

Never piss off a witch.

"And you'll be paying for it for a long time to come," she said fiercely.

"If you hate me so much, why don't you kill me?" he challenged her in frustration. "Just end this. Let me go, or kill me."

Because if she didn't, he'd go mad. He was sure of it.

"Come on, set me free. You can trust me. I'm a doctor." He flashed her his most charming smile.

She rolled her eyes.

"Let me go, or end this," he urged her.

Her gaze flickered, then she masked her expression behind a cool, brittle smile. "Oh, but we're only just getting started."

"Red, if you still want me around after five months, maybe it's not revenge you're after," he said softly, suggestively. He knew he was poking the bear, but she started it.

"You think I won't hurt you?" She shook her head as she stepped even closer, and he measured the decreasing distance between them.

"Oh, I think you could," he said, leaning forward ever so slightly. "But I don't think you'll kill me." The realization hit him like a spark of lightning, and he wondered why the hell he hadn't figured that out much earlier. "You've had five months to do it—but you haven't." He tilted his head. "I wonder why not?"

Something flickered in her gaze, and her lips tightened. He'd hit a nerve. Triumph washed over him. God, he'd finally found a crack, a weakness. "You. Can't. Kill me." He drew the words out slowly. "Am I paying for your daddy issues, little girl?"

Her eyes narrowed, and that was all the warning he got—it was all the warning he needed. She swung at him. He caught her wrist, pulling her around with one hand as he yanked at the chain tethering his other.

There was a loud crack. Bricks crashed to the floor as the old pulley tore away from the ceiling, and then he had her back pressed up against him.

"Tut-tut, Red. You got too close."

Chapter 3

Melissa didn't quite know how he did it, but the bastard broke his chain. Just one, but it was enough to give him dangerous freedom. With one arm around her neck and the other wrapped around her waist and trapping her arms, he lifted her clear off the floor. She experienced a brief flare of panic. She tried to kick, tried to dig her heel into his instep, but he dodged her easily.

"Let's end this now, Red. One way or another. Let me go, or I'll snap your pretty little neck."

"Let me go," she gasped past the press of his arm against her throat.

"What? You don't like to be held against your will? Try it for *five months*," he muttered, his lips near her ear, then grunted as she lashed out with her foot. She made contact, but her kick had no force behind it.

The strength in his arms was frightening, yet he just held her. The breadth of his shoulders easily bracketed her own body, and she could feel his muscles bunch as he bore her weight. He could crush her. He could easily do as he threatened and snap her neck—but he didn't. He held her. Then he did something that shocked her.

He leaned forward and rubbed his chin against her neck. His beard brushed against her sensitive skin, at once soft yet prickly, and the rough sensation set her trembling. "Come on, Red. You know you don't hate me."

Her breath hitched, and her nipples peaked at the tingles that spread down her neck, bringing a warm flush along with it. His naked chest was a wall of heat against her back, and his hips cradled her butt. Awareness, sharp and consuming, swept over her. She could feel him against her, every ridge of muscle against her back, the strength of his thighs and something that throbbed and moved against her, which created an answering pulse deep in her core. Her breasts swelled. *No.* She wasn't— she couldn't—*no.*

She stiffened in his arms. "No, I *loathe* you," she said through gritted teeth. She twisted her wrist until her palm could make contact with his muscular forearm, and she latched on, pouring every inch of her resentment into that contact. She whispered a spell. Heat seared between them, and she tightened her grip. He grunted. Hissed. His arm moved slightly, and she managed to move her other arm until her hand could press against the outside of his thigh, and she clutched him, focusing her power on those two points of contact. The heat increased. She could feel his skin blistering under her hand, smell the fabric of his jeans burning.

His breath hitched, then he let her go, pushing her away. She whirled, hands raised, and an invisible force threw him against the wall behind him, holding him against the brick surface.

"Argh!" He tried to pull away, tried to reach for her, and she curled her fingers until he threw his head back in pain. "Stop it!"

She'd captured him initially with the help of her brother—and that was only after Hunter had exhausted himself in a battle first against his brother, and then his Warrior Prime of a father. Keeping the pyro jerk imprisoned on her own was proving a challenge. If it wasn't for the iron cuffs he wore that bound his light warrior magic, he would have already overpowered her.

Melissa retreated and didn't let up on the force she was directing against him until she reached the door. She clenched her hands and shoved her fists in a downward motion, and her prisoner collapsed to the floor. He moaned as he clasped his head, curling up into the fetal position, and she stormed out into the tunnel. With a flick of her fingers, the door slammed behind her, the lock sliding home. She strode up the corridor, fuming.

She'd gotten too close. She should have known better. He was like a viper, waiting for you to get within striking distance. Five months ago she'd been tempted by him, by his devilish smile and wicked brown-eyed gaze when he'd walked into her store. He'd been so confident, so darn cocky, saying he'd heard she was the best witch in Irondell with the best supplies, best spells, best concoctions—and the best strain of wolfsbane, and she'd swallowed his flattery, hook, line and sinker. She'd taken him into her apothecary, just like he'd taken her in with his false compliments.

She'd been thinking how gorgeous he was, and was even returning the flirty banter as she'd opened up her order book. Then her world had exploded. Fire, heat, and those brown eyes shot with burning flecks of red amber as he'd cast his flames throughout her little store. Then he'd backed out and closed the door, closing her inside her inferno.

He'd used her. She'd found out later he'd been trying to turn to ash any evidence of his brother's involvement in a murder. He'd smiled at her. Teased her. Tempted her.

Torched her.

She pulled herself up the steep staircase that led back to her apothecary, trying to shoot strength into her shaking arms. That comment, though…the one about her father…that was—weird. For the past few weeks she'd been dreaming of the night he'd left—and other nightmares. She hesitated. Could he…? She shook her head. She didn't know that anyone could do *that*. She closed the door behind her, engaging all the locks and wards, and then sagged against its surface, craving the unmovable support.

Tears burned beneath her eyelids. For a moment, ever so brief…she shook her head. No. Not *that* guy. Not ever.

"You look like you've seen a ghost," a woman's voice murmured from the gloom.

Melissa startled, then peered across the room. A figure moved away from the wall, stepping into the soft pool of light. Melissa closed her eyes briefly. She wasn't in the mood for this.

"Mother," she greeted the woman with resignation. "What are you doing here?"

"I came to see how your…" Her mother hesitated briefly, then continued "…project was coming along."

For a moment, Melissa thought her mother was talking about the renovation. Then almost laughed. Right. The last time her mother had shown any interest in her life was five months ago, when they'd had a terrible argument.

Over the pyro jerk downstairs.

"Well, as you can see, the apothecary is coming along nicely," Melissa said, deliberately taking the obvious direction for conversation.

Her mother's green eyes flared briefly. "I meant our little light warrior," her mother stated succinctly, folding her arms.

Melissa glared at her. "He's not *our* little light warrior, Mother. He's mine." She frowned at the possessive phrasing, realizing it probably sounded completely different than the way she intended. "And he's not so little."

She closed her eyes. And yep, that could be taken out of context, too. Her heart still pumped at being held against that large body, so much stronger than her own. She told herself the elevated heart rate, the sensitive... she folded her arms over her chest. Adrenaline. That's all it was, adrenaline.

"Please tell me he's still alive," Eleanor Carter didn't bother to hide her exasperation.

Melissa faced her mother reluctantly. "What if he's not, Mother? What if he's dead? How would that make you feel?"

"Do not play with me, Melissa," Eleanor snapped. "He is a light warrior, for heaven's sake. Do you know how rare that is?"

"With the way they make enemies? Trust me, Mother, it's as much a surprise to me as it is to you this one has survived as long as he has." She walked across the room to the door and the stairwell that would lead to her shop.

"He would make a useful ally, Melissa. He's in our debt. Use it to your advantage—and for God's sake, don't screw it up," her mother ordered as she followed closely. "You know we have to nurture this relationship."

Melissa halted at the door. "That is so ironic—you talking about nurturing." She bit off a brittle laugh.

"Melissa! You never stand back to look at the big picture. He is valuable."

Melissa whirled. "What about me, Mother? What value do you have for *me*?" Anger flared to encapsulate her hurt. "He tried to kill me, Mother, and all you can talk about is creating an alliance with the pyromaniac psychopath. What about *me*? Don't I matter in this? Why aren't you angry that he tried to kill your daughter? And if not your daughter, at the very least one of your coven. Why aren't you knocking down that door to tear his heart out?" *Why won't you fight for me?* She turned and stomped up the stairs.

The door at the head of the stairs slammed shut, and Melissa halted, pursing her lips. This is how her mother had dealt with conversations when she was a teen, for Pete's sake. She turned around to face her mother, arms folded.

Eleanor Carter slowly walked up the stairs until they were on the same tread and they could meet each other's gaze on an equal level. "Do not lecture me on defending my coven, Melissa," her mother stated in a cold tone, and Melissa realized she was no longer talking to her parent. "You may be my daughter and a Coven Scion, but you are still only a second-degree witch, and I am your Elder Prime. Do not presume to discipline *me* on coven matters." Eleanor lifted her chin. "You are popular with the humans, and you are gifted, but you still behave like a liability, whereas that light warrior is an asset. *That* is why I'm not tearing his heart out."

Eleanor flicked her fingers, and the door opened.

She walked into the bookstore, chin up and shoulders back, looking every inch the coven regent she was. Melissa stayed in the stairwell for a moment, blinking back the burn. God, she was so pathetic, always hoping her mother would for once put her daughter before her coven.

Should have known better.

She stomped up the steps and slammed the door shut behind her, closing off all thoughts of the "asset" downstairs, and the humiliating pain that her mother valued the man who'd tried to kill her more than her own daughter.

Hunter held out the remains of his sandwich to the rat. "You better fill up while you can, Steve. Might be a while before we get another feed."

He winced as he shuffled back against the wall. His body ached. Everywhere. His burns were almost healed, though. It had taken him a few hours longer than usual to mend—a sign of his low reserves. He grimaced. "Mental note—knock her out, next time. She hits like a...witch." He tilted his head back against the brick behind him. She hadn't brought down the evening meal. He supposed he deserved that. He hadn't intended to start anything with her today. It had just...happened.

He frowned. Things just happened a lot around him. She'd been right. Her surviving their meeting in her apothecary was purely based on her luck, not his design. He'd had one thought—protect his brother. He hadn't spared the witch any consideration when he'd obliterated all records of her orders.

He and Ryder hadn't been on speaking terms when Jared Gray, Alpha Prime to the Alpine Pack, had died in his brother's surgery, poisoned by wolfsbane. His first instinct was to slap some sense into his brother for committing a crime that could be so easily traced back to him. His second instinct was to hide any evidence connected to the case. If they couldn't prove his guilt, they couldn't convict his brother.

How was he supposed to know his brother wasn't the coldhearted murderer Hunter thought he was? Okay, so it didn't help that his brother had thought the same thing about him. Turns out, they were both wrong. Their father, on the other hand, could account for at least two murders. Hunter didn't want to think about the probability that there were more. He eyed Steve. The rat held the morsel of the sandwich in his front paws, nibbling at it delicately.

"Such petite table manners, Steve. You know, I think folks underestimate you rats." He shifted again, getting a little more comfortable in his stone-and-brick cell. He forced himself to relax. It was night. He wasn't quite sure what time, but he could sense the sun had set. Over the last few weeks he'd gone dreamwalking. He'd learned quite a lot about his temperamental prison warden as she'd slept. He'd managed to crack the locks on some of the memories she'd tried to shield. She'd been happy, once. A red-haired sprite with a cheeky sense of humor. That had changed, though, the night her father had left. He'd played that one over a few times, just to try to understand it, but it was a garbled mess in there. Her emotions were too jumbled to get much of a read.

Perhaps tonight he could find out why she hated the shadow breeds so much? If he could find that key, he could use it to his advantage.

Closing his eyes, he regulated his breathing, allowing himself to slip into slumber, his consciousness drifting away from his body as he started his dreamwalk. It didn't take long to find her subconscious—he'd made the trip enough times he could find her easily enough.

Melissa carefully picked her way down the steps into the grand ballroom. Oh, wow. She hadn't been to a Reform society debutante ball since, well, since Theo. Couldn't quite figure out why she was at one, now. Where was Theo? There was something bothering her, but she couldn't quite put her finger on it. She tried to remember how this had come to be, but each time she tried to recall how she got here, her thoughts danced and flitted, and she couldn't follow anything down to its source. She sighed. She felt like she should be worried, perhaps even alarmed, but even those thoughts zipped away, as though dancing with the wind.

She glanced around the opulent ballroom. As a teen, she'd thought it was a romantic event, magical even—a sign of maturity and acceptance. Then she'd discovered what a tedious torture they were, with all the Scions of the Prime classes gathered in some sort of archaic custom of forging alliances among the Reform elite.

She tripped, bracing a hand against a nearby wall to catch herself. She glanced down. What the…? She gaped. She was wearing an emerald green gown, with a strapless beaded bodice and flowing skirt. She couldn't see her shoes, and her hair was such a heavy weight on her head, she didn't want to bend over too much in case she overbalanced. But she could look down enough to see her outfit. She was wearing a bodice that seemed to cover only half her chest. Oh. My. God. She straightened to prevent displaying her full assets. She wasn't wearing a bra, but the bodice support was gravity-defying.

She fingered the satin of the skirt. It was quite simply the most beautiful thing she'd ever worn. And the most feminine. She wished Theo could see her in it. But he wouldn't. Regret bloomed, stiff and uncomfortable. Why wouldn't he? Again, the flutter of something at the edge of her consciousness teased her. She blinked, and her eyelashes brushed a solid edge. She raised her hands to touch her face. She was wearing a mask. She had no idea what it looked like, but she could feel the crystals on the surface. Her wrist caught her eye. Where was her tattoo? Two years ago her brother had etched it into her skin—painstakingly and way too gleefully, she'd thought at the time. But now, the inside skin of her wrist was smooth and unmarked. Confusion and concern for the missing mark teased at her, like the gossamer wings of a dragonfly, before fluttering away.

She stepped farther into the ballroom, her gaze flickering from one elegant sight to the next. Waiters bearing crystal flutes filled with champagne—or blood for the vampires. Her lips tightened. She could see them, despite their masks, their alabaster skin a dead giveaway. The lycans, too, were easy to spot, with their longer, thicker hair, the rebellious attitude they all seemed born with—and their obvious antipathy toward the vamps.

Her fingers curled as she raised them, and she startled when a waiter stepped in front of her, offering her a glass of blush pink champagne. She accepted it, sighing brusquely. Her mother would not like it if she used magic against a fellow Scion. It was encouraged for the offspring of the Prime leaders to get along—at least at the ball. She glanced around the room. An elegant cage full of monsters.

"What are you looking for?" a deep voice murmured above her right ear. She managed not to flinch, although she couldn't quite hide the shiver that tingled down her back at the low masculine voice so close to her ear, the whisper of breath across her collarbone.

"An escape, perhaps?" she commented casually as she slowly turned, raising the glass of champagne to her lips. When she faced him, she forgot to drink.

He was tall, his black jacket perfectly tailored for his broad shoulders and muscular arms. The dark vest he wore over the white dress shirt emphasized his narrow waist and lean hips, and the black bow tie highlighted the strong column of his throat. He looked like a tall drink of handsome, barely contained strength poured into a dark suit. The mask concealed the upper half of his face, but the strong jawline and sculpted lips she could see were tantalizing, attractive, with an inherent pout that was undeniably sexy—and frustratingly familiar. Recognition—just like the memories of how she wound up here tonight—dipped and danced out of reach. Her gaze lifted. His dark hair was cut short, but still long enough for her to play with—if she'd just reach up and…

Her fingers tightened around the stem of her glass. If he was at the ball, he was a Scion. She didn't play with Scions. That would delight her mother and she made a practice of not delighting her mother. She refused to participate in the woman's political power plays.

The dark eyes behind the mask turned assessing, and he tilted his head. "They all seem nice enough," he commented, inclining his head to the crowd behind her.

She stared at him. His skin was tanned, a healthy complexion that didn't suit a vampire, and he didn't give off a lycan vibe. She was curious, but that in itself was enough of a warning for her. She hadn't been curious about a guy since Theo. Wasn't ready to be curious about a guy. Not now, and hopefully not ever. She glanced around the room. Where was Theo? She wanted to go home.

"It's just not my kind of scene," she murmured, and sipped from her glass.

His gaze flicked to the open French doors and he smiled. "Then why don't we change the scene?" he suggested, lifting his hand to indicate the terrace outside in a graceful gesture. For a moment she stared at his hand. Long fingers that looked courtly in their gesture, yet masculine, and a steady palm that showed a solid, stable strength. The hands of a musician with the strength of a warrior. The thought came out of nowhere, distracting and disturbing, and she shook it off. She was the Scion of the White Oak Coven; she could more than handle herself with any man in this room.

She clutched her skirt, lifting it slightly to step outside without falling flat on her face. The night air was warm, with a slight breeze that was like a sensual trail of ethereal fingers across the skin. Her brows dipped. Surprisingly balmy for December—but Reform balls were always held in October. She was sure it was snowing outside…again, something fluttered in her mind, easily ignored. Small starbursts of color bloomed in the pots evenly spaced along the balustrade, white roses unfurling under the stars.

She stepped out of the light of the doorway to face the stranger. "So tell me, which Prime family are you associated with?"

He shrugged. "Does it matter?" He grinned, and she stared at the sexy tilt of his lips, the flash of white teeth. "Honestly, I never really got into these events. Always thought they were too pompous. Didn't realize the company could be so beautiful."

Her cheeks warmed as his dark eyes flared with a

heated appreciation that was hard to miss, despite the mask. An appreciation that was returned. Despite her champagne, her mouth felt dry, and something lazy and sensual uncurled deep within her.

"So, you're not really a fan, huh?" she whispered, intrigued someone else viewed the marriage mart and alliance negotiations with as much disdain as she did. Intrigued by a man who seemed neither vampire nor lycan—or any of the other shifter breeds.

He took the glass from her hand and placed it on the ledge of the stone balustrade that bordered the terrace, his gaze dropping to focus on the cleavage revealed by her low-cut bodice. His lips curled higher, his gaze grew hotter and her heart thumped in her chest. "I could be changing my mind about that," he whispered, raising his hands to cradle her face, turning her until the base of her spine pressed against the balustrade. Her heart thumped a little faster. She didn't feel physically threatened, but something whispered to her, something full of warning and wickedness, and yet it didn't frighten her. It excited her.

His scent, something wicked and musky, with patchouli and a faint undertone of amber, enveloped her, entrancing her, and she slowly raised her hands to his broad shoulders—not sure yet whether she was pushing him away or drawing him closer.

Then he lowered his lips to hers.

There was no soft teasing or gentle awakening, Melissa realized. His mouth demanded, and she delivered, parting her lips as his tongue swept in to rub against hers. His hands delved into the intricate curls on top of her head, angling her head so he could deepen the kiss. Over and over, his mouth moved against hers. Her pulse began to throb in her ears as a sensual warmth swept over her. He pressed against her, and she could feel the breadth of his shoulders, the strength in the biceps that bunched as he pulled her closer, ever closer. She moaned softly, tilting her head back as he explored her mouth, her heart thumping in her chest, her breasts swelling as arousal, hot and hungry, flared within her.

He bent down, his hands sliding over the back of her skirts, and she felt the earth shift as he lifted her up and settled her on the balustrade. His lips left hers to trail a hot caress down the side of her neck, and moist heat gathered between her legs as she tried to wrap her thighs around his waist, the cumbersome skirts an aggravating barrier between their bodies. Cool air teased against the moist trail, and her nipples tightened at the sensation. He pressed his hips against hers, and damp heat flared between her thighs. She tilted her head back as he rubbed himself against her in a carnal dance that had her aching for more. *Now.*

The erotic heat spread from her chest to her thighs, and she writhed against him, craving skin-on-skin contact and deliciously frustrated by their clothing. He nipped, his teeth sharp but delicate, causing the pinpricks of sensation to dart down to her nipples and farther. He licked his way across the swell of her breasts to the edge of her beaded bodice, hot licks that had her trembling, her breasts swelling even further at the attention. Desire, arousal, a deep yearning couched in hot hunger flooded through her, hot and demanding.

Her eyes opened, and she glanced down as her nipples tightened, craving his touch—any touch. His dark hair was so stark against her pale skin, like some carnal demon having his wicked way with a virgin.

She smiled. Only she wasn't a virgin. Her hands slid

to his hair and she tugged, tilting his head up and claiming his lips with a hunger that rivaled his. Their tongues tangled, dueling for domination. This…this was heady, wanton… She'd never felt this free, this shameless, with anyone. Not even Theo.

Theo. The last time she'd been to a ball, she'd been with Theo.

But this wasn't Theo.

She tore her mouth from his, panting as she stared at the handsome face, his lips wet from her kisses. She knew those lips.

"No," she gasped.

Chapter 4

Melissa jolted awake, her body tight with need, craving a satisfaction she'd just denied herself. She rolled over in her lonely bed, groaning with frustration.

Her heart pounded, her nipples were tight and longing for the touch of a man's hands and her thighs were damp. She sat up in bed, her eyes wide as her chest rose and fell with her pants. What. The. *Hell?*

Realization dawned, and she dived out of the bed, stomping out of her bedroom and through her small apartment above the bookstore. That bastard. She didn't know how he'd done it, but he'd taken one of her memories and twisted it. She remembered that night, damn it, and she sure as hell hadn't been out on the balcony kissing an anonymous stranger. She flung her front door open, then slammed it shut behind her. That...*jerk*. The relief at realizing she wasn't willingly fantasizing about her prisoner was quickly consumed by rage. She ran barefoot down the stairwell to the corridor that led to the external street access, her pink nightgown streaming, the silk unfurling in her wake as though caught in an invisible tempest. Two steps down the hall was the internal security door to her store. She didn't bother to manually key in the code. She snapped her fingers. The door swung open. She stormed through her bookstore, disregarding the books flying off the shelves and falling to the floor behind her as her power raged around her. Anger poured through her, and she could feel her power building within her. She should scale it back, temper it a little, but she just wanted to let loose.

She swept through the door at the back of the store, chanting as she scampered down the stairs. The door to her apothecary burst open before her and she stalked across the underground room. The cupboard hiding her fire hose reel caught her eye, and she halted, seething.

Yep, this would do the trick. She yanked open the doors and pulled on the head of the hose, flicking the lever at the base of the hose reel. She turned to face the mural. A flick of her hand, a quick, fiercely muttered incantation, and she unlocked her wards. The painted door flung open. She didn't stop for the torch. She climbed down the stairwell, tugging the hose along with her. The bare concrete floor felt cold beneath her feet, but she didn't pause until she came up to the steel door. She used her power to slide the lock and thrust the door open. It made a resounding clang as it snapped back to the wall.

Her prisoner jolted awake, blinking as he pushed himself up from the floor where he lay.

"You need to cool down," she snapped, and yanked the lever on the hose.

Ice-cold water shot across the room, pummeling the man on the floor. He roared, trying to gain his feet, but she kept the hose trained on him. He slipped, tried to rise again, but the force of the water was too powerful, and he fell back against the wall.

He bellowed as he tried to twist away from the high-pressure blast of water, but she didn't give him any relief. After a long moment, she shut the hose off.

"Stay the hell out of my head," she yelled, and whirled around, the door slamming shut behind her, the lock sliding home.

Anger was good. Anger she could hold on to, anger she could use. She pulled it around her like a cloak. Because if she didn't have anger, all that would be left would be guilt at the fantasy that betrayed her fiancé's memory, and the shame of betrayal, of giving in to temptation from one of *them*. She climbed the stairs and locked up, but paused when she entered the bookstore. It looked like a mini-tornado had whirled through, leaving devastation in its wake.

Just like pyro jerk. That dream, that wicked kiss—that had devastated her. She had to get control. Of herself, of her powers…of her reaction to him. She would not give in.

Sniffing, she knelt down to start picking up the scattered items throughout the store, restoring order to the shelves as she calmly restored order to her thoughts.

Hunter shook the water out of his eyes, then glared at the door as he leaned back against the wall. That cold shower had cooled his desire for the damn woman. He made a fist and hit the floor beside him, and a spray of water hit him in the face. Damn it.

Arousal, tight and unrelenting, gripped his cock, stirred his pulse. He hadn't expected that. Hadn't planned it. His lips tightened as he rubbed at the hard ache. That cold shower had been painful, like ice bullets against his ardor. He swore. He'd meant to lurk, that was all, let her lead the way. He'd sent her a subliminal suggestion. Why did she hate the shadow breeds?

He hadn't expected her to take him to a Reform society ball. He'd given her a gown straight out of his imagination, one that hugged that siren figure yet had hidden her secrets. Classical yet incredibly sexy. That had *not* been his intention. Usually he just contented himself with being a mere witness to memories—like the dreams he'd previously walked through as Melissa had slept. His father had often played with suggestion, as had Hunter when first learning his dreamwalking skill. But what had just happened—that wasn't normal. He couldn't tell if that scene on the balcony was driven by his subconscious or hers. Whose suppressed desire had shanghaied that dream? Goose bumps rose on his skin as the chill night air caressed the icy water that drenched him, leeching at his desire. She'd surprised him, though. When he'd asked her subconscious to reveal the source of her hatred for shadow breeds, she'd shown him a scene of society's civility, and instead of following that clue, he'd been distracted. The muscles in his jaw felt so tight he had to consciously relax them. He wished he could blame it on the icy drenching, but he practiced deluding others, not himself. He was painfully horny, damn it. For the bitchy witch.

He shook his head, droplets of water flicking off his head like a shaggy dog. A damn Reform ball.

He'd heard all about them, but had never attended one. He should have—he was the eldest son of a Warrior Prime, and the ball was a social event to gather all the Scions of each Prime family in one spot, as a celebration of Reformation Day. It was also where connections were made, alliances were forged and some strategic pairings were made among the sons and daughters of the Primes. As a Warrior Scion, he had a right to attend. As a light warrior, a shadow breed that kept its very existence secret, though, there was no way his family would ever participate in such an event.

They had other ways of making alliances and wielding power, and it was far more delicate and discreet than the obnoxious gatherings of the Reform elite.

He rubbed his bare arms. He was chilled now. His lips curled. And yet, he was also energized. Strange. Usually when he dreamwalked, it was to find out secrets and implant suggestions, or fake memories—even make people forget... He'd never once thought to use it to entice, to seduce. Light warriors drew energy and power from all sources of light, except for created fluorescence. They were also able to pull power from sexual energy and emotions. He'd always believed there needed to be a physical proximity for that to work, though, not something that could be accomplished through an unconscious connection. Apparently he was wrong.

He'd connected with the witch, and with just one dreamy kiss she'd revitalized some of his stores. Totally worth a cold shower. He idly wondered what a real kiss with the woman would be like, then shook his head. He didn't think her reaction would stop at just an uncomfortable, near-Arctic dousing.

Two days later, Melissa stared at her pale features in the mirror of the store's bathroom. She pinched her cheeks, blinking her eyes open wide as she tried to wake up. She glanced at her watch. One hour. One hour before she could close the shop. Part of her wanted to curl up under the counter and sleep for a hundred years. Another part of her wanted to inject caffeine and never close her eyes again.

She was going to kill him. Sure, her mother would be disappointed, but she'd be able to *sleep*, damn it. He was tormenting her, and no matter what spell she conjured up, he managed to get past her defenses and dance through her dreamscapes.

She turned the tap and splashed cold water on her face. Last night had been bad. Over and over again, she'd relived the night her father had left. She eyed herself in the mirror, the haunted memories surfacing so easily now, as though her mind no longer obeyed her command to bury it.

She and her brother, Dave, had crept out from their rooms, eyeing each other warily in the darkened upstairs hallway as their parents had argued downstairs. It was the eve of Melissa's sixteenth birthday, when she would graduate from adolescent to Initiate and attend her first Reform ball.

"She's too young, Eleanor, and you know it."

"She's the Daughter-Scion, Phillip, and she has to start behaving like one."

"She's *sixteen*. She's our daughter. You can't marry her off, not yet."

"She doesn't have the luxury of just being our daughter, and you know it. We have to form that alliance. I don't want to be at the mercy of the Armstrongs, or the Marchettas, or any other Reform family. We need to ensure our witches have strong representation within the Senate, and this merger will ensure that. You know we can't use David, but we can at least use Melissa as an asset."

David pulled her away from the banister and tried to drag her back into her bedroom, but she shook her brother off, her blood chilling at the argument down-stairs as she returned to the railing. An asset? That's how her mother saw her?

Their parents were in the living room, oblivious to the listening ears upstairs.

"Why the Hawthorns?" Her father's question was laced with frustration and exasperation.

Melissa's eyes rounded, and she glanced up at her brother. The Hawthorns? They were known to dabble in blood magic. Hadn't one of their ancestors given in to the blood-craze? She shook her head. No, surely not. Surely her mother wouldn't ally the House of White Oak with the House of Hawthorn…she turned toward the head of the stairs, but Dave yanked her back, lifting his finger to his lips in caution.

"The Hawthorns are strong, Phillip, and because of their—proclivities—they count some vampire colonies among their allies." Her mother's answer was haughty, as though offended she had to explain herself.

"Do you hear yourself? Vampires? We don't want to align with the bloodsuckers, Eleanor."

"Why? Are you afraid of them?"

Melissa frowned at the blatant scorn in her mother's tone.

"I am wary of them. I don't trust them, and neither should you. Anyone slave to the blood thirst will always be an enemy to the humans and witches, Eleanor, and you know it."

"Well, I'm not scared of them, Phillip. It's done. I've already discussed it with Marcus Hawthorn. He is will-ing to formally introduce his son to Melissa at the ball tomorrow night."

"So, you've gone ahead and done it without discussing it with me." Her father's tone brought tears to Melissa's eyes. It was so brittle, so cold.

"I do not need, nor seek, your permission, Phillip. I am the Coven Elder, and in this my authority is absolute. Deal with it."

"I won't stand for this, Eleanor."

Her mother laughed, a cold little tinkle that sounded like broken glass cascading over stone. "There is nothing you can do, Phillip. It's already arranged."

"I won't stand by your side and watch this. You've gone too far—you should have discussed this with me. We could have come up with an alternative."

"You're my Consort, Phillip, not my confidant."

Melissa flinched at the sound of breaking glass, and then her father stormed out of the living room and into the front foyer.

"Well, you won't have to worry about that anymore, Eleanor. I'm renouncing this farce of a marriage. Do as you will—you always have." He gave a sharp, cruel bark of laughter. "You're so worried about your standing among the society, I'm almost interested to see the spin you'll put on that, but I find I really couldn't care less."

Her father yanked his coat down from the hook behind the door. Melissa broke away from David, tears streaming down her face as she started to walk down the stairs.

"Daddy, please don't go."

Phillip Carter turned around, and she could see his struggle to contain his anger in front of his children. Finally, he smiled sadly and shrugged as she approached him. "Sorry, poppet. I just can't do this anymore."

He gave her a hug, then gazed up at David. Father and son looked at each other for a long moment, and then Phillip finally nodded, as though there was some meaningful, silent exchange.

And then her father left.

When Melissa turned away from the open front door, she saw him, a shadow in the corner of the foyer, his brown eyes watching the scene intently. He hadn't been there at the time, but he was there, inside her memory, replaying it for her again and again. There was something predatory about his gaze that suggested his name was more than just something handed down to him at birth, but more a characteristic of his personality.

Damn pyro jerk. Just for that, she'd cast an elemental spell and had made it snow in his cell for the rest of the night. He was still shivering when she'd tossed him his sandwich at lunchtime.

Melissa looked away from the mirror and grabbed the hand towel hanging from a loop attached to the wall. She dabbed her face dry, her teeth clenched, that last image of her father storming off into the night haunting her. Neither she nor Dave had seen him since. She wasn't going to cry. Not again. She'd wasted too many tears, remembering that night.

She fluffed her hair, pasted a fake smile on her face, then turned to the door that led out to her store. She had a client coming in to pick up a hex pouch, and another one due for an extremely diluted solution of wolfsbane. It wasn't enough to kill a lycan, but it was enough to make the man's abusive werewolf wife feel poorly enough to leave him alone.

Her hand rested on the doorknob. That night memories of her father weren't the only dreams she was having. She frowned. She'd have to do something about her prisoner. She didn't want these dreams, didn't want these painful memories resurfacing at his whim, not hers. She didn't think she could let him go, though. Who knew what chaos he would wreak on the unsuspecting and vulnerable if let out. He showed no real remorse for his actions, no consideration for others, but continued to push his own agenda. She wasn't allowed to kill him, but she had wanted to teach him a lesson. Her shoulders sagged. Perhaps he was unredeemable.

Right now, though, she was too tired to care.

Straightening her shoulders, she swept into her store, a fake smile on her face as she greeted her customers.

A while later, after the two customers had left, she was almost deliriously happy to shut her front door, swinging the sign to Closed. She switched the light off over the display window and rubbed the back of her neck as she walked down the aisle toward the internal door that opened near the stairs that led to her apartment.

A furious tapping on the door at the front of the store had her turning, her brows dipping as the tapping became thumping. She walked back toward the store entrance, then started running when she caught a good look at one person propped up against her store window and another person struggling to keep him up. Melissa unlocked the door, and Lexi sobbed, nearly hysterical as she draped her brother's arm over her shoulders.

"Please, Melissa. We need your help. Lance is hurt—bad."

Chapter 5

Hunter hugged himself. The snow flurries had melted within his cell, but there was still a leftover chill from the witch's retaliatory snowstorm. How apt that she took an icy approach. She probably thought he'd been replaying that particular memory out of spite, but he wasn't.

Okay, so maybe there was a tiny bit of spite in there, but he'd really wanted to find out more about his captor. She'd been so young in that memory, not even an Initiate—untried and untested with her powers. He'd seen her hurt flare when her mother discussed her as no more than a resource for the coven, sensed her fear and anxiety at being married off, seen her blanch at the mention of the Hawthorns. The White Oak Coven... He racked his brain, trying to remember what he knew of the family. He knew of no current alliance between the Hawthorns and the White Oaks, and managing and orchestrating alliances and enmities were part of a light warrior's toolbox, as his manipulative father had taught him. Arthur Armstrong had made it his business to understand, and even to influence, the partnerships and negotiations within Reform society.

When he saw Melissa's dream of the ball, though, she'd been close enough to her current age—definitely an adult, and not some sixteen-year-old on her first introduction into Reform society. What had happened with the Hawthorns? He knew enough of Eleanor Carter's reputation to know the Coven Elder was politically savvy and extremely powerful. What had happened to Melissa's arranged marriage? It was an archaic custom, and one that couldn't be enforced. If the Scion didn't wish to be married off, there were opportunities to withdraw without causing insult, but he couldn't remember hearing of anything involving the White Oak Coven. Hell. It wasn't like Melissa was the kind of woman who could be discreet and diplomatic in that kind of situation, so surely he would have heard of some shock or scandal…?

Every time he learned something of his captor, it just raised more questions. Not that a broken engagement was any help to him getting out of his prison… He was just…curious.

He settled himself back against the wall. She was tired. His dreamwalking was disturbing her sleep. He regretted that. Her face had been pale and drawn when he'd caught a brief glimpse of her as she'd tossed him his lunch. If she wasn't craving a nap, she'd be going to bed early tonight. He frowned. Goose bumps rose on his arms. He realized there was a chill in the air, but he also knew excitement when he felt it—and he was strangely excited by the prospect of seeing her in her dreams. She was unguarded there, and hadn't quite figured out how to block him, yet—although he'd had to exercise more effort last night, so she was getting there. He saw her in all her vulnerable, awkward and naive glory. So far, though, he still couldn't understand why she was such a hard-ass when it came to the shadow breeds. To be fair, he'd behaved badly toward her, and all thoughts of protecting his brother aside, he should have factored her into his firestorm, and was ashamed he hadn't. She had a right to be angry with him, but he sensed there was more to the anger than just him nearly killing her—although some might think that was enough of a reason.

No, he sensed there was more behind that anger, a bitter sense of betrayal he just didn't understand—and now he couldn't use it to get the hell out of here.

He closed his eyes. She might be avoiding him, tossing him his food from the door, and not speaking to him at all, but she couldn't avoid him in her unconsciousness—and he'd be ready and waiting for her tonight.

Melissa grimaced as she and Lexi struggled to carry Lance's massive form over to the bed in her spare bedroom. It had been quite the challenge for both her and Lexi to get him up the stairs from the bookstore in his semiconscious state, but she had no place to lie him down in the store.

God, the blood. There was so much blood. Lance's complexion was almost gray, and his eyelids kept fluttering, as though he was struggling against a tide of unconsciousness that threatened to claim him.

"I haven't seen him in ages, and for some reason, I just felt this need to touch base with him," Lexi said between ragged breaths, her words stumbling over each other. "I found him like this—" Lexi shook her head, unable to continue.

"Get his legs up," Melissa instructed as she lowered

him onto the bed. She glanced at the young woman. Apparently the ring was doing its job. "There are towels in the bathroom and a bucket under the sink. Fill it up with water—don't worry, it's clean, and then bring it all in here."

Lexi's hands were shaking as she hoisted her brother's feet up onto the bed, and Melissa touched her shoulder. The young woman turned to her, her blue eyes glistening with tears and bright with fear.

"It's okay, Lexi. You did good, bringing him here. How did it happen?"

Lexi shrugged. "I don't know. I was on the way to his place, and found him in the park down on Addison Road. You were the first person I thought of for help."

Melissa patted her shoulder reassuringly. "He'll be fine."

Lexi nodded, took a deep breath, then hurried to the bathroom down the hall.

Melissa opened Lance's leather jacket and sucked in her breath. His shirtfront was dark and shiny with blood, so much that she couldn't rip the damp material, and had to slide the buttons out of holes to peel back the fabric. His chest rose and fell rapidly, as though he couldn't quite fill his lungs, and his body was bathed in a cool perspiration.

She gently rolled him onto his side, wincing as he groaned. There was blood on his back, as well.

Her mouth dried when she saw the extent of his injuries, and her gaze flicked up to Lance's face. He stared at her, his green eyes dull with pain and sadness, a weary acceptance stamped on his features.

"It's fine, Mel. I know."

Melissa shook her head, blinking back the tears. "Don't say that, Lance. You're going to be fine. We'll fix you." This man had worked quietly and diligently in her store, had listened to her rants about her mother, had gotten drunk with her and her brother on the odd occasion, and had been there when Theo had died in a way no other could have been. "You're going to be fine," she repeated in a whisper, gazing at the cuts on his chest, and the hole that looked too close to his heart.

It took an effort, but Lance covered her hand with his bloodstained fingers, and she flinched at the cool touch. "I've been shot, Mel. I'm dying. You can't fix this."

Lexi entered the room with a bucket of water and towels, and Melissa lifted her chin toward the bedside table. "Good woman. Now, there is a cupboard at the end of the hall, with a basket on the bottom shelf. Go get it for me quickly." Lexi jogged out of the room, and Melissa turned to her friend.

"Who did this to you, Lance? Who did this?" She hissed the words at him softly, conscious of Lexi just down the hall.

Lance smiled weakly. "It doesn't matter."

Melissa's eyes narrowed. "Oh, it does, because we are going to deliver a whole world of hurt on them." She dipped a hand towel into the bucket, squeezed it, then started to clean his chest. She needed to see exactly what she was dealing with here.

Lance's smile fell, and he shook his head, just once. "No, stay out of it, Mel. Look after Lexi for me."

Her gaze flicked up to meet his. She wasn't ready for this, wasn't ready to say goodbye to one of her best friends, wasn't ready to take on his burdens. "Oh, no you don't," she whispered harshly. "You don't get to dump that high-maintenance chick on me. *You* can clean up her messes." She wiped away most of the blood, although it still pulsed, slowly, from some of his wounds, so red—unnaturally so. The lacerations were deep, but it was the hole near his heart that most concerned her. A bullet wound, through and through, with an exit wound in his back. Lance was a dhampir, with a metabolism that aided self-healing, but the fact that he was healing so slowly suggested he was, indeed, gravely injured.

She brushed his dark blond hair back from his forehead. "But for now, you need to sleep." She whispered a sleep spell, and his eyelids drifted shut, his dark lashes forming crescents against his cheeks.

Lexi ran back into the room, and halted when she saw her brother. "Oh, God, is he—?"

"No, he isn't, and he won't, not if I've got anything to do with it." She took the basket from Lexi and opened it up. Inside were her essentials—her emergency magic kit. This wasn't the first time an injured person was brought to her. "Round up as many candles as you can and bring them here. You'll find them everywhere throughout the apartment."

Elements helped her focus her magic, and as she wasn't near a watercourse or a garden, and she didn't want to subject Lance to a gale, not in his state, then fire was her go-to element.

She worked quietly, cutting Lance's bloodstained clothing away from his body, and Lexi helped her clean him up. She frowned. His cuts weren't healing. As a dhampir, Lance had the ability to heal fast—which wasn't happening.

"Help me place the candles around him," she told Lexi. Using the furniture setup of the room, she and Lexi placed the candles on the surfaces so that they formed a rough circle around the bed. With a flick of her fingers, all the wicks of the candles lit up, and Lexi turned off the overhead light so that candlelight was the only illumination within the room.

"Sit over there," Melissa instructed, pointing to the chair in the corner, and Lexi hurried over, her face pale and anxious as she watched her brother on the bed. Melissa climbed up near the head of the bed, gently lifting Lance's limp head and resting it on her knees. Closing her eyes, she took a deep breath, calming her heart, evening out her breathing and summoning her powers. Placing her fingers at Lance's temples, she let her magic flow over him.

She frowned. She could sense something inside him, something small, but sharp, with a shadow that was slowly spreading. Whatever it was, it wasn't letting him heal. She tried to battle it, tried to conquer it, then tried to confine it, but she could sense it diffusing through his system.

She didn't know how long they remained like that—Lexi sitting quietly on her chair in the corner, Lance breathing harshly into the silence and Melissa holding on to her friend, trying desperately to pull him back from the brink of death. She poured her own strength, her essence, into helping him. It slowed down the creeping shadow, but it didn't stop it. This was some sort of natural poison that she couldn't halt. She focused on that small, sharp object, the source of the toxin. It was so close to his heart. She tried to draw it out of him, using her magic like a magnet, but Lance moaned softly with pain. Melissa felt the raw edge of agony stiffen his muscles. She was only hurting him further.

She sagged back against the head of the bed and opened her eyes. The room was almost dark. She'd burned through many of the candles, and only a couple still flickered with light. Her legs felt numb. She must have been sitting there for hours. Lexi was staring at her, her expression of anxiety and hope like a suffocating weight on Melissa's chest.

"I can't do this," she whispered brokenly, shame and desolation washing over her as she stared at her friend's sister. "It's not—it's not responding to my magic." Admitting that she couldn't help her friend felt like a betrayal, an abandonment. "He needs medical help."

Lexi stared down at her brother in confusion. "What?"

"He's a dhampir, Lexi. In some ways, he's the strongest being I know. In this, though, he is as weak and vulnerable as the rest of us humans. He's got a bullet fragment inside him, and I can't get it out."

"No." Lexi shook her head, tears streaming down her face as she rose from her chair. "There has to be something you can do, Mel. Please. Whatever it is—I'll pay."

Briefly, anger flared within her at the suggestion she would receive payment for helping a friend, but she quashed that anger. Lexi loved her brother and was desperate. She'd do anything to save him, and Melissa could relate to that—she'd do anything to save her own brother as well as her close friend. No, it was better to save her anger for those responsible for this—whoever shot Lance. But they weren't going to be able to wreak any vengeance if they didn't know who pulled the trigger, and in order for that to happen, Lance *must* survive. Only, she couldn't help him.

Her gaze drifted down to the man lying on the bed, his features so still. She knew someone who could, though, and the very thought of asking him for help burned like acid in her stomach. The thought, though, that Lance would die was even worse.

Melissa dredged up her remaining stores of magic. The work she'd already done on Lance had been draining. She pressed gently against his temple and whispered a dormancy spell. It wasn't quite as effective as a suspension spell, but putting the half-human Lance into a suspended state would halt his heartbeat, and a continuance spell may not work without that vital pulse. A dormancy spell allowed his body and mind to go into a state of hibernation, still sustaining life, but limiting the spread of that toxin, whatever it was.

"I, uh, I need to step out," she said, her voice husky with strain. She blinked. Her vision was blurry and gray. Dormancy spells weren't easy, and they took a toll. "Stay with him. Talk to him, Lexi. I've put him in a coma, to stop…it." Death. She'd put him in a coma to stop death. Her mother would freak if she found her playing with the natural order of things. Magic could be used, but once you used it against nature's course there were consequences. Melissa mentally defended herself against the imaginary conversation with her Coven Elder. She'd delayed death, not contravened it.

She knew one person, though, who could prevent it—and he was currently shivering in a cell in her basement.

With each step she took down to his prison, she argued with herself. Was there another option? Could anyone else help? What about Dave? No. He'd encounter the same issue she did. Lance needed medical help, not magical. How long could she keep Lance dormant? Perhaps she could wait just a little longer, until someone more suitable could be reached? The stairs leading from her store down to her apothecary spun for a moment, and she clutched the wall for support until her vision settled and she could enter her secret store.

A dormancy spell worked differently to most. For it to continue its effect, it had to siphon energy from her own reserves, and she'd drained most in her efforts to heal

Lance and to halt the toxin. It was almost too much effort to despell the wards on the mural door. She reached for the torch and carefully made her way down the steep stairs, clinging to the railing as she went.

She halted before the dark door and took a deep breath, composing her features. She hated this. *Hated* it. She swung open the door and the torch cut a swathe of light through the darkness.

Her prisoner sat on the floor, his back to the wall, and he lifted his head. His lips curled in a wicked smile.

"Hello, Red. Come to make a deal with the devil?"

Chapter 6

Hunter eyed the witch, his eyebrows dipping slightly. She looked like hell. He saw the blood on her shirt, saw her sway, and he rose to his feet. He had one only cuff that was anchored, but if she collapsed, he wouldn't be able to reach her. "Are you okay?" He gestured to her shirt. He didn't know who was more surprised by his concern, the witch or him.

The witch looked down at herself. "Uh, yeah, I'm—I'm—it's not mine." Her voice was huskier than usual, a slight rasp that was like velvet against skin.

She stepped inside the room and rubbed absently at her forehead. He masked his concern with expectation. He'd seen her angry, mildly curious, angry, exasperated, angry, wary, more angry…he'd never seen her so… flustered. Yeah, flustered.

She put her hands on her hips and looked down at her

boots—those same killer heels—then looked up at him. "I need your help."

His eyebrows rose. Okay. That was unexpected. She looked so damn uncomfortable, he almost laughed, yet her obvious exhaustion, the blood…she wasn't here to ask him to stop dreamwalking, as he'd thought, as he'd hoped. His intention had been to wear her out so that she would be begging him to leave. "What kind of help?" he inquired smoothly.

She moved her arms, halted, then folded them against her body, as though unsure what to do with her limbs. "I, uh, I need a doctor."

His heart thudded in his chest, and he stepped closer. "Why? What's wrong with you?" He looked her up and down. She was a mess. Her hair was tangled, and dark shadows rested beneath her eyes. Her lips were tightly pursed, and her shirt…all that blood. He wanted to check her, make sure she really was all right. The instinct surprised him. He told himself it was his medical training taking over…although he wasn't really the nurturing type.

"Uh, not for me. For a friend. I need your help for a friend." She couldn't quite meet his gaze.

He raised an eyebrow. "Really? You have a friend?" Melissa Carter, bitchy witch, had a friend. He'd have to see it to believe it. "You?"

She frowned. "Yes, *me*," she said through gritted teeth. "I have a friend, and he needs help."

He. Her *male* friend needed help. His concern shrank, swallowed by a darker emotion. He shrugged. "Then take him to a hospital."

"There's no time, and the transfer could kill him," she said quietly, at last meeting his gaze directly.

His eyes narrowed. "So…you *need* me." He leaned

back against the wall. Hmm. She was in a position of demand, and he was in a position of supply. He liked where this conversation was going. "What exactly do you *need* from me?"

"You have a reputation for being good at what you do," she said brusquely, although her tone suggested she found it hard to believe. "I want you to fix him. Heal my friend."

"And what do I get in return?" he asked her, a smile teasing at his lips. She was direct. He'd give her that.

"What do you want?" she asked, shrugging.

He blinked. She was asking him to name his price? He tilted his head. "This friend must mean a lot to you." She struck him as being so prickly, so quick-tempered, it was fascinating to see this side of her, this loyal, protective side.

She tilted her head back, and he watched her red hair slide over her shoulder. "I'm too tired for games, Hunter. What do you want in return for healing my friend?"

Hunter. Not pyro jerk or any of the other monikers she'd given him. It was the first time she'd used his name. Things were serious. He rubbed his chin, the remaining chain clinking with his movements. "I want you to release me," he said simply.

Those green eyes flared with anger, and he met her gaze intently. Did she care more for this friend, or for her own revenge? Her lips tightened, then she dipped her head. Once.

"Fine. You heal my friend, and you can walk away."

"And then you and I are done, right? No more snakes or snow or spiders?"

She nodded. "No more snakes or snow or spiders."

His eyes narrowed. Yeah, she wasn't the first witch he'd ever dealt with. "Or any other form of revenge or retribution from you for what I did. It was wrong, I'm sorry, we're moving on."

Her pouty lips tightened even further, and he saw the anger, the reluctance to let go of her punishment. She nodded. "You do this, and we're done. Moving on."

It was so obvious she hated this whole discussion. His curiosity deepened. Who was this friend, and why was he so damn important to this witch? Not that he cared, it would just be nice to know what reasoning had bought his freedom. He held up the chained cuff.

"Release me," he said softly.

She stepped closer, and her eyes narrowed. "The deal is you heal him. If he dies, or if you kill him—"

"I'm not in the habit of killing folks," he interrupted in exasperation.

"You tried to kill me," she pointed out, and he grimaced.

"Okay, so just that one time…"

"You've attacked me five times."

"Nobody's perfect."

"You don't get to leave until my friend is well," she snapped. "If he dies, you die."

He stared at her for a moment, reading in her eyes the worry she tried to hide. He tried to think of someone who would do this for him, sacrifice their own vengeance for his well-being. Sadly, no name came to mind. "If he has a pulse, he'll live." His reputation was understated. He wasn't just good, he was the best.

Her eyes narrowed. "You sound cocky."

"Oh, you have no idea. Now, if you want me to save your friend, I suggest we stop flirting and you release me," he said, taking extra care to pronounce his last two words clearly as he jangled the chain.

She raised a finger, then paused. "If you try to attack

me, or harm me or my friends, whatever you try to do will be visited a hundredfold back on you."

"You have my word as a gentleman," he promised, bowing. He kept the triumph out of his voice, his expression. He was getting the hell out of here.

"You're not a gentleman."

He raised his hand, parting his fingers. "Scout's honor."

"That's not a scout's—"

"I promise," he growled, then sighed. He dipped his head to meet her gaze directly. "I promise to heal your friend," he told her, all attempts at levity gone. "You'll have to trust me." He waggled his eyebrows. "I am a doctor, after all."

Her gaze flickered away, and it was so clear she didn't trust him. He straightened. He guessed he deserved that. "What else can you do for your friend?" He knew already she couldn't do anything else, because sure as hell, he would have been her last resort.

She blinked and looked away. Were those—were those tears? She really was worried about this guy. This time it was Hunter who looked away, unprepared for the spark of envy for a dying man.

"Do we have a deal?" he asked roughly. "I don't hurt you, you don't hurt me, your friend lives and we go our separate ways?"

She nodded. "We have a deal."

"For this to work, you'll need to do as I say. You'll need to be my—nurse." He smiled. "See, we get to play doctors and nurses."

The witch didn't crack a smile. At all. He needed her promise, though. He got the impression that promises were important to her. "Your word—I don't want to argue over treatment, I just need you to do as I say."

Her lips tightened. "Fine. With regard to Lance, I'll do as you say."

He didn't miss the qualification but didn't comment. He jangled the cuff, eyeing her suggestively. She waved her hand casually and the cuffs around his wrists snapped open and fell to the floor. She turned and led the way to the door.

He nodded as he rubbed his wrists. "Neat trick."

She didn't look over her shoulder. "Oh, you have no idea."

Melissa walked into her apartment, conscious of the man who followed behind her. Her shoulders were tense and she occasionally glanced over her shoulder warily. This man had tried to kill her, and now she was letting him into her home, her haven.

God, what the hell was she thinking? But what choice did she have? She'd understated Hunter Armstrong's reputation. No, wait, he was Hunter Galen now. She'd been hiding in the next room when he'd renounced his father's name. Hunter wasn't renowned simply for being adequate, or even good at his job. He was widely reputed to be the *best* at his job. Surgeon. General practitioner. Specialist. If anyone was to work on Lance, she'd want him to be the best.

She'd also want him not to have homicidal tendencies.

She led him into the spare bedroom, and Lexi looked up from the bed. She rose to her feet, frowning. "Who's this?"

"A friend."

"A doctor." Melissa eyed him. They'd responded simultaneously, and he'd called himself a friend. Friend? Good grief. If he thought this was friendship, she'd hate to see the man's enemies.

No, wait, they were probably all ashes, somewhere.

"This is Hunter Galen. Hunter, this is Lexi, and that's her brother, Lance," she said, indicating the bed.

Lance's chest rose and fell rapidly, and sweat gave a sheen to his body in the muted candlelight. Gauze and bandages covered his chest, and although she'd seen Lance's injuries, and had treated his wounds as best she could, the sight of his damaged body was still a shock. She glanced away. Only three candles remained burning, the rest had long since blown out or burned out.

Hunter stepped closer, his bulk casting a shadow over Lance's body. Hunter touched his patient's forehead, then raised the man's eyelids. He placed his fingers at the side of Lance's neck, as though taking a pulse, and a faint frown marred his brow.

"What is it?" Melissa whispered.

"Talk to me. Tell me what happened," he commanded.

Melissa drew in a breath. "I don't know." She glanced over to Lexi, who shrugged, her eyes wide. "This is how he was found. I asked him what had happened, but he wouldn't tell me."

"Oh, so you two are close, huh?" Hunter commented dryly.

"He doesn't want me to go after who did this," Melissa whispered, ensuring Lexi didn't hear her. Hunter's gaze met hers briefly, then flicked over to Lexi and then back to his patient.

"He's been cut. Doesn't look like claws, though. And he's been shot."

Hunter peeled the gauze off Lance's chest and grimaced. "Yikes. That's nasty."

"There's—there's something near his heart," Melissa told him, pointing to the bullet wound high on Lance's chest. "A fragment, maybe."

Hunter leaned down to peer closely, not at all bothered by the blood. "Uh-huh."

"But you can heal him, right?" Melissa stepped up to stand beside him. She'd meant it to sound like an order, not a plea. It was such a contrast, her friend, pale and sickly on the bed, and the light warrior, so damn vital and strong, next to her. Hunter flicked a quick glance toward her, and his eyes darkened as he noted the short distance between them. He finally nodded.

"I believe so."

Her shoulders sagged with relief.

Hunter frowned and placed his head on Lance's forehead. "There's something not quite right here," he muttered.

"I, uh, I think that bullet is creating more damage with every breath he takes."

Hunter raised an eyebrow at her. "Oh, so now you're a doctor, too, huh?"

She frowned. "No, but I am a witch, and I sensed something dark in there, like a shadow that is expanding inside him."

Hunter nodded. "Poison. Looks like the bullet was possibly tainted. If the bullet had just passed through him, he would have been really sick. With that bullet fragment in there, and the sustained exposure to the toxin, it's killing him. His body hasn't got a chance to rejuvenate with that thing eating at him." Hunter tilted his head. "But that's not quite what I meant. There is something…unnatural here."

"Oh, that would be me. I worked a dormancy spell." She couldn't think of anything else to do for her friend, and the knowledge of her limitations was excruciating.

She met his gaze, and was surprised by the flicker of approval she saw there.

"Smart move. It slows the spread of the toxin, but still keeps his system active." Hunter folded his arms. "A dormancy spell, huh? I'm surprised you're still standing. So, he's human, or at least part human? I mean, I have to assume that, otherwise you would have used a suspension spell, right?"

He seemed to possess an uncomfortable amount of knowledge on witchcraft. The suspension spell could be used on most of the pure-breeds, like full-blooded vampires, and those that were undead in their natural state. She nodded. "He's a dhampir."

She saw his brown eyes widen.

"A dhampir? As in, vampire hunter? But that would make him a shadow breed." Hunter's brows dipped with confusion. He'd never seen a dhampir in action before. Sure, he knew the basics; they consumed vampire blood. Their human nature still desired food and drink, but to build their strength and other enhanced physical qualities, they had to consume the blood of the undead. Nature's solution to the vampire abomination. Half human, half vampire, they became a natural-born vampire hunter. Most didn't survive to maturity, having been killed off by the vampires before they could become a true threat. Those who did survive that long spent the rest of their lives with a target on their back, hunted by the entire vampire breed. It was an interesting relationship, but one of equal footing, the hunted also becoming the hunter.

"But you hate shadow breeds, remember? You go on and on about how you wish we'd all die." He rolled his hands as he spoke. "On and on."

Melissa lifted her chin. "Dhampirs hate vampires just as much as I do. Dhampirs want vampires dead. Ergo, that makes them the good guys."

Hunter gazed absently at the wall behind her as he considered her words. "So you don't hate *all* shadow breeds, then, huh?" He leaned forward. "*Ergo*, there's hope for me yet," he whispered in her ear.

"No, there isn't." She pulled back a little, ignoring the little kick-start to her pulse. No. No way in hell would she be going there. She checked behind her to avoid stepping on Lexi. He was so big, and warm, and...cheeky, damn it. "What do you need to get started here?"

Hunter turned around the room, taking an instant visual inventory. "We're going to need more water, for starters. Towels, bandages, scissors, tweezers, needles, candles—lots of candles." He counted off the items on his fingers. "And alcohol. Bourbon, preferably." He glanced meaningfully at Lexi, who nodded and hurried out of the room.

"Bourbon?" Melissa's brow wrinkled as she tried to remember the medicinal purposes of the liquor. Maybe sterilization?

Hunter nodded. "Yeah. That'll be for me." He shrugged. "Five months..."

She folded her arms. "You can't—"

"Tut-tut. Whatever I asked, remember?"

Her eyes narrowed. She knew he was going to take advantage of the situation. She guessed she should be relieved it was just a drink or three. "Don't screw up," she warned him.

Hunter grimaced. "Can't promise that. I'm renowned for screwing up, just ask my brother."

Melissa took a deep breath, praying for patience, and he waved a hand at her. "Relax. I'll be fine. Soon."

"Soon?" Oh, hell, now what did he want? What cockamamy demand was he going to make? His words finally registered. He'd be fine *soon*. Which implied he wasn't fine *now*. Her mental alarm bells started to ring. "What do you mean?"

Hunter turned to face her. "You've kept me locked away," he said coolly, and took a step toward her. She eyed him. He was going all predator on her. She took a wary step back. Uh-oh. He wasn't chained to a wall anymore.

"Five months in the dark," he grated, and she saw the muscles in his jaw clench. He stepped closer again. Damn it. He was going to try to kill her again. This had all been a ploy for him to get out of those iron cuffs. She cast her gaze toward Lance, unconscious on the bed. He couldn't help her. Her fingers tensed.

"I'm dry," he told her, his stare intent.

She hesitated. Frowned. "Dry? What do you mean, dry?"

"I have no energy," he told her quietly. "Your friend— he's going to need some serious energy, and I don't have it at the moment because you've kept me in the dark for so long."

She blinked. "Oh." She'd researched, but there wasn't a great deal of information available about light warriors. Any records that mentioned them were notoriously sketchy. They siphoned energy from the sun, flame, some light—but they couldn't draw energy from the blue fluorescence. She backed away again, only to come up against the bedroom wall. "Uh, what—what do you need?"

"Candles," he told her, and rested his palm against the wall, right beside her head. She swallowed. He was close. Really, really close. The corded strength of his arm was right there, tendon, sinew and muscle covered in golden skin. He even smelled...clean. She guessed the fire hose and a mini-blizzard had that effect on a man.

There was no aftershave, no cultured scent, just him. He smelled pleasant, with a hint of amber and male musk.

Nope, she wasn't going to think about musk.

She snapped her attention back to the conversation. "Uh, well, Lexi will bring some in shortly."

Hunter nodded, placing his other hand on the wall on the other side of her head, effectively hemming her into a space within his reach that was growing smaller with every breath she took. She could sense the warmth of his body, so close, that naked chest just inches away from her own form. Warmth and heat. Heart pounding. Male musk. Muscles.

"Fire," he told her, his gaze on hers, and she could see the flare of heat there, too, as though he could feel the sizzle between them.

"Fire?" she repeated, then cleared her throat at the hoarse sound. "Fire?" she repeated, this time in a stronger voice. Oh, dear. That chest, those muscles, covered in that smooth, golden skin.

"I need fire," he said, and her eyes widened. Did he mean he was going to set her place on fire again?

"I need to draw energy from fire," he told her, apparently reading the concern in her gaze. He bent his elbows, drawing himself even closer, his gaze lowering to focus on her neck, her shoulders...her chest. "I'm a light warrior, Melissa. I need light to do what I do." His voice had dropped to a whisper. "Light. Warmth. Heat. I draw energy from it. It's like blood for vampires—I need it to survive."

She swallowed. Well, she could certainly help him with the heat. Her cheeks were hot, her mouth dry. "Oh. Uh, well, those candles..."

"Your friend is going to need a lot of energy, Melissa," Hunter said, and dipped his head toward her neck. She heard him inhale.

"Uh…" Good grief, he wasn't even touching her, but her nipples were tightening in reaction.

"It's going to take time for me to rejuice, heal, rejuice, heal," he told her. His chest was so close, all warmth and naked skin. If she took a deep breath, they'd be touching, breast to breast. She swallowed.

"There is a way I can get some pure energy, fast," he whispered, his breath against her neck.

She closed her eyes. "There is?" Good grief, he was so *there*, so big, so…sexy. All tall and broad shoulders, male musk and—

Something delicate and damp flicked against her neck, and her eyes sprang open. He'd licked her. He lifted his head, his gaze meeting hers.

She gasped. His eyes. They'd gone from dark brown to warm hazel, with shards of golden amber flecking his irises. Even as she watched, her gaze never leaving his, he pressed closer, his chest coming into contact with hers, separated by her cream blouse and lacy bra. His eyes brightened. Not with emotion, but actually brightened. Sparks of amber brightened to flecks of gold, and his eyes glowed.

They *glowed*. His expression looked stunned for a moment. "You're so—hot," he whispered finally, and lowered his lips to hers.

Chapter 7

This was no dream. His lips were warm and supple against hers, and she closed her eyes as he kissed her. Even with her eyes shut, though, she could sense his heat, a sensual haze creeping over her, through her. Her heart thumped in her chest, and he changed the angle, drawing back for barely a moment before pressing his mouth to hers again, his tongue darting in to tease at hers.

The sensations were at once familiar and alien. She remembered passion, she remembered arousal, desire... she just hadn't felt any of that in so long.

Her breasts swelled, and he sighed as he rubbed his chest against hers, her nipples peaking at the delicious contact. His tongue caressed hers, causing a tremble to start low in her stomach and ripple outward...down to her core and up to her breasts. His kisses were well practiced, expert—drawing a response from her, a surrender she wasn't prepared for. She was panting, trying to catch her breath, but not wanting to relinquish the sweet, hot hold of his lips. She realized her hands were pressed against the wall by her sides, as though she was trying to hold herself back.

Screw that.

She raised her arms, and his hands left the wall, his fingers intertwining with hers. He raised his head, panting, his beautiful golden eyes staring down at her. He looked like he was going to come back for round two, and then he blinked. The golden fire in his eyes banked, and the passion of his expression cooled into a remote mask.

"Thank you," he said politely, taking a step back.

She gaped at him for a moment, feeling a chill wash over her. "What for?" she whispered hoarsely, although glimpsing the glow and golden flecks of his previously dark brown eyes, she thought she knew.

"I, uh, needed that." He licked his lips and stepped back again.

"Needed what?" she asked, strength returning to her voice, her limbs. Despite the passion and excitement of a few seconds ago, she felt drained, exhausted.

"A small recharge." He indicated Lance on the bed behind him. "You know, to look after your friend."

She hid her dismay. All thoughts of Lance had fled her mind as soon as Hunter's lips had touched hers. She'd been swept away. Excited. Horny. Hell. She hadn't kissed anyone since...

She blinked once. Twice. No. She clamped her lips tight, as though they could keep her horror, her pain and her shame hidden away inside her. She'd kissed Hunter, and she'd forgotten all about Theo. She'd been totally lost to the passion—with Hunter, of all people. A light warrior—a damn shadow breed. And he'd just been using her to "recharge." Guilt hit her like a solid punch to the gut. She wasn't going to tear up, damn it. She wasn't going to give pyro jerk the satisfaction.

She took a breath, sagging back against the wall. For a moment, the room swirled, and she flattened her hands against the wall for balance.

"Melissa," Hunter spoke softly, stepping back toward her, his hand raised.

She hit it away. "Don't touch me," she rasped. "Not ever."

He halted, something flashing in those eyes that looked almost like hurt, but she ignored it. He was incapable of empathy. "You need to break the dormancy spell," he told her. "You're—drained." His gaze flicked away for a moment. "You need to break away from Lance."

She shook her head, but he nodded, his chin lifting. "You have to. I can't do what I need to do if he's dormant. Let him go."

She eyed him. If she let him go, Lance's injuries would flare up. He'd feel pain. The poison would spread. He could die.

"Trust me," he told her softly.

She blanched. After what he'd just done to her, he expected her to trust him? Anger flared, and if she'd had the energy, she would have punched him. She wanted to lash out, make him hurt as much as she did.

Hunter dipped his chin, meeting her gaze squarely. "I will heal your friend, Melissa, but you need to trust me to do it."

She fixed him with a glare, pouring as much anger and bitterness into it as she could. "If anything happens to him, I will kill you."

He nodded. "Understood. Now, let go."

She closed her eyes, her head tilting back against the wall. She was so gosh-darn tired. She didn't want to argue anymore, didn't have the energy. Summoning up the dregs of her power, she whispered an incantation that severed the magical link between her stores and Lance's life source. It was like a small burst of light disappearing into the darkness.

She opened her eyes, and startled. Hunter had stepped right up to her, his face close to hers.

"You need to rest," he whispered, touching her forehead gently. She tried to move away, to open her mouth to protest, but a warmth rolled through her mind, a comforting blanket of white that stole her consciousness, and then she knew nothing.

Hunter caught her as she started to slide to the floor, scooping her up and carrying her to the chair in the corner her friend—what was her name?—had sat in. He placed her gently in the chair, pulling up one of the cushions that had fallen to the floor and carefully placing it against the wall. He tilted Melissa's head into a comfortable position, making sure the cushion was placed to prevent a crick in the neck, and squatted there for a moment, gazing up at her.

She looked so peaceful, so damn luscious. It always surprised him how a woman with so much sass and attitude could look so angelic. He took advantage of the moment, staring at her without worrying about her hissing, spitting, kicking or smashing his head in, because he'd sensed that was where she was headed when she realized he'd used her.

His mouth pulled down at the corners. He hadn't lied to her. Light warriors needed sources of light to fill their energy stores. Sexual energy, though, was like a pure shot of adrenaline, a caffeine triple hit. It could also be draining for the source, if the light warrior was feeding and not careful. Most light warriors learned how to consume the energy without bringing their source to the brink of death, although it was possible to kill a partner if the light warrior didn't stop.

Melissa's energy was like an inferno. He wondered if that was because she was a witch. Regardless, her energy was a seduction in itself, especially with him being half-starved. With her lack of sleep, though, and the magic she'd expended on trying to heal her friend, she was dangerously low on power. It had felt so good, but despite their shared passion and it was shared—she'd reciprocated, he hadn't imagined that—he could also sense the lethargy stealing into her limbs. He'd had to pull back.

Normally he wasn't quite so—enthusiastic—in a light feed. He knew control, he knew discipline. He blamed it on subsisting on torchlight for the past few months, and not on any kind of magnetic attraction he might feel for the witch.

Her friend entered the room, carrying a bundle of towels and a bucket, steam curling up from the water. She halted when she saw Melissa sleeping in the corner. "What's wrong with her?" Her expression showed her alarm, and Hunter rose, holding his hand out in a soothing gesture.

"She's fine. She's just really tired after working on your brother." He took the towels from her. "Thanks..." He racked his brain for her name, but honestly, he'd been kind of focused on Melissa, and checking out her home, more than anything—including his new patient.

"Lexi," she supplied. She indicated the candles. Some were just hardened puddles of wax, some could be relit.

"Melissa used all of her candles earlier. Do you need me to run out and get some?"

He nodded. "Please." He was good to go, but working on Lance was going to take some time and energy, and he'd need to top up and rest. Lexi nodded, then paused, clearly hesitant to leave him alone with her brother and Melissa. "He's going to be fine," he said, hoping he was right. There was never any guarantee with a patient, there were too many variables, but he would have promised Melissa anything to get out of that cell.

"Uh, okay. Well, I'll go get some candles," Lexi murmured, backing out of the doorway. She eyed his chest for a moment, and he saw the curiosity flare in her eyes before she glanced at her brother. "I'll bring some clothes, too. For both of you."

He smiled. "Thanks." He didn't offer her any explanation for his half-naked state.

Lexi left, and he heard her light tread on the stairs. He glanced around the room. Lance was still unconscious on the bed and Melissa was sleeping deeply in the corner. The whole apartment was filled with an eerie silence. He couldn't even hear the tick of a clock. At present, he may as well have been alone.

He turned and eyed the door. He could leave. Lance was out cold, and couldn't stop him—although the guy looked massive enough to present a challenge if he'd been alert. Melissa was in a forced sleep. She would waken when she was fully rested, her energy restored.

He stepped out into the hallway, turning in a full circle. There was absolutely nothing to stop him leaving. He eyed the door at the end of the hall.

He could just up and leave. Step through that door and escape.

* * *

Melissa stirred. Her eyelids flickered. Something fluffy made her nose itchy, and she put her hand up to rub it, her eyes opening. Pale blue wool filled her vision, and she frowned. She was covered in the fringed blanket she normally draped across the back of her sofa, and it was the strips of heavy yarn that teased her face. She lowered the blanket to her waist and straightened, frowning as a cushion behind her shifted and fell into her lap. She yawned and stretched. God, she'd needed that sleep. She felt so...refreshed. Then she remembered how she'd fallen asleep. Her muscles stiffened. That rat bastard. She glanced about her.

Everything around her was cast in a golden hue. Candles sat on every surface. Many, many candles. It would almost be romantic if it wasn't for the bloodied rags she spied on the floor. Hunter stood with his back to her, his feet planted shoulder-width apart, his back all smooth and golden. He held his hands out over Lance's unconscious body, his arms and shoulders roped with muscle, and her mouth dropped.

Tendrils of light glowed and snaked from Hunter's palms to the bullet hole in Lance's chest, and she could see the radiance moving beneath his skin, as though glowworms pulsed inside his body.

She rose from the chair, the blanket falling to her feet as she stepped toward the bed. Lance's body was covered in perspiration, and he'd been stripped, cleaned and covered with a sheet. His complexion was still gray, yet his chest and limbs looked flushed. Every now and then he would groan softly, and Hunter would draw his hands away, the threads of light dimming, before continuing. She glanced at Hunter.

His eyes were closed, his face pale and perspiring,

and occasionally his brow would dip, and the stream of light would pulse beneath his palms. Melissa glanced at her watch, and her eyes widened. Four hours had passed since she'd last glanced at it. It was well past two in the morning.

Hunter was silent, his attention focused inward, and Melissa didn't want to distract him. She folded her arms and moved to stand at the foot of the bed.

She did it to watch over her friend, not to get an eyeful of Hunter's bare torso.

She focused on Lance, but every now and then her gaze would return to the light warrior, to his hands...his chest...his lips. She found herself staring at his mouth.

He'd kissed her.

She'd kissed him back.

It had felt incredible. They'd barely touched, really, but he'd managed to stir something in her, hot passion and a soft vulnerability she didn't know quite what to do with. Bury it. Showing this man a weakness like that would only lead to pain. Maybe even death.

Her lips tightened. He'd done it again, damn it.

She couldn't believe she'd allowed him to get close to her again. She'd been totally sucked into that kiss, and he'd just been using her to drain her energy and fill his own stores. She lifted her chin. Well, she knew what the jerk was capable of. She would make damn sure he never used her again, that he never fooled her again.

Lance flinched in his unconscious state, emitting a low moan, and Hunter rolled his lips in, his brows drawing into a deep V. He curled his palms, his fingers dancing as though playing an instrument, and Melissa was mesmerized by the grace and fluidity of his movements.

Lance's breathing sped up, and Melissa bit her lip. She had no idea what was going on, but it looked like

Lance was in tremendous pain. Hunter rolled his hand over, as though grabbing the tendrils of light in his fist, and raised his hand, as though pulling on a fishing line.

Lance's features contorted and his body arched off the bed. Melissa shifted, not sure what to do, and then she heard a soft, moist squish and something slid out of Lance's chest. Her eyes rounded as Lance's body subsided back on the bed, his head lolling to the side, his features relaxed once more. His eyes remained closed, but his breathing changed. No longer panting, his breaths slowed down, deepened.

Hunter's eyes opened, and the tendrils of light disappeared, winked out of existence. He reached for a clean hand towel near Lance's head and used it to pick up the bloodied bullet fragment that lay on Lance's chest, a smile of triumph curling his lips.

Melissa stepped forward, and Hunter turned, as though surprised for a moment to see her. His expression changed from triumphant to wary in the blink of an eye.

"You're awake," he noted, his voice a soft murmur in the room.

She raised an eyebrow. "I am." No thanks to him. She kept her voice and expression cool. She'd wanted to throttle him when she awoke, but watching him work had mollified her anger somewhat. She was still angry, just not violently so. Besides, revenge was a dish best served cold, right? She stepped closer toward him, eyeing the small item resting on the hand towel.

"Is that part of the bullet?" She reached out, but he pulled the hand towel out of her reach.

"Careful, it's tainted, remember." He tipped the fragment into a glass on the bedside table. "Hemlock, if I'm not mistaken."

"Easy to get your hands on," she commented. It was

one of the first toxins she'd been able to restock, although it wasn't necessarily a high-demand plant. Mainly because you could find it growing on roadsides and near water sources everywhere.

"Nasty, especially if you're dipping your weapons in it."

She nodded, making a mental note. If you wanted to kill a vampire, you dipped your weapons in verbena. If you wanted to kill a werewolf, you dipped your weapons in wolfsbane. If you wanted to kill a human—or a dhampir—you used hemlock, or any other common poison at your disposal. Lance wasn't shot by accident. Someone had wanted to hurt him, and knew what would do the trick.

"Where is Lexi?" She finally realized Lance's sister was nowhere to be seen.

"She ducked out for some supplies, but then I sent her home for a rest. She'll be back sometime in the morning."

Melissa raised her eyebrows. "I'm surprised you convinced her to leave her brother." The young woman had remained in the room when Melissa had worked her magic.

Hunter shrugged. "She needed a little convincing, but she was tired, there was nothing she could do here and, quite frankly, I don't like a cluttered workspace."

She eyed him for a moment. Needed a little convincing, huh? She wondered if light warriors possessed a talent for compulsion, like vampires did. She thought about her dreams. Maybe they had some skill with mind bending.

Another reason to hate.

Then she realized she'd been alone with Hunter—and she'd survived. No infernos, no explosions, no retribution for locking him up for five months. Not only had she survived, he was still here. She hadn't thought to put up any blocking wards to prevent him leaving.

She turned her gaze to her friend. He was breathing easier now, and although his flesh still looked damp with perspiration, color was beginning to return to his complexion. But he still looked weak and unwell. "Why isn't he waking up?"

Hunter threw the hand towel onto the soiled linen by his feet. "Because I'm a light warrior, not God." He folded his arms, staring down at his patient, and she forced herself to ignore the way the muscles in his arms and chest bunched with the movement. "He was badly hurt, Melissa. That poison has spread through his body. I've been able to remove the toxin, but traces still remain in his body. It's not going to kill him, but it's going to take time for his metabolism to burn through it, especially in his weakened state."

"So do something to speed it up," she told him.

He dipped his chin. "I'm beat."

"No." She stepped away from him. She wasn't going to go anywhere near him when he needed to "recharge." He held up his hand to halt her, correctly interpreting the reason for her retreat.

"Relax. Lance needs a break from the treatment. Too much light force too fast, and I could end up killing him. He's had enough for now, as have I. I'll start working on him again in the morning, once we've both rested." He smiled at her, and for a moment she stared. There wasn't anything wicked, or calculating. Rather, it was a tired, sincere smile, and utterly without guile. "I'd love a shower, though...?"

And there it was. A vision of him, naked, in her shower, water sluicing over those abs, droplets trailing down his body. She bent over and scooped up the linen, hiding her flushed cheeks.

"Bathroom is at the end of the hall, towels are in the cupboard underneath the sink. You can look after yourself. You're not here as a guest." She didn't look at him to see his reaction, but stalked down the hallway to the cupboard that cleverly hid her laundry. After a moment she heard him behind her, shifting aside to let him pass her to the bathroom. He carried a dark bundle of clothing, but he shut the door before she could inquire about them.

She busied herself with the laundry, determinedly shutting any vision of his wet, naked body from her mind as she heard the water turn on in the shower. She heard him moan and realized this was his first real shower since his capture. Those bucket washes had consisted of cold water and a cloth.

Her lips curled as she poured some stain remover and detergent into the machine, then switched it on. The machine shuddered, then she heard the reassuring noise of water filling the tub.

A choked cry came from behind the door, and she heard a series of thumps, as though he was recoiling against the wall. A series of curse words were bellowed, and then nothing but the fall of water in the shower.

She walked down the hallway to her bedroom, her hips swinging, and she shut the door.

Nope. Not a guest.

Chapter 8

Hunter scooped up the eggs and slid them onto the three plates on the table. He was wearing an apron he'd found in a kitchen drawer. Either Melissa or someone she knew had a sense of humor, because the apron had the words *I kiss better than I cook* across it. It was true, though. Melissa did kiss a hell of a lot better than she cooked, if her prison food was anything to go by.

Lexi poured the juice, and he was moving the plates to the set places on the tiny round kitchen table when Melissa walked into the kitchen.

He almost dropped the plate, and fumbled to catch it.

She was all sleep-tousled and rosy-cheeked, her eyes blinking as she took in the domestic scene. She wore loose-fitting slate blue cotton pants and a matching top that looked soft from many washings, and pink-and-black polka-dotted woolen socks that looked like they'd been knitted from the hair of a Persian cat, all fluffy and spiky.

She looked adorable. Before, when she'd stormed down to his cell in her silken nightie, she'd looked all womanly and sexy, like a dangerously sexy siren. This morning, she was girl-next-door, scoop-me-up-and-screw-me cute. Like a sleepy tomboy stripper. He put the plate on the table with a thud.

"What's going on?" Melissa asked, her voice all husky and soft from sleep. That voice. It still had that same effect, curling deep inside him with an insidious desire. Her brows dipped, her lips were pulled into a sexy little pout and she looked adorably grumpy.

"I noticed you had barely any food in your fridge and brought some groceries," Lexi informed her as she took a seat at the table. "Hunter cooked breakfast."

Melissa padded over to grab the coffeepot off the warmer and fill it with water. "Did he just?" she muttered as she placed the pot back on the warmer, scooped coffee into the filter and jabbed the button to turn it on.

"You're a morning person, I see," Hunter commented dryly as he lowered himself into the seat.

"I'm a coffee person," she muttered, as she sank into the remaining seat. She eyed the food on the table with suspicion. Hunter's stomach growled, but he held up his cutlery politely, waiting for the ladies to start eating.

Green eyes met his, narrowed and mistrustful. "After you," she said coolly.

He tilted his head to the side. "It's not poisoned," he told her.

Lexi laughed as she chewed on some bacon. She swallowed. "It's delicious. Besides, he's a friend—and a doctor. I'm sure he can cook something without killing us."

Hunter waggled his eyebrows. "See, Melissa. I'm a friend. And a doctor. I wouldn't hurt you."

She glared at him, and he sighed. She really didn't

trust him. "Fine." He scooped up some egg and put it in his mouth. "Hmm-mmm. Yum."

Melissa finally raised her cutlery, twirling her knife meaningfully as she met his eyes, then began to eat. He saw the soft flare of surprise in her expression as she tasted the food, and he smiled. "I didn't think you'd mind me cooking for once. I mean, I know how you love cooking for me, but I wanted to return the favor." No more peanut butter and jelly sandwiches.

Lexi's eyebrows rose. "Oh, so you two are—"

"No," Melissa interjected shaking her head.

"Not yet," Hunter stated, enjoying the flare of annoyance in her green eyes.

"Not ever."

Lexi glanced between them. "Okay," she said slowly, before focusing on her food.

Melissa rose from her seat, and Hunter watched as she crossed over to the cupboards. "Does anyone else want coffee?"

"No, thanks. I'm trying to go no-caffeine," Lexi said as she pierced some bacon with her fork and ate it.

"Yes, please," Hunter said, mostly because he'd gone five months without the stuff, but also because he knew it would annoy her, serving him. She shot him another hard stare and poured the freshly brewed coffee into two cups. She placed one in front of him with a thud. He had to move his hand to avoid the hot droplets that spilled with the movement. She gestured to the bottle of milk on the table and the pot of sugar.

"Help yourself," she told him sweetly, then resumed her seat. She sipped from her cup, eyeing him over the rim. Her gaze drifted down to his clothes, and he straightened his shoulders, then almost laughed at himself, puffing up his chest like a courting parrot.

"Where did you get those clothes?" she asked brusquely.

"I brought them over," Lexi answered, then drained her glass of juice. She rose from the table. "I figured I'd have to bring some over for Lance, and Hunter looks about the same size."

Hunter's eyebrows rose. She thought he was the same size as that hulk in the spare bedroom? He turned his arms, looking at his biceps. Maybe he'd bulked up in his prison, but he didn't think so. The gray long-sleeved T-shirt was loose, but comfortable. "Thanks," he said, smiling.

Lexi winked as she rose from the table. "Hey, I've had to do the walk of shame enough to recognize one when I see it. No dramas."

Hunter chuckled softly as Melissa choked on her coffee, but Lexi didn't seem to notice as she dumped the dishes in the sink and left the kitchen. He waited until Melissa stopped coughing and leaned back in her chair. He met her gaze as he raised the cup to his lips.

"You didn't tell her I was your prisoner." It wasn't a question. Lexi had treated him like a friend-by-association, easygoing and open. She'd brought him clothes and bacon—even some toiletries so he could shave, and for that, she had a new friend for life.

"Neither did you," she pointed out, folding her arms. That top looked so soft, and it showed off her breasts. His mouth dried. She wasn't wearing a bra.

Good God. He could feel himself swell in his hand-me-down jeans. He raised the coffee to his lips, trying to distract himself, but all he could think about was how those breasts had felt against his chest last night, and how he wanted to kiss her again, and this time not stop.

"Why didn't you?" he asked her. Talking felt like he

was trying to push his voice over rocks, so tight and dry was his throat.

She arched an eyebrow, and she went from gloriously tousled cutie to seductive vixen. His lips quirked. If she knew where his thoughts were going, she'd probably do some of her witchy-woo voodoo on him, make him a eunuch.

"Because Lexi is already worried enough. She doesn't need to know the man healing her brother tried to incinerate me in a fireball. Where did you sleep last night?"

"On your sofa." He put the cup down on the table. Her couch may have been a piece of furniture about a foot too short and not quite wide enough for his frame, but after sleeping on stone for the last five months it was almost bliss.

Almost.

It also faced a hearth. Would have been nice to have known that last night, too. They'd lit up Melissa's spare bedroom like a fairy wonderland, when he'd had a perfectly good fireplace in the living room down the hall. Had she been trying to limit his access to light? Still, he got the recharge he needed when he'd kissed Melissa, and he didn't regret that, not one bit.

Knowing that a soft and sleepy Melissa was just down the hall had been torture. He'd wanted to go to her. He'd had to keep telling himself it was because he'd been in captivity, months without a woman, and Melissa was right *there*. He almost believed himself, too, but as he didn't share the same hunger for Lexi as he did for Melissa, it wasn't quite convincing.

She was silent for a moment, then she flicked her hair back over her shoulder. "How is Lance?" she asked, her gaze on the table. He pursed his lips. She really did care for this friend.

"He's resting. I checked on him when I woke up. He's still battling the poison, but he's breathing easier." He eyed the kitchen for a moment, and a photo frame on top of the fridge caught his eye. He rose from the table. "Who's this?" He gestured to the frame. He'd seen other photos around the living room, some featuring the same guy. In this one, Melissa was sitting at a table, leaning against the guy whose arm was slung around her shoulders. She looked…younger. Not agewise. He guessed it was a recent photo, within the last couple of years, judging by her age. No, it was the easygoing smile, the carefree twinkle in her eye, the absence of…anguish. He blinked when he recognized it. Melissa carried a darkness within her now, something that she hadn't possessed at the time this photo was taken. The photographer had caught the couple in midlaugh. They looked relaxed, and very comfortable in each other's space.

She rose from the table and grabbed the frame. "None of your business." She held the frame behind her back, and lifted her chin to eye him squarely. "What do we need to do about Lance?"

His lips pursed for a moment. Whoever the guy was, he was important to her. As important as the guy lying unconscious in her spare room? How many men did this woman have dangling around her? Just the thought she was a player made him fold his arms and match her brusqueness.

"I'll work on clearing out the rest of the toxin, but I might have to halt after that. With the extent of his injuries, he's going to need a slow rehab." He made a split decision. "This could take a while." It wasn't quite a lie. He could justify it. He could speed up the process, but right then, he decided to take his time, take a little extra care.

She frowned. "A while? How long is a while?"

He shrugged. "A couple of days."

"Days?" Her expression was a combination of surprise, horror and frustration.

He smiled. "Yep. Guess we're going to be spending some quality time together." This was an opportunity to discover more about the woman who had held him captive. He should move on, but he convinced himself this was a strategic move—and nothing to do with a developing fascination for the woman. He'd initially sought her out to destroy any evidence that could convict his brother of murder. Now his desire to stay had nothing to do with Ryder, and everything to do with the complicated woman standing before him. She treated him as though he should behave better—as though she believed he was capable of being better. Everyone else took him at face value. He frowned. No, he mentally corrected himself. He was staying because he needed leverage against someone who could match him. The witch had managed to capture a light warrior and hold him prisoner. She knew his vulnerabilities. He needed to find hers to level the playing field—because he sure wasn't going to go through that hell again.

Her lips pursed, and his gaze dropped to her sexy little pout. She could be so sexy in a snit. "Just—just heal him, Hunter. As fast as you can."

He bowed his head. "But of course. A deal's a deal. I'm a man of honor."

She rolled her eyes and snorted as she turned to leave the room. "Please, we both know that's not true," she muttered as she walked down the hallway to her room.

He brooded as he watched her go. She was right. He took what he wanted, when he wanted, and it had served him well in the past. He'd almost killed her trying to hide what he thought was evidence against his brother.

When an Alpha Prime had died in his brother's dental surgery, he knew it was just a matter of time before his brother was punished—either through the Reform court, or through the Alpha Prime's werewolf pack. He'd seen the autopsy results, knew that the highly concentrated dose of wolfsbane that had killed the lycan leader could have only come from Irondell's premier apothecary. Even during their disconnection, he'd wanted to protect his little brother, had felt the need to look out for Ryder. Maybe it was a throwback to a time that was no more, when the boys had behaved like brothers, and there had been love and camaraderie between them. Or maybe it was a deep-rooted sense of duty as protector after his mother died. Either way, he'd done it because he'd believed it to be the right thing to do. A bad act for good reasons. He frowned. Sometimes, he did bad things. Sometimes he regretted it. Sometimes he didn't. It wasn't a question of honor; it was a matter of expediency. Sometimes those virtues couldn't coexist, and he'd never lost any sleep over it.

He eyed the closed door between him and Melissa. For the first time last night, though, he'd had trouble sleeping.

Melissa entered the spare bedroom carrying two glasses of water and halted. Her apartment was toasty. Like, the warmest she could remember. Candles were lit everywhere, and the fireplace in her living room was in full flame. She figured he'd find it sooner or later. While she might not know much about light warriors, she knew they needed light or flame, and with that they could create their own light and flame. She wanted Hunter to have the strength to heal her friend. She didn't want him to have the strength to level a city block.

Hunter now stood over Lance's still-unconscious body, but he looked different. He'd shaved, the dark beard gone to reveal a chiseled jaw. His hair had been trimmed, too. Gone were the dark, loose waves, and instead his hair was shorter. It was still long enough to curl, still gave him that rough edge, but the shaggy style made him look casual and presentable. She turned an inquiring gaze to Lexi, who nodded proudly, gesturing to the scissors that lay in the first aid basket.

Lexi had cut his hair. Melissa set the glass down on the bedside table. He didn't look like the man who'd been kept in a cell for five months. He no longer looked like her prisoner. Didn't look rough and dangerous, but instead looked much more civilized. Like a guy she'd pass in the street and probably turn to look at twice. Who was she kidding? She'd been thinking of him most of the day. Ever since that kiss, she couldn't get him out of her mind. She'd look more than twice if she passed him in the street. Honestly, she'd probably do more than just look, after that kiss. And that frustrated the hell out of her.

She stepped back. She didn't like the false air of civility he wore—and she knew it was false. He may have his hair trimmed neatly, be cleanly shaven and wear presentable clothes that clung to those broad shoulders before draping down to hide the washboard stomach she knew existed beneath. But that was the problem. She knew exactly what strength and lethal power were now hidden behind the facade of propriety—and she didn't trust him. Not. At. All.

She'd pushed her nightstand against the door last night, and since waking she'd installed spelled wards around her home and shop. He wouldn't be able to leave the premises—he couldn't get past her apartment's front door, but she'd taken extra precautions with her access points in the store below. He wasn't going anywhere, no matter how hard he tried. He wasn't in a cell any longer, but he was not free. He wouldn't be until Lance was healed. She was still in control.

Although, she hadn't been in control last night… Oh, there it was again, that mental image of him kissing her against the wall. No, damn it, he was her prisoner, not the hunk of her dreams. She refused to start thinking of him like that, kisses be damned.

She handed the second glass to Lexi, her gaze remaining on what Hunter was doing. She could see those light tendrils snaking around her friend's body. She'd had to go downstairs and open her store, and this was her first opportunity to return to check up on her friend. She wouldn't have left him alone in Hunter's care, but Lexi had taken up temporary residence watching over her brother—and playing hairdresser, apparently. That left Melissa able to tend her business.

Although all morning she'd been distracted, wondering how things were going in the apartment above the store. She told herself it had nothing to do with this good-looking angel of death, but everything to do with her friend.

"How is he?" she whispered to Lexi.

Lexi sighed. "He's improving, but Hunter is taking it slow so as not to hurt him more." The woman shook her head, her straight blond hair shifting with the movement. "I have to tell you, Mel, I've never seen anything like this. I don't know what he's doing, or how he's doing it, but Lance is improving." She raised the glass to her lips.

Melissa leaned against the wall. "He's a light warrior," she told her. Lexi coughed on the water, her eyes wide. She wiped her chin, and glanced between Melissa and Hunter, who seemed oblivious to their conversation, so focused was he on his patient.

"Are you serious? I thought they were extinct."

Melissa shook her head. That was the common belief and, until recently, it had been hers, as well. "Apparently, the reports of their demise are greatly exaggerated."

Her brother's friend, Vassiliki Verity—a half-blood vampire, and an annoying one at that—was defending a shadow breed dentist on a murder charge, and had tracked him down to the home of his brother—Hunter. The man who'd destroyed her apothecary. Hunter Galen and his brother were having an argument when she and Dave had arrived, and they'd hidden, managing to over-hear snatches of the conversation. She and her brother had been astounded when Arthur Armstrong, a Prime of the human faction, had arrived. Armstrong was as wealthy as he was powerful, an active participant in the intrigues of the Reform elite—and father to Hunter and Ryder. Just as his light warrior ancestors before him, Armstrong had kept the light warriors' existence secret. Everyone assumed that Arthur Armstrong and his sons were highly skilled healers among the shadow breeds. Nobody had guessed it was their light warrior powers that helped them be so.

Armstrong had been manipulating various members of the shadow breeds for years, during their treatment appointments. Melissa stared at the man standing over her friend. Who knew what he'd done with his patients. Was he as sick and twisted as his father?

She folded her arms. Of course he was. He'd tried to kill her, hadn't he? Then he'd used her dreams against her, and finally he'd used her to recharge his inner battery by kissing her. Everything this man had done to her had been one form of deceit and betrayal after another.

"Don't leave Lance alone, okay?" Melissa told her friend quietly.

Lexi frowned, concern darkening her gaze as she stared at the man standing over her brother. "Why? What would he do?"

Melissa pursed her lips. "I have no idea, and that's what scares me."

Hunter lowered his arms, extinguishing his light, and turned to face them. He really was too damn good-looking. "I think that will do for today. Any more and I might overload him." His gaze was friendly, and mildly tired. He hadn't heard their whispers in the corner.

He saw the glass of water on the bedside table and his brows rose in surprise. "Thanks, Melissa." He reached for it and drank, swallowing the contents in two gulps. He smiled, holding up the empty glass. "Thirsty work. Appreciate it."

She nodded. "I have to go back to work. Let me know if you need anything," she told Lexi meaningfully, and left the room.

"Oh, wait," Lexi called, and stepped out into the hall behind her.

Melissa turned to face her, her hand already on the doorknob to leave the apartment. "What's up, Lex?"

Lexi grimaced. "I'll, uh, I'll need to head back home tonight."

Melissa's eyes narrowed, and her gaze dropped down to Lexi's hand. The green snakeskin jasper ring was still on her finger.

"I need to have a chat with my boyfriend," Lexi told her quietly. "I'd put it off, but after what's happened with Lance, I think there are some things I need to address."

Melissa nodded solemnly. "I understand. What time

do you need to leave? I'll make sure I'm back here by then."

"Five?"

Melissa hesitated, then nodded. "Sure. I'll get Jenna to close up. I'll be here."

"Thanks. I'll stay the night at Lance's place," Lexi told her, her hand gesturing toward the rest of Melissa's apartment. "It's pretty full here. Is that okay?"

While Melissa would love the buffer between her and Hunter, she realized Lexi's words were true. All available beds or furniture were taken with Lance and Hunter here. Besides, Lance was a dhampir, and his home was probably the best option for Lexi to stay at if she was leaving her vampire boyfriend.

"That's fine. Will you be all right?"

Lexi waved a hand casually. "I'll be fine."

Melissa frowned. She may have thought Lexi was annoying or frustrating, and perhaps a little insecure, but after witnessing the care and love the young woman held for her brother, Melissa was warming to her, a new respect dawning behind the exasperation. Trying not to, but she couldn't quite help it. Lance had asked her to look after Lexi, and she would, but now she'd do it possibly as much for Lexi as for Lance.

"You call me if you need me," she told the young woman, her tone serious.

"Oh, Mel—"

"Don't 'oh, Mel' me. If you're in danger, you call me. I don't care what time, okay?"

Lexi smiled. "Okay, but seriously, I'll be fine."

"Just call me when you get to Lance's place, okay? Promise?"

"Promise."

Melissa nodded, moderately satisfied, and left the apartment.

Hunter listened to the whispered exchange in the hallway. His hearing was acute, and he had no trouble hearing the conversation near the front door, nor the one that had occurred earlier in the room.

He frowned. Why would Lexi need help? Why was Melissa concerned? The fact that Melissa was so protective of Lexi was a surprise. Hell, he'd been surprised ever since Melissa had told him she had a friend, and one that she was prepared to surrender her own need for vengeance in order to assist. Now she was going all motherly protective over Lexi—admittedly in a fierce, kick-ass kind of way.

Lance stirred on the bed, his eyelids flickering, before his eyes finally opened.

Hunter was next to him immediately, and gave him a friendly smile. "Whoa, hey, you need to rest," he whispered, gently touching the dhampir's temple, and the man's green eyes glazed over, and he drifted off into unconsciousness. "Back to sleep, bud."

No, he wasn't ready for the dhampir to wake just yet. He still wanted to find out a few things about the witch, and Lance unconscious and still not quite healed was exactly the way things needed to be for now.

Chapter 9

Melissa hadn't needed to get Jenna to close up, after all. The weather had turned foul outside, with winds gusting and flurries of snow whirling down the street. Her store had emptied about an hour ago, so she'd sent Jenna home early. She was climbing the stairs when Lexi met her halfway.

"How is Lance?" Melissa asked without preamble.

Lexi smiled. "He's doing well. It looks like Hunter has been able to neutralize the poison, and he's working on the deep tissue cuts tomorrow. I think he's wiped out, though. He was passed out on your sofa when I left."

Melissa nodded as she turned to walk back down the stairs with Lexi. "Good. I'm not quite sure how it works, but I guess it can be exhausting, expending all that energy." They walked down the corridor to the door that opened out onto the street. Melissa had bespelled and warded this access point, too. She twisted the locks and hauled the heavy door open. It wasn't long after she'd set up her apothecary that she'd discovered some people viewed her store like a pharmacy, and she'd had a few break-ins, early on. Of course, when she'd tracked down the perpetrators and meted out her own form of punishment, word got out about what happened to those who tried to steal from a witch.

She didn't get burgled anymore.

Still, she'd learned personal and property security was important, and preferred to err on the side of extreme caution. She wasn't going to be vulnerable to attack. Never again.

She stepped aside to allow Lexi to leave. "Don't forget, call me if you need me."

Lexi nodded. "And you call me if anything changes with Lance. I'm not too far away."

Melissa waved, slamming the door shut and engaging all the locks.

She was almost at the base of the stairs when she heard the pounding on her door.

Hunter quickly settled himself on the floor next to the bed. Lance was breathing deep and even, a sign of the dhampir's rapid recovery. Lexi had just left the apartment, and Melissa would be up very shortly. He only had a brief opportunity to dreamwalk through Lance's subconscious, learn a little more about her, before her arrival.

He closed his eyes, allowing the rush of unconsciousness to sweep over him. In moments, he walked through Lance's memories. It was as though projector screens surrounded him, each playing different memories. He noted the darker one tinged with red—the one where he'd been hurt. He'd be interested to take a side trip into that, but later. Now he whispered a suggestion to act as a shortcut to the information he wanted to access.

Melissa.

Instantly, the screens flickered to life, and he selected the one furthest away. Their first meeting. Everything around him changed, and he realized he was in a back alley. It was late afternoon, the sky bathed in swathes of crimson and orange, but it was already getting dark in the alley. He glanced around, trying to get a read on the location, and noticed the Better Read Than Dead Bookstore lettering painted on one of the roller doors. The alley behind Melissa's bookshop.

Lance stood, leaning against a wall, his pose casual. He kept his gaze trained on the street, as though waiting for something—or someone.

Hunter heard the squeak as the door was rolled up, and he could dimly make out the figure of someone hauling down on the chains inside the dock as the door rose. Melissa.

She was younger, though. Early twenties, her red hair tied back into a ponytail. She wore a ratty T-shirt and jeans and scuffed sneakers, and already looked dusty.

Lance turned and frowned as Melissa emerged, glancing at her watch. "Go back inside," he called to her.

Melissa paused, noticing the man at the end of the alley for the first time. She folded her arms.

"I'm waiting for a delivery, bozo. You might want to move on, yourself."

"I said, get the hell back inside," Lance growled, his fists clenching, his shoulders slightly raised in a dominant pose.

Hunter's eyebrows rose. He looked threatening enough. He glanced to see what Melissa would do next.

She folded her arms, her eyes narrowing. "Get lost, before I call Reform Authority."

Hunter smiled. Ah, there was the shrew he knew so well.

Lance took a step forward. "It's dangerous out here. Go inside."

Melissa laughed, a sexy little tinkle as she stepped toward the edge of the loading dock. "I know this place far better than you, alley rat."

Something skittered at the mouth of the alley, and Hunter turned as shadows seemed to emerge from the encroaching darkness.

"Well, what do we have here, boys?" A masculine voice called out from the darkness, and a form stepped forward. He was tall, with blond hair and dark eyes. "Looks like the book witch has a new friend."

Hunter eyed the men stalking down the alley, and that's what they were doing, stalking. Their movements were smooth and predatory, and he watched cautiously as they fanned out in a strategic move that looked well practiced.

A vampire pack. Five in all, and very determined.

A second vampire stepped forward. He had dark hair, brown eyes and a coldness that seemed to emanate from his pores. "You were right, Ty. She is out tonight."

Hunter glanced back to the dock. Melissa eyed all of the vampires. He knew there would be no way for her to close the roller door in time, and the narrowing of Melissa's eyes suggested she'd arrived at the same conclusion.

Then she did something that surprised him. She laughed.

"Is that you, Dick? Did your little underling come crying to you? Is this your idea of some big, bad retribution against the witch?"

"I did try to warn you," Lance muttered as he shifted, subtly putting himself between Melissa and the vampires.

"Rick," the blond corrected through gritted teeth.

"Well, if the name fits…"

Rick laughed, showing his elongated fangs, as he nodded. "You're right. You might be a witch, but I'd prefer to call you dinner."

He opened his mouth in a snarl, and he and his pack moved as one, all springing toward the woman on the dock.

Melissa peered through the peep slot of her door, frowning. After a few minutes she turned to retreat up the hall, but then she heard a sound.

Sobbing. A painful, woeful, sorrowful sobbing, as though someone was mortally wounded, or their heart was cleaved in two. It was the kind of sound that reached deep into a person's conscience, and Melissa whirled back to the door. She craned her neck, twisting from side to side, peering into the darkness.

There.

Someone lay in the gutter, rocking, as the snow drifted around. Melissa frowned. It wasn't clear if it was a man or a woman—they were in shadow, their head covered with a knitted cap that even now showed the glitter of wet snow. She could see, though, that whoever it was wasn't wearing a coat.

Damn fool would freeze out there if they stayed much longer.

She opened the door, gasping as the bitterly cold air swept into the front hall. Then she stepped out and hurried to the person huddled in the gutter. She paused halfway across the sidewalk.

"Hey! You can't stay here," she called out. She flexed her mouth, then stepped forward again. "Hey, there, you in the gutter. You need to move on."

The person whimpered. Melissa frowned. It wasn't a normal whimper, she could tell; it sounded almost like a pup in pain.

"Excuse me? Are you okay?" She reached her hand out to touch the person's shoulder. The action seemed to make the person erupt out of the gutter.

Snow flicked in all directions, and the person's form twisted, a pained growl coming from them as they turned. It was a man, only it wasn't—not anymore, as his body morphed into lycan form.

Melissa turned to run back to her doorway, back to the haven that would protect her and prevent his entry, and halted.

Another werewolf had planted himself just in front of the doorway. Melissa raised her hands, summoning her powers as the lycans launched. She screamed as fangs tore into her shoulder.

Hunter watched as Lance and Melissa fought off the vampires. For a big guy, Lance could move like lightning, and if Hunter didn't already know Lance was a dhampir, he would have been impressed. Knowing he possessed similar attributes of strength and speed as a vampire made the brutal clash a little ho-hum, in his book. Still, it was interesting watching Melissa in action. She was like a virago, a whirlwind of red locks, flashing green eyes and hands that caused her opponents to scream in pain and clutch their heads at her softest touch.

Lance, on the other hand, was far more brutal, matching his strength against the vampires, his punches and kicks vicious. His expression was savage as his fangs elongated, and he bit into the necks of his victims.

He grimaced as Melissa touched one of the attackers, and he convulsed, screaming in pain as he fell. Lance ripped out the throat of another, and suddenly the numbers shifted from five to two dead, one who rocked, staring sightlessly at a crack in the pavement, one frothing at the mouth and unconscious, and the leader. Dick.

Oh, wait, Rick. Dick was Melissa's special name for him.

"Wait," she called, as Lance stepped toward the vampire.

He glared over his shoulder at her, eyes an eerie red, and blood smeared on his chin.

"He's lost his guardians. He's powerless now."

"He's a vampire," Lance stated roughly. "He should die."

Melissa strode up toward them. Damn, the woman didn't know the meaning of the word *retreat*. Hunter drifted closer to listen to the exchange.

Rick glared at them both. "This isn't over, witch. You think you can set up shop here and sell your poisons? Ain't gonna happen."

Melissa looked down the alley, then shrugged. "Looks like it just did." She put her hands on her hips, and gave the vampire a slow smile. "So you can go back to your little nest and tell Vivianne Marchetta that she doesn't own everything in Irondell. If she tries to mess with me or my store again, she's going to find out exactly how painful a curse can be."

Rick snorted. "We are going to rain hate down on you so bad—"

Lance reached out, his movements so fast they were almost a blur, and snapped the vampire's neck.

He watched in satisfaction as the body crumpled to the ground. "Sorry. I hate it when they go on, and on." He rolled his hand. "And on. Besides, all these bodies will tell Marchetta exactly what she needs to know."

Melissa assessed the man next to her for a moment. "You're not from around here, are you?"

Lance chuckled. "I was. Once. It's been a while."

"Oh? Where have you been?"

Lance took a handkerchief out of his back pocket and cleaned his face. "Prison." He said the word calmly, but didn't look at the witch.

Melissa digested that for a moment. "And yet you were in my back alley when these guys decided to pay me a visit. Why?"

Lance shrugged. "I've been trying to track this particular vamp, and heard he might show up."

"Dhampir?"

Lance nodded. "Yeah."

Melissa looked down at the bodies strewed around, and nodded. "Good job."

He glanced toward the entrance to the alley. "Hey, you don't happen to know if anyone's got some work going on around here, do you?"

Melissa shook her head. "Sorry, no." She turned, hesitated. Hunter watched her fleeting expressions with curiosity and amusement. First there was resistance, and she actually shook her head as though arguing with herself. Then there was guilt, followed by reluctant resignation.

"Wait." She turned around, and Lance halted. She sighed. "I'm looking for a store clerk. Minimum wage. Interested?"

Lance tilted his head, considering. "I tend to attract vampires."

She gestured to the bodies littering the alleyway. "So do I. I can live with it if you can."

Lance chuckled. "Then you have yourself a clerk."

The scream jerked Hunter awake. He lay on the floor, confused for a moment until he got his bearings. Melissa's spare bedroom.

Another scream, followed by a snarl.

Hunter rolled to his feet and made his way over to the window. He peered out to the dark street below.

Melissa was prone on the ground, one arm outstretched, as two werewolves circled her. Even from this distance, he could see the blood. It glistened down her arm, scarlet drops staining the white snow she lay in, and he could see the fine tremor in her hand as her lips moved. Whatever she was doing was holding them at bay, but they still prowled around her, snarling.

Even as he watched, one of the wolves launched at her.

"No!" Hunter roared as Melissa kicked at the wolf. He bolted through the bedroom, down the hallway, and yanked open the front door—and ran into an invisible barrier.

He growled with frustration, trying to bust his way through, but whatever ward Melissa had put on her home to keep him in was strong. He wouldn't be able to leave her home unless she allowed it.

He ran back to the bedroom, vaulting over Lance's body on the bed and landing at the window. He could open it, but encountered the same issue.

Melissa had trapped him inside her home.

Chapter 10

Melissa kept chanting the buffer spell. They'd caught her by surprise, damn it, and it was the first one that sprang to mind when the lycan's fangs had sunk into her shoulder. It created a small zone of protection, one that the lycans could pierce through, if they figured it out. She was on her butt, and using her good arm and legs to slowly shuffle back toward her front door. The snow was falling thicker, heavier, and the icy wind was numbing her. She was sluggish to move, sluggish to think.

If she could just get inside...the werewolves wouldn't be able to follow her.

She whimpered midchant, and one of the werewolves pressed his advantage, barreling toward her. She started chanting faster, her arm outstretched as she focused her power on the wolves, and she cried out in pain as teeth snapped—and caught—her ankle. Even through the leather, she could feel those sharp fangs pierce her skin, heard the crack of bone, felt the snap deep inside.

She screamed, kicking out viciously with her other foot, the heel of her boot raking across the lycan's snout, and the werewolf recoiled.

She chanted faster, blinking furiously to try to stop the gray creeping in at the edges of her vision.

God, her arm was so heavy, stretched out like this, and she tried not to stare at the rivulets of blood that ran down her sleeve. So much blood. She could hear her heart pounding in her ears, see her fingers tremble as the painful heat of her shoulder started giving way to a cool numbness.

She shuffled back again, reciting the spell, thinking furiously. What else could she do? The shock of the attack was numbing her brain.

She heard a dull roaring from above, and thought for a moment she was going to pass out. A thump, followed by a crack, caused her to glance up.

Hunter was pounding on a window upstairs, his expression fierce. He was trapped. She kicked out again when one of the wolves came too close.

Her wards. If she died, her wards would still be in place. Hunter would be forever trapped—unless another witch managed to break the spells. She sucked in a breath, wincing as the gesture moved her shoulder.

If she broke the seal, he'd be free. Free to leave. He'd fulfilled his promise. If she didn't break the seal, he'd rot inside her home.

It was almost ironic that he'd tried to kill her, but in the end her death would be his undoing.

One of the lycans caught her eye, and she knew. It was going to push through her buffer. Funny how, even in their beast form, they could still telegraph their intentions.

A promise is a promise. Our word is our bond, and the only way a spell has any weight is because of the commitment we infuse in it.

The words sprang into her mind in the voice of her mother, and she bellowed, dismayed that the constant lecture from her mother had such a strong foothold.

The wolf sprang at her, and she raised her arms in a defensive motion as the furry bulk hit her in the chest. Teeth clamped around her right forearm and more teeth caught her on her left thigh.

She squeezed her eyes shut, whispering the words that would unlock freedom for her light warrior.

Hunter could sense when the wards dropped. There was high pressure that built in on him whenever he tried to ram his way through the door, or break through that open window. And then there wasn't...

He launched himself through the open window, sliding down the first-story roof, his hands outstretched as he summoned his light force.

He already had a fireball in each hand when his feet cleared the gutter, and suddenly he was free-falling down to the pavement.

He flung his fireballs at the lycans, and hit the ground in a roll to absorb the shock. He rose to his feet, smiling grimly as he heard the yelps and whimpers of the wolves as they felt the heat.

Melissa cried out, and he frowned. The werewolves didn't turn, didn't slow down. He summoned more energy and created two more fireballs. This time he threw them with force, and the lycans howled as their coats were consumed by the fire. He scooped up Melissa and strode to her doorway, not even bothering to look back.

His flames would finish the job for him. He kicked the door shut on the painful howls and whimpers outside, and jogged down the hallway to the stairs.

Melissa tried to lift her head, and she murmured something.

"Shh," he whispered as he climbed the stairs two at a time. "I've got you."

"A promise is a promise," she whispered, her head lolling against his shoulder. "You kept yours." She gasped in pain as he leaned forward, twisted the doorknob in his hand and shouldered his way into her apartment.

"Take it easy, Mel," he told her. She'd lost a lot of blood; she needed to conserve her energy. He trotted down the hallway to her bedroom, placing her with care on her bed.

"I kept my promise," she told him, her eyes flickering as though she was battling unconsciousness. "You're free."

He frowned. He had no idea what she was talking about. Delirium was setting in. "Shh, I'll look after you."

Her eyelids rose slowly, as though their weight was almost too much for her, and he found himself staring into the most mesmerizing green eyes. Her lips pulled down. "Is it going to hurt?" she whispered. There was just the faintest flicker of fear, and her bottom lip trembled, until she caught it between her teeth.

He stroked her red hair back, such a contrast to her pale, almost gray complexion. He smiled at her gently, wanting to reassure her. "Trust me," he whispered. "I'm a doctor."

He caressed her brow, and watched as her eyelids slid

shut. She went under so fast, it alarmed him. She was so hurt, so damn weak. His lips firmed.

He would look after her. And it wasn't because she was annoying and feisty and had managed to entertain him and challenge him with every breath she took. It wasn't because she was so damn vibrant and lively and luscious. She thought she was dying, and she'd set him free.

Damn it, how could he hate a woman when she put his needs before hers? He frowned. It was just like her to entangle him with guilt, with duty and loyalty. Damn witch.

He got to work.

The dark seemed to waver, lift, waver, lift…it took a hell of an effort, but Melissa finally managed to open her eyes. She stared up at the pressed ceiling. Her bedroom ceiling. She flexed her feet beneath the covers, grimacing at the pull on muscle. Must have slept in a funny position. She was warm. So warm and toasty. She stretched, wincing at the ache in her shoulder and arm. The brush of cotton sheets against her naked skin was oddly liberating, and she sighed softly. Thirsty. She was thirsty.

Her bedroom curtains were open, and sunlight was streaming in. Candles, half-spent, were on every available surface, and Hunter sat in a chair next to her bed, in a pool of light from the window, his arms folded on the bed, his head down.

Hunter. In her bedroom.

Melissa shrieked, hauling her sheet up to her chest as she sat up in bed.

Hunter flinched, his head whipping up, and his chair

tipped back, upending him on the floor. He glanced around wildly for a moment, his hair tousled.

"What are you doing in here?" she screeched at him, her voice hoarse.

He held up his hands, wincing as he moved gently on the floor. He blinked rapidly, as though to get rid of the sleepy cobwebs in his brain.

"Hey, take it easy," he soothed, rising to his feet, grimacing.

"Take it easy? Get out of my room!" She flung her arm up to point to the door.

"Settle down," he snapped, arms out toward her. "You're still going to be tender, and I don't want you to rip open any of my work."

She frowned. "What?"

Even as she said it, she realized her shoulder had begun to throb from the startled movement, and her ankle ached beneath the sheet. She glanced down to her arm and gasped. Pink slashes marked her skin—on her shoulder, her arm… She cautiously slid her ankle out from beneath the sheet. It was mottled with purple-and-blue bruises, with marks that looked a lot like puncture wounds, only they were already healing.

Melissa sat up in bed, dragging the sheet up with her. She frowned, touching her forehead. Last night…

"What do you remember?" Hunter asked as he righted the chair, but set it a cautious distance from the bed. He approached the bed, eyeing her warily, and slowly reached for the glass of water on the nightstand, offering it to her.

She took it from him, gulping it down.

"Easy," he told her. "Just—take it slow."

She eyed him over the glass, wanting to drain it all in one gulp, just because she didn't want to do as *he* said. Reluctantly, though, her stomach was already telling her to be gentle, its roiling and small wave of nausea a warning of what could happen if she didn't. She sipped the water, then held the glass to her chest as she stared at him.

Foggy visions, of him banging on a window and glaring at her. She frowned. "It's a little hazy," she admitted, worry creasing her brow. She normally had near perfect recall.

"That's probably due to the loss of blood," he murmured, subsiding in the seat.

She took a deep breath, focusing on the end of her bed. "I remember saying goodbye to Lexi... I remember your thumping on a window." She glanced at her bedroom window. Despite the sun, snow still clung to the sill, and icicles hung from the roofline.

White snow. Bitter cold. Crimson blood. Lycans. Fangs.

Her gaze flicked to Hunter. "I was attacked, wasn't I?" she said hoarsely. The memories were starting to stir in her mind, of being stalked, of being bitten. Two werewolves. It had been a while since the last attempt on her life. She'd grown complacent. The fuzzy visions were coming into focus, at first jumbled, then slowly becoming a part of a logical timeline. Supplying spells and potions to arm humans against shadow breeds meant attacks were a hazard of the job. She should have been more alert though, especially after what had happened with Lance—although his being a dhampir meant he was even more prone to attacks than she was.

Hunter nodded, and for the first time she noticed the dark circles under his eyes, the lines bracketing his mouth. He looked tired. She turned her arm over again.

The memory of the werewolf sinking its teeth into her flesh warred with the vision of healthy, pink skin.

"You...?"

He nodded.

He'd rescued her. She tightened her grip on the sheet at her chest, not quite sure what to do next.

He'd saved her. She didn't know quite what to say, how to react. Gratitude felt so weird after all this time hating him, being so angry with him. After everything he'd done to her, and after all those things she'd done to him...

He rose from the chair, his hands sliding into the back pockets of his jeans. He looked about as comfortable as she felt, lying in a bed with only a sheet as protection. Sure, it provided adequate cover, but she still felt so damn exposed.

Vulnerable. That was it. She felt vulnerable. She didn't like feeling vulnerable. Not at all. Blast it.

He gestured awkwardly to the door as he stepped around her bed. "I'll, uh, go check on Lance. You need to rest. You lost a lot of blood."

She nodded, then her eyes widened. "Oh, God, my store—" Panic set in as she realized the sun was high in the sky.

"It's Sunday," Hunter reminded her gently, and she subsided against her pillows. Her store was closed on Sundays.

Silence stretched between them for a moment, then Hunter scratched his head.

"I, uh, I need to sit in front of the fireplace. Recharge," he said, backing away.

She remembered another way he could recharge, and her cheeks warmed. His lips against hers. His chest against hers. Their bodies, naked and entwined. She was nude under the sheet, after all. The warmth of her cheeks bloomed to a scorching heat. The thought should have horrified her, but she noticed her natural resistance to getting anywhere close to this guy had drained out of her. The idea that she would willingly be a source of energy for the man, a source of *that* kind of energy... She suddenly knew what those vamp slaves must experience, the eagerness to sacrifice personal safety for extreme pleasure, even if it did come at a high cost... Hunter's eyes flared, as though following her train of thought, and he bumped back into her bedroom door. "So, uh, I'll go. Now."

He opened the door, his heated gaze resting on her lips, her bare shoulders...the sheet she clutched to her chest.

"Why?" she whispered, battling her confusion. His eyes met hers. She wasn't asking him why he was leaving, and he knew it.

His gaze flickered away for a moment, and shadows darkened his eyes. He shrugged.

"You needed me." He shut the door, effectively ending further conversation.

She stared, nonplussed, at the white timber.

Hunter tilted his head back against the door.
You needed me.

Ugh. It sounded so corny, so...banal. He'd rescued her because she'd needed him. His brother would be laughing until he cried if he'd heard that one.

Hunter tried to focus on the last five months, on huddling in a dark brick-and-stone cell, on being chained to a wall by cuffs that singed his skin with every movement. On dirty, ripped clothing. On being chilled and tired and uncomfortable. On never having a full belly or a truly restful sleep. On those spiders she'd poured in through the peephole. Not literally, of course, but he hadn't realized it was an illusion spell. It had felt damn real at the time.

Oh, and the snakes. Let's not forget the snakes.

She'd held him in the dark, intentionally withholding light from him.

And in her last conscious moments, she'd delivered on her promise to him. He dragged a hand over his face.

He was a sad and sorry sap, that one promise could affect him so damn much. He'd tended to her wounds, stripping her, cleaning her, healing her... He'd even ignored her attributes, so to speak, in his focus to heal her. She'd been naked, and he'd been completely professional.

Mostly.

Because she needed him.

He levered himself away from the door and made his way to his other patient. He would check Lance's wounds, ensure he would still remain under the blanket of unconsciousness for the foreseeable future, and then he intended to open all the curtains in Melissa's living room, start the fire and sit there for the rest of the day. He would try not to think about the bravery Melissa had shown in her first meeting with Lance, her kindness—reluctant though it was—in offering an ex-con a job, and her loyalty to the vow she'd made to him, or the fact that she was down the hall, naked.

No, he would not think of that. He would sit in front of the fire, nurse that bottle of bourbon and get pleasantly drunk.

Melissa padded down the hallway, her blush pink silk nightgown flowing behind her. She flicked her hair back over her shoulder. Wow, whatever shampoo she was using was working. Her red locks were artfully curled and all glossy and shiny, cascading over her shoulders. She couldn't quite understand why her hair was perfectly styled so early in the morning, but didn't question it. She entered the kitchen and halted, her eyes rounding.

Hunter stood at the stove, frying bacon. He looked over at her and his lips curled in a sexy grin.

"Hey, beautiful," he murmured.

She swallowed.

He was wearing an apron. *Just* an apron.

The muscles of his arms, shoulders and chest bulged, and she could see the dusky disks of his nipples peeking out on either side of her *I kiss better than I cook* apron—which looked like it was made for a kid when he wore it, revealing more than it concealed.

His broad shoulders tapered down behind the fabric—which ended mid–muscled thigh. His legs were toned, just like the rest of him. She didn't know why she was surprised.

"What—what are you doing?" she breathed. She should be stunned, should be shocked. Instead, she was…interested. Bacon sizzled, and the smell was so damn good, mingling with her favorite scent of well-made coffee.

"Making breakfast," Hunter responded with a wink, then turned back to flip the eggs in the frying pan. "Got to keep your strength up."

Her eyes widened as she saw his muscled back and perfectly shaped butt. Oh, dear heaven. That butt. It was—she lifted her chin, trying to tear her gaze away from his butt—it was gorgeous. Sexy…and her eyes were still glued to his butt.

The kind of butt that made you want to reach out and squeeze it.

"Oh, wait, I have something for you," he said, lifting the pan off the burner and flicking the gas off. Her mind immediately suggested all sorts of wicked somethings he could offer. He reached across the counter and poured—oh, sweet mercy—percolated coffee into a mug for her, and spun with an athletic grace to present it to her, his movements graceful and strong, his lips tilted in a half smile that was all knowing and wicked.

"For me?" she breathed, accepting the mug, the enticing smell of coffee and bacon entwining with his own personal scent of amber and musk. It was heady, and she took a sip, her eyes never leaving his.

"Uh-huh." Hunter's brown eyes flared with the beginnings of those mesmerizing amber flares, and his expression relaxed into a sensual invitation as he watched her drink.

"I'd like to taste some of that," he murmured, and his gaze dropped to her lips as she lowered the mug to the counter next to her.

"Yeah?"

"Yeah."

"Well, what's stopping you?" she whispered, her lips lifting in a smile meant to dare. She couldn't believe she was being so flirty, so relaxed and encouraging.

"Nothing," he breathed as he lowered his head.

Chapter 11

His lips took hers in a searing kiss, his hand delving into her curls, grasping her head and angling it to his liking. His other arm curled around her back and pulled her closer.

Melissa moaned as her body came into contact with his. Over and over, his tongue slid against hers, and her hands slid up those glorious biceps to twine around his neck.

He leaned forward, his hands lowering to clasp her buttocks, and she moaned into his mouth as he pulled her up against him, his groin against hers. She wrapped her legs around his waist, twisting her head to meet his lips, over and over, as he turned and walked them over to the kitchen table.

He swept his arm across the surface, sending plates and cutlery crashing to the floor, then sat her on the edge of the table.

Melissa gasped as his lips left hers to trail a hot, wet caress down her neck. She clasped his head, her fingers delving into his short hair, and he growled softly at the sensual head massage. He tugged her forward, her hips against his, and kissed his way down her neck to her chest as he bore her back down to the table.

She trembled as he flexed his hips against hers. Liquid heat pooled between her thighs, and her heart thudded as he licked and nipped his way across her collarbone. Her breasts swelled and heat bloomed. Everywhere.

She gulped. Who knew that was such a sensitive zone? Her eyelids fluttered open, and she stared sightlessly up at the ceiling as he dragged the spaghetti strap of her nightie off her shoulder and down her arm.

She wriggled her arm, arching her back as he slid the silken fabric down her body, revealing her breasts.

He levered back for a moment, eyeing the bounty he'd just revealed, and those amber flecks in his eyes turned to molten gold.

"Damn, you're beautiful," he whispered, an expression of hot appreciation and something softer, bordering on sincere. She raised her arms to caress his shoulders.

"So are you," she told him, her fingers lightly trailing down to his pectoral muscles, where she gently flicked his nipples. He shuddered, dipping down to take her lips again in an intense kiss before shifting to kiss her chest, brushing his lips over the tops of her breasts as his hands cupped them, lifting them. He swept his thumbs over the peaks of her nipples, and she caught her lower lip between her teeth as her nipples tightened.

He rubbed himself against her, his hips moving with the grace and rhythm of a dancer. But a built dancer, like a stripper, not the ballet kind, she found herself thinking, and then her thoughts scattered. He lowered his lips to

one nipple, and she closed her eyes on a breathy moan
as he drew it into his mouth, lashing it with his tongue.
His erection rubbed against her, finding that place that
needed his attention.

She flexed her hips against his, her head tilting back
as he suckled at her breast. She clasped his head to her,
not wanting him to move, it felt so good. But move he
did, and darn if he didn't make it feel even better.

He released her nipple with a soft pop, switching his
attention to her other breast, his hands sliding down her
body to pull up the hem of her nightie.

Her nails scoring down his back in a slow glide, she
pulled him closer, hands covering that beautiful butt.

He groaned. "I have to be inside you," he whispered.

She nodded. "Yes. Now." She couldn't agree more.
She dragged up the apron, and he positioned himself.
She could feel him, ready at that spot that wept for him,
needed him, and she gazed up at him as he—

Pounding on the door jerked Melissa awake, and she
rolled onto her back, scooting up to the headboard, the
sheet wrapped around her.

Eyes wide, her chest rising and falling with her agi-
tated pants, she glanced wildly around the room.

"Melissa," Hunter roared from the other side of her
bedroom door. "Wake the hell up."

The bedroom door was finally flung open, and an
angry Melissa emerged, shrugging a plaid shirt over
a white T-shirt. She wore jeans and was still jamming
one foot into its sneaker, and her expression promised
punishment.

His body hummed with desire, a painful arousal and
a rage born from shock. "What the hell do you think
you're—?"

"You bastard," she hissed, her eyes spitting green fire. "I told you to stay the hell out of my head."

Hunter's eyes narrowed. "I did," he exclaimed hotly.

"I bet you're all recharged now, aren't you?" she said, her tone accusing.

"Thanks to you," he gritted. She was right. He was. And he was so damn hyped up he could throw a barbecue for the damn city.

Her fingers curled, and she raised them in a way he knew from experience meant pain would follow. He held up his own hands, and flames flickered from the tips of his fingers. "Don't even think about it," he warned, frowning fiercely. He was so damn angry with her, although why the hell she was acting as though *he* was the bad guy, he had no idea.

"I told you to stay out of my head," she hissed at him, fingers curled like claws. He could feel the pain starting in his head, as though her nails were slowly sliding into his brain. "Do you think this is a game? Do you think you can come in and twist my mind to your own devices?" Her voice was climbing in volume.

He blinked, confused on so many levels, and trying to think past the mental burn. "You think *I* did this?" He flicked his finger and a little flame zinged off and around behind her. She squealed, flinching at the hot sting that bit at her butt. It was only brief, and only a warning, but it was enough to distract her, and to eject those talons of pain out of his head. "You think that was me?" He didn't bother to hide his disbelief. "You were in *my* head, Melissa. I don't know how the hell you did it, but I don't like it and it stops now."

Her eyes narrowed and she glared at him, ready to inflict more pain, but his words halted her. "What?" she asked, angling her head, her fingers still poised, eyes full of suspicion and confusion.

She didn't know. Good God, she didn't know. The anger still coursed through him, the shock and frustration, but she was so eager to accuse him, to deliver pain as punishment for something she thought he'd done. She had no idea.

He extinguished his fire, his hands dropping to his sides as he stared at her, incredulous. "I was sleeping," he told her, his voice low and rough. "And *you* walked into *my* head."

Now it was Melissa's turn to be confused. *"What?"*

Her fingers relaxed, but he wasn't sure if it was intentional, or if she was thoroughly distracted. He knew he was sure as hell distracted.

"What are you talking about?" she asked, and he could see she was struggling with the concept. Join the club. He was totally stumped. "I was sleeping, and all of a sudden you were prancing through my dream."

He held up a finger. "One—I do not prance." He raised another finger. "Two—that wasn't your dream, that was mine."

She stared at him for a moment, blinking, and then she lowered her hands. "Wait, so…you were dreaming about…me?"

He frowned. "Yes, damn it." He looked away. Talk about damned awkward.

She rubbed her chin. "I don't understand how this works," she admitted, a little embarrassed. Of course, her little embarrassment paled in comparison to his abject mortification. He took a deep breath. Now that he could see she truly hadn't intended to dreamwalk in his mind, he'd gone from wanting to strangle her straight back to wanting her. Period.

He wanted the bitchy witch. He dragged his hands over his face. "Oh, this is so wrong."

"I don't get it," she said, arms out in a helpless gesture.

His eyes narrowed. "How can you not get it? You just did it." She was more skilled than he'd first thought—and he didn't like underestimating his enemy, damn it.

To his knowledge, only some light warriors had this particular gift. He'd inherited his from his father. He knew vampires could compel others. He knew witches could cast spells and unlock secrets of the mind with incantations and touch, and they could see visions, etc. He'd never heard of another breed being able to do as he could.

It scared the hell out of him. The crapstorm he had going on up there, he didn't want anyone to see. He didn't like the exposure, the lack of control.

"You dreamwalked," he told her. He put his hands on his hips. "Tell me how."

She shrugged. "I have no idea." She tried to step around him, but he blocked her way. He was determined to figure this out—and prevent it from happening again.

"Try again," he growled.

She tilted her chin to meet his gaze, and he couldn't help but recognize the challenge inherent in the movement. "What bugs you more? The fact that I 'dreamwalked,'" she said, wiggling her fingers to parenthesize the word, "or that I busted you dreaming about me?"

He fixed his gaze on the door behind her, clenching his jaw, and she swept past him.

"I don't know how your party trick works," she said over her shoulder, and then she held up her hand. "Although, if I can do it in my sleep, well that kind of implies it's not so tricky."

She laughed, a sound that came out part husky tinkle, part unladylike snort. He thumped his fist against the doorjamb. Damn it.

She'd tiptoed through his dreams. Actually, no, she'd swept through it in a lustful haze, leaving him horny, frustrated and shaken. She wasn't supposed to be able to do that. The only other person he knew capable of dreamwalking was locked up in a Reform cell. Although his father hadn't been able to intrude in Hunter's dreams; his own shields were too strong for that.

But apparently not strong enough to withstand a bitchy witch.

He ducked his head. Fine. This had been fun, but it was time to wrap things up. He didn't quite understand her, or why she was so hell-bent on annihilating shadow breeds in general. Lance was a dhampir, and she considered him a friend—and would go to considerable trouble for him. His lips pursed. That was nice. Sure, he could admit that. What she'd done for Lance, that was nice. Of course, he had to reconcile that with being chained up and locked away in a cell for five months. Not so nice.

He straightened and turned in the hallway. He had that knack for pulling the not-so-nice out of people. His mother had left him—well, okay, she'd died, but his brother had walked away from him, and this witch had imprisoned him. Even Debbie had chosen Ryder over him. There was something wrong with him. He was not-so-nice.

And she was tiptoeing through his dreams. The woman who had made his life a living hell now had access to his hidden secrets. Definitely time to leave. He shouldn't be messing around with the witch, anyway. He should be getting back to work. At least there he was—different. There, there was a little glimmer of light to rail against his darkness. He needed his light. It was the only thing he had going for him. He sauntered down the hallway. Time to wake up his patient.

Melissa sat in the chair in the corner as Hunter did his work. He'd told her that he thought Lance could wake up, and then hadn't spoken a word since. He stood at the foot of the bed, hands clasping Lance's ankles, and Melissa could see the tendrils of light worming their way through Lance's body. She never got tired of watching; it was beautiful.

She glanced briefly at Hunter's back. Who would have thought a man so capable of violence could also be capable of such beauty? He'd taken such care with Lance, so cautious with his treatment. So gentle. It was hard to reconcile this man with the healing light with the warrior who had turned her apothecary into a Roman candle.

Her gaze dropped, and it took her a moment to realize she was staring at his butt. This time it was covered in denim, though.

She blinked and looked away. He did have a great butt, though. She peered at him briefly. At his butt. She still couldn't believe she'd walked through his dream. *That* dream. She puffed her cheeks out on an exhalation of breath. That had been one hell of a dream.

But she hadn't tried to fight him off. Hadn't tried to blast him, sear him, or otherwise make it painful for him. What was up with that? She hadn't been with anyone since Theo… She realized she hadn't even thought of her fiancé during or since that dream. That guilt weighed heavily on her. It felt like such a betrayal. She still didn't quite understand what had happened, though. Did they do the horizontal tango because he wanted it, or she wanted it, or they both wanted it? No, damn it. She didn't want *it*. Not with him. After everything that had happened between them, that would make her pathetic.

Damn, this was giving her a headache. She straightened in her chair. Maybe the dream wasn't supposed to be literal. Some dreams meant something vastly different than the experience they actually portrayed. She sighed. The problem was, she was a witch, and she had a better idea than some when it came to dream interpretation. If a client had come in with that story, her analysis would be…that one or both of them were as horny as a…well, something really horny.

Hunter stood back and rolled his shoulders. He slowly turned to her.

"He's going to be fine. We'll just let him wake up naturally, and then he'll be good to go." He folded his arms. "Which means I'll be good to go."

"When Lance is awake," she clarified. She didn't want Hunter skipping out until she was certain Lance was well and truly fine.

"When Lance is awake," Hunter repeated, nodding.

Melissa looked away. When her friend woke, Hunter's part of the deal would be delivered. Then it would be her turn. A promise was a promise. Hunter would be free to go.

And she would be alone.

She rose from the chair. "I, uh, have to catch up on some paperwork."

Hunter nodded. "I'll wait here."

She left the room and strolled down the hall to her living room. Hunter would be leaving. She frowned. Good grief, she wasn't getting morose about it, was she? She should be happy he was going, and good riddance to him. She may not feel like she'd truly delivered vengeance against the man who'd destroyed her business, her craft, and had tried to kill her in the process—but at least something positive had come out of it. Lance survived what would otherwise have been a fatal attack. She should focus on the positives.

She wouldn't have to make Hunter any more peanut butter and jelly sandwiches, or take down a dinner that even the rats preferred to leave alone. No more being on alert every time she ventured down to the basement. No more having to watch her back, or second-guessing what her prisoner would do.

No more bacon and coffee for breakfast. The thought came out of nowhere, surprising her. No more Hunter and his light. No more fires. No more breath-stealing, resistance-draining, knee-weakening kisses...

She took a deep breath. She wasn't going there. No. If she was distracted or tempted, she'd just have to remember what Hunter had done to her on their first meeting. If that didn't work, she'd think about Theo.

As usual, the guilt flared up, and she almost cried in relief at the familiar emotion. The guilt and the sadness were still there. She couldn't entertain any thoughts about Hunter—about any man. Theo had been her love, and he'd forever hold her heart. This craze with Hunter was just that—a craze. A temporary period of insanity. And then things would finally return to normal when Hunter was gone, back wielding whatever dark power he liked to use in his family's medical clinic.

It was so quiet. She rubbed her arms. So quiet and so cold. She crossed to the hearth and started a fire, then grabbed her shoe box full of receipts, dockets, invoices—a tissue?—and started to sort her paperwork. This was one part of owning a store she did not like. She grabbed the remote and turned the television on, just to have some background noise.

That was one thing she couldn't quite get used to. Her store was generally busy, but ever since Theo had gone, her apartment felt like a crypt when there was only her in it. She couldn't hear Hunter or Lance down the hall. She could have been all by herself. She turned the volume to low. Just having those voices in the background gave the illusion that she wasn't alone in the world.

She'd been working for over an hour when she realized she wasn't alone anymore. Hunter was leaning against the doorjamb, watching her.

"Oh, I didn't see you there."

He shrugged. "I didn't want to intrude. How are you feeling?"

He levered away from the door frame and sauntered close.

She frowned. "Fine."

He lifted his chin toward her shoulder. "How is your arm?"

"It doesn't hurt," she answered honestly. She didn't know how he did it, but it worked.

"Do you need me to—" Hunter hesitated, then tried again. "Will you be safe when I leave?"

She frowned, surprised by the question. "Yes, Hunter, I'll be fine. I can look after myself." She'd been doing it for some time, now.

"Those werewolves…" he began, and she waved a hand casually.

"Oh, that's nothing."

Hunter arched his eyebrow, and she made a face. "Okay, maybe they came close this time, but I'll be more careful next time. It wasn't my first wolf attack, and won't be my last, I'm sure."

Hunter dropped onto the sofa facing the fire, and frowned. "Do these attacks happen a lot?"

She turned back to her paperwork. "I'm a witch, Hunter. It comes with the territory. I give humans some measure of defense against the shadow breeds. My job is to try to even out the balance of power, or possibly tip it in our favor." She shrugged. "That means occasionally the shadow breeds try to take me out. Vampires, werewolves...you."

She lifted her gaze to his briefly, and noticed a flare of something...regret? Remorse? Just as quickly he schooled his features, and she couldn't be sure she'd seen anything.

"Those lycans, Melissa... I hit them first with a flare. It didn't stop them. Didn't even give them pause."

She shrugged again. "Maybe you're losing your touch?"

Touch. She remembered the dream, the way he'd touched her breasts, her thighs... Warmth flared in her cheeks. Okay. Stop thinking about *that*.

"Or maybe there was something else driving them," Hunter suggested. "I know I hurt them, but they kept at it. Almost like they were compelled."

Melissa lowered the dockets she held to the shoe box. "Lycans are supernatural. They can be compelled, but it would take a strong being to get past their natural defenses. I think you're reading too much into it."

It was Hunter's turn to shrug. "Maybe. All I know is I had to kill them to stop them. Just...bear that in mind."

She kept her gaze on the beaten shoe box on the coffee table. "I will."

The fact that she still lived due to Hunter's interference didn't escape her. She opened her mouth, then hesitated. She'd lowered the ward that trapped him. He could have escaped, could have left her to the wolves, but he hadn't. She didn't understand why he'd stayed, or why he'd acted to save her life. She wanted to understand, but was afraid where that conversation might lead, especially in light of their shared dream. Asking Hunter why he'd stayed, when he had every reason to leave, would only lead to an uncomfortable discussion.

For the first time, Melissa backed down from a conversation, and shut her mouth. Leave it alone. As soon as Lance woke up, Hunter would leave, and they could both go on with their separate lives, ignoring each other's presence and pretending this had been but a minor episode in their lives. It didn't have to be more than that.

The buzzer rang, and Melissa looked up in surprise.

"Are you expecting anyone?" Hunter inquired as he rose.

"No."

Hunter nodded, and she didn't know what was more disturbing, that on her one day off she didn't expect visitors, or that Hunter thought that was a normal state of affairs for her.

"I mean, my brother drops by occasionally, but I'm not expecting anyone," she clarified, just so she didn't seem like a complete loser.

Hunter strode to the living room window and peered down into the street. "It's Lexi."

Melissa smacked her palm to her forehead. "Of course. She broke up with that bloodsucking boyfriend of hers last night." She rose from her seat and hurried down the hallway to press the button that would unlock the main door briefly to allow Lexi up.

She couldn't believe she'd forgotten all about Lexi, and the fact she was leaving her manipulative boyfriend. She lifted her finger off the buzzer and opened the apartment door for Lexi. She started toward the kitchen. "I'm going to put the coffee on," she called out to Hunter. "Want one?"

"Sure."

Hunter glanced over at the TV as Melissa puttered in the kitchen. He reached for the remote, turning the volume up slowly. It looked like the price of iron was up, he noted, due to some arrangement between Marchetta Enterprises and the Alpine Pack. Hunter arched an eyebrow. Vamps and werewolves in business together? What the hell had happened while he'd been chained to a wall?

He continued to watch the news report as he heard the footsteps in the hall behind him. Some prisoner killed a security guard and had escaped a Reform maximum security prison. He glanced over his shoulder. "Hey, Lexi."

Lexi halted briefly, scanning the room. "Where is Melissa?"

Hunter's eyebrows rose at her brusque tone, lack of greeting and the determined set of her jaw. "She's getting her domestic vibe on in the kitchen." Thankfully she was only making coffee. He didn't think he could stomach one of Melissa's attempts at a meal.

Lexi left the doorway, and Hunter frowned. He'd come to think of Lexi as something approaching a friend, but this morning she'd barely acknowledged him. Had something bad happened with the boyfriend?

Lexi had always treated him with respect, and despite Melissa's warning, she'd been friendly and trusting. That had been rare for him, and he appreciated it more than she or Melissa would ever know. He rose from his seat. If Lexi needed help, he'd be happy to fry a vamp for her.

"Hey, Lexi, how did it go?"

Melissa's voice was soft, caring, and he halted for a moment, intrigued by the tone. He'd never heard her speak like that before. It was like a warm embrace, something that curled around, attentive and supportive.

"Melissa."

"Lexi? Are you okay?"

So Melissa had noticed their friend's mood. He started to walk toward the kitchen.

"I'm sorry, Melissa."

"Lexi? What's going—where is your ring?" Melissa's voice sharpened, and Hunter frowned.

"Put the knife down, Lexi," Melissa warned, and then Hunter heard a clatter of dishes, the sound of glass breaking and then a shriek. Hunter ran.

"Stop it, Lexi," Melissa yelled, and there was another crash.

He skidded to a stop at the kitchen door. Melissa had raised a chair, both as a shield and as a weapon, its legs pointed toward Lexi.

Lexi stood close, a knife from Melissa's butcher block clasped in one hand. The coffeepot lay in jagged pieces on the floor, and brown liquid dripped from Lexi's arm, leaving a blooming scald mark behind.

"Lexi," Hunter called softly, his arm out, but Lexi ignored him, her attention on Melissa. The woman shook her head, tears flowing down her cheeks.

"I'm sorry, Melissa," she repeated. She pushed the chair legs aside with considerable force and her arm flashed out, the wicked blade slicing through the air.

Melissa dropped the chair and dodged, but Hunter heard her hiss, saw the red mark bloom on her sleeve. She hadn't avoided the blade entirely.

"Stop, Lexi," Melissa cried, her expression a combination of shock, fear and anger.

Hunter stepped in, and Lexi whirled. He jumped back to avoid being slashed across his middle.

"Stay back!" Lexi yelled, her features harsh as she glared at him briefly. His eyes widened.

"Lexi, it's me, Hunter." He'd never done anything to hurt this woman, yet here she stood in the kitchen, trying to kill them both. The woman before him stared at him with wild eyes. There was recognition, but it was like a wall was erected between them.

"Put the knife down," Melissa told her, trying to back away, but Lexi was slowly advancing on her. Hunter watched in horror as the woman he'd decided was a friend went after the witch who had freed him. Torn didn't begin to describe his emotions. Saving one would mean betraying the other. He couldn't get close enough to touch Lexi, to render her unconscious, but if he didn't do something, she was going to hurt Melissa, possibly kill her.

Lexi darted forward, and Melissa jerked out of the way, sending more dishes from the counter spilling to the ground, breaking and scattering across the floor. She managed to deflect the knife, catching and clutching Lexi's wrist.

"Hold her," Hunter called, and stepped forward, his arms raised. He summoned his light force. Large arms wrapped around him from behind, forcing his arms down and lifting him off his feet.

Hunter's eyes rounded as the arms clasped around him tightened, squeezing so hard his lungs couldn't expand fully.

"Do not even think about hurting my sister," a deep voice rumbled against his ear. Hunter didn't have time to let his disbelief take control. He kicked, trying to land against the cupboard door to give him some resistance, some way of shoving against the man mountain that embraced him, but his patient—back to full strength, apparently—shifted, and Hunter's feet kicked at the air.

"Lance," Melissa screeched as Lexi continued to struggle. "Help."

Lexi raised her hand, the blade gleaming in the sunlight streaming into the cheery kitchen, the whites of her eyes visible, and she swung.

Hunter curled his fingers, summoning a small flame in his hands and pushing it at Lexi. The giant holding him roared, flinging him out into the hallway, and his flame caught at the kitchen table instead. Hunter bounced with considerable force against the plastered wall of the hallway and crashed to the floor. He grimaced at the pain, and coughed as his lungs filled with air.

Lance, wearing a pair of jeans and no shirt or shoes, advanced toward him, a dark murderous glint in his eye.

Chapter 12

Melissa ducked under Lexi's arm and brought her elbow up to smash into the woman's back. Lexi screamed in pain and rage as she fell forward against the sink. Melissa grabbed the frying pan that hung from a hook on a frame above the stove and whirled, using it as a shield. Her eyes widened when she heard the scrape of metal on metal, felt the force as Lexi's blade hit the back of the pan that she held in front of her face.

She heard a bellow from the hallway, followed by a crash, and then Hunter skidded into the room again, his face bruised, his arm raised and fury in his gaze. She saw the fireball flare in his hand, and her stomach lurched as she recognized his intent.

"No," she yelled in protest. She held one hand up in defense, then used the pan like a tennis racket and swung it at Lexi's head. She flinched at the clunk it made when it caught the woman on the upper jaw, and Lexi's head whipped around, smacking into the fridge door. She fell, unconscious, to the floor, collapsing among the broken shards of crockery and strewed cutlery. Melissa hurriedly used a tea towel to put the small fire on the top of the kitchen table out, smoke and scorched wood permeating the air.

Hunter frowned fiercely at her. "Why did you—"

A large body crashed against his, and suddenly the doorway was empty as Lance tackled him. They crashed toward the living room.

"No," Melissa yelled, skirting around the inert Lexi, kicking the blade away under the table and hurtling out of the kitchen. She winced as Lance punched Hunter in the stomach with a force that had the light warrior doubling over in pain.

Hunter glared at the dhampir, anger flaring, and Melissa saw the fireball leave Hunter's hands and launch toward her friend. She flung her arm out, muttering a dampening spell that turned the fireball into a puff of smoke.

"Don't," she cried as Lance strode toward Hunter. She sprang in between the two men, arms out. To their credit, both men halted immediately.

"He was going to attack Lexi," Lance gritted.

"He saved your life," she snapped, and Lance halted, frowning.

"She was going to kill you," Hunter grated, gesturing toward the kitchen.

"I'm going to kill you," snarled Lance, stepping closer.

"Oh, bring it on, bigfoot," Hunter challenged, beckoning him with one hand. Lance took another step, and Melissa found herself wedged between two very big, powerful and angry men.

Lance's eyes widened. "Is that—is that my *shirt*?"

Hunter's shirt was ripped open, revealing his toned chest and washboard abs. Not that now was the time to notice his toned chest and washboard abs.

"Stop it, both of you," Melissa said through gritted teeth. She pointed a finger at Lance. "You need to bring it down a notch." She used her other hand to point at Hunter. "And you need to stop trying to set everyone on fire."

She swallowed, then nodded, finally acknowledging Hunter's point, her heart still racing at the threat. "She's under a compulsion," she told him. "Lance is protecting his sister, Hunter." She turned to Lance.

"Hunter was just—" She blinked, still trying to process it. "He was looking out for me." She turned her gaze to Hunter, and he glared at her with an intensity that revealed something she wasn't sure she could identify properly, as her instinct didn't make sense. But she wasn't going to query it. She dropped her gaze but gave a little nod. He'd saved her life yet again.

"Someone better tell me what the hell is going on. Now," Lance demanded.

"Why don't we secure psycho sis first," Hunter suggested. "Then we can catch you up over tea and scones."

Lance narrowed his eyes, and Melissa turned to him, bracing her hands against Lance's chest. "He's got a point. For some reason, Lexi feels compelled to kill me. When she comes to, she'll start again, and none of us want to see her hurt. At least, not more than she is already."

"Let me at her," Hunter said, and she felt his sigh against the back of her neck. His anger had cooled.

Lance shook his head. "That's not going to happen," he muttered.

"No, wait," Melissa said, then turned to face Hunter, curious. "What are you suggesting?"

He was standing so close she could feel his breath against her collarbone. His brown eyes were dark with turmoil, and she couldn't quite get a read on his emotions.

"While she's unconscious I might be able to do a scan, maybe even break the compulsion."

Melissa gaped for a moment. "You can do that?" she breathed. To her knowledge, a compulsion could only be broken by the one who set it, or by their death. To learn that there was possibly another option was like finding an undiscovered loophole in the laws of nature. Exciting and frightening at the same time.

Hunter shrugged. "It's possible," he admitted. "It depends on how deep the compulsion goes."

"I'm not letting this fire-freak anywhere near my sister," Lance stated, folding his arms, and Melissa placed her hand on his arm.

"He's not just a fire-freak." She ignored the exasperated sigh of the man behind her as she gazed up at her friend. "This man saved your life, as a favor to me, and to your sister. If he thinks he can help Lexi, I'd suggest you let him try," she told him softly. "I don't want to hurt Lexi, Lance, but if she comes at me again, I'll be forced to defend myself."

"Trust me," Hunter said, "I'm a doctor." Melissa could hear the sarcasm in his tone, just as she knew Lance could.

The muscle in Lance's jaw flexed, and his gaze shifted between her and Hunter. Her friend's green eyes narrowed. "Are you vouching for him, Mel?" The question was loaded with meaning, and it took Melissa a moment to digest it. Did she trust Hunter? That's what

Lance was asking. Did she trust the light warrior enough to place another friend's life in his hands?

Finally, she nodded. "Yes, I'm vouching for him."

Lance stared at her for a long moment, before dipping his head. "Fine. Do it." Hunter stepped toward the kitchen, and Lance reached to grab his arm. "But if you hurt her..." His expression turned hard and threatening. Hunter flashed him a tight smile.

"I saved you, didn't I?" He shook his arm free and stalked into the kitchen. He scooped up Lexi's unconscious form and carried her out to the living room, placing her gently on the sofa. Melissa and Lance followed closely.

"Why don't you tell me exactly what the hell has been going on here?" Lance asked Melissa in a low voice. "Who the hell is this guy?"

Hunter ignored Lance and Melissa's conversation, although he didn't completely push them from his mind. Largely because he didn't trust the Paul Bunyan wannabe. The guy was massive, and Hunter's ribs still ached from their encounter—he'd felt one crack, but he was healing fast.

He knelt at Lexi's head and gently rested his fingers against her temples. He still struggled with the homicidal vision of her in the kitchen. She'd borne very little resemblance to the woman who'd brought him bacon and eggs, and who had teased him as he'd prepared breakfast in the room she'd just turned into a battleground.

She'd threatened Melissa.

He closed his eyes, summoning his light force to enter her mind. He winced as he noticed her concussion, and he siphoned some energy off to heal her, reducing the swelling as he also delved into her mind.

He didn't dreamwalk—didn't trust Lance enough to slide into unconsciousness anywhere near the dhampir, but instead checked for previous assaults on Lexi's mind. He found plenty, and his lips tightened as he realized how vulnerable the young woman had been. He saw clumsy strokes of coercion with the unmistakable taint of a vampire, but they were aged, and though not completely severed, there was a definite weakening... He angled his head, feeling something warm and protective there. He didn't know why, but Melissa immediately sprang to mind. Had she tried to protect Lexi?

Normally he didn't worry himself too much with this kind of attack on a patient. He dulled trauma, if need be, but it was mainly the physicality of a body that he concerned himself with, believing that if a person exposed themselves willingly or not to psychic attack, then they should deal with the consequences. He had no issue with implanting suggestions. He did it with patients trying to kick addictions or lose weight all the time. Okay, so he may have dabbled once or twice with nonmedical stuff, but that was purely for amusement's sake to see people do things they wouldn't normally do.

Having seen the consequences of downright forceful manipulation firsthand, though, in a woman who had done nothing to deserve the removal of her free will... For the first time, Hunter was annoyed. He severed the coercions easily enough. It was a darker lock on her mind that concerned him. He skirted around the edges, impressed despite himself at the finesse of the block. Someone had implanted a series of suggestions in Lexi's mind with great skill. Every time he tried to unlock it, another barrier revealed itself. His brows pulled together. He hadn't seen this level of artistry since... He stilled.

No. He denied it immediately. It couldn't be. And yet,

there was only one person's persuasion that had ever really fooled him, only one person's prowess that he was unable to break.

He opened his eyes, withdrawing his touch from Lexi's temples.

"Well?" Melissa asked softly. He looked up. Melissa and Lance stood behind the sofa, leaning on the backrest with arms folded, looking down at him expectantly.

"I've gotten rid of the lame attempts from some vampire to control her, but there is something in there…it's so deeply buried that if I try to destroy it, I'll hurt Lexi. Badly." He reached for the remote control on the coffee table and turned up the volume, then flicked through the channels.

"I hardly think this is the time for watching TV," Melissa commented, frowning, but he shook his head, stopping when he found a twenty-four-hour news station.

"I can only think of one person capable of this kind of compulsion," he said absently, reading the newsfeed scrolling across the bottom of the screen. There had been something about…

He sucked in his breath when he saw the headline. "Son of a bitch."

In moments the news anchor announced the story. "In further news, authorities have identified the escaped inmate from the Oodvark maximum security prison as Arthur Armstrong, currently awaiting trial for conspiracy to murder Alpha Prime Jared Gray. Armstrong killed a female security guard during his escape, and is considered armed and dangerous. Authorities are warning the public not to approach this man if sighted, and to call Reform Authority."

"You've got to be kidding me," Melissa breathed. Hunter rose from the floor and crossed to the window.

He placed a finger against the curtain and slowly, gently, pulled back the fabric to peer out.

It was late afternoon, and already the gloom was setting in. The snow was turning to gray slush on the ground. A movement across the street caught his eye. Someone stood in a doorway, flicking ash from a cigarette. Hunter angled his head. A guy who looked like he'd slept in the clothes he wore for a good few months leaned against a shop window farther down, and a couple of men lurked up toward the other end of the street. Even as he watched, he could see a group of men approaching from about three blocks away.

"We have company," he muttered.

Lance went up to the other living room window and peeked out. "Werewolves."

Hunter nodded. "I don't see any vamps."

"It's still daylight," Lance murmured. "Besides, they're not going to come out with this many lycans about. One bite and they'd be dead."

"What's going on?" Melissa asked, coming up behind Hunter.

He turned to eye her. "Either you've pissed off a great many lycans, and—" He held up a hand, saying, "I'll give credit where it's due, I think you're totally capable of doing it, or someone is compelling an awful lot of folks to marshal an attack."

Melissa frowned. This close, he could smell her, feel her warmth, her body so close to but not touching his. He frowned when he noticed the bloodstain on her shirt. She'd been cut. He reached out, clasping her arm gently, and sent a warm tendril of light from beneath his palm to gently heal the wound. Melissa gasped, glancing down at her arm, then up at him. He winked, then turned to stare out the window again.

After a moment, Melissa stepped closer to peer over his shoulder, then shrugged. "They can marshal all they want, but my place is a fang-free zone, current company excepted," she said, indicating Lance. Hunter's gaze flicked over to the hulking giant. What was so damn special about this guy that he got a special hall pass from a witch with a fang phobia? Was there something more than just friendship between them? He wasn't sure. They didn't seem amorously inclined, but she had been able to stay the big guy, just with a frown and wagging finger.

"What about tomorrow?" Hunter asked quietly. "Will you open your shop?"

Melissa lifted her chin in that challenging, stubborn, try-me gesture he was beginning to recognize. "They're not going to run me out of business. They've tried many times, and they'll try more, but they won't succeed. We're not even sure who *they* are."

Hunter rolled his eyes. "Save the pep talk for someone who will swallow that crud," he told her. "Have you ever been under siege? What about your customers?" He pointed to Lexi. "She doesn't have fangs, and she damn near made a pincushion out of you." He folded his arms. "And I think you and I both know who is behind this."

Melissa mimicked his stance, folding her arms. He decided this was his favorite position for her, when her arms pushed her breasts up like an offering. A movement caught his eye, and he dragged his gaze up from Melissa's chest to Lance, who glared at him with narrowed eyes. Lance shook his head ever so slightly, as though in warning.

Hunter smiled. He rarely did as he was told.

"What would your father have against me?" Melissa asked, oblivious to the exchange.

Hunter looked back at her, his brow dipping. "Seriously? Maybe the fact that you and some other witch used your powers to help my brother and me battle our father, which ultimately led to his arrest and incarceration? Or maybe the fact that you kept his son chained to a wall?" He shrugged. "Or maybe he has a thing against gingers, who knows? My father isn't exactly on an even keel, if you get my drift."

"Like father, like son," Melissa muttered.

Hunter wheezed a chuckle. "Like your family is perfect. Pot, meet kettle." He'd seen enough in her dreams of the interaction between her and her mother to know she could also boast of a dysfunctional pedigree.

Lance sighed brusquely. "Well, this is all very entertaining, but what do we do?"

Hunter glanced over at Lexi. She was still unconscious, but her color was good, and she'd probably come to, minus the concussion, within the next half hour or so. "I can't get rid of that compulsion, which means she'll come after Melissa again when she wakes. You need to get her out of here."

Lance shook his head. "I'm not leaving Melissa defenseless against a pack of wolves."

"She won't be defenseless—I'll be here. The wolves can't breach Melissa's barriers. At the moment, they're just waiting for her to come out. If she stays inside, she's safe."

"Not until tomorrow, when any compelled human can come after her," Lance pointed out.

Hunter nodded. "True. So I will call my brother, and he'll come down and help me get rid of them."

Melissa frowned. "I thought your brother was just a dentist?"

"He is, but I don't know anyone who has teeth who isn't afraid of a dentist."

Lance put his fists on his hips. "How are the two of you going to get rid of a pack of wolves?"

"Let's just say my brother and I have a special set of skills," Hunter stated calmly, and brought forth two small fireballs dancing on his palms. He rolled his palm, and the fireball rolled with it, until he gave a flick of his fingers and the fireball disappeared.

Lance frowned. "What the hell are you?"

"Hot stuff," Hunter answered, grinning. Melissa rolled her eyes, then turned to Lance.

"Don't worry, I'm not defenseless, either. We'll be fine, but they're here for me, not you or Lexi. You need to get her out of here before she wakes up and becomes part of the problem."

Lance glanced between his sister and his friend, and Hunter felt a little sympathy for him. Not much, but a little. He could relate—as much as anyone could relate to a giant, blond dhampir who sucked on vamps yet was afraid of what would happen when his kid sister woke up.

Melissa rested her hand on Lance's arm, and Hunter eyed the movement closely. Neither had an issue with personal space, he noticed. "I'll be fine, Lance. You know me. You know I can take care of myself."

Lance sighed, then nodded. "Fine."

Melissa smiled. "Good. I'd suggest going up to the roof. There's a ladder up there we use to stretch across the ally for roof parties with the neighbors." She started to walk toward the hallway. Lance turned to face Hunter, his expression harsh.

"If she gets hurt or killed," he began, his voice soft with menace.

Hunter held up a hand. "Let me guess. If Melissa gets hurt or dies, you're going to kill me." He sighed. "You and Melissa need a new playbook."

Lance leaned forward. "What about this one? Mess with Melissa, and you mess with me."

Hunter rolled his eyes. "I get it." He almost told Lance he was renowned for his messes, but didn't think the big guy shared his sense of humor.

Lance strode over and picked up his sister, hoisting her unconscious body up over his shoulder in an effortless fireman's lift. Hunter shook his head. "You guys are related? Unbelievable." Lexi was tiny in comparison to her brother. But then, most people would be, next to this big lug.

He followed Melissa and Lance, carrying Lexi, up to the roof. The sky was bathed in pink and orange, with indigo and purple creeping in, and already the night shadows stretched across the streets. Hunter helped Melissa place the ladder over the facade edging to bridge the gap between Melissa's building and the next. He frowned at the ladder, then glanced over the edge. It was a long way down to the alley.

"You walk across this a lot?" he asked, eyeing the distance between the buildings. It looked like a whisker away from suicide.

Melissa nodded. "Uh-huh. I generally do Halloween, and Hal over there does Christmas."

"Why don't you just use the door?" Hunter asked as Lance stepped up on the ridge of the facade.

"Where's the fun in that? Besides, I'd have to walk all the way down, then all the way up, and Hal would have to do the reverse. This is much easier."

Hunter shook his head as Lance carefully stepped across the divide. The witch was a daredevil, or just a touch crazy. He held the ladder to make Lance's trek across as stable and secure as possible, and then helped Melissa drag the ladder back, stowing it against the roof's capping. Lance jogged across the roof to the door that led to the interior of the neighbor's building.

"Oh, wai—" Melissa held up a hand, but Lance either didn't hear, or chose to ignore her. He tried the handle, then stepped back and kicked it open. Hunter's eyebrows rose. It had taken the guy just one blast with his foot to break open a security door. It was just as well they were on the same side. He eyed Melissa. Sort of.

He shoved his hands in his pockets and strolled to the front of the building and looked down. The street below was in dark shadows, the sun sliding behind Irondell's northern skyscrapers. The numbers below had increased. Hunter frowned.

So many werewolves—wait. Now there were vampires, too, their pale complexions visible in the encroaching darkness. Hunter's frown deepened. But—but vampires and werewolves didn't work together. They hated each other. A lycan's bite was lethal to a vampire. He shook his head at the weirdness of the sight. He estimated there were a good twenty people gathering in the street. A small group turned a corner, striding down toward the bookstore. *More.*

"Uh, Melissa, we should go in." He didn't like the looks of this, not at all.

"Why, what's up?" Melissa asked, crossing over to him. He watched as a couple of vampires bent their knees, looking up at the roof.

"Inside. Now," he stated, grabbing her hand and pulling her back toward the door that led to the upper level of her building. He heard the soft thud of feet on the roof behind them, and dragged her faster.

Chapter 13

"Oh, my God," Melissa gasped behind him, as she saw the three vampires land on the roof, and then suddenly she overtook him, dragging *him* into the building. She slammed the door closed behind them, muttering a protection spell as she slid the lock home. Thuds and cracks echoed on the other side of the door, and Melissa flinched as the door shook.

"How long will that hold?" Hunter asked. She turned to him. He wasn't even panting, not like she was.

"A little while," she said, and turned to clamber down the stairs toward her apartment. "Those spells are durable against a shadow breed." She shook her head. "They were vampires. I don't understand. Since when are the vamps and mutts in cahoots? They hate each other."

"Well, let's see," Hunter said as he trotted down the stairs behind her. "How likely is it that you would piss off both the lycans and the vamps so much, at the same time, that they would band together against you?"

Melissa drew to a stop outside her apartment door, and bit her lip. Uh-oh. "Well, um…"

Hunter shot her a resigned look. "What did you do?"

"I may have substituted silver for steel cutlery at the Reform ball this year." Silver was toxic for both vampires and shifters, and touching silver was about the same as caressing acid for them. Silver cutlery wasn't enough to kill the shadow breeds, by any means, but it had made everyone who came into contact with it damned uncomfortable. Her mother had been furious, and had banned her from the winter solstice celebrations as punishment.

It had been totally worth it.

Hunter gaped. "Silver? At the Reform ball?" He closed his mouth and gave her an assessing look. "You can be so devious," he murmured, and she blushed at the amused appreciation she saw in his eyes.

She ducked her head. "So you see, it might not be some twisted plan of your father's," she admitted. The cutlery switch wasn't intended as a fatal attack on the shadow breeds, but it had provided enough of a disruption that some of the more secret conversations couldn't be conducted, with everyone eyeing anything that looked remotely metallic with suspicion.

She pulled the keys out of her jeans pocket and slid one into the lock.

Hunter braced his hand against the wall beside the door, and her awareness narrowed down to the bunched biceps so close to her head. "You know, you really are a—"

The loud crashing from one floor below startled them both, and Melissa clutched her chest as Hunter took a few steps down the lower stairwell and peered around the corner.

"It's okay, that door is warded, too."

Hunter looked back at her, his expression grim. "Something tells me that's not going to stop them this time."

She frowned and removed her keys, jogging down the steps to check it out. Her wards were impenetrable. She'd used a lot of magic, and she'd even had her brother, Dave, assist her in creating a blood lock.

"No fangs, remem—" Her throat closed over when she saw the peephole forced off its runner, and a muscular arm slid through to wave around. Yells and jeers could be heard from out in the street.

"Human," Hunter stated. Melissa paled, and she took a step back. Hunter reached for her, his warm hand grasping her arm.

"If we go back up there, we'll be trapped between a human mob and the vampires on the roof."

"I haven't pissed off any humans," Melissa whispered. She frowned. "At least, I don't think so." She glanced up the stairwell. She could still hear the muted thuds from the door on the roof. The vampires were still trying their best to get past the door. She swallowed.

"There's a fire escape in the alley," she said, and her stomach coiled. If there were humans on the ground, there could be humans making their way up to the roof. Hunter was right. They would be trapped.

She whirled and ran down the stairs two at a time. "The store," she muttered. "We can call for help."

She flinched when she heard something launch at the door that led from the corridor into the street. They were going to break it down.

"Hurry," Hunter urged as she fumbled with the lock.

"I'm trying," she rasped. Hunter slid his hand over hers, steadying it, and together they slid the key into the lock. The door at the street buckled under the force of whatever was hitting it.

Melissa twisted the key and turned the knob, and Hunter pulled the door open as the front door at the end of the hall burst open. Hunter shoved Melissa in front of him and followed closely, dragging the door shut and flipping the internal locks as footsteps ran down the hall toward them.

Melissa backed away from the door, shaking.

"Where's the phone?" Hunter asked, and she pointed to the front of the shop.

"Behind the counter."

They ran up the aisle, and when Hunter halted suddenly, Melissa plowed into his back.

"What—"

Hunter pushed her behind him, and started to retreat. "Tell me there is another way out," he said, his voice calm but grim.

Melissa peered over his shoulder, and her eyes widened. A group of men stood at the front door, hands pressed up against the glass as they peered into the store. Neither werewolf nor vampire, they were definitely human.

"Loading dock," gasped Melissa, tugging on Hunter's arm. She started to run to the back of the store, but halted when she heard the thumping from the rear.

"No," she whined, "seriously?"

There was a yell from the front of the store, and then the sound of fists thumping against glass.

"Melissa," Hunter's low voice prodded at her. He pointed to the doorway that led down. She grimaced.

She didn't want to go down. There was a way out, but they'd possibly be facing something far worse.

Glass shattered at the front of the store, and the intrusion forced her decision. She muttered quickly, gesturing with her hands and the door clicked as the locks disengaged.

"Come on," she muttered, grabbing his hand. Maybe they could hide down in the basement until help came.

"Wait," Hunter said, his voice rough, and he turned to face the men now climbing through her broken shopfront, scattering and trampling over the display books. Hunter lifted his hands, palms up, and Melissa grabbed his shirt so forcefully it ripped.

"No!" she cried at him. "They're compelled, Hunter. It's not their fault."

Hunter glared at her briefly, then sighed harshly. "Fine. I'm going to apologize now, though."

"Apologize for what?" She asked warily, then huffed as he pushed her into the stairwell.

"Just remember, I'm doing this for you," he muttered, then raised his arms, hurling the fireballs at the shelves of books.

She gasped in horror as fire tore through her bookstore, and the men screamed, retreating from the flames. Hunter slammed the door shut, cutting off her view of the firestorm. "Lock it," he said fiercely as he stepped past her.

Her eyes burning with unshed tears, she murmured her barrier spell, then shook off Hunter's hand as he grasped her arm. He shot her an exasperated look, then stepped aside, gesturing for her to precede him.

"After you."

She could hear the crackle of flames beyond the door, already feel the heat. He'd effectively cut them off. There was only one way, and it was down. She stomped down the stairs and flung open the door that led to her apothecary.

Hunter watched as she spelled the door, heard the locks engage with a viciousness that made him flinch.

"You can't be pissed at me," he exclaimed as she turned to face him. Her lips were tight, her cheeks flushed, and her green eyes glared at him with fury.

So, maybe she could be pissed at him. Hunter shot her a look of surprised innocence. "What?"

Her eyebrows rose in disbelief. "What?" she repeated softly.

Hunter's eyes narrowed. He'd learned that Melissa was a passionate, vibrant and lively woman, but when she went all quiet, it was like the silence found in the eye of a tornado, with destruction sure to follow.

"You set fire to my store," she said, and took a step toward him.

He didn't budge. He thought about budging, but then realized it would make him look weak—and any hint of vulnerability with this one was like a mouse pausing within reach of a cat's claw. Dangerous.

"Because you wouldn't let me set fire to them," he protested.

She slapped her forehead with her palm. "You can't set everything on fire," she exclaimed.

"Not everything," he argued. "Those men upstairs are fine. They're not dead. Most of them aren't even singed."

She blinked, her mouth open as she tried to find her words—unsuccessfully.

"Hey, you have to admit, that was close," he said, gesturing to the door. "They would have had us if I hadn't done that."

"You set fire to my store," she exclaimed.

"And you can thank me, anytime," he hinted. What the hell was her problem? She was alive, wasn't she?

She made some garbled noise in frustration, closed her eyes and did an intriguing little stomp-dance with her hands fisted by her sides.

"Why are you so angry?" he asked, confounded. "We were surrounded by guys who apparently want you dead, and they would have had their wish granted if I hadn't put them on pause with that fire barricade." He shrugged. "Be angry all you want, but just know the reason you *can* be angry is because I saved your life. *Again.*" He emphasized the last word as her fingers curled, just to make it clear she owed him, and to keep her painful talons out of his brain—or delusions of snakes or spiders or whatever other nightmare she could conjure up.

"Maybe we could have reasoned with them," she said through gritted teeth. "But we'll never know because, yet again, *you torched my shop.*" She yelled the last words at him.

Hunter folded his arms. "There was no talking them down, and we both know it. That was a homicidal mob with one intention. To kill you." He'd seen their eyes. He'd seen the murderous glint, the compulsion. They intended to do Melissa harm. "You can hate me all you like, Red, but you can't deny that I'm efficient. You might not like my methods, but I'll get the job done, and today that job was saving your life." Damn ungrateful witch.

Melissa rubbed at her temples, as though trying to soothe a migraine. Or else she was trying to summon more magic to smite him with.

"That fire won't hold them for long," he warned her,

just in case it was the latter. "It's burning hot and fierce at the moment, but—"

An explosion above them interrupted him, and they both ducked instinctively. Dust filtered through partition boards in the ceiling.

Hunter eyed the door warily.

"What was that?" Melissa whispered. "A gas tank, maybe?" Her hand rose to her mouth. "Oh, my God. All those men…"

Hunter shook his head. "I don't think so." It had been over too quick—a short, violent burst. He knew fire, and that was not a gas explosion. He crossed over to the door and placed his hand on the surface. It was cool. He hadn't expected it to be hot to the touch, but he'd expected some warmth from above. He put his nose to the crack between door and frame. He could smell smoke, but the acrid scent was only mild. He twisted to place his ear against the crack instead, listening intently. He could hear talking upstairs, then the sound of wood sliding across the floor. A male voice, one he recognized, had him backing away.

"Get your sneaky little door open, quick," he ordered Melissa, his muscles tensing.

She didn't hesitate, but turned and did some sort of graceful hand gesture, her lips moving soundlessly. The door that was neatly hidden in the painted mural swung open.

He grabbed her wrist and pulled her toward the dark space.

"What's going on?" Melissa asked as she trotted alongside him. For once, she wasn't pulling back, wasn't trying to fight him. He guided her gently down the steep stairs, grabbing the torch and handing it to her as he turned to grab the door.

"I think I just heard—"

Another explosion rent the air, and the door on the far side of the empty apothecary blew in. The force of the explosion hurled Hunter and Melissa into the darkness, and slammed the mural door shut.

Melissa hissed as she rolled over. Every damn bone in her body ached. Her muscles felt like jelly, and she covered her mouth, trying not to puke.

For a moment, all she focused on was the pain, the discomfort. Her elbows were grazed, her wrist and hip throbbed where she'd fallen heavily at the bottom of the stairs and sharp pain seared through her ankle each time she tried to move it.

Hunter lay across her thighs, and he groaned as he stirred.

He levered himself off her, rolling across her legs in a move that had her biting her lip to stop from screaming. She used her good foot to shove him off her before he did any more damage.

"Ow," he moaned as her foot found his shoulder.

She swore as she tried to roll to her feet. Her ankle gave way when she tried to put her weight on it. She flung her hands up, unbalanced in the darkness, and caught herself against the brick wall. She hopped in a small circle, so that she could lean her back against the surface.

It was pitch-black inside the corridor. Heaven only knew where the torch had landed.

She was totally in the dark. She listened as thumps and thuds and male voices filtered down to them. A lot of male voices. Then she heard the sound of metal scraping, clanging and crashing. They were pulling the shelving apart.

They were wrecking her apothecary. Tears welled in her eyes as she listened to the destruction above. She pursed her lips so tight and held herself so rigidly that she didn't even breathe until she had to suck some air in. Her bookstore was gone, and so too was her clandestine little clinic. She dragged in her breath, a whispered sob in the darkness.

Damn it. She'd worked so hard on that damned space. She'd scrimped and saved, she'd worked on the reconstruction herself, after work and on the weekend, painting, hammering...she, Lance and her brother had worked tirelessly. It was a clichéd statement, but she really had shed blood, sweat and tears in that work.

All for nothing. She flinched as something big and heavy was thrown against the door above their heads.

Her fists clenched, and she could hear Hunter shifting in the darkness.

That bookstore had been her livelihood. There were so many dreams and hopes wrapped up in that business. She had started it, but then Theo had joined her, and together they'd made plans, grand plans, special plans.

And in the space of one evening, her income, her vocation—her future—everything had been reduced to ashes.

It started to unfurl in her gut, a burning rage that turned ice-cold, spreading through her. She raised her arms, readying to pour all her fury into her own destructive spell.

Hunter's hands clasped hers in the darkness. "Don't," he whispered, stepping closer to her until she could feel his body, so close to hers.

"Don't even think about stopping me," she said, her voice so low, but she knew he heard in the darkness. She tried to free her hands, and he pulled them above her head, bracing them against the wall. This time his body did lean into hers, all heat and muscle and strength. His scent drifted to her. She could feel the delineation of his chest muscles against her breasts, and despite herself she reacted, her nipples tightening against the wall of his chest.

"Don't," he told her, his voice husky but clear in its warning. "You can't win. My father is up there, and he's stronger than I am. You try to tickle him with your spells, and he will turn you into ash without a moment's regret."

"Your father?" For a moment, cool reason intruded in on her anger. She'd seen Arthur Armstrong in action. It had taken both Hunter and his brother, Ryder, and Melissa and her own brother, to subdue him, and that was because she and Dave had had the element of surprise on their side.

She wanted to scream in frustration. The man destroyed lives without any conscience. When she most wanted to, needed to, she couldn't just go up and bewitch her way out of a problem. Again. Memories of the only other time that had happened to her, and the way that situation had ended, still haunted her. For only the second time in her life, there was someone more powerful than she, and she had to stay her hand.

And listen to him destroy everything she lived for in the process.

"If it's your father, why don't you just go to him? If this is some attempt for him to save you, he can have you. I'm not holding you back."

Hunter stilled next to her. "He can have me?" he repeated. His tone was mild, but she sensed the tightening of his chest muscles, the rigid set to his shoulders.

"Nobody else needs to be hurt, Hunter. If he's doing

this to get to you, maybe we should just open the door to him and let you go to him." And maybe stop him from transforming her apothecary into rubble.

"I'm not sure how your family works, Red, but blowing up a building is not our usual greeting. My father might be pissed at you, but he would be incensed by what I did to him. No pun intended." Hunter angled his head, his nose brushing her hair aside. "If I go to him, he will kill me. Is that what you want?"

Melissa frowned at the loaded question. Did she want Hunter dead? Five months ago, she would have said yes. Without hesitation. Five minutes ago, she may have said yes, after the stunt he pulled in her bookstore. But with everything he'd done for Lance, for Lexi—even for her... she didn't try to sugarcoat it. He'd saved her life. On the one hand, she was very tempted to let the light warriors duke it out.

But then Hunter might lose. He might...die.

With her own mother being so politically minded, with every move, every word part of a hidden agenda, and having experienced firsthand the hurt and betrayal from a parent, she didn't wish that on anyone—although she didn't think her mother would actually attack her.

"Wow, you really—"

"No," she admitted in a whisper, interrupting him. "That's not what I want," she grumbled. There was silence for a moment, then Hunter chuckled, his breath gusting against her neck. "Careful, I might think you actually care."

She lifted her chin. She didn't want him thinking *that*. "Hardly. My mother would not be happy if anything bad happened to the light warrior within my care—even if it was at the hands of his own family."

"You sentimental thing, you."

The sounds of destruction got louder, as though they were systematically making their way around the room.

"This isn't fair," she whispered, all the frustration, the desolation and the fury poured into those three little words.

"What can you do about that door?" Hunter asked, his lips next to her ear. Her eyes narrowed in the darkness, despite the fine tremble his breath caused in her. Did he not understand the true import of what was happening above them? Did he have no sympathy, not even buried deep in some forgotten place? "My father and his mob will find that door eventually, and they'll come down here. We'll both be finished. Do you have anything in that pretty little head of yours that will help us?"

If she tried to attack the Warrior Prime above them, his retaliation would see them both dead. She could at least do something about the door, though. Her lips lifted. Actually, that would be fun.

She nodded, and for a moment Hunter remained where he was, his chest against hers, his strong hands gently gripping her wrists. He stepped back so slowly it was like an incremental distancing of their bodies.

She clasped her hands together, calling on her magic. There were no elements down here save for the stone bricks beneath her feet, but even that was not natural. She focused inward, feeling the stirring of her essence. She leaned forward, just a little, until her hand brushed the steel supports of the stairs. Using an old spell her brother had once taught her, she could feel the stairs become thin, wavery, insubstantial within her grip. She sent the magic up the railing, mentally wrapping it around the treads as well, until she sensed the door. Keeping in touch with the railing, she spread the magic over the door, letting it embed within its surface. Then she muttered the final verse of the spell.

Beneath her fingertips, the railing disappeared. She added a new line to the spell, adding an extra punch line to it, then she drew back.

"Well?" Hunter asked beside her.

"I've cloaked the door, given it some substance so that even if they do a tap test, it's going to look, sound and feel like wall from the other side. It's not completely impenetrable, but they'll have to be very lucky to find it."

"Which means we'd be very unlucky if they do," muttered Hunter. "Is there another way out of here?"

Melissa considered the tunnels, and grimaced. "Not really." She didn't like it as an option.

"Not really isn't a no. What gives?"

"If we follow that corridor to the end and climb down one level, we can access the tunnels of Old Irondell. We could possibly make our way through the ruins to my brother's shop." Dave's tattoo parlor sat above one of the old caverns, with access to the tunnels, but where she cringed at the underbelly of Irondell's new Reform society, her brother seemed to revel in it.

"Great."

"No, not great. You don't know what's down there."

Hunter leaned forward. "As my father's son, I can tell you it can't be as bad as what is waiting for us above."

"Maybe we should wait. I mean, someone will notice my flaming beacon of a bookstore and come to help." Maybe her brother, for instance. Or maybe Lance, once he'd safely contained Lexi.

"Or, considering all the enemies you've made over the years, perhaps they'll bring marshmallows and sing songs around the bonfire," suggested Hunter.

Melissa pursed her lips, but didn't argue. Sadly,

each option had an equal chance of fruition. Despite the shields she'd put in place, they could still clearly hear the men above. She didn't know how long they could wait it out, how long it would take before her mother decided to pay her daughter a visit and negotiate a truce—because Eleanor Carter wouldn't actually defend her daughter until she'd wrung every ounce of advantage she could out of the situation. And then Melissa would have to listen to her mother's lecture about it being her own fault.

"I wonder what thoughts are whirling through your head," Hunter murmured.

Melissa sighed. It was the thought of her own mother, more so than Hunter's father that made her decision for her. She refused to be beholden to that woman, for anything. If the White Oak Elder Prime had to bring any influence to bear on a situation of her daughter's creation, then her mother would ensure there was a debt for Melissa to pay.

"Fine, let's go."

She took a step forward in the corridor and crumpled, hissing in pain. Her ankle was throbbing, but any weight on it was unbearable.

Hunter was by her side immediately. "What is it?" he asked, his hands moving gently and efficiently over her body. She halted. Did his hands linger on her breasts?

"My ankle. I think it's broken."

His hands still hesitated at the side of her breasts.

"That's not my ankle," she muttered.

"I know," he whispered back, and she saw a flash of white in the dark, and then shuddered when his hands slid around to her front, almost but not quite cupping the mounds. The jerk was laughing. He moved his hands on before she could slap them away, touring down the indent of her waist, the swell of her hips—even there, he paused briefly—and then on to caress her legs through the denim. She heard him sigh.

"Yeah, it's broken, but I can't do anything about it here. My father will sense the light, and then he'll find that door." He pulled her arm behind his neck and helped her up. His arm slid around her waist. "Let's get into Old Irondell first, then I can do something."

Chapter 14

Hunter slid the heavy metal grate across the hole, letting it drop as quietly as possible into place. He snapped his fingers, and a small flame hovered above his hand. He glanced around. They were in a tunnel. A big one. The walls were made of different kinds of brick, and the surface they stood upon was dark and hard. It took Hunter a moment to realize they were in a narrow street, and the wall of bricks was simply different buildings.

His eyebrows rose. Hot damn. Those old stories were true. Present-day Irondell had been built on the skeletal remains of the old city. He frowned. He wondered if all of the stories had an element of truth in them. Like the Darkken.

No. Their luck couldn't be that bad.

He eyed the gaps between the buildings. It was so dark down here. He turned to face Melissa, infusing the flame with a little more light to see her more clearly.

Her face was pale and drawn, the lines bracketing her lips deep with strain. He had to remind himself she was still recovering from her wolf attack the night before. He was surprised by a need to take care of her, make her comfortable. It went beyond his usual attention to patients in need. He frowned. It made him feel soft. He didn't like it.

"Come on, let's find some shelter and get you sorted." Ah, now that had been brusque. Firm. Much better.

She levered herself away from the wall, her eyes wide and anxious as she glanced around. This was the first time he'd ever seen her skittish. "Relax, Red, there is no bogeyman."

"It's not the bogeyman I'm worried about," she whispered. He pulled her arm around his shoulders and tugged her close, trying to bear as much of her weight as she'd allow. She hobbled along beside him until they reached the corner, and he pulled her gently across to the wall, using it as cover as he peered around.

His light force shed a little beam, and he gauged the area. He could hear the drip, drip, drip of water leeching through the bricks from above, could smell the faint scent of rot and decay, and it was blessedly cool—not cold. No breeze stirred the underground. He spied a door in the wall. It was a good ten feet away, but poor Melissa was hurting. He could see the sheen of perspiration dotting her brow, her lip.

Screw it. He lifted her into his arms, hushing her to quiet her protests, and hurried down the alley. The door was locked. No surprise, he guessed. Nobody had officially lived in this part of the city for a good century or two. He turned until his back was to the door and gave a short, sharp back kick. The door bounced open, and he cringed at the noise. This place was creepy quiet. Too quiet.

He stepped into the darker interior, flaring his light force to make sure there were no surprises inside. The place was empty. He glanced around. It looked like the place had once been a diner of some sort. The leather booths were torn, the laminate on the tables cracked, dust and grime coating every surface, but it still looked relatively untouched. A veritable time capsule.

He lay Melissa down on a booth cushion that didn't look as worn, ripped or filthy as the others, then gingerly cradled her foot. She rubbed her lips together, as though trying to stop any noise from the pain. He met her gaze. After her little temper dance and attempt to blast his father away with her magic, she hadn't complained. Hadn't blamed him. Hadn't bitched, moaned or tried to kill him.

She must be in considerable pain.

"It's okay, I can fix this," he whispered, and rolled the pant leg of her jeans halfway up her shin. He slid his hand down her leg. For a moment he was distracted by the sensation of her silky smooth skin, the toned muscle, the warmth...and then he felt the heat, the swelling just above her shoe. Even in the dim light, he could see the dark shadow of substantial bruising blooming above the sock line.

He grasped her ankle gently, and even though he took great care, he still felt her flinch. If they were going to get anywhere close to Melissa's brother, she needed to walk. If necessary, she needed to run.

Closing his eyes, he poured his light force into her. This was going to hurt. He couldn't afford to knock her unconscious—she needed to be alert, but he couldn't expend that much energy, not without a backup source to recharge with. He filtered energy through her, creating a warmth, a lethargy in her that relaxed her tense muscles enough to aid his healing.

He focused on the bruised tissue, delving deeper until he found the bone, and started to knit the calcic fibers back together. It took a great deal of concentration, pulling strands together and fusing them, strengthening them so her bone would be as good as new, if not better.

It took some time, and he could sense her sliding in and out of a daze. Eventually he sagged against the back of the bench seat. Done. He raised his eyelids slowly, battling weariness. Bone reconstruction always took it out of him. First there were the bones, then the damaged blood vessels and tendons...

He withdrew his warmth from her, and Melissa sat up, blinking. She stared down at her ankle, then flexed it cautiously. Her eyes widened at the movement, and then she rolled the ankle, shaking her head.

"Those are some mad skills you have there, Doc." She tilted her head, as though mulling something over, and her brows dipped, just a little. "You healed my broken bone in what, twenty minutes?"

He shrugged. He'd lost track of the time. He'd been focused on her, not the ticktock of a clock.

She swung her legs down to make more room for him on the seat, and he shuffled across gratefully. He'd been perched on the corner, and now he could lean properly against the backrest of the booth. He tilted his head back and closed his eyes. He needed to rest. Just a little.

"Twenty, schmenty."

He could feel her moving, shifting a little in the seat to face him.

"So why did it take you—what, two days?—to heal Lance?" He opened his eyes and stared at the opposite wall of glass that looked out onto a darkened corner. Uh...damn, he must be tired, he couldn't come up with a convincing lie fast enough.

"Uh..." He tilted his head, just a little, to peer at her out of the corner of his eye. She looked genuinely curious.

"I mean, sure, he had more injuries, but they seemed kind of superficial. Except for the bullet wound," she added.

She was too curious for her own good, damn it.

"Poison," he muttered, mentally scrambling. He didn't know how she'd react if she discovered he'd intentionally delayed her friend's recuperation so that he could find out more about the woman he'd once considered his enemy. He drew his brows together. When had he stopped thinking of her as the enemy? "The poison did some damage. Took a while to metabolize it."

She eyed him for a moment, before finally nodding, accepting his words at face value. Relief relaxed his shoulders for a moment, but something niggled at him. It took him a moment before he identified it.

Guilt.

Good grief. Out of all the lies he'd told in his life—and he'd told a few—why did lying to this woman bother him? He had to get over himself.

She twisted to face the same direction as him, gazing at the dirty window that looked out on the darkened street. He dimmed his light force, conserving his energy. Hiding behind the mantle of darkness.

They sat for a moment in silence. He could hear her breath, sense the rise and fall of her breasts, the slide of her hair over her shoulder as she tilted her head against the backrest. Her scent, that same sexy combination of cinnamon and smoke, teased at him.

"Why didn't you leave when you had the chance?" she whispered into the darkness, and his muscles tightened at the question. He could hear the hesitancy in her voice, the curiosity...the vulnerability.

It was a raw question, leading to exposure for her, and for him. He swallowed. He was tempted to lie again, make up something believable—he was good at that. For once, though, he didn't want to go to the energy of creating a lie, of deceiving another. Maybe it was seeing his father in action, the master manipulator... Or maybe he was just tired of trickery and deception.

"You had a chance to go..."

He sighed. "You...you kept your promise."

"Of course I did. You kept yours."

His lips lifted at her statement. As though it was a normal, everyday occurrence. "You were dying." And with her last burst of energy, she didn't try to save herself, she'd tried to save him.

He blinked in the darkness. More than keeping her word, it was that selfless act that had really hit home for him.

"But what about before?"

He frowned. "Before? When?"

"When I showed you Lance, and you—" Her words halted.

When he'd kissed her, and stolen some of her energy. When she'd gotten him so damn aroused it had been the hardest thing for him to pull back. When their passion had, ever so briefly, made him feel and act like a different man.

"When you put me to sleep," she finished in a low voice. "You made Lexi go home, Lance was unconscious and I was out of it. You had every opportunity to leave.

I couldn't have done anything to stop you. You didn't think about it?"

"Oh, I thought about it," he admitted, his lips twisting in a smile that held no humor. "Contrary to popular belief, I do actually keep my word. Every now and then," he clarified. "But don't worry. I figure there's a cure for that."

She chuckled softly, and he nearly jumped when her hand brushed his in the darkness. "Maybe, Hunter, some things don't need to be fixed."

He turned to her, wishing he could see her expression in the darkness. What exactly did she mean by that? Did she—did she mean that she thought he was…okay? That he wasn't a completely irredeemable bastard?

Her fingers tightened around his, and he sensed the tension radiating up her arm. "I just saw something move," she whispered.

He swung his head to the window, and caught a vague impression of a darker shadow, streaked with gray, moving at speed. Then the glass window broke, and a dark mass exploded into the diner, barreling toward them.

Melissa didn't have time to scream before Hunter shoved her down along the seat. He rolled over the top of the table, legs lashing out, and she heard a grunt—although whether that came from Hunter or whatever the hell was in the diner with them, she couldn't say.

By the time she peered up over the rim of the table, Hunter was grappling with a figure. It was about the same height as Hunter, but bulkier. That was about as much as she could make out. She saw the light blur as Hunter's fists struck out, his torso a paler shadow in the dimness.

She heard flesh strike flesh, and the figure stumbled

back against the table, before righting itself, squaring up against Hunter. Melissa didn't think. She climbed up on the seat and launched herself at the back of the creature.

She hit with enough force it shocked her as much as the creature she tackled, and they both crashed down to the floor.

"Melissa," Hunter yelled, and light flared.

Melissa blinked at the sudden brightness dispelling the dark, and the creature beneath her recoiled, covering its face. She could feel the muscles move beneath her, and she frowned. She looked up at Hunter. He had a small fireball in his hand and was raising his arm as though to hurl it.

"No, wait!" she cried, flinging up her hand.

Hunter's eyes widened midswing, and he had to jerk back, pulling his fireball with him.

"What the hell?"

"I think—I think it's human," Melissa said, levering herself off the figure beneath.

The figure curled up on its side, hiding its face from the light, but she could feel the frame beneath the heavy garb. Definitely human.

"*It* attacked us," Hunter rasped, his fireball churning and writhing in on itself, as though fueled by fury.

The figure on the floor shook visibly, and it emitted a garbled noise, somewhere between a keening wail and a harsh sob.

"Hey, shh," Melissa crooned, reaching out tentatively to touch his back. She could finally see enough of it, in the light cast by Hunter's fiery glow, to see that it was a man. Long, dark, oily hair, face and hands covered in grime, and a stench that could make your eyes water.

"My house," the man sobbed, curling into the fetal

position and rocking. "My house, my house." He kept crying it, holding his knees tight, his eyes squeezed shut.

Melissa sighed as she backed away. "He lives here," she whispered.

"He still tried to kill us," Hunter said, his eyes narrowed as the fireball flared in his hands.

"You're scaring him," she snapped as the man on the floor whimpered. She flicked her fingers, using her signature dampening spell to turn Hunter's fireball into smoke.

Hunter turned on her, his face angry. "You need to stop doing that."

"Doing what?" She hissed at him. "Stop you from setting everyone who threatens you on fire?"

"No, you need to stop thinking I will back down from a fight just because you want me to," he grated at her. "I'm not some torch for you to flick on or off at whim. I'm a light warrior, damn it. Fire, light, this is who I am."

She gestured to the vagrant on the floor who was still rocking, but his sobs had quieted down to hiccups. "This is who you are? Some big bully who uses his powers against those weaker than himself?" She didn't want to remember what he was like. She wanted to hold on to the guy who healed her ankle, who would talk quietly and hold her hand in the dark.

"If someone comes after me, or those I—" He halted for a moment, his fierce gaze wandering over her face before he swallowed, and continued, "or those I am with, I will fight back."

Her eyes narrowed. That wasn't what he'd been about to say. As though sensing her suspicion, her doubt, he stepped up to her, his expression ruthless. "I can heal, but don't mistake that for weakness, Red. I can also destroy. Yin and yang, baby. You don't get one without the other. You need to remember that."

"Why?" she whispered, her gaze trying to read his emotions behind the rigid mask he was now using.

"Because I am not my Goody Two-shoes brother, or some noble knight. Never was, never will be. So stop looking at me like that's what you want me to be, and neither of us will be disappointed."

He looked down at the man on the floor, then extinguished his fireball in an exasperated sigh. "Now you've ruined the buzz. Let's go, before any of his friends decide to defend their territory."

He strode toward the broken window, glass crunching underfoot as he stepped through the opening. He paused on the street, and turned in one direction, then the other. His torn shirt framed his torso, and for a moment that was all she could see—an indistinct pale blur framed in darkness.

"Which way to your brother's?" he called softly, but she could hear the impatience in his voice. She gazed down at the figure on the floor, and winced.

"Sorry," she whispered, then jogged over to the window, stooping a little to avoid any jagged pieces of glass still in the frame. She glanced around briefly, trying to get her bearings. Old Irondell didn't come with a map, and she was trying to figure out where her store was, and where they needed to head in order to get to her brother's tattoo parlor.

"This way," she said finally, indicating right, and Hunter nodded, striding briskly down the street.

She followed, but stopped short of catching up with him. Was he right? Had she started to think of him as a noble knight? The thought was laughable. Hysterical, even. Hunter Galen, her knight in shining armor.

He had saved her life, though. Twice. And he'd saved Lance's life—although that had been part of a bargain to earn his freedom. She watched him walk, his long legs eating up the distance in the darkness, the torn shirt swinging to reveal glimpses of pale skin in the darkness.

Did she really expect him to behave differently? Was she trying to hold him to a forced, false ideal?

An explosion shook the earth, and glass shattered in nearby windows. Hunter dived for her, tackling her to the ground and rolling her under him as bricks and crumbling mortar tumbled to the dark street around them, and Hunter covered her body with his, protecting her from any debris.

It took a while for the dust to settle, but Hunter finally lifted his head. He gazed around in the darkness, his body tense, his expression alert. "What the hell was that?" he whispered.

"It looks like your father found the door," Melissa said, shrugging, although she didn't try to hide the triumphant gleam in her eye.

Hunter's eyes narrowed. "What did you do, Red?" he inquired silkily.

"I added some extra zing to the cloaking spell," she admitted.

His lips quirked. "You're actually quite proud of yourself. What did you do, exactly?"

"I added an element of reflection, and then magnified it."

His head tilted. "And for those of us not criminally witchified, what does that mean?"

Melissa smiled. "It means that whatever your father threw at that door was reflected back at him, a hundredfold." The light warriors may have set fire to her bookstore and apothecary, but she'd just flattened the building. "I'm hoping your father burned right along with it."

Hunter shook his head. "Sorry, but a light warrior can't be killed by fire." He levered himself off her, and held out his hand, pulling her to his feet. He gazed around the street. Broken glass, timber and bricks littered the area. It looked like a war zone. He shook his head, whistling soundlessly. "I am so turned on by you right now," he admitted, eyeing the destruction.

She rolled her eyes and started walking, stepping over a partial wall that had collapsed. "Let's go."

She was trying not to think of the way he'd grabbed for her, covered her with his hard body to bear the brunt of any damage. He'd put his body between her and danger. Again.

It would be easy to believe he was exactly as he claimed—a man who could kill or cure with no conscience.

She realized her ankle didn't hurt. At all.

He'd healed her. He'd taken away her pain, and he'd protected her from a bomb of her own making. Was that good in him really just a front for his bad, or did that good go just a little bit deeper?

Chapter 15

Hunter plodded along, stopping every now and then to look at Melissa for guidance. She hung back, reluctant to walk beside him. He nodded to himself. This was for the better. Every time they encountered anyone, she expected him to behave like some damn hero.

He was no hero. He did bad things. Most of the time to people who deserved it. He pursed his lips. He'd tried to be good, once. It didn't work out. Even now, when he thought of Debbie he felt the instinctive shame, the guilt.

He had to tell himself it wasn't entirely his fault, what had happened to Debbie, but it was hard to break the cycle of self-hate. He had loved her. Well, he thought he'd loved her. It turned out he'd loved the false impression she'd made.

He didn't blame her, though. She'd been but a pawn in his father's machinations. For a while, he'd hated her, and that had just increased the guilt a hundredfold when he'd discovered the truth. No, that blame fell squarely on his father's shoulders. He clenched his jaw so hard it began to ache. His father had cost him so damn much.

He and his brother had met Debbie at one of the many parties his father had thrown in his endeavors to force the powerful Reform elite to accept them into the higher echelons of society, but without revealing their true identities. As the only light warriors in Irondell, and as the head of the Armstrong family, Arthur Armstrong was by rights the Warrior Prime of their clan. It was ironic, really. His father craved the power, the recognition of being a Prime, but could never claim it without exposing the existence of light warriors to Reform society, and potentially making them vulnerable to attack. In his bid to be the strongest, his father's secret in effect made him the weakest.

So his father decided manipulation, deceit and trickery would be their stock-standard weapons when dealing with others, and had drilled those lessons into his sons.

When Hunter had met Debbie, she'd been his kind of gal. He should have known there was no such thing, but, well, she'd convinced him otherwise. His brother had thought the same, though, and they'd fought bitterly over her. Debbie had eventually chosen Ryder.

Yeah, well, the less time spent on those memories, the better. He kicked at a pebble in the darkness, and it skittered across the road, disappearing into the darkness. They'd come to another fork in the road. Every now and then a manhole in the tunnel roof let in weak moonlight. He turned around. He didn't know how long they'd been walking for, but he was exhausted. He glanced up at the dark roof, spying the faint lightening of the gloom from what looked like a stormwater drain above him.

The only light he had access to was moonlight, and it was weak, at that.

"How far to your brother's?" he asked Melissa as she came up to stand beside him. She looked around, her eyes narrowed as she peered through the gloom.

"I'm not sure," she admitted. "Irondell and Old Irondell don't share the same road map. I think maybe another half hour or so. If we're going in the right direction."

His eyebrows rose. "If? What do you mean, *if*?"

"Look around, Hunter. We can't really ask anyone for directions."

Her tone was cool. She was still pissed about the homeless guy. He ducked his head. Not his finest moment, he must admit. Still, the guy had *attacked* them. He would not feel guilty for defending himself, or for defending Melissa. Maybe next time the guy would think about using his words first.

He took a deep breath, held it, then exhaled. "Which direction do you suggest we take, then?" he asked, keeping his tone mild.

He could sense her movements in the dark. She was twisting this way, then that.

Great. She had no clue.

"I think—"

A growl echoed down the street, and both of them froze. Now he could see the whites of her eyes in the darkness.

Another growl rolled through the darkness. This time it was closer.

Ah, crap.

Ever so slowly he turned, and he reached out to grasp Melissa's arm as she did the same. "Easy," he whispered.

They stared down the street, and Hunter edged them

slowly, silently over to the side, closer to the wall of a building. He was tempted to light up the street, but figured that would seem more like an invitation for whatever was out there. Something farther down the street shifted. He could see the movement, but not the detail.

He tried to push Melissa behind him, but she resisted, stepping up next to him. He frowned, but when he heard the pad of paws on the pavement he tugged on her, spinning around as something snarled and launched at his back. He fell to his knees, the scent of fur and something foul assailing him.

Hunter hissed as teeth sank into his shoulder. Melissa screamed, but it was more from anger than fear, and then the creature flinched behind him. He heard the enraged snarl, felt the werewolf turn, as though getting ready to attack Melissa.

"Come on," Melissa yelled, and out of the corner of his eye he saw movement, as though she was about to attack the lycan.

Hunter summoned his light force, and let it rain like cascading fire down his back. He heard the snarls turn into whimpers, and groaned as claws dug into his back momentarily as the lycan hunkered down, then jumped away from him.

Hunter rolled over, hissing at the burn of torn flesh in his shoulder and back, and squinted, watching the lycan skitter away.

Melissa curled her hands over, her teeth bared as she gritted out a spell in some archaic language, and the wolf recoiled. It stumbled back, panting, then flinched as Melissa raised one hand. She clenched her hand into a fist, then twisted it.

Hunter flinched when he heard the bones crack, saw the lycan's head twist, the neck snap at an unnatural angle, and then the lycan collapsed, its tongue lolling out, its eyes glazed and empty. Dead.

Melissa hurried over to him and slid her hand around his neck. "Why didn't you kill him?" she asked, her face pale and anxious as she smoothed his hair back from his brow.

For that moment, Hunter thought he was in heaven. It was either that or blood loss. Her clear worry, her tender touch... Then her words registered, and he frowned.

"Don't kill people, kill people," he said, wincing as he tried to sit up. "Make up your mind, woman."

"I thought you weren't my torch." She put her arm around his back, helping him get upright. "For the record, shadow breeds are fair game."

"I'm a shadow breed," he muttered as he rose to his feet. Damn, he hurt. His back felt like it was on fire.

"As you say, you're not perfect. Can you walk?"

He started to nod, but stopped when the world tilted. "Yeah," he lied.

Melissa pulled his arm over her shoulders, and he chuckled when she nearly fell under his weight.

"You're falling for me," he wheezed, then hissed as her arm moved around his back.

She gasped. "Hunter, you're bleeding, I can feel it."

He snorted as he concentrated on putting one foot in front of the other. "Funny, so can I."

"We need to find some shelter. I'm pretty sure that wasn't the only stray in Old Irondell, and we don't know what else might come out at the scent of blood."

Hunter grimaced. His vision was blurring, and his limbs were so heavy it was like he was wading through mud, but he could still recognize common sense when he heard it.

His toe dragged across pavement, then metal, and he halted. "Here." It was a drain in the gutter.

"You've got to be kidding. It'll be filthy. I need to get you someplace clean to patch you up. No, wait, you can heal yourself."

He shook his head, and then clung to Melissa like a drowning man to a life preserver. "I'm tapped out. I used a lot of energy in your bookstore, then on you, and all the friendly folk we've met in Old Irondell." He swallowed. His mouth was so dry. "We need to hide—I can't protect you at the moment."

Melissa gave an unladylike snort. "I think I've got this." She slid his arm off her shoulders and stepped toward the drain. Without her support, Hunter stumbled, then fell to the ground, groaning softly as first his knees, then his palms, hit the pavement. She glanced over her shoulder. "Oh. Sorry."

She bent over the drain, and he crawled over to help her lift it. He wasn't sure if he did actually help, he just knew his hand was on it, and the grate moved. With a little maneuvering and a lot of swearing, they both disappeared beneath the surface of the road.

Hunter must have blacked out for a moment, because he came to as Melissa was dragging his body down a dark tunnel. This one was narrower, with a lower roof. The original stormwater drainage system of Old Irondell.

Now, it was bone-dry, having not seen a storm for a couple of centuries. Hunter tried to look up, but his head lolled back, and he found himself staring into the glittering dark gaze of his witch.

"Leave me," he whispered, and he felt her stumble. Her grip under his arms tightened, and he grimaced as she pulled him farther along, panting.

"Shut up."

"Leave me," he said, his voice stronger. "Go find your brother. Then, if you want, you can come back for me."

Although why she would he had no idea. He hoped she would, but wouldn't blame her if she didn't.

She changed angle, and he vaguely noticed the anteroom she was pulling him into.

She pulled them well away from the doorway, then collapsed. He hissed as his back fell against the front of her body.

"Shh," she said, wrapping her arms around him gently. "You just need to rest."

His eyes fluttered open briefly. It was dark. So dark, and cool. The place smelled...old. Musty and dusty, but not foul. That surprised him.

He sagged against her. He was a light warrior. He was starving, and there was no light down here. No amount of rest was going to save him.

He lay there, half on top of Melissa, in the dark, the strong, regular beat of her heart thumping against his torn and bloodied back.

He was going to die. He sighed. He'd always wanted to go out in a blaze of glory, not bleed out in a puff of defeat. He blinked slowly. This wasn't the way he thought it would happen. He smiled in the darkness. Cradled in the arms of a beautiful woman. He couldn't think of a better way to go.

"Fix yourself," she whispered, her voice so close to his ear.

"I can't," he croaked. "No light."

Her chest paused beneath him, as though for a moment she'd stopped breathing. She realized, now. His lips turned down. He'd hoped she wouldn't figure it out until after he'd gone.

Her lungs expanded beneath him, and she leaned forward. Her cheek rubbed against his, and for a moment he felt the tiniest of sparks between them.

"There's another way," she whispered into the darkness.

This time it was his chest that stopped moving. He shook his head, taking a slow, painful breath.

"No. I'm not taking anything else from you, Melissa." He blinked, annoyed by an unfamiliar burn in his eyelids. "I've taken enough from you."

Her finger under his chin forced him to turn his face toward her in the dark.

"You're not taking," she whispered. "I'm offering."

And then her lips covered his.

Melissa moved her lips against his, so gently it was just a light brush of contact. Her heart thudded in her chest, and she startled when Hunter's hand grasped her fingers that were holding his chin.

"I don't want to use you," he whispered to her, his lips moving against hers. She could hear the need in his voice.

She smiled, enjoying the closeness, the shared breath, the contact of their mouths. "That's not what this is," she said honestly. She didn't view this as him taking advantage of her, of her losing her will and becoming just a food source.

He needed sustenance, and she could give it. Put simply, she didn't want Hunter to die. She wanted to do this. She'd had enough of dreams, enough tantalizing…she wanted more. She was doing this as much for Hunter as for herself.

She pressed her mouth against his, moving her lips gently, until his mouth opened beneath hers. She closed her eyes as she slid her tongue in, rubbing it against his.

For a while, that's all they did, lips and tongues moving against each other. He stirred something inside her, something hot and lazy. He let go of her fingers and slid his hand up to trace her jaw. That gentle touch, so delicate, set her to tremble.

It was as if that little telltale reaction, that sign that she was into this just as much as he was, acted as a release for Hunter. His fingers delved into her hair, his mouth widened and, suddenly, he was drinking in her passion.

Her breath caught as heat flooded her. Heart pounding, she cradled his head. He shifted in her arms, rolling to face her, and suddenly she was on her back and he loomed over her. Not once did their mouths break contact. He rose above her, his hips pressing against hers, and she drew her hand down his chiseled chest. He shuddered, and she liked it, so she did it again.

Over and over, he kissed her, lips and tongue tangling with hers. His hands swept over her body, and she moaned at his touch.

He raised himself on one hand, and used the other to cup her breast. His lips left hers, trailing down her neck. She arched her back, giving herself over to his caresses. Her pulse thudded in her ears.

Hot. It was so hot. She panted, trying to shrug out of her plaid shirt. Hunter helped her, pushing the garment off her shoulders. She wore a T-shirt under it, and Hunter's hand dropped to her waist, bunching the material in his fist as though trying to regain some control.

She writhed beneath him, eager to finally feel his flesh against hers. She'd dreamed it, she'd fantasized about it, now she was doing it, and it couldn't happen fast enough.

Hunter's hand slid up under the shirt, and her stomach quivered at his hot touch. Her breasts swelled within her bra, and she moaned with pleasure when Hunter's hand finally reached her there, cupping her through the lace-and-silk undergarment.

Hunter's lips skimmed down her throat, and she shuddered when she felt the hot lick of his tongue in the indent of her collarbone. At the same time his thumb swiped over her nipple, a delicious friction with the lace between them.

"Please," she moaned, not able to form any more coherent words.

"Yes," Hunter moaned back, levering up to drag at her T-shirt. Melissa sat up a little, helping him yank the fabric over her head, her hair falling down against her back.

"Oh, yes," Hunter groaned, as he looked down upon her, and Melissa realized she could see him. She had a brief impression of twinkling lights, like stars floating in the air around them, and then Hunter's lips lowered to hers again.

His hands skimmed over her body, molding her breasts before trailing down to tug at the button of her jeans. Her hips rose to meet his, and she dragged her nails over his chest as he unzipped her fly.

His fingers slid inside her jeans, beneath the lacy fabric of her panties, and her eyes widened as he toyed with her.

"Oh, wow," she gasped, then tilted her head back as he strummed her, the hot, slick slide of his fingers driving her to the edge.

"Yes," Hunter said, lifting his head to kiss her.

"Hmm-mmm," Melissa agreed as she kissed him back. Yes, yes, and hell, yeah. Heart thumping, thighs quivering, she climbed the peak of pleasure, and Hunter expertly pushed her over the edge.

Scorching bliss flooded her, and she floated in a cloud of intense satisfaction. It took several moments for her to catch her breath, and she realized they really were surrounded by light.

Hunter leaned over her. Gone was the pale, clammy complexion, his skin golden once more. His features were tight, his eyes shot with glowing amber flecks and he took a deep shuddering breath as he withdrew his hand from her jeans. She trembled, her body craving more of his touch, despite her recent orgasm.

"Thank you," he murmured.

Her chest rising and falling, she stared at him, astounded. That was—wow. That was pretty amazing.

She gulped. "You're welcome." Her gaze drifted down over his body. His hands were braced on either side of her body, and his chest rose and fell as he tried to catch his breath. The muscles across his shoulders were tight, his rippling abs taut with tension. Lower, his erection strained at his jeans. Hunter sank back on his heels, dragging a hand through his hair.

"Don't you want to…?" Melissa lifted her chin to his groin.

"Of course I want to," he said tightly. "But I shouldn't. I feel bad enough, taking so much from you." He exhaled roughly. Melissa felt disappointment, and her own edge of frustration creeping in, with perhaps a hint of embarrassment. She lay there in front of him, her breasts swollen and needy, her core damp and ready, and he was ready to stop.

He rose to his feet and turned away. His back was smooth once more, and there wasn't so much as a scar from the stray werewolf's attack.

"Oh, okay," Melissa whispered, reaching for her shirt.

Hunter looked at her over his shoulder for a moment,

his features harsh with arousal, and his eyes sharpened, the amber flecks brightening. "No, damn it, it's not okay." His gaze heated as he stared at her lace-covered breasts, then he turned to face her. "No. If I'm going to feel bad about this, at least let's make it worth it."

He strode over to her, dropping to his knees between her thighs, his hand sliding behind her neck to hold her for his kiss. She gasped as his tongue entered her mouth, lashing her with desire.

Just like that, her senses snapped to attention, eager to dive back into the passion. So quickly, Hunter had her panting, drawing her up to his chest, his hands sliding around her to expertly undo the back clasp of her bra. He slid the bra straps over her shoulders, trailing his fingernails softly against her skin, causing her to shudder. He pulled away slightly so he could remove the garment altogether, and he sighed as her nipples brushed his chest.

Liquid heat pooled between her thighs, and she moaned against his mouth as his hands cupped her breasts. She quivered as he gently pinched both nipples, and hot sensation zinged straight to her core.

Hunter's lips trailed down her neck, and he bore her back to the ground, kissing, licking and nibbling his way down to her breast. He drew a rosy nipple into his mouth, sucking on it and laving it with his tongue.

Melissa's eyes widened as sensations, hot and wicked, bombarded her. The lights in the little cavern flared and flickered, dancing above them. She trembled as Hunter released her nipple with a final tug, and switched his attention to the other breast. He was driving her crazy with need.

Well, two could play at that game.

She caressed his broad shoulders, her breath hitching as his hips moved against hers. She trailed her hands down to touch the chest that had drawn her gaze and had been the source of her fantasies for so long. His strength, his heat, was intoxicating.

She flicked his nipples, and smiled when he groaned. He rose up to kiss her on the mouth fiercely, then turned his attention to stripping her jeans and panties off, dragging her shoes off in the process.

She pressed against his chest, and he moved back. Melissa rose, her hands moving to his belt. In moments she had his fly open, and he lifted his hips as she stripped him. Her eyes widened when she revealed his cock, its rigid length drawing her touch. Hunter's head lolled back and he moaned.

She leaned down and pressed a kiss to his chest. His hand rose, fingers spearing over her scalp, and she kissed and licked her way down his washboard stomach. He groaned when her lips closed around him, and she used her tongue, lips and hands until his fingers clenched in her hair, pulling her off him. He drew her up, eyes boring into hers with an intensity that was all revealing, and all seeing. There was no escape from that gaze. That bold, hot gaze that showed her the depths of his desire, a hint of vulnerability and awe, and an awareness that left her nowhere to hide.

"I—" His lips moved, as though he wanted to say something, then he leaned forward and kissed her. Hard.

Something flared within her, something strange and new, a heat that crept over her with wicked intent. He dragged her closer, pulling her into his lap until she straddled him, his biceps bunching as he embraced her, his tongue sliding with the same rhythm as his hips rocking against hers. She could feel him, hot and hard, nudging against her.

She also felt herself, warm and wet, writhing against

him. Her eyes widened at the sensation. Hunter's hands slid down her back, cupping her butt and lifting her.

He slid inside her, and she felt *everything*. Heat built between them, but it was the sensations bombarding her, robbing her of clarity, of logic and reason until all she could do was feel. He slid inside her, stretching her. Her body surrounded him, welcomed him, and she could feel it all. She didn't understand how she could feel him, feel her, didn't have the presence of mind to question it, she just accepted it.

He gathered her close, and she sighed, feeling his strength embracing her, her softness against him, and their joining, exchanging heat, sharing friction. Writhing against each other, their hearts beating in syncopated rhythm, Melissa could sense her orgasm building. She could feel Hunter's pleasure, an exquisite torture as her senses overloaded, and then suddenly she was flying, and whatever connection they had between them kicked them onto a plateau of bliss that fed itself, creating, expanding, re-creating, until she collapsed against Hunter's broad muscled chest, a quivering molten mess.

Hunter dragged a deep, shuddering breath into his lungs. Holy smoke. He wrapped his arms around the trembling woman in his lap, her thighs clasped around his waist. He'd just glimpsed heaven.

He tilted his head, leaning his temple against the top of her head as they both tried to catch their breath.

Holy. Smoke.

He stared at the stone wall of the chamber they were in. He'd lit the place up as though it was Reformation Day, complete with little starbursts above their heads.

Okay, he needed to tone it down, but hot damn that was amazing.

He closed his eyes, drawing in his light force, dimming the room until there was just enough light to see each other. His lips lifted. So romantic.

She shifted, and his eyes rounded. Oh. God. He was inside her and could feel her surrounding him, but he could also feel himself inside her. As he had during the act.

"Oh, no," he breathed. No, no, no, no. no. *Hell, no.*

Melissa stiffened in his arms, and her head lifted, smacking him in the temple. He winced as she stared at him, her eyes narrowed.

"Oh...no?" she repeated.

She moved, and he helped by lifting her off his lap, his hands on her waist. For a moment, he gazed up at her, staring at her sexy body bathed in the golden glow of his light force. Quite simply, the most beautiful sight he'd ever seen, bar none.

And then he saw it. The cord that linked his heart to hers. Only rare, gifted light warriors could actually see a mating bond. Debbie had died before he'd even thought about a bond, but as it was, she wasn't truly his to bond with, anyway. He'd seen the one that existed between his brother, Ryder, and his mate, Vassiliki.

"No, no, no," he said, shaking his head in disbelief. It was a thing of beauty, an ethereal flow of energy, like cascading, dancing ribbons of color, all pinks and purples and—oh, God—white. "Oh, that's not good."

Crack.

His head whipped to the side as Melissa's palm connected briefly and oh-so-sharply with his cheek.

"Not *good*?" She glared at him, furious, but he saw the hurt, the humiliation in her eyes.

He held his hand up. "No, Red, that's not what I mean—"

"Screw you, jerk." She whirled around, her red hair flaring out like a vibrant curtain of fire, and she bent down to retrieve her clothes. Apparently she was completely oblivious to the strand of twisting colors between them. "And don't call me Red. God, what was I *thinking*?" She dragged her underwear on, the elastic of her lacy panties snapping audibly in the stone chamber. He rose to his feet, dragging on his briefs and jeans, hopping from one leg to the other as he dressed.

"No, this is all me," he tried to explain again, then flinched as she whirled to face him.

"Damn straight. I had a great time, and don't tell me you didn't, because we both know you did," she said, her teeth clenched. "You—I—" She gestured between them, her face a comical blend of horror and confusion. "What *was* that?"

"That was you being so unbelievably generous," he told her, trying to use a soothing tone, "and I really, really appreciated it."

Her eyes rounded. "You *appreciated* it?" This time her voice emerged almost as a screech, and Hunter winced. Ah, hell. He was making a colossal mess of this. Like usual.

He held up both hands, palms out. "Hey, it worked. I'm healed, I'm charged and ready to go—"

"You already went," she snapped, and Hunter's lips twitched. He certainly had. Then his humor left in the face of her fury—of her hurt. He'd done that, in his usual, stupid-ass way.

"And you are...okay?" He'd heard about the bond, the feedback of the link. Had never, never, *never* thought he'd ever experience it. But what if it was just talk? What if he still drained her of her energy? Of her life essence?

"Am I *okay*?" She dragged her T-shirt on over her

head and tucked it furiously into her jeans. "No, I'm not okay. I just—" she gestured to the ground where they'd just blown each other's minds, and then gestured to him, finishing "—with you."

She made it sound like she'd broken a law of nature. His lips tightened. "I meant, are you okay, physically? Are your energy levels sufficient to get you out the door, or have I—" he swallowed, finding it difficult to put into words "—have I drained you?"

He stared at her, concerned and just a little panicked. The pleasure, the energy that had been created between them, could have drained her almost to the point of expiration. If he'd taken that much pleasure from any other woman, he could have killed her.

She frowned, resting her hands on her hips. "I'm fine," she growled.

He raised a hand toward her, saw that it was trembling and clenched it into a fist. "I mean it, Mel. What we just did—I could have killed you. Are you okay?" He needed to hear it from her properly, not some glib assurance. God, how could he have let it go so far?

She must have seen his apprehension because she calmed, ever so slightly, and her brow relaxed. Slightly. "Yeah, I'm fine, Hunter. In fact, I'm good." Her eyebrows rose, as though surprised by the truth in the statement. Then she frowned at him again. "And you suck, you jerk."

She shouldered past him, and he turned to grab up the remains of his shirt. After a tussle with Lance, and a tackle from a werewolf, it was torn to shreds, so he dropped it and jogged after her. He cast a muted glow in front of them to light the way.

"Melissa, I'm so—" he began but she held up a hand, not bothering to turn.

"Save it. I don't want to hear it. We did what needed doing. You're all juiced up. Ace. Sorry it wasn't what you expected." She'd started off strong, but her last words were husky, and she cleared her throat, increasing her pace down the tunnel.

"Oh, it was a surprise, all right," he said quietly, eyeing the swirling ribbons of color between them. She turned on him, holding up both index fingers.

"Please. Stop. Talking."

He closed his eyes briefly. Maybe she was right. Every time he opened his mouth, he just made it worse. He nodded and opened his eyes as she continued walking, arms swinging as she set off at a cracking pace.

And the light warrior's mating bond stretched between them. He fell into step behind her. He couldn't be mated. He shouldn't be mated. There was something innately wrong with him. He'd dated women—hell, he wasn't a monk—but he'd only ever really fallen for one woman, and she'd rejected him. She knew what he was like, on the inside. She'd seen his darkness. And she'd died trying to get away from him.

He eyed the woman who was doing her best to put as much distance between them as possible. He should expect that. It hurt, but it wasn't really surprising. His own brother had thought him capable of murder, so Melissa, the one woman who had seen him at his worst, would definitely not want to be linked for life to him. For a moment he entertained the fantasy that perhaps she would, that perhaps this woman who frustrated him and challenged him and would not back down, that perhaps she would see the good just as she'd seen the bad. That she'd want to share more with him than just pity sex.

Her fists swung at her sides, and Hunter shook his head. Who was he kidding? Every woman he'd ever come close to loving either ran away or died. Or both. Mates were supposed to stay together, but out of all the women of his acquaintance, Melissa was most likely to run away. Or kill him. Or kill him and then run away. Their relationship so far hadn't really suggested long-term commitment to him.

Maybe he could fix this…?

He tried to grab on to the link, but it was more of an aura, and completely intangible. He swung his hand through it in something resembling a karate chop, and the ribbons just ebbed and flowed around him. He kicked at it, tried to pull it, then twisted, hoping it would wrap around him and sever.

It didn't. He tried to separate the strands, so intent on disconnecting the link that he almost tripped over Melissa. She stood in the middle of the tunnel, arms folded, a slight frown on her face.

"What the hell are you doing?"

He whipped his hands behind his back. "Nothing," he replied innocently.

Her eyes narrowed, and she looked at him as though he might be just a little crazy. He eyed the bond between them, and he wanted to laugh hysterically.

He wasn't crazy. He was royally screwed. He'd bonded with the bitchy witch.

She shook her head, then turned. She took four steps, and he watched the twisting band between them, and then something gray and fast tackled Melissa to the ground, a guttural snarl coming from its throat.

Hunter roared, shock and rage coursing through him as Melissa screamed, struggling on the ground with the figure. It had arms and legs and a head, and looked like a man—sort of. Hunter reached out, and a spark of light zinged from his fingers, catching the man off guard, propelling him back down the tunnel a good ten feet.

The man's head reared back, his eyes snapping red in the dark, and Hunter's light caught the gleam of his fangs. Hunter grimaced. It looked like a vamp, but not like any he'd ever seen. The gray vampire let out a howl, tipping his head back and letting the screech reverberate through the tunnel.

Then the vamp launched at them again, and this time Hunter didn't hold back. He let fly with a fireball that engulfed the man. Hunter grabbed Melissa's hand and took off running in the opposite direction, the agonized screams of the vamp following them, like a rolling wave of sound.

Only the sound didn't ebb, as it should have. Hunter glanced over his shoulder, and his eyes widened. More were running down the tunnel behind them. Gray-faced vamps with murder in their red eyes. Hunter swore, then tightened his grip on Melissa. He would not let them hurt her. They approached an intersection in the tunnel, and Hunter tugged her down the right fork. They rounded the corner, and Hunter skidded to a halt.

Before them stood a man. He stood with his feet shoulder-width apart, his hands at his sides. This one didn't have gray skin, though. He stood roughly the same height as Hunter, with broad shoulders, and strength that was evident from the tightly roped muscles in his arms and torso to his powerful legs. His complexion was pale, almost ghostly white, and his eyes glittered an eerie pale blue, although there was a glazed, unfocused look to them. Long white hair was tied back in a braid, and Hunter warily eyed the defined wall of muscle framed by the black leather vest he wore.

A white eyebrow arched, and the movement spurred

Hunter into action. They had a gray army bearing down behind them, or this single blind albino blocking their path. He knew which odds he preferred.

He flung a fireball at the albino, advancing forward to move around him, when the albino reacted, holding up his hands, and a dark shadow grew between them, capturing the fireball Hunter had thrown at him and dousing it effortlessly.

Hunter halted, shocked. "What the hell are you?" he snapped.

The albino smiled grimly, his vague stare victorious. "Your worst nightmare." The tall man turned his hands palm out to them, and a roaring cloud of darkness swept over him and Melissa, swallowing them into the pitch-black.

Chapter 16

Melissa cracked her eyelids open. Her vision whirled, and she wasn't sure if it was her head or the rest of the world that was spinning. She clung to stone, her fingers curled as she dug them into a crack to stop from flying away, and slowly her world settled. She was lying on the floor, her cheek resting on the blessedly cool surface.

"Well, hello, darlin'."

The deep voice rolled over her, and she blinked before she shifted her head. The albino sat on an intricately carved chair. A fire roared behind him in a hearth that could hold her whole kitchen. The hall they were in was massive, with walls inset with timber framing, and a large stone frieze above the hearth depicting a battle of some sort. What the hell was this place?

"Leave her alone." Hunter's voice was forceful, implacable, from somewhere beside her. She didn't have the energy yet to turn and look at him, but he sounded fine. Angry, but fine.

"What did you do to us?" she croaked at the albino.

He smiled, and there was something that caught her attention, something that seemed so familiar, yet she knew she'd never met this man before. Man. Vampire. Her muscles tensed. She was caught by a shadow breed. She didn't know what the hell he was, just that he wasn't an ordinary human. Goose bumps rose on her arms, and she had to swallow her fear. She wouldn't give in to the panic. This would not be like last time.

"I stopped you from hurting any more of my people," he told her softly, and she heard the menace in his tone. He tilted his head, his unfocused gaze curious as it flicked between her and something—or someone—beside her. Hunter, she presumed. She had no idea how much this man could see, perhaps it was just movement, but he seemed to be able to track both her and Hunter unerringly. "I must admit, it's not often we receive guests. What brings you into my territory?"

"Who the hell are you?" Hunter snapped from beside her, and finally Melissa raised herself into a sitting position. The grogginess was beginning to fade, leaving a faint headache behind. She glanced behind her. Hunter was on his knees, his arms twisted behind his back and held by two of the gray vamps. The hall extended beyond them, and flaming torches were set in intricate iron wall sconces that were placed at regular intervals. Enough to reveal the masses gathered behind them. Positively medieval.

Yet no guards held her. They probably thought she wasn't a threat, after Hunter taking fiery action—*again*. Yet another lifesaving debt she owed him.

Hunter met her gaze, and behind the fury she saw

his relief at her awakening. She gave him a small smile to reassure him that she was fine, then turned back to the albino.

The man rose from his seat and moved to stand beside it, his elbow resting on the carved backrest. "They call me the Dark Lord," he told them, smiling politely.

Hunter snorted. "Rather flashy, don't you think? Not to mention the contradiction..."

Melissa couldn't believe Hunter was calling out the albino for being...an albino.

The Dark Lord's pale eyes flared with something that was borderline humor, but mostly exasperation. "A little. But my clan seems to think it fits." He held out his arms. A cloud of darkness descended from the ceiling, and a coolness entered the room, the fire stuttering beneath the mantle of gloom.

It rolled over them with the weight of a heavy blanket, and Melissa blinked, trying to peer past it. She panicked when she realized she couldn't, and her hands rose to try to wave it away, like a fog.

There was the snap of fingers, and the dark cloud disappeared. A chill settled in the room. The fire had died in the hearth.

He swaggered down from the platform, his gaze on Melissa. "So, tell me, darlin', what brings you a-visiting?"

Melissa glanced around the hall and swallowed. A large crowd had gathered. All of the people had dark hair and varying shades of gray skin. Most had dark eyes, although she saw varying shades of eye color, as well. Good grief, the tales were true.

The Darkken. A race of savages living in Old Irondell, eking out a living from the land without light.

Although they didn't look terribly savage. A little girl

peered out from behind her mother's jeans. Her skin was pale gray, with a marbling effect of darker and lighter grays. It should have looked ugly and alien, but instead the blending of color was beautiful. The little girl popped her thumb in her mouth in a universal need for comfort.

No, the Darkken looked...almost normal, in a grayscale kind of way. Normal and alert.

Melissa frowned as she returned her gaze back to the Dark Lord. "We're just passing through," she told him. She didn't see any purpose in hiding their objective from the albino. She hoped he'd let them pass. She feared he wouldn't.

The Dark Lord frowned, and he stepped down toward her. "Well, see, here's the problem. You've killed one of my guardians."

"*I* killed one of your guardians," Hunter interrupted. "She hasn't done anything."

The Dark Lord tilted his head, switching his attention to Hunter. "Ah, yes. The fire starter." He rubbed his chin. "You killed Orion." His expression became harsh. "Orion was a good man, with a wife and a baby on the way."

"Orion was trying to kill *us*," Hunter pointed out. "It was self-defense."

"You were trespassing," the Dark Lord said, his tone mild. Melissa watched the exchange warily. Both men looked and sounded like they were having a casual debate, but there was nothing casual about being held captive by the Darkken.

The Dark Lord sighed as he folded his arms. "What am I to do with you?"

"You could apologize for attacking us and let us be on our way," Hunter suggested hopefully.

Their captor's eyes narrowed. "Or we could kill you now for your crimes," he suggested roughly.

"My crime," Hunter corrected again. "Let her go."

Melissa's eyes widened as she turned to gaze at Hunter. His shoulders were back, his chin lifted. For a moment, her vision blurred, and it was another man on his knees, his dark head tilted back as he begged for her life. She blinked rapidly, shaking her head. No. Hunter was not Theo. It didn't have to end the same way.

"But you're a couple," the albino said, glancing between them. "One in, all in, right?"

Melissa frowned. While she didn't agree with the Dark Lord's interpretation of their relationship, she wasn't about to abandon Hunter. Despite what had happened between them in the tunnel, Hunter had still fought for her, time and time again. He'd saved her life, and was now trying to negotiate her freedom at the risk of his own.

Just like Theo, damn it.

"I just want to go to my brother's place," she said, interrupting their exchange, calling the albino's attention back to herself. "That's all we want. We don't want any trouble…" Well, she didn't know about Hunter. He always seemed so ready for a fight. "We just want safe passage to my brother."

The Dark Lord's eyebrows rose. "Is he a resident of Old Irondell?" he inquired politely.

Melissa shook her head. "No, he's…above."

The Dark Lord frowned. "He's one of the Others…" He glanced down at his feet, his hand out as he gestured casually to her, palm up. "So, if you're from above— which I can clearly tell that you are, and he is above… why are you below?" He turned his wrist in an elegant roll to point at the floor.

Melissa looked at Hunter briefly. Hunter shook his head, just a little, but the Dark Lord caught the movement. He gave them each an assessing look, then leaned forward, his freaky pale blue eyes on direct level with Melissa's. "I have news of a light warrior who has ventured into Old Irondell, and is looking for a man and a woman. You wouldn't happen to know anything about that, now, would you?"

Melissa's eyes widened. "He's down here, too?"

The Dark Lord's eyes flared. "He's issued an alert. He seems very eager to find you."

Hunter lifted his chin. "We'd rather he didn't."

The Dark Lord smiled grimly. "I bet. But you see, he's sworn to kill a resident of Old Irondell for every hour it takes him to find you."

Melissa's eyes widened in horror as she thought of the vagrant they'd encountered. Old Irondell was home to the Darkken, and all manner of creatures, but also to humans who were homeless and vulnerable. She had no idea how many lived below, but from the numbers here, it could be substantial. Strays, the homeless…the Darkken. How could Arthur Armstrong be so angry with them that he was willing to kill so many?

"So you can see my dilemma," the albino said softly, and this time there was no mistaking the menace in his voice. "Not only have you killed one of my men, you're also responsible for the death of more people under my protection."

"Your protection doesn't seem to be worth much," Hunter commented sourly.

The albino didn't even turn. He lashed out, his fist catching Hunter square in the jaw. "I think I'll just kill the both of you and be done with it. Problem solved," he snarled.

Hunter's eyes narrowed. "Fine, kill me. I'm the one he really wants, but let her go."

"Hunter," Melissa gasped. Why was he on a kamikaze mission?

The albino stepped up to Melissa, and she tried to dodge his hand as he stroked her hair. "You're quite the catch, aren't you, little one?" he commented softly. "A light warrior prepared to kill for you, and another prepared to die for you..." He tilted his head, his pale blue eyes considering. "What makes you so special?"

She met his gaze solemnly. "Do you really want to find out?" She focused on the Dark Lord, calling to her magic.

"Melissa," Hunter warned in a low voice.

She ignored him. This—creature—hell, she wasn't sure what he was, exactly. He didn't have the blending of grays in his complexion like the rest of the Darkken, and his blue eyes were startling, mesmerizing. With his snowy white hair, he should have looked old, but his clear pale skin pulled tight over high cheekbones gave him an ageless appearance. She'd never seen anyone pull darkness forth like that, but she and Hunter needed to claw back some footing from this man, and from the Darkken. They were vampires, of a sort, that much she knew...but she also knew they were a breed apart. Living below as they did in Old Irondell, they were the very essence of a shadow breed, dwelling without direct access to light, other than what they could create.

And she didn't cower to the shadow breeds. She would never yield to the shadow breeds. Never. She focused her magic on the large man standing beside her.

The Dark Lord's eyelids flickered, and then he winced, raising his hand to his temple. She pictured her magic leeching into him, gently spreading like tendril roots from a plant, curling and sliding, delving into his mind. She did it gently, but she saw his eyes narrow, then his grimace as he held his hands to his head.

She expanded her reach, and the two men holding Hunter suddenly clutched at their heads.

"Stop it," the Dark Lord growled, peering at her with eyes that started to glow with silver flecks.

"Let us go," Melissa growled back at him. "We don't want any trouble. Let us go."

"I said, stop it," the Dark Lord argued, his voice rising with menace. Darkness started to curl up from the floor, and she could feel it pressing in on her knees, her thighs, as it slowly rose. Perspiration beaded on her lip as the darkness rose on a level with her chest, embracing her with a strength that was almost crushing. She panted, trying to catch her breath, but didn't release the grip of her magic.

"Leave her alone," Hunter exclaimed as he rose to his feet. He clasped both hands in front of him, and a swathe of light appeared, cutting through the fog of darkness that was even now trying to swallow Melissa. The surrounding Darkken gasped, some calling out in surprise and fear.

The Dark Lord turned to Hunter, and Melissa felt the darkness lift around her, just a little, as the albino warrior focused on the man who managed to split his gloom with the sharp length of light.

She could see the strain on the Dark Lord's face as he battled both Melissa's psychic attack and Hunter's physical one.

"Stop it, all of you," a woman's voice commanded from the side of the room. Footsteps echoed across the stone parquetry, and Melissa noticed boots with narrow heels stride into the corner of her vision, followed by two shapely legs covered in dark leather, and a coat that almost touched the floor.

"Mother," the Dark Lord growled, his expression fierce as he eyed Hunter, both of them battling to overpower the other with their talents. "This does not concern you."

"Of course it concerns me," the woman snapped, and Melissa tore her gaze away from the men to briefly eye the newcomer. Her dark hair hung like a curtain down her back, threaded with streaks of gray. She was an older woman, slim and still attractive. She eyed the two men with something that bordered on exasperation. "It concerns me when my son tries to kill his brother."

Both Hunter and the Dark Lord blinked, and Melissa's eyebrows rose as Hunter twisted to peer over his shoulder. The light in his hands flickered out, and his face paled in shock.

"Mother?"

Chapter 17

Hunter shook his head. No. It couldn't be.

The woman who approached smiled, her brown eyes sad. "Hello, Hunter."

He blinked, and his thoughts stuttered to a halt. She—What—? How—?

"No." He backed away from the hand she lifted toward him, and he saw the hurt that flickered briefly across those eyes, so similar to his own. "No, it can't be. You're dead." The face that stared at him was exactly as he remembered it; lines around the corners of her eyes and mouth that deepened with her smiles, the soft skin of her rounded cheeks that pinkened like a cherub with her laughter, the softness of her lips for when she'd kiss him and his brother good-night...

No. This could. Not. Be.

"My brother?" The Dark Lord extinguished his black cloud, and turned from Hunter to his mother, and back again. Hunter could see the incomprehension in the man's crystal blue eyes. At least the albino was just as surprised by this as he was.

"Griffin, this is your older half brother, Hunter," the woman said softly. She eyed both of the men for a moment. "Hunter. You have a new baby brother."

Hunter shook his head. "I don't want a baby brother," he exclaimed, and his mother gave him a tender smile tinged with humor.

"That's what you said when I brought Ryder home to you," she told him softly.

"Clear the hall," Griffin called, and one dark-haired vamp standing closer than the others nodded, then started guiding all of the gathered Darkken out of the hall.

Hunter stepped back as his mother reached for him, holding his hand up in warning.

"No. You *died*," he said fiercely. "I went to your funeral, damn it. I even wore a tie." It was such a trivial detail, but he'd always fought against the conservative, against anything expected of him—except for the day they'd entombed his mother. He would have done anything, worn anything, said anything, promised anything, to have his mother back.

She'd died, and he and his brother had mourned. He shook his head. This just didn't make sense. "Was this all a lie?" His shoulders sagged at the thought. She'd drowned when the car she'd been driving plummeted over a cliff and into a lake. The rescue crews were fast on the scene, but he was told she'd been dead when she'd been pulled from the water. "Whose coffin did I cry over?"

Amelie tilted her head, her brown eyes stared at him solemnly. "Oh, I died, Hunter. That you can believe."

The muscles in Hunter's jaw clenched, and he lifted his hand to point from her head to her booted toes. "And yet, here you are. Riddle me that, Mother Dear."

"My lover saved me," Amelie admitted, and for a moment he saw his mother's gaze flicker away. Then when she looked at him, her eyes glowed red, and her incisors lengthened. He heard Melissa's gasp behind him but all he could do was stare at the woman who had once tucked him into bed and sung lullabies to him. The woman who was now a vampire. He shook his head, trying to make sense of it all. Then her words registered.

"Your lover?" Oh. My. God. That was news. It was the first he'd heard of his mother's infidelity, and he wouldn't have believed it if the detail had come from anyone else. But here he was, staring at what should have been a ghost. He ran his hand through his hair and turned away, meeting Melissa's stunned gaze for a moment. She looked confused, confounded. Well, welcome to his hell. She stepped closer to him, and as he turned to face his mother again, he felt her hand slide into his. He almost pushed her away. He wasn't the type to lean on anyone, to depend on anyone. He didn't need anyone. His father had taught him that. Yet his fingers curled around Melissa's, and he drew her a little closer to him.

"Explain," he gritted. He lifted his chin. He was trying to hang on to his sanity, his calm, when all he wanted to do was release his light and screw the consequences.

"Yes, Mom, please do," the Dark Lord urged softly as he folded his arms. No, what had she called him? Griffin? He eyed his so-called brother briefly. His brother. Seriously? Admittedly, the guy looked about as comfortable with the connection as he felt.

Amelie walked over and rested her hand on the Dar—Griffin's shoulder. Hunter refused to call his brother by some fancy title. "I loved your father, Griff. Make no mistake." She turned to face Hunter, grasping her other son's hand. "I loved your father, too, Hunter, but I had no idea what he was really like until after the wedding."

She lifted her chin. "He was quite cruel," she stated calmly, and Hunter swallowed. He didn't want to hear this. He knew his father could be a dick. Present situation, case in point. Knew he was a difficult man to live with, to please…but hearing the intimate details of his parents' marriage was like sitting next to a banshee. Painful to the ears. Melissa's thumb caressed the top of his knuckles, and he realized he was squeezing her hand tightly. He tried to relax his grip.

"Arthur was lovely at first. The perfect gentleman." Amelie smiled dryly. "And then, on our wedding night, I discovered—"

"Mom, no, please." Hunter held up his hand. He did not want to hear about their bedroom antics.

"I discovered the real reason your father married me was for my money," Amelie finished in exasperation. "He made no secret how he viewed marrying the Galen girl and accessing her wealth was his biggest victory, so far." Amelie shrugged. "He had such grand plans for building up a medical empire that would have all the shadow breeds relying on him… He loved manipulating people, me included." She tilted her head, and Hunter watched the dark hair tumble over her shoulder, and the memory of her sitting at a dressing table, brushing the silken strands repeatedly, flared in his mind. He blinked and looked away. He wasn't going to get sucked into some nostalgic fog that blurred the reality of what he was now facing. His mother had left. *By choice.*

"Your father treated me like a piece of art, to be trotted out to impress when needed, and to be ignored for the rest of the time. If I was lucky," she added, her lips twisting. "And if I wasn't—well, let's just say your father had a unique way of using light."

Hunter shuddered. He could only imagine, and damn it, he didn't want to, because then he'd have to feel sympathy for his mother. He wouldn't be able to give in to the anger that fluttered inside him.

"You cheated on him." He said it as a statement. There was no accusation. His father was a jerk. He knew that. Accepted that. His mother and father were not a bonded pair.

Amelie smiled. "I fell in love," she corrected. "Besides, I was not the first to sleep outside the marriage bed."

Hunter grimaced. "Please. Don't." He did not want to hear or think about his parents' sex life—or lack thereof. He was already going to need significant therapy after all of this. He drew his shoulders back. "So you found love and left your sons." He nodded. That pretty much summed it up.

Her eyes narrowed. "I *died*, Hunter. The car I was driving went over a cliff, and I drowned. I did not leave you willingly."

Hunter smiled grimly. "And yet, you didn't come back. All this time, you've been living down here, and we've been living up there." He gestured to the ceiling. "And you never once thought to come for your boys." He glared at the albino. "But you stayed for him."

He wanted to feel hatred for the man who had stolen his mother, but more than anything, the anger he felt didn't even begin to compete with the hurt. "Was I so bad, Mother?" He whispered the words, and Amelie flinched in horror.

"No," she breathed, shaking her head as she stepped

toward him. Again, he retreated. He didn't want her touch, didn't want to crumble. His mother clasped her hands together, almost in a symbol of prayer. "Oh, Hunter, no." She swallowed. "The night I died, it—it wasn't an accident," she whispered.

Hunter's brow pulled into a deep V. "You did it on purpose?" Oh, hell, that was even worse.

"No!" Amelie's lips tightened in exasperation. "No, I was murdered. My car's brake lines were cut. I had no brakes as I went around that curve." Her clasped hands shook and her eyes darkened as though focusing on a chilling memory. She looked over at Griffin, and smiled. "I was pregnant, and your father found out, knew the baby wasn't his. If Griffin's father hadn't found us, both of us would have stayed dead." She turned and met Hunter's gaze evenly. "Just as your father planned."

Hunter shook his head in disbelief. His father was a bastard, and yes, a man capable of murder, but to kill the mother of his children…? He swallowed, then dipped his head. Well, yeah. He could see that happening, sadly. "My father seems to be capable of the worst acts," he commented, looking briefly at Melissa. Her green eyes were dark with shock.

"But when you—" He gestured to his mother, asking, "what, undied? Shifted?" He shook his head. That didn't sound right. He'd treated vampires for all sorts of ills, and didn't have any issues with them—or any of the other shadow breeds, really. He understood the mechanics of becoming a vampire. You needed to be fed a vampire's blood by the next full moon after your death, and then had to feed by the full moon after that to complete the process. He had no name for the procedure, though.

"Metamorphosed," his mother supplied.

He inclined his head. "Metamorphosed." Of course.

Like a caterpillar becoming a butterfly. "When you metamorphosed, why didn't you come back for us? You probably could have kicked the old man's ass..."

Amelie smiled, but this time there was no denying the sadness and guilt in her gaze. "I tried. By the time I felt strong enough to face him, everything was legalized. I was dead. My will was read, my inheritance disbursed. It would have been terribly inconvenient for your father if I'd approached Reform Court for a reclassification." She took a deep, shaky breath. "And he threatened to kill you and your brother if I came forward. I had two choices. I could try to claim you, try to rescue you, and you would die, or I could live below, with Griffin's father, and all of us could live in peace."

Hunter laughed, the sound harsh and tight in his throat as he remembered his childhood, about the continuous challenges his father had set for him and his younger brother, the constant attempts to gain his father's approval and never quite winning it, and the woman his father had brainwashed in a twisted attempt to have his sons compete against each other to prove each other's mettle.

"We didn't live in peace."

Amelie's lips rubbed inward, and she nodded. She would have known what she'd left behind, what she'd left her sons to face on their own. He wondered what life would have been like, living with his mother instead of his father. Well, it was no use wishing for what couldn't be—that ship had sailed long ago. He didn't want to think about it, didn't want to deal with it.

Didn't want to face the fact his mother hadn't died. She'd left.

Hunter faced the big, muscled albino. He already had a brother, damn it, and even that relationship was strained. This brother had powers like he'd never seen, but he suspected it was a result of the vampirism of the man's sire warping the light force of his mother. Fine, he was curious—purely from a medical line of inquiry, he told himself. He'd survived this long without his mother, without the brother he didn't know he had. He could plod along just fine without them.

"Now what?" he asked Griffin. Let him go, kill him for his crime—at this point in time, he really didn't care. He was done. "Are you going to let us go, or punish me for defending myself?"

Griffin shrugged. "Beats me. I've never had to kill a brother before." The albino folded his arms, his gaze assessing.

"And you're not going to kill one now," Amelie snapped. "You know the circumstances. Orion should have brought them to you, not tried to kill them on sight."

"He was defending the perimeter," Griffin growled. "And now we have a psychotic light warrior prepared to kill everyone he comes in contact with until he gets his son."

Amelie faced her white-haired son, and Hunter could see the fury in her gaze. "That psychotic light warrior killed your mother," she rasped. "What do you think he'll do to your brother?"

"Stop calling him that," Griffin snapped. "Just moments ago he was trying to kill me, him and his mate."

"You started it," Hunter called, and his younger brother rolled his eyes.

"You deserved it," Griffin retorted.

"Oh, bite me," Hunter returned.

"With pleasure," Griffin said, his pale blue eyes darkening to a fiery purple, his teeth lengthening.

"Enough!" Amelie held up both her hands, eyes flashing. "For heaven's sake, you're acting like children." She turned to Griffin. "Instead of focusing on your brother, focus on the real threat to your people, and you," she said as she turned to face Hunter. "You will both be our guests—"

"Mother," Griffin began, and Amelie shot him a dark look.

"Our guests," Amelie repeated strongly. "Show them to a guest room, Griffin, so that they can rest. From what I understand, they've been on the run for some time."

Hunter smirked as his brother rolled his eyes, the muscles in his jaw clenching as he beckoned over one of his men.

"Go to the light warrior," Griffin instructed him. "Tell him I'm prepared to parlay, but if he kills any of the Darkken, I'll hunt him down."

The Darkken nodded, then strode from the room. Griffin glanced over at Hunter, not bothering to conceal his irritation, then lifted his chin in a jerky motion, indicating they follow him.

Hunter pulled Melissa along behind him. There was no way he'd leave her side while they were "guests" of the Darkken. His brother may have them under some sort of control—something he didn't quite understand—but he didn't trust them. Nothing personal, he didn't trust anyone, really.

He glanced over his shoulder at the red-haired witch behind him. Except for one, maybe.

Melissa warily stepped past Griffin into the room he'd assigned them. She knew he had some vision limitations, but the man had an uncanny awareness, and a dark side that was more than just a thirst for blood. A shadow breed of a new dimension.

"What *is* this place?" Hunter asked, and Melissa looked away from the albino to take in the room. She gaped.

There was a large fireplace, with a roaring fire that provided the only illumination in the room. Still, the firelight was enough to see the four-poster bed butted up against one wall, with heavy golden drapes hanging from its canopy. A tapestry covered a large portion of one wall, and there was a leather settee and matching armchair facing the large fireplace, with a magnificent Persian rug covering most of the floor. A small lamp table sat between the chairs, and it bore a tray of bread, cheese and what looked like wine. A half-opened door revealed a private, marble bathroom. Melissa turned slowly.

It was— Wow.

Griffin smirked. "Apparently this belonged to some eccentric actor, back in the time before The Troubles. He built this mansion based on some castle in Old Scotland." He glanced up at the ceiling. "I hear there are mansions just as ostentatious above." A pale eyebrow rose as he looked over at Hunter for confirmation.

Hunter stepped over to the fireplace, holding his hands out. "Have you ever been? Above, I mean?"

Griffin's expression grew somber, and he nodded. "Once. Didn't like it."

Melissa looked at the albino with curiosity. He sounded so serious, almost sad. Griffin straightened. "Anyway. Rest. I'll have someone drop off some clothes for you to change into after you've slept. See you in the morning." He backed out of the room before they could say anything, slamming the door shut and sliding the lock home.

Melissa frowned. "So much for being a guest," she said dryly. She turned, and her eyebrows rose.

Hunter stood in front of the fire, and the flames seemed to arc and dance toward his fingertips, almost as though he was sucking in the energy through his pores.

He flexed his fingers, then turned to her. "Are you okay?" he asked her quietly. Her eyes widened, just a little. After everything that had happened in the hall, he was asking her if *she* was all right?

"I'm fine, Hunter," she told him. Admittedly, being surrounded and "hosted" by vampires was not on her bucket list, but she was living, she was breathing, and if she just kept reminding herself of that, she wouldn't lose it.

He frowned. "We're in the home of the Darkken, and I know how you feel about us shadow breeds."

She gave him a half smile. He had no idea how she felt the shadow breeds. Not many did. She also noted how he classed himself as a shadow breed, yet she'd seemed to have forgotten that fact, or at least subconsciously decided to ignore it. She professed to hate the shadow breeds, but she feared them, too, and it was that fear that had almost frozen her when the Darkken guardian had attacked.

She was still trying to stop the memories from surfacing, but even now, she had to ruthlessly block out the echoes of her screams from her mind, of Theo's agonized cries…of what came next.

"I'm fine," she said, her voice stronger. She wasn't going to cave in to the panic. She wasn't going to surrender, not to any shadow breed. She eyed the dark-haired man as he turned to stare back down at the fire. She'd surrendered a lot to this particular shadow breed. More than he'd ever know.

He was the first man she'd lain with since Theo. She subsided into the armchair facing the fire, letting its warmth slowly chase off the chill of her anxiety, her fear. For the first time since she'd stormed off from him in the tunnel, she let herself face that fact. She'd made love with Hunter. The warmth blooming in her cheeks couldn't be fully attributed to the fire. Even now, those heated, whispery memories were swamping the other scenes that were trying to get airplay in her mind.

She'd made love with a light warrior. A shadow breed. The kind of guy she'd sworn to annihilate, not...love. She should feel guilty. She'd betrayed Theo's memory in the worst possible way. Not only had she lain with another, he was one of *them*.

And yet, the guilt was...missing. Maybe she was still in shock. Maybe, on some level, her mind was already running through survival scenarios. One thing it wasn't doing was wallowing in guilt, or shame. What she and Hunter had shared in that tunnel—well, it wasn't shameful. It had been beautiful. She was trying to grapple with the softer feelings that came along with that coupling.

And then the big jerk had reacted as though he was the one to experience regret. That gave Hunter a whole level of conscience she wasn't prepared to recognize. He'd tried to kill her, for crying out loud. And she'd made love to him? It was a habit she really needed to break. How could she forget a minor detail like attempted homicide?

And yet, the man who'd tried to kill her had saved her life more than once since. He'd had plenty of opportunity to leave, but instead he'd stayed. He'd sacrificed his own freedom for her survival. And he'd made love to her with a passion and care she'd never experienced before—and that she wanted to experience again. She swallowed. Now they were held hostage by the Darkken, and Hunter's father was going on a homicidal rampage to find them. She shouldn't be thinking about sex. No, not sex. Making love.

Oh, and Hunter had been reunited with his undead mother. She shouldn't forget that little gem. She lifted her gaze from the flames to Hunter. The firelight flickered, a play of light and shadow across his handsome features.

He still didn't wear a shirt. Not that she was complaining. Yet, right now, gazing at his profile, she could see the tightness around his lips, the tension in his jaw. She didn't quite understand how, but she could sense his shock, his...hurt. He didn't want to talk about it, though, she could tell.

Well, you didn't always get what you want, because otherwise they'd be trying out that massive bed.

"So, you have a mother, after all..." she commented. "I always thought you were the spawn of the devil, but it looks like you entered the world in the customary fashion."

Hunter blinked, his lips parted, and the look he gave her was a charming cross between grumpy and humorous. His lips curled in a wry smile. "Yes, it appears my dearly departed mother isn't so departed, after all." His smile dropped, and he returned his gaze to the fire.

Melissa stretched her arms toward the fire, letting the warmth curl around her fingers. She didn't play with the flames, though, not like Hunter did. This fire had to be recharging his batteries. Which meant they didn't need to make love again, not for that reason, anyway. Melissa frowned as she glanced down at her fingers.

She cleared her throat. "You know," she began softly, "even though she, uh, gave you guys some distance, it seems she loves you." She had seen the woman's pain, her sorrow and sadness, and her very real shame at leaving her family behind. It had been fascinating. Probably because she'd never seen anything like that from her own mother.

Hunter drew back from the fire to collapse on the settee. "She didn't 'give us distance,' Red. She left us."

"She died."

"And then she came back, but only for her white boy," Hunter pointed out.

"She loves you."

"She loves the white boy more."

"Stop calling him that, he's your brother."

"I don't want another brother. I have enough problems with the one I've got already."

Melissa sighed. "I've got a brother, and I'd be damned lucky if I had another sibling like him."

"Well, there's the difference. You and your sibling actually like each other."

"You don't like your brother?" Melissa leaned back into the depths of the armchair and raised an eyebrow at the handsome man lounging across from her. "You set fire to my apothecary for your brother. You tried to kill me for your brother. Don't try to tell me you don't have some feelings for your brother."

Hunter's mouth turned down at the corners. "It's complicated."

"Oh, seeing your family in action—a father who killed his wife, and tried to kill you and your brother, and who is now killing innocents in the underground until he can kill us, a mother who didn't stay dead, and a half brother you never knew existed and who seems to be an equal match for your powers—I'm beginning to think complicated comes with the territory when it comes to you."

He shot her an exasperated look. "It's not the kind of tale you tell by the fire," he said, casually gesturing to the fireplace, the rug and the room in general. The movement caused the muscles of his arm to flex, and his pectoral muscle bunched. She eyed his nipple for a moment, then lifted her gaze to meet his. She wanted to feel his body against hers again. She wanted to feel all those wonderful sensations he'd given her back in the tunnel, but more than that, she wanted to ease the pain she sensed in him, soothe all the anger, the hurt.

"Don't worry, I don't believe in fairy tales. Besides, what else are we going to do, trapped in this room until your brother figures out what to do with us?" She tilted her head to gaze at him in inquiry.

"Half brother," Hunter corrected.

She inclined her head, accepting his qualification. "Half brother."

Hunter sighed, then glanced around the room. She could think of something else to do than talk, and she knew the same thought had occurred to him when Hunter's gaze flicked from the bed, then back to her. His gaze darkened with arousal.

Then he blinked, composing his features as he sat up on the settee and leaned over to grab the bottle of wine and the two goblets.

"Well, if I'm going to tell this miserable tale, we're both going to need to get drunk."

Chapter 18

"So, your father compelled this woman to be the perfect woman for you, and the perfect woman for your brother, just to see who could win her over?" Melissa had curled up on the armchair, her legs tucked under her, her elbow on the armrest as she cupped her chin. He'd just poured her third glass of wine, and Hunter nodded as he emptied the bottle into his own goblet.

"Yep. Sick, huh? He said it was to give us purpose." Hunter shook his head. *Purpose.* He had been quite happy, working in the clinic. Sure, he may have planted subliminal suggestions in some patients that had ended up benefiting him, but he'd never done anything that had been detrimental to his patients, and that was a record he was proud of. Healing people may not have had all the glory and fanfare his father was hoping for, but it was a good vocation. "My work, healing people, that was purpose enough for me," he admitted quietly.

He'd never said it aloud, not to anyone. It made him sound like some sort of benevolent tool, and he knew he wasn't benevolent. This work was entirely selfish. It made him feel good.

Melissa traced the rim of her goblet. "I overheard your conversation with your brother," she admitted. "The one you had with your father."

Hunter's eyebrows rose. "So you saw our dysfunction firsthand." Wonderful. His mate had seen how sick and twisted he and his family truly were. He eyed the bond between them. It still flourished, still weaved and rose, like a beautiful collection of ribbons. His mother had left him, and everyone seemed to think the maternal bond was the strongest. If his own mother couldn't stick around, why would Melissa? He wasn't being maudlin, just realistic.

"How did she die?" Melissa asked quietly.

"My mother?"

"No, the woman you loved."

There was so much weight in that sentence. He had loved Debbie. He wasn't a monk, he'd had girlfriends, and he'd made sure he was careful with how much he consumed of them in their relationship, but Debbie... Debbie had been different. Special.

"My father threw her off an upstairs balcony."

Melissa coughed on the wine she was sipping. When she'd caught her breath, she stared at him with a deep sympathy that darkened her green eyes. "Oh, Hunter."

He shrugged. "I didn't know it, at the time. I thought, with this fierce contest between my brother and me, that Ryder had done it."

"Oh, that makes it much easier to process," Melissa muttered as she shifted in her seat.

His lips curled briefly, but his memories were depressing enough to rob him of his humor. "She chose him," he said quietly.

There was silence in the room, and he turned his head to gaze at the fireplace. The fire was dying. He rose, placing his cup on the tray, and crossed over to the pile of cut logs neatly stacked against the wall next to the fireplace. He picked a good, thick piece of wood and gently placed it on the embers. It came naturally, the little breath of light force that urged the flames to stir once again.

"She was compelled by your father. You have no idea what she really felt."

Hunter shrugged. "She came to me, the morning before she died. Told me she'd made the biggest mistake, and that she should have chosen me over Ryder." He sat down again. "I should have taken her away, then and there." He frowned. "Debbie might still be alive today, if I had."

Melissa set her goblet down on the tray with a distinct clink. "Did you say Debbie?" she asked, and Hunter's eyes narrowed at her oh-so-casual tone.

"I did."

Melissa nodded slowly. "I thought that's what you said."

She slid her legs down to the floor and rose to walk over toward the fire, her hands out as though trying to warm herself. Hunter noticed her hands were trembling, and then she quickly clasped them together.

Realization dawned, and Hunter sagged against the backrest of the settee. "My father mentioned Debbie visited a witch, one that blocked his ability to compel her. That was you, wasn't it?" Melissa was the most well-known witch in Irondell, with a solid reputation. The bookstore witch was rumored to be the best, if he was honest. If Debbie was going to visit a witch, it would have been her. What a cruel coincidence.Melissa turned to him, her expression haunted. "I had no idea, Hunter," she said, and her breath hitched. "I had a client, Debbie Philips. She came to me because she kept having black-outs, and found herself caught between two men, and not understanding how or why."

Hunter tilted his head back to gaze up at the ceiling. Talk about six degrees of separation. Melissa had been the witch to protect Debbie from further compulsion. How damned ironic.

His father had admitted he and Debbie had been ar-guing upstairs at the family home, and in the ensuing struggle his father had pushed Debbie over the railing. She'd died from her injuries moments later. Because he could no longer compel her.

"So, you knew where her heart really lay," Hunter commented.

Melissa caught her bottom lip between her teeth, and shook her head. "Don't. Hunter, please, don't."

"Which one of us did she truly love?" Hunter asked, ignoring her plea. "I don't know what was real and what wasn't anymore. Was she still under compulsion when she came to tell me she'd made a mistake picking my brother over me, or was that her real instinct?"

"Hunter—"

"Tell me, Melissa," he said as he rose from the settee. "Which of us did Debbie really love?"

Melissa gazed at him, her expression miserable, and she shook her head.

"Tell me," he insisted, his voice louder.

The woman standing before him looked like she wanted to crawl into the fire itself. She rubbed her lips together for a moment, then met his gaze.

"Neither," she told him in a whisper.

She may as well have shouted it at him. "Neither." He chuckled, the sound harsh to his ears. He really was fundamentally flawed. He swore softly.

Melissa strummed her fingers against her denim-clad thigh. "She, uh—she liked you both, thought you were good guys, but whatever your father did to her, those moments she was being the perfect woman to both of you, she was being someone she wasn't. The connections she had with you and your brother were built on a lie. She told me she had to do right by both of you, and end it."

Melissa grimaced. "I'm sorry, Hunter," she whispered.

He held up a hand and shook his head. "Don't be. First my mother, then Debbie. I'm beginning to see the pattern." The women he'd loved with all his heart didn't love him in return. Or at least, not nearly as much. For some reason, he couldn't make them want to stick around.

He glanced at the mating bond stretching between Melissa and himself. It was only a matter of time before Melissa left him, too. He pasted a fake smile on his face. "I'm fine. Trust me, I'm a doctor. I know how to get through stuff like this." Only, he couldn't dream-walk through his own mind and switch off those painful memories.

For some reason, though, he suspected Melissa's leaving would hurt him far greater than his mother and Debbie combined. He cleared his throat. "Uh, I'm tired. Think I'll turn in." He indicated the settee he was sprawled over. "I'll take this, you take the bed."

Melissa's glance flitted to the bed that easily dominated the rest of the room. "There seems to be plenty of room for both of us," she suggested softly.

He met her gaze. There was empathy, there was

sadness, but there was also invitation. God, he was so tempted. So tempted to just once lie next to a woman, be held by a woman, be loved by a woman. *This* woman.

But that would just make the mating bond stronger, and more difficult to break. And break it would. He was a shadow breed, and despite her warm sympathy and listening ear, Melissa would never see him as anything more than that, and would never allow a mated commitment. He knew he was in for a fall, big-time, when she left. He just had to make sure it was something he could survive.

He shook his head. "We both know that if I get into that bed with you, neither of us will get much sleep." Even saying that, he couldn't stop his gaze from touring over her willowy body, those long legs that felt so right wrapped around his waist, the breasts that were made to fit his hands. He swallowed. God, he wanted her, and he wanted her to want him—for more than just pity sex. "It's better this way."

Melissa looked away and nodded, then made her way over to the bed. She tossed him a pillow and the extra blanket that was draped across the end of the bed.

"Good night, then," she whispered as she kicked off her shoes and slid beneath the covers. She'd taken his rejection so calmly, but he knew otherwise. Through their shared connection he could sense her hurt, her embarrassment. He stretched out fully on the settee, punching the pillow.

The connection was on a feedback loop. At the moment, Melissa was totally oblivious to it, and he wanted to keep it that way. He didn't want her to sense it, didn't want her to be aware of it—she'd probably kill him when she found out... But for now, she was in the dark. What she didn't know couldn't hurt her. He'd get her to her brother's place, make sure she was safe from harm, safe from his psycho father, and then they'd part ways. He sighed. A light warrior mated once in a lifetime. How fate had selected a fiery, sassy witch for him, he'd never understand. A fiery, sassy witch who hated all shadow breeds. Fate had a very twisted sense of humor.

Melissa sighed from the bed behind him, and he heard the linen rustle as she rolled over. She was lying there, mere feet away from him, all warm and relaxed and voluptuous, and he was sleeping on a settee that was about half a body-length too short, all because he was trying to be noble and not lock her into a bond she couldn't, wouldn't accept.

See, this was why he'd never tried to be noble before. Noble sucked.

Melissa woke in the darkness, the rocks beneath her digging into the bare skin of her shoulders above the back of her gown. She reached instinctively for Theo, and he grasped her hand.

"Stay calm," he whispered.

"Are they coming for us?" she whispered, trying to keep the terror out of her voice. The stiff fabric of her ball gown rustled as she sat up cautiously.

"I'm not sure," Theo said as he, too, sat up. "But don't worry, Mel. We'll get through this."

"I don't think I can go through it again," Melissa whispered, ashamed to admit her fear, her lack of courage. She swallowed. It had hurt so much...she hadn't been able to do anything to stop them, there had been too many of them.

Where was her mother? Or Dave? Surely they should have been rescued by now. She and Theo had been snatched as they'd left the Reform ball—what, nearly two nights ago? She shivered, and Theo took his jacket off and slung it around her bare shoulders.

"We're going to get through this," Theo whispered, staring straight into her eyes. She nodded. "You and me, Mel, we're strong together. We can han—"

"Oh, it's so sweet, listening to these two lovebirds," a feminine voice purred in a soft, Baltic accent, and the cellar door creaked as it opened.

"Yeah, so sweet, I think I might throw up," a masculine voice responded, the accent slightly stronger, harsher. Melissa flinched as the two vampires descended into the root cellar. She knew them. Had encountered them several times at the Reform balls and other Prime families' events. Natalia and George Petrovski. Melissa gazed past them. She'd counted seven vampires since their capture. Most were of the Saltwash colony, just like the Petrovskis, but two were from the Iron Peak colony, and she didn't know their names. Two colonies separated by hundreds of miles, yet united in their torture of her and Theo. She didn't know where they were being held. She'd just glimpsed a decrepit farmhouse in the darkness when she and Theo had been taken from the car and forced to enter the root cellar.

George Petrovski lifted a lantern, and beckoned to them. "Come, come closer."

Theo edged between her and the vamps. Melissa swallowed as the other five vamps climbed down the rough steps into the root cellar. No, not again. They'd fed on her and Theo until they'd both passed out, then had fed them vamp blood to heal their bite wounds so they could start all over again.

"Stay back," Theo warned, holding his hand up.

"Or what?" Natalia asked, then laughed, her eyes flashing red as she stepped closer. "You still have vamp

blood in your system. Your magic is useless until your enzymes break down the V-juice."

"And then we'll just feed you some more, and then some more, and then..." one of the Petrovski cousins interjected from behind, then chuckled. "Well, you get my drift."

Goose bumps rose on Melissa's arms as she stared at the advancing vampires. Two of them held lanterns that they hung up on hooks from the low ceiling. They were right. Both she and Theo were powerless against the vamps. She glanced wildly about the root cellar. The only way in or out of their prison was up the flight of rickety stairs to the double doors that hung open. They'd have to get past the vampires first, though.

Melissa slowly clutched hold of her skirts. The fabric was stiff from the dried blood—so much blood, but she was ready to run when Theo gave the signal.

"Why are you doing this?" Melissa asked, gazing at Natalia. She had no quarrel with this woman—at least, not until now. But these vamps had broken the sanctity of a Reform ball. "My mother will—"

"Your mother will negotiate for your release," George interrupted. "Everybody knows Eleanor Carter will work a situation to her advantage." He shrugged. "Sure, we'll get a slap on the wrist, something that will make it look like we're not getting away with..." He smiled, his incisors lengthening, as he finished, "...what we're getting away with."

Theo kicked the lantern out of George's hand, and Melissa sprang at Natalia, hands fisted as she punched the vampire in the jaw. She kept swinging until her arms were caught, and she screamed as fangs sank into her neck, and more fangs sank into her wrists. Her pulse pounded in her ears as she tried to struggle, tried to thrash against the vampires holding her. With every beat of her heart, though, she could feel herself weaken, feel the chill creep into her limbs, feel the blood draining from her.

"Enough," Natalia shouted. "We want her conscious."

Hands dug into her hair, and she winced as her head was roughly turned so she could see Theo.

She was held by Natalia and two of her cousins, while Theo was held down on the ground by the other four vamps. He cried out in agony as they ripped at his flesh with their teeth. Melissa screamed, trying to go to him, to help him, but the vamps held her back. He glanced at her, his complexion sickly white, his lips gray, his blood a dark crimson against his white dress shirt. George looked up, grinning when he saw he had Melissa's horrified attention.

"Hold," the vamp told the others feeding on her fiancé, and the other vamps reluctantly stopped, their eyes flashing red in the dimly lit room. They hauled Theo up to his knees, supporting him when he would have collapsed. Theo tried to talk, but only a garbled groan emerged. George smiled as he peered over Theo's bloodied shoulder.

"We don't think this witch is the right match for you," George said, grinning.

Melissa shook her head. "No, please don't." She could feel warm liquid streaming down her cheeks, her neck, confused between tears and blood. "Leave him alone."

"Should have thought of that before you accepted his ring," Natalia crooned in her ear. "We don't like the Sassafras Coven. Nobody likes the Sassafras Coven. Hawthorns are much better."

Melissa's jaw clenched. The Sassafras Coven was

good enough for Theo, it would be good enough for her when she married him and left White Oak. There was no way she'd go anywhere near the Hawthorns after this.

"Let her go," Theo croaked. "Please, take me, but let her go." *He looked so broken, yet he'd never seemed braver to her, there on his knees, his blood draining from him as he pleaded for her life.*

"Theo," *Melissa cried, again trying to reach him, again being held back. His blue eyes met hers, and she could see the glassy stare, the weakness creeping over him as his wounds continued to bleed.*

"But we're not cruel," *George whispered.* "We'll put him out of his misery." *He reached for Theo's head, and twisted his neck. Melissa flinched at the audible snap and screamed as the man she loved fell to the floor, dead. If it wasn't for the vampires holding her up, she would have collapsed.*

"Tut-tut," *Natalia tsked.* "Now look what you've done. You'll have to fix that."

George nodded, then bit at his own wrist, tearing at the skin. He knelt down to Theo's corpse, and placed his wound against Theo's lips.

Melissa's eyes widened, and she shook her head. "No. You can't."

George stood, the wound on his wrist healing so quickly he could pull his shirtsleeve back down without staining it with blood. "I just did."

"But—oh, God, what have you done?" *Melissa yelled.* "You monsters."

Theo's body flinched, his back arching as the vampire blood worked its way through his system.

"Have you heard of the old story, Romeo and Juliet?" *Natalia inquired politely.* "This is our version of it."

Theo's eyelids opened, and his blue eyes stared

blankly up at the ceiling for a moment, then he coughed, dragging in deep, ragged breaths.

Melissa shook her head in denial. Oh, please, no, no, no.

"Did you know, the metamorphosis kicks in quicker, the sooner after death you receive our blood?"

She could hear various cracks, and she shuddered when she realized Theo's vertebrae were slipping back into place. Theo sat up, rubbing his neck, and frowned.

"What the hell?"

"It takes a few minutes for the memory to kick in," George explained to Melissa in a conversational tone.

Theo glanced at George, then his eyes widened. "Why, you bastard!"

He launched himself at George, but the vamp tossed him off easily. "Easy, buck. You'll need a feed before you can fight a vamp."

"And fortunately, we have one here for you," Natalia said.

Theo stared at Melissa and shook his head in horror. "No." He rose to his feet, glancing around at the gathered vamps. Melissa trembled as she watched her fiancé's wounds slowly close, until not so much as a scar remained to tell the sordid story of his death.

"Yes," George said, *grabbing on to Theo's shoulders and forcing him to face Melissa. The vamp tilted his head at his sister. "What say we make this interesting? Our new baby should learn to hunt, yes?"*

Natalia chuckled. "You are so twisted, brother, I love it." She ran her finger along Melissa's neck, and Melissa tried to pull away, then watched in horror as the bitch vamp walked over to Theo.

"You need to feed," she told him, *and Theo shook his head, gritting his teeth.*

"No."

"You won't be able to help it," Natalia told him, drawing her finger along his bottom lip.

Theo's nostrils flared as he caught the scent of her blood, and Melissa's horror gave way to true fear as her fiancé's pupils darkened to crimson.

"Let her go, boys. Let's give her a sporting start," George called, and the vamps who still clutched Melissa shoved her toward the stairs leading up from the root cellar.

"Theo," she cried, hoping she could reach him, hoping she could stop this.

"For God's sake, Melissa, run," Theo called to her, and she glanced over her shoulder to see that the vamps were trying to hold him back. From her. His eyes were bloodred, and he cried in pain as his incisors lengthened, his nostrils flaring as he stared up at her. He looked—blood-crazed.

Melissa gathered her skirts and ran up the stairs, sobbing, as she burst out into the night. One shoe fell off her foot, and she stumbled in the dark. She kicked the other shoe off, bundling her skirts in her fists, and pelted across the yard. She winced, gasping as sharp rocks in the dirt poked her feet, but she kept running.

She didn't see it in the darkness, didn't know the fence was there until she ran into it, bruising her chest. She wheezed in pain, her fingers reaching out to clasp the wooden railing. Oh, hell. She started to run alongside it, her fingers trailing along the wood. Her skirts were too full to squeeze through the slats. Hopefully she'd find a gate or something that would give her an avenue of escape.

"Run, Melissa," Theo yelled behind her, and Melissa

picked up her skirts and ran. Moonlight gleamed on a metallic surface up ahead. A gate. An open gate.

Her breaths coming in harsh pants, she bolted along the fence line, hearing with every beat of her heart the pounding of her fiancé's footsteps behind her. She was almost at the gate when something hard and heavy thudded against her, and they crashed through the fence, timber snapping with the force of the hit.

Melissa hit the ground with a thud and wheezed, trying to catch her breath. Theo straddled her legs.

"Theo, fight this," she begged him. He gazed down at her, his expression tortured, his eyes red with bloodlust.

"I'm trying," he moaned as he dodged her fist.

"Try harder," she rasped, struggling beneath him.

"You're bleeding," he gasped, and he shuddered as he inhaled. Melissa stretched out her hands, looking for something, anything to slow him down. Her fingers found a piece of the fence, and then Theo's head whipped down to look at her. She trembled. His skin was drawn tight over his cheekbones, his eyes were red and glazed, and his mouth—the mouth she knew so well now belonged to a man no longer her fiancé.

He snarled, his teeth glistening in the moonlight as he dipped his head down to her neck. She screamed as fangs sank into the tender skin, and panic, anger and adrenaline flooded her as she pushed hard, trying to shove him away.

His body flinched, and he slowly raised his head, her blood dripping from his fangs, a stunned expression on his face. He rose above her, and she looked at him with confusion, until her eyes swept down and she saw the shard of wood she'd thrust into his chest. Her eyes widened in horror as she realized what she'd done.

Theo's hands shook as he clutched the stake in his

heart, his complexion graying as death crept over him, and he slumped over to the side. The bloodlust leeched out of his eyes, returning them to the blue she knew so well, until the eyes staring back at her were once more those of the man she loved, and not the crazed feral creature who'd attacked her.

"I'm sorry, I'm so sorry," she whispered over and over as she stroked his cheek and patted his chest so ineffectually. "I'm so, so sorry," she sobbed softly as her heart broke with remorse, and with guilt.

His lips curled as the gray crept up his neck. "Thank you," he breathed as the gray stole over him, stealing his dying breath.

Melissa squeezed her eyes shut, blocking out the sightless eyes as she felt the coolness creep into the body beside her. What have I done? *She sobbed quietly, trying to deny what she'd done, what had happened. It wasn't until she felt the ground dampening beneath her with her dead fiancé's blood that reality intruded, and she tilted her head back, letting out a heartrending wail of agony to the peaceful, moonlit sky above.*

"Red, Red, oh, God, Melissa, wake up, honey," a masculine voice intruded on her grief, and her eyes snapped open. She stared up at a familiar face, a face that didn't belong to the man she'd killed, but to the man she now loved.

Hunter.

Chapter 19

Hunter swept Melissa into his arms, rocking her as he pulled her out of the nightmare. His heart pounding in his chest, he swallowed as he held her tight, whispering nonsense into the hair that brushed his nose.

Hell. He squeezed her gently, rubbing his hand down her back in soothing circles. "It's okay, Red. You're okay." That dream had scared the crap out of him.

She trembled in his arms, and he heard her gulp. He rose from the bed and hurried into the bathroom, throwing a pale orb of light so he could find a glass and run her some water. He hurried back to the bed, holding the glass out to her, and she accepted it with trembling fingers. He watched closely as she drank the water, then took the glass from her when she was finished. He leaned over and placed it on the ornately carved bedside table, then gathered her in his arms again.

"I'm so sorry that happened to you," he commented

as he rubbed her arms. That had been one hell of a night-mare. He closed his eyes. He could still feel her terror, her sorrow…her guilt. He wished he'd been there for her, wished he could have helped her—and her fiancé. It was a horrific experience to endure, for the both of them. Even if the guy was his mate's love.

"You saw," she whispered, tucking her head against his chest.

"I saw," he admitted. "Not intentionally, though. We seem to be sharing dreams." He shifted, pulling her into the space between his thighs so she could lean against him, his heart thudding against her back. "I'm glad, though. That's one dream you shouldn't have to walk through alone."

She took a deep, shuddering breath. "I think being around the Darkken triggered it."

He nodded. He could see why being surrounded and held captive by vampires could remind her of a previous traumatic vampire experience.

"Lance went and tracked each one of them down," she said into the darkness. "They won't ever do that to another person."

Hunter had a new appreciation for the big lug.

"Theo helped me build the apothecary," she whispered, and he closed his eyes. "It was our vision. We were going to marry, and develop the apothecary so that folks could come and get the help they needed from the witches." She sniffed.

He gently bumped his head against the massive carved headboard. And he was responsible now for it going up in smoke not once, but twice.

He was silent for a while, then dipped his head to kiss her temple. "I get it now," he whispered.

"Get what?"

"Why you don't like us shadow breeds." She'd lost her lover twice. She'd lost her business. She'd lost the dream she'd worked so hard to achieve. The shadow breeds had taken pretty much everything from her.

"You keep saying that," she whispered into the dim room, and he frowned.

"What?"

"Us shadow breeds." She rubbed his arms, and he held her closer. "I—I haven't really thought of you as one of 'them' for a while now."

He arched an eyebrow. "How have you been thinking of me, then?" Naked, he hoped. Sweaty. He'd settle for naked and sweaty. In each other's arms would be better. He held his breath, waiting for her answer.

She shrugged, the lightest lift of her shoulders. "Just Hunter. I think of you as Hunter."

He stared at the tapestry on the opposite wall. Hunter. Just Hunter. Not pyro jerk, or any other name she'd called him since he'd woken up in her cell. Hunter. Not Light Warrior Hunter, not Shadow Breed Hunter, not Tried-To-Kill-Me Hunter. Just...Hunter.

He swallowed. Cleared his throat. "I owe you an apology," he murmured, and she turned to look at him. Her face was pale in the light cast by the fire, her eyes glittery green from her tears.

"What for?" she asked softly.

Well, he was building quite the list with her, but he needed to set something straight, needed to make right some of his wrongs, especially with this woman. He needed to say it, and she needed to hear it. Not some half-assed, lame attempt, either.

"I'm sorry for setting fire to your apothecary," he said, his gaze meeting hers. She moved, but he caught hold of her chin. This was about as genuine as he ever got with anyone, and he didn't want her to miss it. "I'm so sorry for nearly killing you," he continued softly. "What I did—" He cast about for the right words, but there weren't any. "It was wrong. I shouldn't have done it—I'm so sorry, and I'm so relieved you didn't die," he whispered. "Because—" He hesitated, swallowed. His gaze swept over her face. "Because I was so lost, and I didn't even know it until I found you."

Her eyes rounded, and she stared up at him, surprised. "I never thought I'd hear you say it," she admitted in a whisper. "Not for real."

And that was shameful. He dropped his gaze to her throat. "It shouldn't have taken five months," he conceded. "That was not—cool. Not cool."

Her lips twisted, as though she was trying not to smile. He frowned. "What?"

"I don't know if a fire starter could ever be cool," she murmured, her teeth catching her lower lip, but the smile still curved upward. "I think you're too hot for that." Her green eyes flared with something warm, something that was an undeniable invitation. An invitation he no longer had any intention of rejecting. Screw noble. Being disgraceful was so much better.

He arched an eyebrow. "Oh, you think I'm hot, huh?"

She twisted in his arms, her gaze never leaving his. "Uh-huh."

She leaned up to kiss him, her hand cupping his cheek. "I think you are so much more that you give yourself credit for," she whispered, and right then, he knew. He was gone. Totally, irrevocably lost to this woman. She raised her head to his, and he opened his mouth to her kiss.

She kissed him gently, she kissed him hotly, she kissed him until he was breathless and panting and wanting so much more than just a kiss. The fire flickered, then roared, its flames creeping just a little higher, spreading a golden glow throughout the room.

He cradled her head as she straddled and leaned over him, his tongue sliding into her mouth as he dragged her shirt aside from her neck. The fabric halted his exploration. He was tempted to tear it from her, but tried to slow down, to regain some control. He pulled back for a moment, whipping her T-shirt over her head, rising slightly off the bed to take her lips again as he undid the clasp of her bra and slid the straps down her shoulders.

Her hands slid down his chest. He moaned against her lips, enjoying the sensation of her touch. Sliding, caressing, her fingers glided over his torso, teasing him, pleasing him. She rolled her hips against him, flicking her thumbs over his nipples, and his heart thudded in his ears, heat building between them.

His arms slid up her back, her hair brushing his skin, sensitizing him. He moaned as her lips drifted to his jaw, nipping and licking down his neck. He could feel the heat between them, their hips rolling and writhing as though dancing to an unknown beat. She was so damn generous, so giving, offering him such intense pleasure so easily. He flinched when her teeth grazed his nipple. He was so damn hard, so ready for her, but he wanted this to be about her.

He rolled them over, and she gasped at the movement, then sighed as he took her lips in a hot kiss, their tongues curling, caressing.

He skimmed his hand down her body, his hips resting between her legs. He loved the soft feel of her breasts, loved it when she trembled at his touch. He trailed his lips down her neck, and she arched against him, as though offering herself up to him. He dipped his head to one rosy peak, laving it with his tongue, his hand cupping her other breast, and she moaned. He switched his attention to the other breast, satisfaction at her impassioned cries giving way to his own building desire.

He nipped and licked his way down over the gentle swell of her stomach, unbuttoning her jeans and sliding them and her panties down and off her legs as he went. He kept kissing her, and she gasped when he breathed against her warm, damp core. Her eyes widened, and she looked down at him.

"Wait," she gasped, and he smiled, a wicked need ensnaring him. Her cheeks were flushed, her red hair tumbled over her shoulders and her green gaze was dark with arousal. He clasped one of her hands in reassurance.

"Trust me," he said, and winked. "I'm a doctor." He lowered his lips to kiss her, his gaze on her as her head tilted back, the cords on her throat standing out as she cried in ecstasy. He made love to her, kissing her with a desire and reverence he'd never felt before. He loved this woman, and he was determined to show her. For once, he was determined that his bad was going to be very, very good.

Warmth rolled over him, and he realized he was surrendering to the mating bond again. He could smell her, taste her, touch her, yet he could feel his breath on her, feel the wicked sensations that flooded her from her core, and the awareness flooded his own groin with desire, their combined arousal building. He could sense her tightening, sense the climb, experienced the rush of her orgasm right along with her as it swept over her, and she screamed in pleasure, bucking against him.

He rose up over her, unable to hold off any longer. He thrust inside her. Felt the cradle of her core, the heat surrounding him, and felt her. Felt his length sliding inside her, sensitizing her anew. Light flared around him, little sparks that flickered and twinkled, creating a magical skyline inside their room. He plunged, again and again, and she met his thrust with abandon, twining her legs around his waist, clenching him. The tingle started at the base of his spine, and heat crawled over him, spreading outward in an explosion of exquisite pleasure that ricocheted between them. Her pleasure, his pleasure—he wasn't sure where one ended and the other began, it just rolled on, setting off minor explosions as they eventually subsided, panting, on the twisted sheets.

He slid to the side, rolling them over until Melissa covered his body like a sensual blanket. He could feel her heart pounding against his, and his lips lifted in a smile. For the first time ever, he knew true contentment.

He kicked at the sheet until he could grasp it with his hand and pull it up over her back, tucking her in on top of him. She lifted her head, her smoldering green eyes meeting his briefly before she yawned. Like a cat. She'd played hard, and now she was sleepy. He smiled again, cuddling her to him. She made a halfhearted effort to roll off him, but he stayed her, his hands on her hips.

"No, stay. I'm not letting you go anywhere."

Her head dropped to his chest, and she snuggled against him, her thigh sliding up against his waist. For a while, they lay like that, hearts beating against each other as their muscles relaxed. Hunter gazed up at the canopy of the bed, his arms enfolding the woman he loved. He couldn't let her go. Wouldn't let her go. If she tried to leave him, well, he'd just have to leave with her.

Melissa toweled her hair dry. The only reason she knew it was morning was because her watch read 7:32 a.m. They'd been woken up at six-thirty by a knock at the door and a delivery of clean clothes. Her cheeks pinkened. As soon as the door had closed, and the lock had slid home, Hunter had scooped her up and carried her to the bed to make love to her again.

Her teeth caught her bottom lip in a smile as she dropped the towel and scooped up the denim and underwear. Her body ached, but it was a glorious ache, one that told her how her body had been loved long and hard during the night. And in the morning. As well as the shower.

She'd dressed and was finger-combing her hair when she heard a sharp rap on the door. She peered out of the bathroom, and Hunter rose from the armchair by the fire. He wore fresh dark jeans and a white long-sleeved T-shirt that draped his body, emphasizing his broad shoulders and lean hips.

The door opened, and a Darkken vampire peered around the room until he saw Hunter. He beckoned him. "You need to come with me."

Hunter slid his hand into a back jeans pocket and leaned casually against one of the corner posts of the grand bed. "I don't need to do anything with you," he said dryly.

Melissa emerged from the room, plaiting her hair as she walked.

The Darkken frowned. "You need to come with me," he repeated.

"I'm not leaving her alone," Hunter said, inclining his head toward Melissa. She came up next to him, watching the Darkken warily.

"She stays here, you come with me," the vampire said, anger edging his tone.

"No."

"What's going on?" Melissa asked, eyeing the vampire with curiosity. The Darkken's lips tightened, then he sighed brusquely.

"The Lady Amelie wants to see her son. In private," he added.

Melissa glanced at Hunter, saw his hesitation, his curiosity, his wariness. "Go," she told him. "I'll be fine here until you come back."

Hunter turned to her, reaching for her hand. "I don't want to leave you alone," he murmured huskily. His need to protect her made her feel all warm and tender and, oh, damn it, fuzzy.

She met his gaze. "You need to do this," she urged. "You have a mother who wants to make things right with you." She glanced down at their clasped hands. "You don't know how precious that is, Hunter. Don't throw it away."

Whatever she said must have struck a chord with him, as Hunter nodded reluctantly. He dipped his head, ignoring the vampire in the room to kiss her lingeringly. "Be careful, Red," he murmured as he lifted his head, and didn't move until she nodded her promise.

"I will."

She watched as Hunter left the room, and she stood there for a moment after the door closed and the lock was engaged, her fingers keeping his kiss warm on her lips. She watched the ribbons of light that flowed from her chest to beyond the door. He still hadn't mentioned the bond, and she wasn't sure why. She'd felt the tug of it in the tunnel, had been surprised at each of Hunter's attempts to tame it, control it. Hadn't actually seen it, though, until last night. Which meant Hunter had seen it earlier, and hadn't mentioned it.

She sighed, twirled, then flopped back on the bed. She had a bond mate. A bond mate who didn't actually want to talk about their bond. She spread her arms out on the bed. She should be angry. Horrified. Running in the opposite direction… Instead she made a sheet angel, moving her arms and legs on the bed until she could feel the linen bunch beneath her. She was a witch. She'd heard of mating bonds, had even seen the glorious auras of some, and had envied those who shared one. She may not understand all of the laws of magic, but she knew only an idiot tried to ignore the laws of magic.

She giggled. She wasn't an idiot. She didn't think she could ever find love again, not after Theo. Didn't think she'd find a man worthy, and didn't think she'd get over the guilt. Sure, it hadn't been the best start to a relationship, but perhaps that was the universe's idea of a joke. Show the worst of the mate before slowly revealing the best.

She frowned. It had been a really slow reveal, though. She stared up at the canopy. Hunter hadn't said anything, hadn't indicated anything, had even tried to hide it from her. She should feel insulted, but she thought she understood him a little better now. First he'd discovered the woman he'd loved had been a lie, as was their love. Then he'd learned his mother hadn't actually died— well, she had, but that wasn't the reason she wasn't in his life. She'd left him. Unwillingly, but she could see he'd taken that news hard.

She lifted her chin. She'd just have to show him that not all women ran away from him.

Poor Hunter. He had no idea who he was up against.

Hunter frowned as he followed the Darkken vamp down a dark passageway, and then down some stairs. This wasn't the way back to the hall. He'd tried to memorize as much as he could, but they'd turned away from the hall about three corridors back.

"Where does my mother want to meet me?" he asked the vamp as they stepped down into another hallway, and rounded a corner.

"In hell, where you'll see her in good time," the Darkken commented.

Hunter halted, but something hard and heavy crashed into the back of his skull, and darkness snatched him away from consciousness.

Chapter 20

Melissa heard the bolt slide in the lock, and her eyes flickered open. She must have dozed off. Not surprising, considering her lack of sleep. She jackknifed off the bed, summoning her magic as the door swung inward, ready to annihilate any vamp that attacked her.

Lady Amelie's eyebrows rose in surprise, and she lifted her hands, palms facing her. "Good morning."

Melissa lowered her hands, but didn't completely relax. The woman was still a vampire. "Sorry," she said lamely. It wouldn't be the done thing to zap the mother of her bond mate.

Amelie glanced around the room. "I was hoping to talk with Hunter, if he was willing."

Melissa frowned. "He is. He was on his way to you."

Amelie glanced toward the door, a frown marring her brow. "What?"

"That vamp came to collect him—" Melissa glanced

at her watch. "Uh, nearly an hour ago. He said you wanted to talk to Hunter."

Amelie shook her head. "I sent no one for Hunter. I don't need anyone to act as an intermediary between my son and me. There are already too many misunderstandings and lost words between us."

Alarm grew in Melissa. "Well, someone came here and told him you wanted to see him, and he hasn't been back since."

Amelie reached for Melissa's hand, and Melissa stepped back. Amelie's surprised gaze slowly transitioned to understanding. She beckoned instead. "Come, we have to let Griffin know."

"How do we know Griffin didn't organize this?" Melissa asked as she followed Amelie into the corridor.

Amelie snorted as she strode along the hallway. "If Griffin wanted Hunter dead, he wouldn't be sneaky about it. He'd just kill him and be done with it."

"Oh," Melissa responded faintly. "Good to know."

Amelie shook her head. "An hour. A lot can happen in an hour." She broke into a trot, and Melissa increased her own pace to keep up with her. She followed the older woman through the labyrinth of corridors until they jogged into the great hall.

Griffin was on the dais, listening to a report from the vampire who'd urged everyone from the hall the night before.

"What do you mean, there's another witch?" Griffin exclaimed, his tone exasperated. "I feel like someone's declared Old Irondell as a top holiday destination. There are too many tourists traipsing around, damn it."

"He's searching for a woman," the Darkken supplied. "He identified himself to one of the perimeter guardians, and requested parlay."

"Parlay." Griffin shook his head, lips twisted. "Well, that's seems to be a loose term at the moment." He paused, then sighed roughly. "I'll still honor it, though. We're not allowed to kill him now. At least, not until he leaves Old Irondell." The Dark Lord waved his hand, a disgruntled expression on his face. "Fine, bring him in."

"Griffin," Amelie called.

Melissa gasped as she saw the crowd of Darkken part, and a familiar figure with shaggy dark blond hair, biker leathers and sunglasses stalked into the hall.

"Dave," she exclaimed, running toward her brother. Two Darkken vamps stepped between them to halt her, preventing her from reaching her brother.

"I'd suggest you get your hands off my sister before I remove them for you," Dave said calmly, but there was no mistaking his fierce expression.

"Let her through," Griffin called, then grumbled something to his Guardian Prime. The Darkken dropped their hold immediately, and Melissa launched herself at her brother, and he swept her up in a bear hug.

"Griffin," Amelie called, this time sharply.

Griffin rubbed his temple. "Yes, Mother?"

"Oh, it's so good to see you," Melissa breathed as she clutched at her brother.

"You don't call, you don't write," Dave responded, chuckling. "Don't you think leveling a city block to get my attention was a little overkill?"

Melissa paled. "Was anyone hurt?"

Dave grimaced. "Well, if you're talking about your business neighbors, seeing as it was a Sunday night, nobody else was around. But if you're talking about a whole bunch of vamps and lycans…yeah. There were a few fatalities."

"They were attacking me," she said defensively. Dave pulled back to gaze down at her.

"I figured that much, just by the sheer numbers. When they didn't pull your body out, though, I've been trying to figure out where you got to. Didn't think you had the guts to brave Old Irondell on your own, though, kid. Smart move."

"I wasn't alone," Melissa said, then turned toward the dais, pulling Dave along behind her.

Amelie was already talking with Griffin, who rubbed the bridge of his nose.

"What do you mean, he's gone?"

"He's been taken."

"Well, if he's silly enough to get himself nabbed…" Griffin halted when he saw his mother's expression, and he folded his arms as he faced off against her. "I got a delivery today. Do you want to know what it was? Gavin's head." His expression showed his pain, his anger. "I sent Gavin to your dear husband to invite him to parlay, and the psycho killed him. Do you want to know how many he's murdered since then? Six. Six people, Mom. All in the time it would have taken for Gavin to return. While. We. Slept." He said the last words through gritted teeth, then took a deep breath. "How many lives is your precious son worth?"

Amelie tilted her head to the side. "I would risk everything for all of my sons. We have to help him, Griff."

Griffin shook his head. "No."

"Yes." Amelie's eyes welled with tears. "I have already lost Hunter and his brother to this man once, Griff. I should have done something, all those years ago. I can't just sit by and let Arthur do this."

Griffin gazed at his mother, and his eyes shifted to stare blankly toward Melissa as she and her brother drew up close to the stairs of the dais. He was silent for a moment, thinking, assessing, before he finally leaned forward in his chair.

"I'm sorry, Mother, but I won't risk any more of our Old Irondell family than we've already lost."

Melissa blanched as Griffin rose from his seat. "I offer no protection to Hunter Galen. He has no claim to Old Irondell."

"Griffin! What you do..." Amelie shook her head in horror. Griffin stepped toward his mother and clasped her hands.

"Trust me to know exactly what I'm doing," he told her quietly. He turned to face Melissa and her brother, and Dave stepped forward, thrusting his hand out.

"Dave Carter—" He glanced at his sister and Melissa shrugged, as he had no formal title to add to the speech. Dave shrugged. "Tattoo Artist Extraordinaire, formally requests—"

"Save it. Parlay, I know." Griffin nodded. "You wanted to find your sister, she wanted to find you, you've both found each other, everyone's happy, you're free to leave," he said, and bowed. When he straightened, Melissa stepped forward.

"Are you seriously not going to look for your brother?" she asked.

Griffin nodded. "Seriously. And flippantly." He turned to go, but Melissa touched his arm.

The Darkken Guardian Prime stepped forward, but halted when Griffin held up his hand. "Yes, darlin'?"

"You know what this means, don't you?" she whispered.

The albino tilted his head, and his unblinking gaze met hers. His brows pulled into a slight V. "I'm curious. Tell me."

"It means that while Hunter was a guest in your home, one of your kind betrayed your hospitality, and your will."

Griffin didn't blink, but smiled tightly. "As I said, you're both free to go." He stepped back, arms out. "Hear this. The witches have free passage to leave. They will not be bothered."

He strode toward the exit, and Amelie stepped down off the dais. "Griff," she called in protest.

The Dark Lord held up a hand but didn't stop. "Can't talk now, Mother. You know how it is. Things to do, people to see. Old Irondell doesn't run itself." The albino strode from the hall, his Guardian Prime following behind.

Melissa covered her mouth. Hunter's brother wasn't going to lift a finger to help him. Dave glanced between Melissa and the doorway.

"Why do I feel like I'm missing something?" he inquired.

"Hunter's father is the one behind the attack on my store," Melissa informed her brother, and started striding down the hallway to the main exit. The Darkken crowd parted. True to their leader's word, neither she nor her brother was hassled as they left the hall of the Dark Lord. "He's come down into Old Irondell, looking for us." She halted, frowning. "But will he still be looking for me, now that he has Hunter?"

Dave looked back at her and shrugged. "Doesn't matter. After what he did to you and your store, I'm going to look for him. He's walking dead." Dave started to walk toward the main exit, but Melissa grabbed his arm.

"Wait, I can find him," she said, looking down at the coiling ethereal ribbons.

Dave arched an eyebrow. "You want to do a locator spell? Do you have something of his?"

"Kind of. I have his mate."

Dave waited for her to continue, then his jaw dropped as he finally realized what she was saying. Despite his sunglasses, she could still read the shock on his face. "You didn't," he breathed.

"Oh, I did," she said, nodding. "Quite a few times, actually."

Dave clapped his hands over his ears. "Lah-lah-lah—"

Melissa grabbed his arm and tugged him around the corner. "We go this way."

"You realize Mom is going to freak when she hears," Dave muttered as he allowed her to drag him along.

"She'll be ecstatic," Melissa corrected as she followed the bond link. "Which sucks. I really didn't want to make her happy at all. She thinks Hunter is a valuable asset, and will be overjoyed when she hears the news."

"You might get a shock when you get back above," Dave said as he trotted along beside her.

Melissa frowned as she halted at a door. She twisted the knob. It was locked, damn it. "Why?"

Dave drew her back, then placed his hands on the keyhole below the doorknob. He murmured something briefly, and an electric shock sizzled between his hand and the door. The lock clicked, and Dave twisted the knob, pushing the door open. He waggled his eyebrows. "Impressed?"

"Hardly. You're a witch. I'd be disappointed if a simple door lock foiled you."

"It foiled you," he pointed out.

Melissa shook her head. "No, I was winding up to blow it to smithereens."

Dave smiled. "Sometimes subtlety works better."

"I'll remind you of that if we ever have to save your mate," she responded brusquely as she stepped through the doorway and jogged down the stairs. "Why would I get a shock above?" she prodded her brother.

"Well, a lot of shadow breeds died outside your store, and some humans died inside," Dave said as he trotted along behind her. "They want justice for their dead."

Melissa didn't stop, but she frowned at her brother briefly, and he held up his hands. "I know," Dave said, "it wasn't your fault, but Mom is in damage control."

This time Melissa did halt. "No." Denial, disbelief, dismay—they all battled for supremacy.

He sighed. "Yep. She's negotiating."

White-hot anger coiled inside her, and she shook her head. "She's going to be very disappointed when she realizes it's all going to be undone."

"She's your Coven Elder, Mel."

"I'll withdraw from White Oak, if necessary."

"Melissa—"

Melissa shook her head and continued. "No. This is it. I'm done. You're not bound by the coven, so I won't be, either."

"You know it's not as simple as that. I'm different."

And didn't she know it. Melissa had grown up knowing her brother was "special," and not subject to their mother's rules. All duty and obligation had fallen to her, as the only child of the Coven Elder inside the coven. But if Dave could live outside the coven, so could she, damn it.

She lifted a finger, using it to punctuate her words. "She will get my loyalty, and she will get my respect, but only when she's worthy. I'm not going to worry about it now, though. I have a bond mate to locate."

* * *

Hunter opened his eyes, wincing at the jackhammering inside his head.

"Ah, finally. You do so like to laze about, don't you, Hunter?"

Hunter tried to lift his head, but hissed as an iron collar singed his neck. He frowned.

His arms were cuffed above his head, and if the burning at his wrists was any indication, he was bound by iron, chained to yet another wall. His shoulders felt like they were gradually tearing out of their sockets, bearing all of his weight as his feet dangled above the ground.

Cuffs were overrated.

He winced, trying to move his head without touching the collar to get an idea of his whereabouts. It looked like it was some sort of outdoor area of a tavern, covered over long ago. Tables with bench seats, flowerpots with nothing but dirt and what could have been a bar. There were at least a dozen men gathered, a motley crew of vagrants, vampires and a lycan or two.

Movement caught his eye, and he finally caught sight of his father. Arthur Armstrong stood before a brazier, flames flickering through the grate. His gray hair was smoothed back, his blue eyes brittle as he met his son's stare. He wore a suit, and was pulling on leather gloves. Hunter sniggered.

"You're a little overdressed for the occasion, don't you think?"

Arthur's lips tightened. "That's one thing I couldn't really instill in you, wasn't it? An appreciation for grooming."

Hunter shook his head, then grimaced at the hot kiss of iron on his skin. "You tried to groom me," he said, and smiled. "But you failed."

Arthur pulled a rod out of the brazier with a gloved hand, and Hunter's smile dropped when he saw the glowing tip. "Actually, you failed, son. I gave you the perfect opportunity. Ryder was going to go to prison—or die, whichever came first—and you would have been the sole Armstrong heir."

Hunter blinked, stunned at his father's words, at the deceit in them. "You do realize I was there, right? In the same room? You know, when you admitted to plotting to kill both Ryder and myself to get your hands on our trust funds?"

"One, that's my money, I earned it. Two, that's a charge I'm not guilty of," Arthur said as he stepped toward him.

"Only because you escaped from prison before your trial," Hunter pointed out.

"A prison you helped put me in," Arthur remarked conversationally, then drove the hot poker into Hunter's side.

Hunter growled, hissing in pain as the iron speared beneath his skin. Arthur withdrew the poker and tilted his head to the side as Hunter panted.

"I'm impressed. You're doing your own dirty work these days," Hunter gasped. Up until now his father had sat back like a master puppeteer, compelling and manipulating folks to do his evil deeds, so that he could keep his hands clean and claim innocence. Except for now. Hunter was almost flattered that he was the catalyst for his father getting directly involved, but the searing hot pain in his side removed any sense of levity.

"You should know by now," Arthur said as he turned away, handing the rod over to a vampire who walked back to put the iron poker back into the brazier's flames. Arthur turned to face him, his hands behind his back.

"We're light warriors. I am your Prime. You do not punish me—I punish you."

"Punish me for what?" Hunter shouted, incredulous. "What did *I* do? God, you are such a dick. You kill Debbie, you conspire to kill your sons—you killed your *wife*," Hunter spat. "You're not normal, Arthur."

Arthur's eyes narrowed. "Ah, I see you've found your mama. Did you also meet the white whelp? Did you know he's just removed you from his sphere of protection?" Arthur pointed to the vamp who'd lied to him to lure him out of his bedroom earlier that morning. "He's renounced any ties you have with his family, I've been informed." Arthur shrugged. "But I digress. Your mother abandoned us. She betrayed me, and she was going to birth another man's breed. Can you imagine the scandal?" Arthur shook his head. "No. I've worked too hard, for too long, to have our reputation or standing tarnished by a woman who couldn't keep her legs together."

"Please. It's not like you're some paragon of virtue." Hunter didn't hide the contempt in his tone, or his expression. Listening to his mother talk about her life, he may not have accepted her words immediately, but he knew, deep down, that living with Arthur Armstrong must have been hell for her.

Arthur smiled. "I'm the Warrior Prime of House Armstrong. It's my duty to spread my seed, to build a strong legacy. It was your mother's duty to be loyal."

Hunter's eyes narrowed. "Spread your seed? Hell, do you actually hear the rubbish that comes out of your mouth?" Then the words sank in, and he blinked. "Are you saying—do you have more kids out there?" Shock chilled his blood. He knew he was flawed, that he continually had to fight the darkness in him, but what if his father had had another child, one that didn't fight the darkness? One that was just as evil and arrogant as his sire?

Arthur nodded. "Of course. When I'm finished here, I will go introduce myself to my daughter. She's been brought up by her mother in the wild, sadly, completely unaware of her true family." Arthur shrugged. "It's such a pity you won't get to meet your half sister, Hunter. Just think, there is a light warrior out there, full of raw, untrained power. She's unconstrained, totally free to indulge in her nature." His father's hand rolled elegantly. "Of course, she'll need some guidance, some instruction, I daresay basic etiquette training will be a necessity, but I will make her my heir."

For a moment Hunter just stared at his father, unsure of how to process the wealth of information he'd just learned. He had a sister. A sister who apparently had no idea of her madman of a father, or her brothers. A sister who maybe had no other light warrior around to help her. And she would be his heir. Hunter accepted his father wanted to kill him, but there was still Ryder.

"You're still planning to kill Ryder," Hunter said. His hands fisted, and he ignored the hot bite of the iron. "You are a sick man, Arthur. You need help."

Arthur sighed. "I'm your father. Call me Dad." He turned and gestured to the gathered men, all filthy, grimy and waiting for his next instruction. "And I have all the help I need."

Hunter's eyes rounded. "I will call you a lot of names, you sick son of a bitch, but I will never again call you Father."

"Oh, you think you're such a good son?" Arthur exclaimed.

"Yes," Hunter responded. "As a matter of fact, I think I was a better son than you ever deserved. I tried so hard to please you, playing all those stupid mind games, working with you. Ryder left you. He struck out on his own, and I wouldn't go along with all those strategic plays you wanted to do with your patients in your clinic. But you couldn't handle that. You decided to kill your sons as soon as they started to show some independence. Do you know what that says about you, Arthur?"

Arthur nodded at the vampire at the brazier, who stirred the coals. The flames danced and dipped. "What, Hunter?" he asked, his tone bored.

"It tells me that you're a scared little man who can't allow his sons to separate from him because then it means he's no longer their number one. It means you're not as strong as you like to think you are, that if you can't control with an iron fist, then you've completely lost control—and that means you're weak."

Hell, how had he not seen this before? He thought his father was a cruel bastard. He'd never thought he'd be capable of all this death and destruction, though. How much of his father was in him?

"Shut up," Arthur roared, and gestured to the vampire. The vampire yanked the rod out of the brazier and strode toward him. "Shut up. You betrayed me, Hunter. You, of all people. You worked with me. You were by my side, nearly 24/7. I gave you a home, an education—a career, damn it, and this is how you repay me, by siding with your brother against me." He grasped the iron poker from the vampire, and drove it into the top of Hunter's left thigh. Hunter growled again, snarling at the man as he slowly withdrew the hot rod. His leg—the pain, the excruciating, burning agony, actually gave him a chill. Hunter realized his body was going into shock.

"You really have a selective memory, don't you?" Hunter breathed, beads of perspiration sliding down the side of his face and between his shoulder blades. He gritted his teeth, tried to ignore the pain, but damn it hurt like a bitch. He wasn't healing. The iron was constraining his light force, including his ability to regenerate. He blinked, glaring at the man who even now handed the iron rod to the vampire, and he watched the poker get shoved once again into the coals, stirring up the embers. He shook his head. His father's distortion of the facts was stunning. "You wanted to kill me, remember? Before my birthday?"

Hunter blinked. His birthday. He'd turned thirty while chained to the wall in Melissa's cell. Quite the nonevent, admittedly, but it had still happened. "My trust fund," Hunter breathed. He frowned. "Is this about revenge, or about the money? This attempt to kill Melissa, to track us down..." He didn't have a will. Had never really thought about it until the night his father's plots were revealed—and then he'd been taken prisoner by Melissa, and there hadn't been an opportunity to organize one. Not that it had been a priority for him over the last few months.

"Melissa?" Arthur frowned as he thought, then his brow smoothed. "Oh, the witch. No, I was doing that as a favor to you. Nobody locks my son up for months and gets away with it."

Hunter tilted his head back, grimacing as the collar shifted around his neck. "Great. The 'I want to kill you, but God help anyone who hurts you that isn't me' mind-set." He wheezed with weak laughter. "You know, there's a term for people like you," he said, gazing up at the ceiling. He had no idea where they were, but he didn't think he was anywhere near his brother or his mother—or Melissa. He swallowed. He was going to die. He didn't want to die. He wanted to let his mother know he forgave her. He totally understood why she'd fled his father. He wanted to tell Melissa he loved her, tell her about the bond, and live a long and happy life with her. He wanted to repair the relationship with his brother Ryder. Hell, he even wanted to get to know his ever-expanding number of new siblings. But instead, he would die from being used as an iron pincushion. Perhaps it was a fitting end for all the bad things he'd done. Melissa's face swam in his mind's eye. He wanted to spend the rest of his life doing right by her.

"What is it?"

Hunter blinked. Arthur was standing in front of him again, glowing poker in hand. Had he zoned out, just a little? He knew he'd lost a lot of blood.

"What?" He wrinkled his brow, trying to keep up with the conversation.

"You said there is a term for people like me. What is it?"

"Completely fu—" He broke off as the iron rod speared into his other side, and this time he bellowed with the pain before darkness swept over him, giving him some relief.

Chapter 21

Melissa halted at the low, long cry of pain, her blood chilling in her veins.

"Oh, my God, that's Hunter," she gasped, and started to run.

Her brother caught up with her, pulling her to a stop. "Be smart, Mel. We can't just burst in on a Light Warrior Prime. We have to find out what's going on first." His head twisted to the side, and he hesitated for a moment.

"We have to hurry, Dave," Melissa pleaded, trying to drag her brother along. "That is my mate, and he needs me, needs us."

Dave held a gloved finger to his lips, then rolled his hand. Melissa frowned. He wanted her to shush, but... keep talking? Dave backed up the tunnel, and made a beak with his hand, opening and closing it. Keep talking.

Melissa frowned in confusion, but did as her brother instructed. "I—" Her mind went blank. She normally didn't have a problem talking, but talking on cue took the spontaneity out of a conversation. Dave frowned, his beak-hand flapping open and closed faster.

"I love him," she stated abruptly. "I love Hunter, and I want to help him. I intend to spend the rest of my life with him. He's…not perfect, I'll admit—but then, neither am I."

Dave backed up against the wall just before a bend, and nodded. She continued. "I know he can be a little impulsive—but we can all be guilty of that sometimes, right?" She eyed her brother. "He's a good man. He's been hurt, and he's had to live with a cruel father, so I understand he's—adapted." That was probably the nicest way she could frame it. "But, Dave, he's strong, and—believe it or not—he's fiercely loyal, and very protective. He may sometimes get it wrong showing it," she admitted, "but I realize now, deep down, he's doing what he thinks is the best for those he loves." She hesitated. "And I would do the same," she admitted. "I would do the same crazy crap if it meant protecting—"

Dave whipped his hand out, grasping the arm of the person who had crept up to the corner of the tunnel, and slammed them back against the wall.

Amelie Galen gasped, her arms coming up to grasp the lapels of Dave's leather jacket.

Dave relaxed his grip immediately, but didn't let her go. "What are you doing?" he asked Hunter's mother calmly.

Amelie looked between the harsh expression of Dave, and over to Melissa, before swinging her gaze back to the big man who held her, gently but implacably, against a wall.

"I'm helping you," Amelie responded.

Dave arched an eyebrow. "By following us like a shadow, creeping along behind us?"

Amelie lifted her chin toward Melissa. "Griffin says she is my son's bond mate. I can't see the link, but I figure she's using it to track down Hunter. I want to help you save my son."

Dave pursed his lips for a moment, then grimaced. "And just how do you think your other son would view my taking his mother to a fight with a deranged light warrior, hmm?"

Amelie arched her eyebrow, and her eyes flashed red, ever so briefly. "I'm not defenseless. I ran away once, and left my sons in Arthur's hands, and that decision will haunt me forever. I will not do it again. I will not let that bastard kill any of my children."

"This is wasting time," Melissa interrupted. "She is responsible for her own decisions, Dave. Let her come, if she wants, but either way, let's go."

Dave let go of Amelie, stepping back with his gloved hands up. "Fine. But we do this my way. My rules. No innocents get harmed. Understand?" Amelie nodded, but Dave stepped closer. "That means you don't go off on some bloodlust craze," he said quietly. "Arthur had both lycans and vamps working together for him. The only way that happens is if they're compelled. They aren't in control of their actions."

Amelie nodded again. "Understood."

Dave nodded, satisfied, then strode toward Melissa. "Okay, sis, you're up. Show us where this mate of yours is." He shook his head as he fell into step alongside her.

"What?" Melissa asked.

"I can't believe you fell for the firebug. The guy tried to kill you."

Melissa nodded. "And I chained him to a wall for

five months. Neither of us is proud of what we did to each other."

"How the hell did you go from putting your little pyromaniac in chains to becoming bonded mates?"

"Long story," Melissa replied, as she broke into a jog, following the twisted ribbons of color through the darkness.

"I look forward to hearing it, when this is all over," Dave whispered, then pulled her against the wall as they came up to an intersection. Amelie followed suit. He crept up to the corner and peered around the brick wall. He quickly jerked back, then leaned over so that his lips were close to her ear. "I think we've found him."

He silently shuffled back so Melissa could take her place at the front, and she peered around.

Her mouth opened in a silent gasp of horror. It looked like the back alley of a row of what used to be restaurants. At the far end was a courtyard, braziers burning. A group of men were clustered about—vamps, vagrants, some Darkken...and a lycan? All either sat on the bench seats to watch the proceedings, or gathered for a closer view. An unconscious Hunter was chained up on a wall, his feet dangling three feet from the ground. Even from here, she could see the bloodstains on his white shirt, almost black in the dim light. She covered her mouth to stop from screaming, and watched as Arthur held out his arms, light arcing from his hands to the son chained to the wall.

Hunter's body flinched and jerked, his skin glowing, until finally his eyes opened, and he glared, gasping at his father.

The light flickered from Arthur's fingertips, extinguishing as the older man smiled triumphantly.

"Ah, much better. Now we can start all over again."

Melissa recoiled, darting back behind the brick wall. "We have to do something," she whispered to her brother.

Dave nodded. "If we make a move on Armstrong or Hunter, that little posse out there will take action. We'll have to take out Armstrong's men first."

"How? There's at least a mixed dozen out there. I can't touch them all at once." Melissa's favorite weapon was her sleep spell, but it usually required physical contact. "You're strong, but even you can't knock them all out at the same time with a spell."

Dave nodded. "So we'll have to go with shock and awe." He turned to Amelie. "When you metamorphosed, did you retain any of your light force?"

Amelie shook her head. "No, I fed it all to my son, to keep him alive during my death, and then the rest of the pregnancy. I'm just a vampire now."

Dave shook his head. "You're never 'just' something. Okay, here's what we'll do."

He quickly outlined a plan. Melissa's eyebrows rose. She knew her brother could be ballsy, but this was out there, even for him. They were outnumbered, and possibly outpowered with the full force of a Warrior Prime.

Dave grasped her shoulders. "That's your bond mate out there, Mel. You can do this."

She nodded. She could. Or she'd die trying.

Hunter stiffened, waiting for the hot poker to again burn through him. He glared at his father. The man was sick, and if anything, Hunter was so appalled by his actions, so disgusted, he took a small measure of comfort knowing he could never do what his father did, could never be his father's son. His body ached, but Arthur had healed his wounds so that he could start the torture all over again. He didn't know how long this would last for, but he was determined not to show his father his pain, or his worry for his mate. He'd left Melissa alone. He smiled bitterly. Based on his experience, he'd been so worried that she would walk out on him. He'd never once thought he'd be the one to walk out on her.

His gaze dropped to the curling, ethereal ribbons waving and fluttering from his chest. His father hadn't noticed it, couldn't see it. His father had no idea Melissa had become his bonded mate. Thank God. If Arthur knew, he'd go after Melissa in order to discourage any claim to his fortune. At least he would die knowing that she'd be protected from his father's cruel attention.

As though responding to his thoughts, the ribbons brightened a little. He saw them shift direction. They wavered, rising at an angle, then falling, but all the time transferring from his right side to his left. Uh, what was going on?

"Now, where were we?" Arthur said conversationally, the rod with the glowing tip in his gloved hand. "Ah, yes. I was telling you what a colossal failure you were." His features hardened. "How dare you think you can box me up?"

"Well, you boxed me up, I'd call that fair."

Hunter's head swiveled at the sound of the feminine voice, his eyes widening as he watched his mother walk down the alley behind the tavern's outdoor area. She wore that leather coat, the one that flared out like a long dress, her booted heels clicking on the surface of the road.

Arthur turned, his expression surprised for a moment. "Amelie."

She smiled, arms out to the side as she inclined her head in a courtly manner. "In the flesh, so to speak."

Arthur's eyes narrowed, and he scanned the area. "Where is that white freak of yours?"

Amelie's expression hardened. "My son doesn't share my consideration for Hunter," she admitted. "It's just me."

Arthur rolled his eyes, lowering the iron poker to lean on it like a walking stick. "Come, Amelie, do you honestly think I'd believe you'd come here alone, to face me?"

Her lips curled in contempt. "Oh, you don't scare me, you pathetic little man. Always using others to do your dirty work for you." She gestured to the men she passed as she entered the dead garden area. "Look around you. None of these men are loyal to you. None of these men care whether you live or die. You've had to compel them to follow you, to do your bidding. A true leader doesn't lead by trickery, Arthur—but that's something your tiny little brain couldn't quite grasp, isn't it? Seeing as you can't get your way by any other method…"

Arthur's lips tightened, and his eyes narrowed. "Why are you here?"

"I'm here to save my son," Amelie said, as though it was obvious.

Hunter turned his fists in the cuffs. He had no idea what the hell was going on, but this— His brain was grappling to process his mother and father, in the same spot, after all these years.

Arthur chuckled. "And how exactly do you plan to do that? You—against all of us, against *me*?" He shook his head, incredulous. "It hardly seems fair."

"I'm offering a trade," Amelie said, her hands on her hips. She glanced around at the men, shifted a little as they started to edge closer. "Let my son go, and you can have me."

Arthur set the iron poker against the wall, and folded his arms. "And why would I do that?"

"Because you can't stand the fact that I walked away," Amelie said, her voice succinct. "I left you. Can you imagine what your peers would say to that if they knew? How would that affect your standing with them, Arty?"

"Don't call me that," Arthur growled.

Amelie lowered her head to glare at her former husband. "Let my son go, *Arty*. Take me instead. I'm sure there are some lessons you think you can teach me."

"Why would I let him go, when I now have both of you?"

Amelie smiled derisively. "You never really had me, Arty."

Arthur sneered, and Hunter noticed the bond link move again. It fluttered, it writhed and it moved. Arthur held up his hands, and Hunter grasped hold of the chains above his wrists, gritting his teeth against the burn.

"No," he yelled.

Fireballs appeared on Arthur's palms, growing, expanding, roiling. The older man smirked. "This is going to be such fun." He threw the balls at Amelie, and Hunter roared in panic.

The fireballs smashed against some invisible barrier, roiling back in a wall of flame that flung Arthur back against the wall.

Hunter reacted, entwining his legs around Arthur's neck. He heard cries and grunts, registered the flare of fire, but concentrated on keeping his legs—and his father—exactly in the position they were. He glanced up briefly.

His mother was moving in a blur, her dark coat whirling as she dodged the men. She went after all the vampires, snapping their necks in lightning-fast moves that would put a light warrior to shame.

Arthur struggled against his legs, using his hands and twisting this way and that to try to break free. "Fight," he wheezed to his men. "Kill them."

Hunter tightened his hold, gritting his teeth against the searing pain in his wrists, fists and neck. Then he heard the chanting.

Melissa strode down the alley from the opposite direction, arms out, eyes focused on Arthur as she spoke some sort of spell. Meanwhile a tall, broad-shouldered man wearing biker leathers and sunglasses ran up to one of the homeless humans and jumped, landing with a heavy punch to the jaw.

Hunter froze, muscles clenched. *Melissa*. He'd thought never to see her again, and he had to blink to make sure he wasn't zoned out in some fantasy again. She was here, and she was coming for him. She'd had the opportunity to walk away, to leave, but here she was, facing off against his father and the shadow breeds who terrified her. For him.

God, he loved this woman.

One of the men snarled, his eyes beginning to glow as he stripped his shirt from his body and toed off his shoes. Even as he slid out of his jeans, he morphed into his werewolf form. With his teeth bared and a growl low in his throat, the wolf started running toward Melissa. Hunter yelled, and the man wearing sunglasses whirled, chanting something as his fist lashed out to punch the lycan off course. Hunter heard the whimper, then saw the lycan.

His mother cried out in pain as a vampire finally brought her down, his arm twining around her neck as he curled his hand over, ready to strike at her chest.

"No," Hunter yelled, then bellowed as Arthur finally managed to free himself. The Warrior Prime fired off a fireball at Amelie, and started running toward Melissa. Melissa's eyes widened, and she turned to Hunter, flinging her hand up as she muttered a chant. The restraints that held Hunter in place snapped open. Hunter dropped to the ground, crashing hard against the concrete.

He heard screams and glanced up. His mother had managed to turn and use the vampire as a shield. The vampire who held her was now on fire. His mother was trying to struggle free. His head whipped around to look after Melissa. She'd started running, and was dodging the flaming spears his father was throwing her way. She burst into an open doorway and ducked as a fireball crashed against the timber, setting the door alight. Then she disappeared into the dark opening, his father in pursuit.

Hunter rose to his feet and stumbled toward the alley. He would not stand by and watch his father kill the woman he loved, the woman he intended to spend the rest of his life with.

Chapter 22

Melissa raced up the interior stairwell, heart pounding as she heard Arthur burst into the foyer below. She'd made it to the second floor when she heard his steps on the stairs below. She glanced down into the stairwell, then jerked back as a fireball landed above her. She dived for the door on the second-floor landing, yanking it open, hurtling into the hallway and slamming the door behind her.

She glanced first in one direction, then the other, trying to catch her breath. It looked like some sort of old apartment building. There was a window at the end of the hall, and despite the grime and dust that covered it, she could make out the murky frame of a fire escape. She started running down the hall.

This wasn't part of Dave's plan. Well, not quite. The plan was to create a distraction, draw Arthur's attention away from Hunter long enough, distract the rest of the men for long enough, so that she could create a release spell for his chains. She'd used her reflection spell to protect Amelie, but didn't have enough to protect herself as well as free Hunter. She made it to the window and tried to lift it open, but centuries of disuse and grime had sealed it shut. She heard the door clang open back down the hall, and cast about wildly. There was a fire extinguisher strapped to the wall. She grabbed it. It was so old, it was highly unlikely it would work, and the irony didn't escape her as she lifted it to smash the glass as she tried to escape the enraged light warrior behind her.

She heard the roar behind her, and she dived out of the window, landing roughly on the grate outside, below the windowsill. A cloud of flame billowed out of the window above her, and she screamed as the explosion curled over her, then rose above to billow out over the alley. She crawled to the ladder, but screeched when a hand pulled at her hair, yanking her away from the escape route.

"You meddling bitch," Arthur seethed as he pulled her to her feet. He grasped her shoulders, twisting her around to face him. "You should have learned the first time, it takes more than just a weasely little mirror spell to best me. I'm a—"

Melissa rolled her eyes. "Yeah, we all know. You're a Warrior Prime." She kicked him swiftly between the legs. His eyes rounded, his breath wheezed out in a high-pitched squeak and his fingers clenched on her shoulders. "You have to learn that doesn't give you a hall pass to be a dick."

His face became mottled, and Melissa felt the heat building on her shoulders. She tried to beat him off, but the searing heat singed her skin where his hands touched her. She muttered her dampening spell, concentrating on using the light force as an element to build on her incantation. The more he tried to burn her, the more effective her dampening spell became.

"Leave her alone," Hunter yelled from beneath them, but Melissa didn't take her eyes off Arthur's face, muttering her spell over and over as he tried to burn her.

Arthur growled in frustration, backing her up against the railing. Her eyes rounded as she felt the pressure against her. Arthur pushing against her shoulders, the railing at her waist. She tried to kick out, but Arthur dodged her feet, the whites of his eyes visible as he shoved at her, and then her feet left the ground, and she felt herself falling.

"No!" Hunter yelled. She reached for him, panic rising inside as she briefly saw his face as she fell toward him. The ground raced toward her. Hunter stretched out his hand, leaning out over the fire escape, and then a black cloud raced up and billowed over her.

Time seemed to slow—or at least, the speed of her fall did.

She screamed as she felt something hard grip her hand, and the muscles in her shoulder tore. Her other senses were ripped away from her. Sight, sound—she couldn't even tell which way was up or down. Slowly the black fog drifted away.

Hunter was half-over the railing, and he gasped with relief when he met her gaze, his hand holding hers tight. She hung suspended, caught by Hunter's death-defying grip, the ground still some twelve feet below.

Arthur screamed with rage as Hunter slowly pulled her up to him, the muscles in his arm bulging as, hand over hand, he transferred his grip from her hand to her wrist, her forearm, her upper arm, until he could finally clasp her under the shoulder and pull her over the railing to him. He enfolded her in his arms, and she collapsed against his chest, wincing at the awkward, heaving feel of her arm hanging by her side.

Arthur raised both hands, fireballs sparking on his palms as he took aim at them both. Hunter shifted Melissa behind him, facing his father.

"You're not going to win this time, Arty."

Arthur's eyes narrowed. "Watch me." He hurled the two fireballs at them, and Melissa even dodged behind Hunter, then frowned when nothing happened. She peered over Hunter's shoulder.

Arthur stood on the fire escape above them, and the confused expression on his face was comical. Sparks flared again, and he aimed them at the couple below. Melissa watched as little dark clouds danced over and swallowed them up.

Hunter chuckled. "Have you met my brother?" He pointed to the alley below.

Melissa glanced down. Griffin stood calmly below, arms folded, muscles bulging, his pale blue gaze trained on the scene above him.

"The white brat," Arthur seethed, and flung a fireball down at the albino. Griffin gave a flick of his fingers, and the ball of flame disappeared in a puff of black. Arthur frowned and clasped his hands together, a small explosion that fired down at Griffin with breathtaking speed.

Griffin curled his fingers, and black tendrils caught at the fireball, ripping it apart and consuming the flame. Griffin chuckled. "This is fun. I could do this all day."

Arthur growled, spreading his arms out, and Griffin sighed. "You really don't learn, do you?" Griffin raised his arms, and the tendrils of black fog leaped from his hands, spearing into Arthur's palms and slamming him back against the side of the building.

Arthur grunted, trying to free himself from the dark power that now trapped his hands against the side of the brick wall.

Griffin gave a swift yank, and Arthur flew from the landing, tumbling to the street below.

Hunter climbed down the fire escape as fast as he could, running over to where his father lay in the middle of the alley, his limbs bent at unnatural angles. Arthur blinked, as though trying to figure out, as much as his damaged brain would allow, what had just happened.

Hunter skidded to a stop as Griffin approached Arthur. The strange man who had knocked out a werewolf approached from the tavern garden, his arm around Amelie's waist as he helped her hobble along beside him. Melissa came up behind him, and her hand touched his shoulder. They all stared as the albino stood over the broken man on the ground, his expression harsh.

"You came into my home, and you killed my people," Griffin spoke quietly, calmly. "Your first mistake was entering Old Irondell and thinking you could do whatever you wanted. Your second mistake was compelling my man to betray me. Your final mistake was to attack my family."

Arthur's gaze shifted to Hunter, and Griffin nodded. "Yeah, he's my family, too." Griffin knelt on one knee by Arthur's side, his elbow resting on his other bent knee. "You see, we do things differently down here in Old Irondell. There is no Reform law, there is no tribal law. There is just me. My judgment is sound, my punishment is swift." He leaned closer, those pale blue eyes staring blindly at the man on the ground. "It's time for you to go."

Griffin placed his hand above Arthur's chest, and a dark blade, glistening in the fire from the distant braziers, emerged from his palm and speared through Arthur Armstrong's heart.

Arthur flinched, his expression stunned, before his mouth sagged open and his eyes glazed over as his skin turned to black. His head lolled to the side.

The man with the sunglasses grimaced. "Effective," he commented, his tone dry. Amelie stared down at the man who was once her husband, and shook her head, but said nothing.

Hunter stared for a moment, shocked, as his half brother rose to his feet. "You killed him," Hunter said, his voice low.

Griffin turned to him. "Did you want that privilege for yourself?" The albino's pale blue gaze flicked between the man at his side, and the corpse in the alley, and he finally placed a hand on Hunter's shoulder. "I have no doubt you would have killed him, brother, but hear me when I tell you this—no man should have to kill his father." Griffin raised his finger. "Trust me. You may feel the hate, and you may feel the justification, but killing a parent—that haunts you forever." He patted Hunter's shoulder, and Hunter stared at his younger half brother. He spoke with a weary wisdom beyond his years.

Griffin lifted a hand to Amelie. "You weren't supposed to be here."

"Well, you weren't going to do anything," Amelie retorted. "I had to do something."

"I told you to trust me to know what I was doing."

"You told me you weren't going to help your brother."

"No, I told you *we* weren't going to help my brother,"

Griffin corrected her. "You were supposed to stay back at the hall, all grumpy and righteous." He pointed to the Darkken who had lured Hunter away, and Hunter grimaced. His neck was twisted at an awkward angle. He felt no pity, though. The guy was a vampire. He'd regenerate, and awaken with a sore neck, but at least he'd still live. As much as the undead could live. Hunter took some comfort knowing his father's compulsions died with him.

"Knowing that one of my men had removed one of my guests without my say-so—I had to remove Hunter's protection so whoever was responsible would bear the news to Armstrong." Griffin shrugged. "And we followed."

Hunter arched an eyebrow. "Sneaky." He tilted his head. "I like you."

Griffin's lips twitched, and he indicated Amelie. "And you can heal my mom. I like you." Then he frowned. "Is that my shirt?"

Hunter glanced down at the bloodstained, ripped shirt. "Don't know, but I don't have a good track record with borrowed shirts." Then he frowned as he gazed across at his mother. "You're hurt?"

She waved a hand. "I'm fine, just got a little singed on my back."

The big man with the sunglasses shook his head slightly, and Hunter nodded, interpreting the man's silent signal. His mother was hurt more than she let on. He turned back to look at Melissa. Her complexion was drawn and pale, and one shoulder sat lower than the other. She'd dislocated her arm in the fall. She needed his care, too. He gathered his mate close. "Well, let's get everyone back to the hall. I'm going to need fire. Lots of fire."

"And beer," the man wearing the sunglasses suggested. "Lots of beer." He turned to help Amelie, but Griffin lifted his mother into his arms and strode down the alley in the direction of the hall.

"Who *are* you?" Hunter asked as he lifted Melissa into his arms, ignoring her halfhearted protests. "Shh, each step you take will jolt that shoulder."

Melissa sighed, then lifted her chin to the man who fell into step alongside them. "Hunter, this is my brother, Dave. Dave, meet Hunter."

Hunter nodded. "Ah, you're the witch brother."

Dave slapped a hand hard on Hunter's shoulder, and Hunter winced. "And you're the pyromaniac who nearly killed my sister and has now bonded with her." Dave jerked him closer. "Hurt my sister again and I'll kill you." Melissa's brother gave him another friendly pat on the shoulder that could have flattened a lesser man. "Welcome to the family."

Hunter halted, his gaze dropping to Melissa's face. She stared up at him, an eyebrow arched in challenge. Oh, hell. She knew. What's worse, her brother with a fist that could knock out a werewolf knew.

"I was going to tell you," he said quickly. "I just— I just—"

"Spit it out, hot pants," Dave muttered, and Hunter gave her brother an exasperated look, before turning back to the precious woman in his arms.

"Every woman I've ever loved has left me," he told her quietly, and her eyes filled with understanding.

Melissa sighed. She stared up at him, her smile gentle. "I promise you, I will never, ever leave you." She looked at him meaningfully. "And you know me—a promise is a promise."

She'd used those same words when she'd used her

energy to remove her wards instead of fighting off the werewolves. Hunter halted. This woman would literally die before she left him. She cupped his cheek. "I love you, Hunter. I'm not going anywhere."

"Likewise," Hunter breathed, and dipped his head to kiss his mate. "Let's get married."

Melissa nodded. "Let's," she said, just before his lips took hers.

Dave groaned and started walking. "Get a room, you two."

Epilogue

"**C**an I look now?" Melissa asked, arms outstretched. She wriggled her nose, trying to dislodge the blindfold. Chill wind tousled her hair and danced with her skirt. They were outside, but she had no idea where.

"No." Hunter guided her, his hands on her shoulders.

"What about now?"

He sighed, and his breath gusted past her ear. "Patience, wife."

She smiled. "I love it when you say that."

"What? Patience? Yeah, I feel like I say that a lot with you."

She elbowed him in his muscled stomach behind her. "I meant *wife*."

His hands slid down her back and around her waist, pulling her back against his broad chest. "I love it, too," he said as he nipped her neck. They'd been married for nearly three weeks. Her mother had been overjoyed to hear her daughter was marrying the light warrior, until Hunter had insisted she tear up any agreement she'd negotiated as recompense with the pack who had attacked his mate in her bookstore. Eleanor had discovered she had as much influence over the new family asset as she did over her daughter.

Which was zilch.

Hunter's breath gusted past her ear. She trembled, and he nipped her again, trailing his lips up to the sensitive spot behind her ear. She tilted her head to the side, giving him better access, and her breath hitched as his hands slid under her jacket to cup her breasts.

"Is this what you wanted to show me?" she said breathlessly, rubbing herself against his arousal pressed against her butt. He'd made her put on the blindfold as soon as he got her into his car, and she had no idea where they were, or who could possibly see them. It was Sunday, it was chilly, and she'd rather be back at their home, heating up the bedsheets with her sexy husband.

"Oh, I've got something to show you, Red," he whispered in her ear, then growled in frustration. He flicked her nipples with his thumbs, just once, then drew his hands away. "But I've got something else first."

He guided her along, her booted heels clicking on the pavement. She sighed. It had been a busy three weeks. Hunter, with Ryder's agreement, had sought and successfully petitioned Reform Court for a family status. It had caused quite the sensation when the public learned that light warriors weren't an extinct breed, after all.

And now she was Consort to the Galen Warrior Prime. An impatient, blindfolded Consort.

She heard the rattle of chains, the clink and groan of something that sounded like a gate, and then Hunter guided her farther. "Careful," he told her, "it's a little messy." She could feel the dirt and rocks under her feet, and her heel sank into soft earth.

"Okay, stand still." Hunter's hands untied the blindfold, and he pulled it away. Melissa blinked in the light. Christmas had come and gone, but gray snow was still on the ground in some parts. She looked down into the great big hole. She could clearly see the neatly poured concrete foundations, the spray-painted markings that delineated zones, the pipes that protruded from the slab. She glanced around in surprise. It was her building. Well, the place where her apothecary and bookstore had once stood.

"What's going on?" she asked, confused.

Hunter stepped beside her to gesture to the staked-out markings. "That's your wedding present."

She arched an eyebrow. "A slab of concrete?" A chill breeze drifted through the chain-link fence and scaffolding that edged the lot. A tattered cover lined the fence, blocking the view of the site from the street. She folded her arms, hugging herself.

"No, this is your new store," Hunter stated. He folded his arms, his navy blue sweater pulling taut across his chest.

"Okay," she said slowly. He'd been working on expanding his clinic since their return above—or so she'd thought. It was as though his time away from tending people had renewed an energy, creating a drive in him to work. He worked hard—and then he came home and played hard. He reached for her hand, and dragged her over to the site office. He unlocked the door, pulled her in and shut out the wind behind her. In minutes he had lights on and the heater going. She glanced around. The desk was surprisingly neat for a construction zone. Plans were pinned to the wall, and Hunter gestured to it.

"Here it is," he said huskily. "Your new store and apothecary."

Her eyes rounded. "What?"

He clasped her one hand in two of his. "You lost your apothecary because of me and my family." He nodded to the plans. "I wanted to give it back."

"Are you serious?" she gasped, glancing between her husband and the schematics drawn on the wall. She was still trying to get her insurance claim completed for her building. This—this was—wow.

Hunter nodded. "Uh-huh." He stepped up to the drawing. "See, you have a separate area here, on the lower level, for you to mix all your witchy-woo potions and lotions, and a separate consulting room here if you want it. I've added some storage there, for your supplies," he said, gesturing to some markings. "And the stairs are wider, but you also have an elevator if you need to move supplies between the floors. Your apothecary will be made from reinforced concrete—it's going to be a bunker that can withstand the end of the world, if need be," he muttered, waving his hands casually. "And here are the plans for the bookstore, with some event space if you wanted to get authors in for a talk or signing, or something…" He turned to her, and for the first time his expression was unsure. "And if you want, you can change anything you like."

"Hunter, this is so generous," she gasped.

He rolled his eyes. "Well, not quite. My family destroyed your clinic twice, so it seems only fair we should rebuild it, and—" He grimaced. "This makes me feel better after what I did to you, so it's completely selfish." He leaned down and kissed her quickly on the lips, before drawing back and holding up his hand. "I was going to attach your apothecary to my clinic, but then realized your patients wouldn't want to be anywhere near mine, but really, if you want to build somewhere else, that's fine, too—whatever you want." He drew her closer. "I just want you to be happy," he murmured. He lifted his gaze from her lips to her eyes. "What do you think?"

She smiled. "I think it's wonderful. Thank you."

Hunter closed his eyes in relief and tilted his forehead against hers. "Thank God. I wasn't sure if I was over-stepping the mark, or—"

She rose on the tips of her toes and kissed him. "It's wonderful," she reassured him. He nodded, pleased.

"I find I like making my family happy," he said huskily, and despite the warmth in his gaze, she also saw the fleeting concern.

Melissa squeezed his hand. "We'll find her, Hunter. Soon."

Ever since Arthur had mentioned the missing sister, Hunter and Ryder had been searching for her. They were slowly wading through Arthur's papers in an effort to discover the name of the woman who had birthed him a daughter. Griff was helping, too, and Lance. With so many searching, it was only a matter of time before they located their unknown sister.

He nodded and winked. "We'll find her," he repeated, his expression grim with determination.

She looked at him in inquiry. "Wasn't there something else you wanted to show me?" she said suggestively.

His lips curled in that wicked, sexy way of his, and those golden flecks in his eyes flared. "Why yes, yes there is."

He leaned over and flicked the lock on the site office door, and stepped closer to her.

"You know what they say about a new office, though, right?"

"This isn't my new office," she pointed out.

He nodded. "True, but we can practice."

The golden flecks glimmered in his eyes as he stopped in front of her.

Melissa shook her head. "Practice what, Hunter? What do they say about a new office?"

"That you should christen it at the very first opportunity," he murmured as he dipped his head. He took her lips in a scorching kiss as he slid the jacket down off her shoulders. She shrugged out of the garment, then slid her hands up his arms, enjoying the dip and flex of muscle as he started to unbutton her blouse.

His lips drifted across her jaw to her neck. "I hadn't heard that one," she admitted breathlessly as he opened her shirt, kissing his way over her collarbone and down to the lacy edge of her bra.

"Oh, yeah. It's a tradition." His hands caressed her back, unsnapping her bra strap and drawing the garment down her arms. He turned briefly and fired it like a slingshot at the top of a filing cabinet set against a wall. "You have to christen the desk, the chair—the floor."

He dipped his head to take a rosy peak in his mouth, and she trembled, heat flooding her as arousal built. "Oh, I had no idea," she murmured, then moaned as he drew down on her nipple, nipping gently with his teeth before laving it with his tongue. He cupped her other breast, alternating his attention between the two.

"Oh, yeah," he said huskily. "Then we have to christen my office."

"We do?"

He rose up and kissed her, bearing her back down on the surface of the desk. "Uh-huh." He pulled his sweater over his head, and she sighed as his muscled chest came into view.

"I like your traditions," she said, trailing her hands over his pectoral muscles. He grasped her hands, kissing each before placing them over her head so that she clasped the rim.

"You're going to need to hold on," he whispered, and she shuddered. He drew the palm of his hand down from her neck to the waistband of her skirt. He waggled his eyebrows.

"There are lots of them," he told her, and she frowned, trying to keep track of the conversation and not drown in sensation.

"Lots of what?" she asked as he rolled her hips to the side so he could access the zipper of her skirt. The sound of her zipper in the small office was loud and full of carnal promise. Her nipples tightened, and she could feel herself getting damp.

"Traditions," he told her as he slid her skirt down her legs and off, along with her panties. His eyes flared when he saw her garter belt and stockings. "Holy smoke."

She smiled at his appreciation. "What other traditions?" she prodded him as she turned back to face him.

"Oh, we have to christen each new moon," he said, dipping low to kiss her navel. She heard the slide of his zipper, heard the soft thump as his jeans hit the floor. "We have to christen each sunrise," he murmured as he kissed his way farther down her body. "Oh, and every time we open a new cereal box. Lots of traditions."

She shuddered as she felt his breath against her and her head arched back. She had to remind herself they were in a site office of a construction zone. What if one of the builders turned up? "Uh, Hunter, should we be doing this?" she murmured, eyeing the door. It was locked, but still, if the site supervisor turned up for any reason... She had no idea how busy a construction site could be on a Sunday, or whether people were likely to walk in and interrupt what was going on in the about-to-be-christened practice office.

She glanced down, and Hunter met her stare, his brown gaze wicked with promise.

"Trust me," he murmured. "I'm a doctor."

He dipped his head, and then she didn't care who saw or heard what as her husband showed her just how much he knew about the female anatomy. All she knew was that she loved this man, loved his sexy traditions, as well as the quirky little fireworks he set off each time they made love. He challenged her, he protected her—but more than anything, they were true partners. Mates for life. Her orgasm swept over her, and she cried out her release as Hunter entered her, and then it was star-bursts and sparkles everywhere.

* * * * *

WITCH HUNTER

This book is dedicated to all the readers who have supported me by reading this series. You have no idea how meaningful and humbling your consideration and time have meant to me.

And thank you to Coleen, for the inspiration that has become Dave Carter, tattoo artist and witch hunter.

Chapter 1

"Why do you have so many tattoos?"

Dave lifted the tip of his needle from his client's inner wrist and gently dabbed at the skin. The woman was looking up at the ceiling, and she was exhaling slowly through her lips, as though trying not to flinch. Scream. Pee. Puke. Whatever.

"I'm a tattoo artist. Perks of the job." He eyed the intricate linework he'd inked onto her wrist. He just needed to close the top of the loop of one twist of the knot, and he was finished.

He dabbed at the skin again. He was only doing a simple line tattoo for this woman. It was her first tattoo, and she didn't think she could stand a lot of shading. He had to agree. The whole time she'd breathed as though she was in a Lamaze class. He was surprised she hadn't hyperventilated.

"I can't quite make it out...?" Her tone was raised in query.

He leaned forward, gently pressing his foot on the pedal, and the woman snapped her gaze from the mark on his arm to the ceiling again. The skin on his left breast itched.

Damn.

"I can, and that's what matters," he said, smiling at the woman as he carefully pressed the needle against her skin. He focused intently, despite the itch that was getting more annoying—and bound to become more so.

He worked as quickly as he could, his lips tightening as the itch became warm. He didn't have long.

"Are you sure you can see with those glasses on?" The woman bit her lip as he wiped petroleum jelly across her wrist to hydrate the skin, and then pressed the needle against her, concentrating on drawing out the ink.

"I'm nearly finished and you're asking me that now?" Dave raised an eyebrow, but didn't stop his work. The itch began to heat. Sweat broke out on his forehead and upper lip, and he worked faster, gritting his teeth at the burn.

He finished the line perfectly, closing the loop and preventing any breach to the protection spell he'd drawn into her tattoo.

"Right, that's done," he rasped, reaching for the anti-septic liquid soap on his table. He washed her skin and gently held her arm so that she could see the intricate linework. It looked like a delicate lace band around her wrist.

"And this will stop him...?" she asked tentatively.

He nodded. "He won't be able to raise his hand against you." He worked quickly, placing low adherent bandages over her new tattoo and taping them carefully into place. "Leave those on for about twenty-four hours—or until tomorrow morning at the earliest. It will probably look shiny and gross—don't worry, that's normal." Damn, what had started as an itch now felt like someone was directing a heat lamp on his chest. "Shower and soap it up—antiseptic soap only, nothing scented, and for God's sake, no scrubs, and don't scratch it."

Ow. Crap. The burn! He'd run out of time.

He reached over with his left hand to pick up a flyer he'd had printed. "Here are the instructions for aftercare, call me if you need anything and leave your money on the counter on the way out."

He rose from his wheeled stool, and she gaped at him, her gaze dropping to his torso. "Hey, are you all rig—?"

"Fine," he said brusquely, leaving his room and jogging down the hall. He flung open a door marked Private and ran down the metal stairs to the apartment below his tattoo parlor, below street level. He raised his hand, pushing the door at the bottom of the stairs open with his magic, and then flicking it closed behind him. He jogged down the rock-hewn corridor to the door to his private quarters, and thrust it open, kicking it closed behind him, swearing in a soft hiss as he pulled the fabric of his gray T-shirt away from the blooming stain over his left pectoral muscle. He lifted the garment over his head, moving his left arm gingerly as he removed the T-shirt.

He always left the lamp next to his armchair on in his subterranean quarters, and it gave out a low, warm light. At the moment, it was just enough light to show him the damage.

The skin on his breast was blistered, bleeding. He

sucked in and held his breath, trying not to yell or scream as it happened again.

The marking glowed as it seared into his skin, and he gritted his teeth, closing his eyes and tilting his head back as his skin was branded. The name was scorched into the very fiber of his being, and he let out a soft, pained growl as the searing seemed to continue forever. He started breathing like his recent client, short hitched gasps that stopped him from crying like a baby. The heat, the pain—it was excruciating, and left him temporarily powerless until the etching was complete.

He opened his eyes and stared at the bare-chested figure in the mirror on the wall by the door. The glow was beginning to darken, and he tried to slow his breathing down as the mark was completed, the wound glistening with his blood. He swallowed, his shoulders sagging.

Christ. That was a long name.

He stumbled closer to the mirror, and tilted his head to the side as he translated the script. *S. U.* double letters...more double letters. He turned back to the natural-edged hardwood table that was his dining table, kitchen prep, spellcasting, office desk and anything else he thought to use it for. He grabbed the pencil and notepad, then turned back to the mirror.

S.U.L.L... He jotted down the letters, gaze flicking between the notepad and the mirror, until he was sure he'd gotten it right—because he sure as hell couldn't get this wrong. Of course, it would be much easier if the Ancestors would try scripting their messages in English, and not in a language that hadn't been spoken in seven hundred years.

He held the paper in front of him and closely compared the lettering. Yep, he was right.

It was damn long name.

Sullivan Timmerman.

Dave's lips tightened. So what was Timmerman's crime?

He removed the sunglasses he always wore and took a deep breath.

"Sullivan Timmerman."

Bright light lanced his vision, and then all of a sudden he could see not his rock-walled apartment beneath his tattoo parlor, but a dark alley instead, as he gazed through Timmerman's eyes. He gazed down at the body he knelt over, and removed the blade from the man's heart. Dave watched as gloved hands picked up the limp right wrist and used the intricately carved blade to incise a rough X into the skin, and held a— Dave squinted—a horn?

Timmerman drained some blood into the horn and— Dave's stomach heaved as the killer drank the blood. He couldn't hear the words that were uttered, but the X on the wrist turned an inky black—and then Dave's vision went dark, and he blinked, his vision clearing to reveal his dim apartment.

What the—how had Timmerman kicked him out? He was usually able to piggyback on the vision of the killer until he could identify his location. This time, though, Timmerman had consumed the blood, said a few words and then blocked him.

Dave pressed his lips together. It was easy to see the witch was using dark magic, and he'd taken a life. No wonder the Ancestors had assigned him a new target.

Well, tracking the damned was part of his job, and he was good at it. He'd start looking—right after he'd patched himself up. He winced as he looked down at the brand that was already beginning to heal. Damn. It was over his heart, too. He shook his head as he stalked over to his bathroom door. The Ancestors didn't seem to care where he got the message, as long as he got it. Well, he'd received it, loud and clear.

He had a witch to kill.

Sully Timmerman glanced cautiously about the schoolroom.

"Relax, Sully. The kids are having their lunch outside," Jenny Forsyth said with a smile as she set out test papers on the students' desks.

"The day I relax is the day I get caught," Sully said, then smiled as she leaned her hip against the teacher's desk. "How are the munchkins?"

Jenny smiled. "They're good, right now. They don't know they have a math test this afternoon."

Sully grinned. "You are such a cruel woman."

"And you love it." Jenny put the paper on the last desk, then strolled toward the front of the classroom. "How is work going?"

Sully nodded. "It's slowly picking up. I have a delivery in the car for the diner, and it looks like the mayor's wife wants a new set of cutlery for their anniversary."

"Cutlery? For an anniversary?"

"Twenty-five years, silver." Sully shrugged. "Hey, it's an order, so I'm happy." Being a cutler was a dying art. There were so many cheaper options for pretty cutlery in a home, but Sully's reputation as a master cutler was finally beginning to bring in some new business, and now that she had a website, she was getting orders coming in from all over the place. She glanced at her watch and winced. "I'd better get going. I want to get Lucy in between the lunch and dinner rush."

She picked up her satchel, and the not-so-subtle

clink reminded her of the unofficial delivery in her bag. "Oops, nearly forgot."

She pulled the heavy cloth bag out of her satchel, and set it down on Jenny's desk with a dull chink. "Better find a good place for this lot."

Jenny's eyebrows rose as she undid the drawstring and peered inside. She whistled. "Wow. That is a lot of silver dollars. That will help quite a few families," she said quietly. She lifted her gaze to Sully's. "You take a big risk, you know."

Sully shrugged. "Hey, every little bit counts, right? It's not much, but if it helps, than that's the main thing." She was satisfied with this particular delivery. She'd counterfeited over two thousand dollars, this time, and that bag contained only about half that. Jenny would make sure it got to those who most needed it. This null community was struggling, more so than most, and if the offcuts from the pieces she made could help put food on the table for some of these people, then the risk was worth it. She pulled her strap up over her shoulder as the school bell chimed outside, signaling the end of the lunch play period. "Now, hide it, or we'll both be in trouble."

Jenny opened her desk drawer and dropped the bag inside as the door to the classroom burst open, and her students swarmed inside. Their eyes brightened when they saw Sully, and she was nearly bowled over when the twenty or so seven-year-olds rushed to her. She hugged as many as she could as she made her way through the throng to the door.

"Hey, Sully, you want to join us next month for the school fete?" Jenny called.

The school fete was scheduled to coincide with the Harvest Moon Festival. Sully turned as the kids

cheered, and she folded her arms and frowned. "I don't
know. Is it worth it, Noah?" she looked at the young
red-haired boy, who nodded, his blue eyes bright. Noah's mother, Susanne, was another of Sully's friends.

"It is, Sully. We've got rides and *donkeys*."

Sully's eyebrows rose. "Donkeys?" She glanced over
at Jenny.

"Petting zoo," Jenny explained. She leaned closer.
"Jacob will be there, too."

Sully shot her friend an exasperated look. Jenny had
been trying to fix her up with her brother since she'd
moved to Serenity Cove, and to date Sully had successfully avoided the hookup. Jacob was nice—good-
looking, too, but she just wasn't interested. In anyone.
She turned back to Noah.

"Donkeys, huh? Oh, well, I'll have to come for that."
She winked at him. "Tell your mom hi from me." She
waved to the kids as she closed the door behind her,
grinning. A day surrounded by nulls? Yes, please.

She strode out of the two-story building that was elementary, middle and high school to the resident null
community, and over to her beat-up sky blue station
wagon. She sat in the driver's seat for a moment, enjoying the peace, the quiet. All the kids were back in
class, but she was still close enough she was affected
by their presence.

She closed her eyes. She was surrounded by…noth-
ing. It was so beautiful. Dark. Silent. Peaceful. It was
the absence, the void, that embraced her, and she loved
it. She knew most witches avoided nulls like a hex, but
she found there was a tranquility in their presence that
she couldn't find anywhere else.

She opened her eyes, and shored up her shields, making sure that there were no cracks, no fractures in her

defenses. When she was satisfied her mental walls were strong, and no light could cut through, she started her engine and drove the ten minutes into Serenity Cove.

She pulled the box out from the back of her car, lifting the tailgate with her hip. She didn't bother winding up the window or locking it. Anybody with half a mind to steal her car must be desperate, and welcome to it. Besides, everyone in town knew this was her car, and you didn't steal from a witch. The resulting curse wasn't worth it.

She walked up the steps to the Brewhaus Diner, and her flip-flops made a smacking sound on the veranda. She pushed through the door and the tinkling sound of the bell above the door brought an almost instinctive response as she stepped inside. She put a smile on her face as she ignored muffled emotions knocking at her protective walls.

Cheryl Conners, the waitress, was hiding her hurt that Sheriff Clinton was absorbed in his phone and not her. Sheriff Clinton was worried—but that seemed to be his default setting. Harold's gout was troubling him, Graham, the cook, was tired and his feet hurt, Mrs. Peterson was fighting off a strong cold, and Lucy—

Sully halted at the diner counter. Lucy wasn't happy. No, she was…heartbroken. She couldn't see the woman, but she could feel her pain—and that was with her shields up.

She placed the box on the counter and looked over at Cheryl as the waitress walked over to her.

"I'm here to see Lucy," Sully said softly. She glanced toward the swing door that led to the kitchen and the office beyond. "Is she okay?"

Cheryl shook her head. "She got some bad news."

She lifted her chin in the direction of the sheriff. "They found Gary's body last night."

Sully gasped, then lifted her hand to cover her mouth. "Oh, no."

Gary Adler was the coach over at the null comprehensive school, and Lucy's longtime boyfriend. No wonder the woman emitted the feel of devastation.

Sully patted the box on the counter. "Look, I'll leave these here, we can talk about sorting stuff out later. She's got enough on her plate, tell her not to worry about this. We can talk when she's ready, but don't stress over it." She adjusted the strap of her bag on her shoulder. "When is the funeral?"

"Won't be for a few days, yet," Sheriff Clinton said, glancing up from his phone. "We've got to wait for the autopsy."

Sully nodded. Gary had watched what he ate, exercised regularly, and apart from that one Christmas festival, didn't drink much. She wasn't aware of him suffering from any illness. They'd have to do an autopsy to find out what had made a relatively healthy man drop dead.

"Any ideas what the cause was?" she asked the sheriff.

He grimaced. "We're guessing it was the stab wound to the heart that did it."

Cheryl's jaw dropped. "What?"

Sully's eyes widened. "Are you saying he was murdered?"

"Well, it didn't look like he fell on the knife, or stabbed himself," the sheriff commented dryly.

"Oh, no, poor Lucy," Sully murmured. "I'll go home and put together a tea for her." She nodded to herself. "I should go visit with Gary's mother, too." Gary's mother lived in a tiny cottage on the northern tip of the seaside town, along with the bulk of the null community. "She'll be devastated."

Sheriff Clinton nodded. "Yeah. I'm sure Mary Anne would appreciate a visit, but I don't think a tea will help her."

Sully smiled sadly. "Not in the usual way, but herbs can still affect a Null, just like any other person, and there's always a little comfort to be found in a shared brew."

She waved briefly to the sheriff and Cheryl, and was nearly at the door when she snapped her fingers. She walked back over to Mrs. Peterson, and gently placed her hand over the older woman's.

"How are you, Mrs. Peterson?" she asked loudly so the woman could hear.

"What's that, dear?" Mrs. Peterson leaned forward.

"I said, how are you?" Sully said as loud as she could without shouting at the woman.

She opened her shield a crack and pulled in some of the pain she could sense in the swollen knuckles, and fed some warmth through in return, laced with a little calm.

The older woman's face creased like a scrunched-up piece of paper when she smiled up at Sully.

"I'm doing well, Sully," she said in her wavery voice.

"You're looking nice today. I like your dress," Sully said, gently patting the back of the woman's hand. She could already sense the easing of tension in the old woman as her arthritic pain subsided.

"What mess?" Mrs. Peterson glanced down in confusion at the table.

"Your *dress*," Sully repeated. "I like your dress." Pity

she couldn't do anything about the woman's hearing—but she was an empath witch, not a god.

"Oh, thank you, dear," Mrs. Peterson said, and her face scrunched up even further as her smile broadened.

Sully nodded and winked, then turned in the direction of the door, cradling her hand on the top of her satchel. She closed her mental walls, ensuring nothing else leaked in she wasn't ready for. She walked on toward the door and waved at Harold when he signaled her. "Don't worry, I'll bring you something back later, too, Harold." She wagged a finger at him. "But you really do need to lay off the shellfish."

She pushed through the door, her smile tightening as the pain in her hand throbbed. Poor Mrs. Peterson. That really was a painful condition.

She skipped down the steps and dusted her hands as she walked to her car. To anyone else it looked like she was shaking black pepper off her hands as she discarded the pain she'd drawn in from Mrs. Peterson.

She considered the teas she'd make for Lucy and Mary Anne Adler as she climbed into her car. Lemon balm, linden and motherwort, she decided. They each had a calming effect, and the motherwort would be especially helpful with the heartache and grief. She waited for a motorcycle to turn across the intersection in front of her, and then pulled out. She sighed. Poor Gary. Murdered. Who would do such a thing?

Chapter 2

Dave pulled his motorbike into a spot on Main Street, and slid his helmet off his head. He looked around. So this was Serenity Cove, huh? The town was picture-postcard quaint. Victorian cottages, cute little boutiques and stores, and lots of white picket fences and ornate trim. Lots and lots. This place looked so damned sweet, he could feel a toothache coming on.

There were a few people wandering around. Admittedly, he thought there'd be more. It was summer and Serenity Cove had a fishing marina, nice little beaches—if his online searches could be trusted—but for some reason there wasn't the usual vacationers drifting around with beet-red sunburns and sarongs. A local bar also seemed to be missing from the scene. He eyed the diner across the street. In lieu of a bar to visit and source information, this place would have to do. Maybe someone in there could tell him where the bar was—after he got some intel on Sullivan Timmerman.

He swung his leg over the bike and placed his helmet over the dash and ignition, uttering a simple security spell. It never paid to mess with a witch's stuff.

It had been surprisingly easy to track down the witch. The guy had a website, for crying out loud. It was obviously a front, though. A cutler? He'd never heard of the trade. Most people just went to the store and bought their cutlery. Who would have a set made?

He crossed the street and entered the diner, the tinkling of the bell over the door causing the patrons to look up. He didn't remove his sunglasses, but then he didn't have a problem seeing inside. An older man, an even older lady and—oh, good. A sheriff. Dave sighed. He wasn't sure if it was the bike leathers, or the tattoos, but the law always seemed to want to chat with him.

He strolled down to the opposite end of the diner counter and slid onto a stool. The solitary waitress bustled over to him, a smile on her face. Dave smiled back. He read her name tag. Cheryl.

"Hey, stranger, can I get you something?" She leaned a hand on the counter and gave him a wink.

He grinned as he removed his gloves. "That depends, Cheryl." Her smile broadened at his use of her name. "What can you recommend?" He kept his tone light and flirtatious, and out of the corner of his eye he saw the sheriff lift his gaze from his phone.

She folded her arms on the counter and leaned forward. "Well," she said, drawing the word out slowly. "I've just put a fresh pot of coffee on, so I haven't had a chance to burn it, yet, and the peach pie is pretty good."

He nodded. "I'll take that. For starters," He winked

back at her. She was pretty, she was nice and liked to flirt. Serenity Cove might be all right, after all.

"What brings you to Serenity Cove?" The sheriff put his phone away and directed his full attention to him. His tone was casual, conversational, but the look in the man's eyes was anything but.

"I'm looking for someone," Dave replied as Cheryl placed a plate in front of him. She reached for the coffee carafe and poured him a cup, and he took care not to touch anything until she was finished. He waved away the cream and sugar she offered.

"Who?" the sheriff asked. This time his tone wasn't so casual or conversational.

"Tyler," Cheryl chided. "Be nice to our visitor."

"No, it's okay," Dave said. If there had been a murder, this officer would know about it—had to, in a place as small as Serenity Cove. He needed information from the man, and he didn't want to seem threatening or dangerous, because that would lead to an entirely different conversation.

"I'm looking for a friend," Dave said, flashing a smile at the sheriff in an effort to appear friendly. "I was in the area, so I thought I'd catch up."

"You have a friend?" the older man sitting at a booth near the door piped up. "Here?"

Dave kept his face impassive. Was the guy surprised at the idea of him having a friend in Serenity Cove or having a friend at all? "Yeah."

"Who?" Cheryl asked as she leaned against the counter. She didn't bother to hide her curiosity.

"Sullivan Timmerman."

Cheryl's eyes widened. "You know Sully?" her expression was incredulous as she looked him up and down.

"How do you know Sully?" the sheriff asked, his brow dipping.

Sully, huh? Dave took a moment to slip a bit of the peach pie into his mouth as he thought about his response. He always had an explanation ready for barflies, but talking with law enforcement required finesse and strategy. He swallowed the mouthful of pie—and Cheryl was right, it was pretty good.

"Are you an old boyfriend?" the older guy in the booth asked.

Dave coughed into the coffee mug he held to his lips. Boyfriend? Sullivan Timmerman had boyfriends?

"We went to school together," he responded cautiously once he'd cleared his throat. He hoped to hell Timmerman hadn't gone to school around here, although the information he'd found online suggested probably not. Timmerman had set up his business four years ago, but he hadn't been able to find any mention of the guy in the local schools' hall of fame lists for athletics or other clubs.

"Did you date?" Cheryl asked, waggling her eyebrows.

"Uh…" He ate some more pie as he thought of an appropriate response.

"What's that about Sully?" the old lady called out, cupping her hand to her ear.

"This guy used to date Sully," the guy in the booth yelled back.

"Why do you hate Sully?" the woman asked, horrified.

Dave blinked as Cheryl leaned over the counter. "Date, Mrs. Peterson. *Date.*"

"Oh." The old woman looked him up and down, then raised her eyebrows. "You don't say."

"You just missed her," Cheryl told him, then waved toward the door. "She left about five minutes ago."

Her. *Her.* He dipped his head for a moment. Phew. Then he frowned. He'd somehow felt a masculine energy in his vision and had assumed he was looking for a man. In his line of work, he couldn't rest on assumptions. The radio on the sheriff's hip squawked, and the man sighed as he levered himself off the chair.

"Gotta go." He grabbed his hat off the seat next to him and put it on his head. "How long are you intending to stay in Serenity Cove?" he asked Dave.

Dave waved a hand. "Oh, I'm only passing through." This kind of job never took long.

The sheriff nodded, satisfied, then turned to walk out the door.

"Bye, Tyler," Cheryl called. The sheriff didn't turn back, but lifted his hand in a casual wave of farewell. Dave caught the fleeting look of disappointment on her face before she masked it with a smile. "So, you used to date Sully, huh?"

Wow. These people were good. He bet that by the time he got back to his bike, he and this Sully would be in a serious, angst-ridden relationship. Which could work for him, really.

"Yeah," he said, folding his arms on the table and leaning forward conspiratorially. "I want to surprise her, though. Uh, do you know where I can find her?" He sent a compulsion spell in Cheryl's direction.

"She lives out at Crescent Head, north end, overlooking Driftwood Beach," Cheryl responded automatically, then blinked.

"Thanks." Dave scooped up the last of his pie, and nodded farewell as he rose from his seat. He donned his gloves and waved politely to the older patrons as he passed them.

He halted outside the diner. Two youths were checking out his bike. One of them even had the audacity to reach for the handlebars and pretend to steer. He frowned. His security spell should have knocked the kid off his feet. He flicked his fingers at him, but encountered...nothing. He frowned and tried to again.

Nothing.

He grimaced. Great. Nulls. He glanced about. Where there was one—or in this case, two—there were always more. Hopefully, though, it wouldn't interfere with what he had to do.

He sauntered across the street, and the teens took off as soon as they noticed him. He might not be able to cast a spell on them, but at least he could still look fierce.

Good. Because he had a witch to hunt.

Sully ignored the sparks as she ground the steel against the wheel. She turned the arrowhead slowly, shifting now and then to avoid smoothing the sharp angles she'd hammered into the steel. She pulled back, lifting the arrowhead to the light. Just a little more off there...

She held it back to the wheel and evened out the side, sliding the steel across the spinning wheel. When she was satisfied, she took her foot off the pedal and switched off the grinder.

She crossed over to the forge she'd made out of a soup can, sand and plaster. She'd turned the torch on a little while ago, so it was now ready for her. Using pliers, she carefully placed the arrowhead inside the forge, and then waited for it to glow. She stepped back and lifted her mask to take a sip of water from the glass on the shed sill. It was hot in the shed, and she was sweating profusely.

It didn't take too long before the arrowhead was glowing. She reached in with the pliers, and carefully dunked it into her bucket of oil, pausing for a long moment before withdrawing it.

Sully smiled. The arrowhead was in the square-headed bodkin style. Sure, the broadhead arrows were sharper and caused more damage, but every now and then it was a nice change to go for a classic shape. Besides, it had worked for the Vikings, so it wasn't completely useless. And it was exactly what Trey Mackie wanted—he wanted to try hunting just like his computer game avatar did. When the set of arrows were completed, she'd have to have a word with him about aiming at folks. She didn't make weapons for "fun". Weapons weren't toys. She'd bespell them, but she also wanted to make sure the youth used them responsibly.

She placed the arrowhead on the bench next to the other four she'd made that day. Damn, she must reek. She'd go for a quick dip before heading out to see Mary Anne. She shut down the torch on the forge and cleaned up, then quickly strode across her back garden to her cottage. Within minutes she'd donned a bikini, then threw on a peasant-style top and her long, flowing skirt. She didn't bother to fasten the belt that already twined through the loops on her skirt. The loose clothes were her stock standard wardrobe, especially for summer. She grabbed a ratty old towel, slipped her feet into her flip-flops and trotted to the end of her street. A path led from there to the stairs at the top of the cliff, and then down to the beach below. She paused at the grassy verge at the top of the stairs and took a moment to tilt her head back and let the sun shine down on her. This was one of her favorite spots, offering a one-hundred-and-eighty-degree view of the ocean. She could feel the kiss of a breeze against her skin, the heat of the sun as it beat down on her. The smell of salt and grass and the summer blossoms in her garden… The waves crashing on the beach below. This was one of her recharge places, where she could give herself up to elements of nature and restore her own energy. She gazed out at the vista. Dark clouds were gathering on the horizon. Whether a storm was coming, or about to pass, she couldn't tell. She sighed and then headed for the stairs.

Driftwood Beach was pretty much deserted. She saw a man walking his dog down the other end, but it looked like he was at the end of his walk, rather than the start. She was the only other person to walk across the sands. Most folks preferred the more sheltered Crescent Beach for a swim, just on the other side of the headland. Occasionally surfers would venture this far north out of town, but the surf at Caves' Beach was much better. She hadn't necessarily been looking for a private beach when she settled here at Crescent Head, it had just worked out that way. And she loved it. The less people she had to deal with, the better.

The surf was crisp and cool, exactly what she needed. The water embraced her, shielded her. She couldn't feel when she was fully immersed in the water. It was just her and the deep void, the occasional sea creature and strands of seaweed that always startled her into thinking it was a shark. For some reason, though, she was never bothered by the predators of the sea. No matter how far she swam out, it was like the sea provided a shelter for her. Buoyant, enveloping…peaceful. She let herself go, relaxed her mental shields and surrendered to utter unguarded enjoyment. This was as good as being surrounded by nulls, and the void their presence created.

After diving beneath a couple of waves she strode out of the water, lifting her knees so she could walk faster. Within minutes she'd patted herself dry, pulled her clothes on over the top of her swimsuit and fastened her belt. She stood on the beach, looking out over the water. By now it was late afternoon. She'd like to stay a little longer, maybe watch the sunset, but she'd promised teas for Lucy and Mrs. Peterson, and Harold something for his gout. She decided she'd take a double-prong attack with Harold. Something to rub on his toe for instant comfort and a tea to start working from the inside.

She remained where she was and closed her eyes. She mentally pictured her shutters rolling down to shield her mind. As she was going to be visiting grief-stricken women, she added a couple of extra layers to ensure she was protected from the waves of heartbreak she'd encounter. Once Sully was sure she could stand calmly in a room with them both and not crumble to the floor, curl into the fetal position and sob at the overwhelming pain, she opened her eyes.

A movement in the corner of her vision made her turn her head. A guy was walking along the beach. No, walking was too gentle a word. He was striding purposefully, his gait even and rhythmic. His broad shoulders moved with each step he took, like the slinky stalk of a predatory big cat. Graceful. That's what it was. Little puffs of sand rose at each step, catching in the breeze to dance a little before falling back to the beach. The man moved with a physical grace that suggested he was used to moving, with an added strength that made him look dangerous.

And way sexy. Sully took a moment to enjoy the

view. He was built. Like, stripper-at-a-bachelorette-party built, with broad shoulders and lean hips, and thighs that looked... Her lips curled inward. Strong. Despite the heat, the man wore leather pants, boots and a black leather jacket over what she hoped was a T-shirt, for his sake. His hair was cropped short, and the sunglasses hid his eyes. She briefly wondered if he looked just as good out of them as in them. She'd once dated a guy, Marty, who looked hot in his shades, but when he'd removed them he'd revealed his sunken eyes, the dark shadows beneath and the enlarged pupils of a drug addict—which was never a good combination when mixed with his witch talents—such as they were.

Sully shook her head as she turned her back on the leather-clad man. Cute, but she wasn't interested. She sure knew how to pick 'em, as her grandmother would say. Marty was the reason she'd moved clear across the country and settled herself in a Null-saturated area. Never trust a guy who hides his eyes.

She scooped up her flip-flops and started to trudge along the waterline in the opposite direction, toward the timber stairs that hugged the cliff and led to the cliff-top walk.

She normally cut her herbs at either sunrise or sunset, when they were most potent. She'd have to hurry so she could collect all the ingredients for the teas she planned to make for her patients. Clients. Whatever you wanted to call them.

A soft breeze, warm and whispery, teased at the hem of her skirt. She grasped some of the fabric in her hand, lifting the skirt as she waded through the shallows, her lips curving at the rhythmic, refreshing chill of the waves washing over her feet.

"Sullivan Timmerman!"

Sully frowned at the sound of her name and glanced over her shoulder. The man in black was closer to her, his expression—well, it didn't look flirty or friendly. No, he looked determined.

"What?"

"Are you Sullivan Timmerman?" the man asked again, and Sully nodded, although the movement was more a cautious dip of her head. She halted, but still looked over her shoulder at him, ready to bolt if need be. At this distance, though, she could see more of his face. He was unshaven, but not unkempt. The dusting of a beard along his jawline was closely trimmed, but it didn't hide the strong line of his jaw, or the sculpted shape of his lips. His cheekbones were balanced, his sunglasses revealing tiny lines at the corners of his eyes that could be from laughter, or scowling, she had no idea. Although she couldn't see his eyes, she could feel his stare boring into her.

There was an intensity about this man, a focus, that sparked a flare of attraction, yet the overwhelming impression she got was one of danger. She instinctively bolstered her shields with more protection. Whatever this guy was going through, she didn't want to feel it.

And yet…she knew she'd never seen this man, but there was something familiar about him, something she couldn't quite put her finger on, but it was intuitive, a bone-deep recognition she couldn't quite fathom.

"Uh, yes," she answered. She turned to face him warily. "Who wants to know?"

The man raised both of his arms out from his sides, palms up, fingers curled slightly. He started to murmur in a low voice, and it took Sully a moment to realize he was talking in the Old Language. She frowned as she struggled to decipher his words.

"…for your dark crimes, and the Ancestors call upon your return to the Other Realm, to a place of execution—"

Sully's eyes widened in shock. Holy crap. A memory, lessons long since learned and nearly forgotten, fluttered in her mind, but it was dread that hit her, followed by comprehension.

"—until you are dead. May the Ancestors have mercy upon your soul."

His wrists rolled as he brought his arms around in front, toward her, and still clutching her flip-flops, she brought her own arms up, crossing them in front of her chest to brace against the magical blast that rolled over her.

Her feet created long burrows in the sand as she was pushed back under the force—a force that should have crushed her, but was mostly deflected by her shields.

The man blinked when he realized she remained standing.

"What the—?" Sully gaped at him, stunned dismay warring with anger. The Witch Hunter. He was here. Now. For *her*.

The man tilted his head. "Hmm." He raised his arms again, and Sully narrowed her eyes.

"Oh, no you don't." She refused to be at another man's mercy. She summoned her own magic, drawing from deep within and hurling her own cloud of badassery in his direction. Their powers met with a thunderous clap. Sully's shields coalesced into swirling colors as his magic rolled over her safeguards, and she twisted, guiding the force around and beyond her. Away from her.

Holy capital H.C. Crap. The Witch Hunter. One of the most powerful witches in existence, and he wanted to return her to the Other Realm.

She sidestepped another supernatural blast, deflecting it right back at him. He grunted as it hit him, sending him stumbling for a few steps. It gave her enough of a respite to bolster up her shields. She didn't have the juice to kill him—and she couldn't begin to fathom the karma that would come from killing the Witch Hunter—but she might be able hold him off long enough to—*oh, crap.*

It seemed he'd figured he couldn't pierce her shields, and had decided a more direct approach was in order. He roared something that could have been a battle cry in the Old Language—or perhaps a curse word—then lowered his head and charged straight at her.

Sully dipped to the side and started to run, but he flung out his arm and caught her around the knees. She hit the sand hard. She tried to wriggle away as he pulled her toward him.

Chapter 3

Dave swore as the witch flung a handful of sand in his face. What the—how the hell was Timmerman so damn strong? She'd shaken off his initial blast like a dog shaking off water.

She muttered something, and then her bare foot connected with his chest, sending him flying. A percussion incantation. Damn it. He flung another blast in her direction, but saw the sparks as it rolled over the armor she'd shielded herself with. Any other time he'd admit to being impressed, but right now he was annoyed. He had a duty to perform, and her impressive damn barriers were preventing him from doing it.

He murmured a spell, raising his hands, fingers splayed, satisfied when he felt the erosion spell spread over her shield like a wave of acid, eroding her safeguards.

She flinched, her face paling, and she murmured

something. A wall of sand rose around him, enclosing him. He uttered a quick spell, and the sand erupted away from him.

A flip-flop slapped him in the face. His head whipped back at the sting. He blinked, shaking his head, then focused on his—where the hell did she go?

The beach was empty. He narrowed his eyes, scanning the sand. There. His lips curved. The damn witch had covered herself with an unseen spell, but that didn't mean she didn't leave tracks.

He saw the footprints and the little puffs of sand as she ran up the beach. He took off after her. He gritted his teeth. He hated running in sand. It always felt like it was clawing at you, pulling you back, slowing you down. He angled across the wet sand, where it was firmer under foot, then growled. *Screw it.*

He raised his hand toward her, murmuring a restraining spell, and a lariat of power lashed from his hand, encircling his target. He heard her surprised cry when he yanked her back. The sand was forming thrashing mounds, until finally she couldn't hold her invisibility *and* fight off his magical restraint, and her concealment gave way to show the struggling woman as he dragged her toward him.

A wave of water edged around his boots. Damn it. His favorite boots were getting a bath in salt water.

He grasped her thighs, and she roared—*roared* at him, her fist connecting with his jaw. His teeth snapped, and he blinked, then jerked to avoid the feet that kicked uncomfortably close to his groin. He tugged her farther along the sand.

"Sullivan Timmerman," he panted, straddling her thighs to keep her from turning him into a eunuch. "You have been found guilty of—"

He closed his eyes instinctively as her hand flashed toward him, catching him on the cheek in an open-handed, stinging slap. By the time he focused again, she held a short but wickedly sharp blade in each hand, one pointed at his groin, the other against his throat.

He froze, and his eyebrows rose. "Well, aren't you full of surprises?" That was an understatement. The woman had deflected his power with a skill he hadn't seen before, and now had him at a slight disadvantage. Only slight, though. He outweighed, outmuscled and outpowered her. If outpowered was a thing.

"This is a little extreme for some coins, don't you think?" she panted up at him.

He frowned. "What?" Coins? What? The memory of her victim, the man in the alley with the *X* carved in his flesh…the draining of his blood. The blade in his chest…he didn't recall seeing any money. What the hell did all that have to do with coins?

"What the hell do the Ancestors have against the nulls?" she demanded.

His frown deepened. What the—? He was having trouble keeping up with the conversation. And why were they even having this conversation? Was she completely mad? Did she seriously not comprehend the damage she'd done—to an innocent, to the balance of nature itself? He'd never really had a witch withstand justice before, at least, not long enough to challenge the Ancestors. The blade at his neck pressed against his skin just a little harder.

"Get off me. Now." Her blue eyes glared at him, and her slightly lopsided mouth formed a tight pout. Her hair hung in a tangled curtain behind her, dark and wet and…okay, maybe a little bit more than mildly sexy. She was attractive, slim yet curvy beneath him. Her cotton top clung to the wet triangles of her red bikini, and despite the toned strength of her arms and the thighs he straddled, she still had a softness about her that would have had him buying her a drink in a bar under different circumstances. Very different. Like, without the execution directive.

Maybe that was one of the reasons this woman was so damn dangerous. She looked like some sexy beach goddess, but he'd seen the blade in the man's heart, the carving on his wrist, and...ugh. His eyes flicked to those pouty little lips. She'd drunk his blood. She'd killed a human. And it hadn't been in self-defense. It hadn't been to protect others. It had been calculated and cruel. It was intentional harm to an innocent, to the personal benefit of the witch. He had no idea *why* she'd killed the man, or why she'd murdered in the manner she had, but he was the enforcer, his authority was recognized by Reform society and by the witch population. No matter how damn smoking hot sexy the witch was, she'd committed a crime against nature, against all of witchery, and she had to be punished.

He held up his hands, palms out, in a nonthreatening manner as he rose. She shuffled out from beneath him, her daggers still held in a guarded, defensive position. He eyed her outfit. Loose sleeves, loose skirt—where the hell had she hidden those blades?

He let her back up a little. She thought she now had the upper hand. She was so wrong, but for now he'd let her go with it.

"This is not fair," she hissed at him as she took another step backward.

His eyebrows rose. "Not fair? Do you think I haven't heard that before?"

She shook her head, frowning at him. "What I did—

sure, some might consider it a crime, but I was doing it for the greater good."

He shook his head. "Yeah, I've heard that before, too."

"Damn it, I mean it. There was no harm done!"

"No harm?" he repeated, incredulous. His brows dipped. "Are you kidding me? You think that what you did was *harmless*?"

"I was doing a service for the community," she snapped back at him.

"A service." His lips tightened, and he had to look away for a brief moment. Her words sparked a flare of anger in him that he didn't normally let himself feel. "You want to talk service? I live my life in service, and what you did—" he wagged a finger at her. "You should be ashamed. You've brought darkness to all of witchery for your actions."

Her eyebrows rose. "Darkness? To all of witchery? Wow. They've really set the bar low, then, haven't they? What I did, and how it affects others, should have no bearing whatsoever on all of witchery. For the Ancestors to call upon the Witch Hunter over such a trifling matter—that's extreme."

He gaped at her. She talked about murder so callously, as though it was of such little consequence. He couldn't begin to imagine the damage this woman could do if she wasn't stopped.

He took a step forward, and she shifted, angling the blades toward him. "I can defend every damn thing I've done," she said in a low voice.

Disappointment, hot and sickening, roiled through him. "You defend the indefensible," he said. "And for that, the Ancestors call you to—"

He dived for her, thigh muscles bunching as he

launched himself at her. He caught her hands and raised them above her head as he tackled her to the ground. Her breath left her in a grunt as she hit the sand. He spread his body over hers, using his weight to anchor her beneath him.

That's when it hit him. It was as though their powers met and coalesced in a sensory explosion. Her scent, salty and sweet, clouded his mind, as though blanketing him in an awareness of the woman beneath him. Her hair, wet and dark, still showed the odd strand of burnished gold. Her skin, smooth and warm, her eyes so blue and stormy, and her mouth—a delicate, lopsided pout that drew his attention.

For a moment, they both halted, staring at each other. Her mouth opened, and her expression showed her confusion, her surprise. His gaze dropped down to her lips, and he could hear his heartbeat throbbing in his ears— or was it her heartbeat? He couldn't tell. He lifted his stare to hers, dazed. He blinked—and time snapped its fingers, speeding up through the last few moments, folding itself over so that he felt a little unbalanced, a little bereft and a whole lot shaken.

She was supposed to be a hit, damn it. As though she was also catching up to speed—or perhaps she hadn't felt whatever the hell that was—the woman beneath him frowned up at him and started to struggle again.

She was surprisingly strong, and tried to free her arms, those blades glinting in the light from the setting sun. His grasp tightened on her wrists until she whimpered slightly and released her hold on the short daggers.

He stared down at her. Her cheeks were flushed, her blue eyes bright with outrage and perhaps a tiny bit of fear. Her chest was heaving beneath his, her breasts brushing against his pecs. His legs were tangled with hers, and as his gaze drifted down her body, he saw the fabric of her skirt had hiked up in the struggle, revealing a shapely calf and toned thigh. He'd have to be a dead man not to find the woman attractive, and it was with a heavy heart that he returned his gaze to hers.

She was young. Passionate. Highly skilled. What a waste of a witch. She could have done so much good, and yet she'd acted against nature, against humanity—the vulnerable people they were charged to protect from the shadow breeds.

"Please, don't," she whispered, shaking her head.

"I have to," he told her quietly. "This brings me no joy."

Her pouty lips trembled, and she nodded. "I know."

He blinked at the unexpected concession from the witch he was about to kill. He eyed her face, the resignation in her expression, despite the resistance in her eyes. He wished... He shut that thought down. That way led to madness. Wishes were for fools. His lips firmed, and he sucked in a breath.

"The Ancestors call upon your return to—"

"The Other Realm, yeah, I know the drill," she said. "I remember the First Degree classes. Why don't we skip the speech and get to it?"

He frowned. She had just fought him off with skill and power of an elder, she'd almost gotten away from him, had pulled a knife—two, actually—on him, and now she wanted him to hurry up and kill her. This woman was doing his head in.

"Why are you suddenly so eager to die?" He dipped his head to gaze directly into her eyes, despite his sunglasses. Admittedly, this was possibly the most conversation he'd ever had with one of his hits, but he couldn't help it. She was an intriguing package of contradictions.

"I just realized that death isn't all bad," she said softly, lifting her chin.

He tilted his head, surprised. "You do realize that being summoned to the Other Realm is kind of...*bad*." It was hell—at least, a witch's version of it. Being summoned by the Ancestors who watched from beyond the veil was most definitely not good. The Ancestors had been there long enough to know how to tailor punishment to an excruciating degree for the individual witch who dared to act contrary to the beliefs and morality of the universal covens.

Her expression softened into one of sadness, a weariness that was a stark contrast to the young, vibrant woman she'd seemed just a short while ago as she'd tried to kick his ass.

"I'm ready."

He hesitated. He didn't often come across a target resigned and accepting of their fate. This particular hit was proving a first on many fronts. He nodded. "Okay, then." His frown deepened. After holding a blade to his balls, this witch was proving to be quite civil.

He moved back, just a little bit, one hand still grasping both of her wrists as he pulled his other hand back, almost as though to strike. "May the Ancestors have mercy upon your soul."

He summoned his inherited powers and sparks flickered at his fingertips.

Heat blazed across his chest. He cried out in pain and grasped his left pec as he rolled off her. He blinked furiously, trying to catch his breath.

What was happening? What the *hell* was—?

"Argh," he growled as the name branded on his chest

flared to life. He shook his head. No. No, this can't be happening. She's here, he was about—

He winced as the wound blistered anew, and pulled at his T-shirt, tearing the fabric from neck to hem. He grunted when the cloth pulled away from the burn.

The witch on the ground next to him rolled, grabbing one of the blades in the sand before she scrambled to his side. She clasped the dagger in both hands and raised it above her head, poised to bring it down on him.

The pain was blinding, all-consuming, and he couldn't do anything to defend himself. When the ancestral fire was branded into his skin, he was powerless. He stared up at the woman above him, confused. She was here, and yet her name was being rebranded into his flesh.

Another innocent had been killed.

But not by this witch.

The woman started to bring the blade down, but she gasped when she looked down at his body.

Sully dropped the knife, her gaze locked on the Witch Hunter's chest. His T-shirt hung in tatters at his side. His chest was broadly muscled, his skin a light golden tan, his toned torso lined with dark tattoos that looked both beautiful and dangerous, but it was the glowing mark that drew her gaze, and made the sweat break out on her brow as she tried resurrect her shields.

Sullivan Timmerman.

It was written in the Old Language, but she couldn't mistake it.

Her name radiated on his chest, searing through his skin as though borne from a fire within, and the cords of his neck stuck out in stark relief as he tilted his head, growling in pain.

Holy capital H.C. Crap. She was too late.

She sucked in a breath at the hot wave that flashed through her, over her. It was *everywhere*. Pain. Tormented heat. Searing agony. Guilt. Self-loathing. Confusion. Loyalty. So many more emotions, too fast, too ferocious to name, bombarded her. The sensations were excruciating.

The Witch Hunter writhed on the ground, his teeth gritted, until she felt the pain drop from excruciating agony to aggravating throb. He gasped as he rolled over and onto his knees, wheezing slightly.

Sully looked away, mustering all the strength she could from within to shakily layer up some protections, although they were weak and tattered. Holy f—

"Sullivan Timmerman," the man at her side gasped, turning away from her as he removed his sunglasses to stare at the sea.

She eyed him warily. She tried to swallow, but couldn't quite get past the lump in her throat. Her arms hung limply by her side and she trembled all over. It didn't seem to matter, though. The Witch Hunter didn't look like he was talking to her, though. He was on his knees, hands fisted in the sand, and she stared at the back of his head as his chest rose and fell with deep, shuddering breaths. How the hell could the man still be conscious after that experience? Her gut twisted, and she felt shaky and nauseous, and quite frankly wanted to curl up on the sand and pass out.

After a moment he dipped his head, then he slid his sunglasses on. Sully rose to her feet, stumbled on her shaky knees and almost face-planted in the sand when she bent over to scoop up her blades. If he was coming for her again, she was going to fight. He'd obliterated her shields, and it would take her some time to rebuild them, but she could still hit.

Right now, though, all she could feel was him. His pain, his shock, his confusion.

He glanced over his shoulder to her, his brows drawn. "Sullivan Timmerman...?"

This time, his tone was uncertain, and she raised her arms in front of her in a defensive block, blades ready. She didn't bother to answer him. She'd almost gotten herself killed the last time she'd responded.

He shook his head as he rose to his feet. "You're not the right one." Even if she couldn't hear it in his tone, or see it in his face, she could feel the shock reverberating through him, the dismay. The guilt.

Her eyes widened, and she gaped at him. "Are you—? What the—? Holy—." She blinked at him. He'd just attacked her. Nearly killed her. And she wasn't the *right one*? She'd almost *died*. For the briefest of moments, she'd *wanted* to die. She squished that thought down deep, buried it under a fragile barrier.

He drew himself up to his full height, and she could see his wound was already beginning to heal, the lettering darkening to a semblance of what she'd assume would become a tattoo that matched the rest of the markings on his body.

He touched his abdomen and dipped his head. "I have made a grave mistake. My duty is not with you. Please forgive me, Sullivan Timmerman."

His apology was sincere, his gestures faintly noble. Courtly. His earnestness was almost tangible, along with a profound sense of guilt, of sadness and of dismayed shock. And pain.

"For—forgive you?" she responded, her mouth slack. She'd practically begged him to kill her.

Her lips tightened, her eyes narrowed. "Screw you, Witch Hunter."

She backed away from him, then turned and headed toward the cliff stairs. He'd tried to kill her, and normally she wouldn't be turning her back on a man who'd just tried to kill her, but she'd felt his remorse, his guilt. His exhaustion. He wouldn't come after her again.

"I'm so sorry," he called after her. She didn't look back as she flipped him the bird, then realized she still carried her blades. She slid them into the slim-line sheath that formed part of her belt, and it wasn't until she put her foot on the bottom step that she realized she'd left her flip-flops behind.

She glanced back at the beach in frustration, just in time to see the Witch Hunter drop to his knees, then collapse on the sand, his unconscious body an inert dark form on the sand.

Chapter 4

Dave's eyes fluttered open. He frowned. Stars? He blinked. Yep. Stars. A cool breeze—not unpleasant—brushed across him, and he could hear the rhythmic roar of waves. He shifted and groaned. His neck was supported by a mound of sand, but it felt like he'd been lying there for hours. He moved his arms and realized a light cloth covered him. He glanced down. Despite it being sometime in the night, the stars and a glimmer of the moon gave enough light to see a little. He picked at the cloth. A towel?

He sat up, hissing at the pull of skin on his chest. He flicked off the towel. A white patch was taped to his chest. What the—? He peeled back a corner of the bandage and caught a whiff of something disgusting. He scrunched his nose up. Ew. He could smell marigold, aloe vera, maybe jasmine and something else he couldn't quite put his finger on, but whatever it was, it smelled gross. He patted the tape back down. Someone had made him an herbal poultice to help heal his wound and limit infection and inflammation. He could think of only one person in the area that would have the plant knowledge for it, yet he couldn't quite believe she'd do that for him, not after what he'd attempted to do to her. Where was she? He glanced around. He was alone on the beach, with just the waves to keep him company.

He rolled to his knees, then his feet, groaning as the kinks in his neck and back straightened themselves out. He shook out his shoulders. Sleeping on the beach worked only if you were drunk and in the company of a woman. Here, he was neither.

His tattered T-shirt fluttered in the breeze, and he shrugged out of his jacket so he could discard the ruined garment. His mouth tightened. Damn. He'd almost killed her.

He dragged his thumb across his forehead. What the hell happened? He'd struggled to comprehend when his chest had started to burn again. He'd had Sullivan Timmerman right where he wanted her, and had been about to send her across the veil, but then...

It was still so hard to accept, to make sense of. Another innocent had died at the hands of Sullivan Timmerman, yet the woman had been right in front of him at the time, ready to accept her fate. When he'd uttered the name and channeled the killer's vision, he'd seen the latest victim. An older woman, tears running down her face as she'd stared up at him with confusion, horror and pain, and then with shock as the blade had pierced her heart. Once again, the killer had carved that mark on her wrist and used that same horn to capture the woman's blood. And once again, Dave had been booted out of the vision when the killer had consumed the blood and uttered his spell—whatever that damn spell was.

He placed his hand over the dressing. He'd had the wrong person. His stomach clenched, and he had to suck in some deep breaths to stop from throwing up. He'd almost killed an innocent—a crime that would send *him* across the veil to the Ancestors. How could that be?

Sullivan Timmerman wasn't a common name. How could he have gotten it so damn wrong? Guilt, hot and sickening, wrung his gut. The woman had answered his call, and had confirmed her identity—she'd even mentioned something about coins, as though she knew she was guilty of some wrongdoing... He looked down as the towel fluttered in the breeze, then rolled a little along the sand. He reached down and picked it up.

Death isn't all bad.

What the hell did she mean? She was so young, so full of life, so full of power when she'd fought him— the first witch to be able to maintain a defense against him...ever. She was also the first witch to halt him in his tracks, midhit. What the hell was that all about? And yet, when he'd had her down on the sand, it was as if all her fight had left her, and she was ready to cross the veil. He'd nearly killed an innocent witch. How...? What...?

He started to walk across the beach toward the trail at the edge of the dunes that would lead him to where he'd parked his bike. He ducked his head as he trudged through the sand. He'd fought with a woman, for God's sake. He—the guy who inked up women with protective spells against their abusers, who was committed to never hurting an innocent, who believed the women in his life, however fiery and frustrating they could be—

and his mother and sister could be plenty of both—should be safeguarded, whatever the cost.

He stumbled. Hell. He'd tackled the woman. He'd threatened her, dominated her. He was no better than the monsters he hunted.

His toe hit something, and he glanced down. A white flip-flop lay half-buried in the sand.

Hers.

He scooped it up, turning it over to look at it. It was well worn, with dents in the rubber from her heel and the ball of her foot. He sighed as he continued along the beach. He'd have to make it up to her. Somehow. He didn't apologize very often, but words couldn't make up for his transgressions against her. Part of his job as the Witch Hunter was to redress the balance, wherever possible—especially by counteracting the misdeeds of the malefactors. What he'd done today with this Sullivan Timmerman—well, he had some counteracting to do.

After he caught the real Sullivan Timmerman and put an end to these murders.

He crested the last rise and walked over to his bike. He slipped the flip-flop and towel into one of his panniers. He wasn't quite sure where to start. All he'd managed to see was the female victim, an older woman, and what looked like a wooden floor beneath her, and the claw foot of a threadbare sofa.

He straddled his bike, started it and flicked up the kickstand with his heel.

Kill one Sullivan Timmerman, then make it up to the other Sullivan Timmerman. He'd better get busy.

Sully boxed up the teas she'd cut for Lucy and Mary Anne Adler. She realized her hands were trembling, and she curled her fingers over. Tears formed in her eyes. She'd been ready to die.

She blinked, sniffing, as she gathered the boxes and grabbed her satchel. She wasn't going to think about it. Nope. She was going to be a good little witch and completely ignore the ramifications of this afternoon's incident. She wasn't going to think about that moment when his body lay across hers. She should have felt threatened, frightened, but she felt—nope. Not going there.

She hesitated at the front door, gazing out at the sea that reflected the light of the moon and stars. From this point she couldn't see directly down to the beach. She'd have to walk to the edge of the headland to be able to do that.

She wasn't going to walk anywhere near the headland at the moment. What if he was still there?

Well, it would serve him right. She slammed the door closed behind her and stalked over to her car. The guy had tried to kill her.

He was just doing his duty.

Screw duty. The man was the Witch Hunter. She climbed into her car and started the engine, reversing out of the drive. All coven children were taught about the Witch Hunter. Much like the bogeyman, the Witch Hunter was someone to fear, someone who would come after you if you did something wrong. You never knew what the Witch Hunter looked like—only that he was out there, and ready to hunt you down if you so much as hinted at violating the universal laws of the covens. Witchery lore claimed there were Witch Hunters in every generation, chosen by the Ancestors, and assigned with the duty of preserving nature's balance. Only a hunted witch could recognize the Witch Hunter for who he—or she—was.

No wonder he'd seemed "familiar".

She drove down the dark road. Her cottage was the last one in a street of four, with a considerable distance between neighbors. They had no streetlights, and the real estate agent who'd handled the sale had told her to be thankful she had indoor plumbing, a landline and electricity. Cell phone reception kind of sucked, though. With the expanse of the ocean on three sides, the nearest cell tower was quite a distance away. She had to go into town to her shop to get access to the internet, and even there connectivity was a little spotty.

She still couldn't believe it. The Witch Hunter had come after *her*. She shook her head as she turned left onto the coast road. The only crime she committed was a pesky little Reform one, and not one against an individual, a coven, or nature. Why the hell were the Ancestors upset by a little coin-making? Sure, counterfeiting was *slightly* illegal, but it was all to help others, so really they should be proud of her, right? Witches blurred the legal lines often, with the making of potions and toxins, and spells designed to reveal or conceal... but she'd never used nature's power to provoke another to an unlawful act, nor had she sought power through the suffering of others, or personal or financial gain at the risk of another. Those were pretty much the deal breakers with the Ancestors, and as far as she was concerned, she'd done neither.

You're not the right one.

She frowned. The Ancestors had gotten it wrong... she grimaced at the memory of the lettering blazing across the man's chest. That had looked painful. Oh, not the chest. No, the chest had looked damn fine, actually. All those glorious muscles... She shook her head. She was lusting after a guy who'd tried to kill her. She

thought she was better than that, now. That she'd grown
some insight, maybe even some self-respect and dig-
nity. She needed her head examined. Or to get laid. She
preferred…neither. She hadn't had a companion since
she'd left the West Coast and arrived in Serenity Cove
four years ago. If she thought the Witch Hunter was a
long drink of sex on the beach, it was either too long
between lovers, or she really hadn't experienced the personal growth she'd fooled herself into thinking she had.

No, damn it. She'd learned her lesson, and wasn't
prepared to make those same disastrous mistakes again.
Ever.

She wound down the driver's window, trying to get
some fresh air, some snap to reality. Her car was so
old it didn't have air-conditioning. She lifted her chin
as the wind ruffled her hair. The warm breeze carried
the scent of salt and brine, and almost as though he had
a homing device in her brain, her thoughts returned to
the man on the beach.

She'd been shocked to see him collapse, and had
reluctantly, cautiously approached him. She'd lightly
kicked him, but he hadn't stirred. She'd tentatively relaxed her shields and discovered he truly was unconscious. She couldn't blame him. That branding—damn,
that had stung like the bejeebus.

She should have left him there for the crabs, or for the
tide. Her mouth tightened. When he'd been poised above
her, ready to deliver the death strike, she'd sensed him.

He'd been fighting his own reluctance to kill her.
She'd felt the burden of his duty, his responsibility to the
Ancestors, to the covens. She'd sensed—of all things—
his honor that gave him a core of steel. She'd felt his
pain, too, over the killing, and his absolute commitment
to delivering her to the Ancestors for her crimes, and

his determination to save the vulnerable from her actions. Having all these emotions, the true metal of his character, she'd glimpsed something she wasn't expecting. She'd seen beyond his actions, beyond his awareness, and she'd seen through the veil. She'd sensed the nothingness. No dark, no light, no pain...no emotion. She'd seen a glimpse of...peace. No emotions to dodge or defend herself from. No effort required to constantly shore up her defenses, to protect her own heart and mind from the pain of others. And for the briefest of moments, that oblivion seemed heaven-sent.

She'd spent so much energy shielding herself, the constant effort to mute the emotions of others on a daily basis was tiring. At that moment, when the veil parted, and time stood still for her, offering her a glimpse of what could be, she'd realized how alone she was, and how tired she was of playing at being someone else for those who thought they were closest to her, yet knew her not.

For that briefest of moments, she was ready to step through the veil into the Other Realm, and accept the solace it offered.

And then he'd received that bodyline text from the Ancestors, and she'd snapped out of it, thank goodness.

She was such a *sucker*. The guy had passed out on her after expending all that cosmic energy fighting her, and then enduring some epic pain, and what had she done? Checked on him. What a sap. She'd gone and made him a darn poultice for his wound. She'd even packed the sand into a pillow for him. She told herself it was to get back on the good side of the Ancestors, by looking after their Witch Hunter.

But she was an empath witch, and she didn't have the luxury of being able to walk away from a person in pain without making some effort to help. That, and he was the *Witch Hunter*, for crying out loud. She couldn't begin to imagine how pissed off the Ancestors would be if she turned her back on their warrior.

She sighed as she rounded a bend in the road. He certainly looked the part. Hard muscles, skin that was warm and smooth, and strong, handsome facial features. She was surprised the Ancestors had chosen such a hunk for their most difficult job. She'd always expected the Witch Hunter to be some twisted, not-so-attractive guy who looked on the outside as mean and harsh as she thought he'd have to be on the inside.

Only he hadn't been mean and harsh on the inside. He'd been determined, yes, and ruthless to boot, but she'd sensed a surprising hint of fairness in him, and a heavy dose of honor. Surprising as she hadn't expected to find either in the Ancestors' assassin.

She turned off the highway, and after a short drive turned onto the street where Mary Anne Adler lived. She frowned at the flashing red-and-blue lights, and slowed to a stop when a county deputy held up his hand.

A man emerged from Mary Anne's house, his hat in his hands, and the sheriff nodded when he saw Sully's car. He trotted down the stairs and over to her car, and she propped her elbow on the window frame. She leaned her head out slightly to look up at him.

"Evening, Tyler."

"Sully. I'm afraid I'm going to have to ask you to move on," he said, resting his hand on the roof of her car.

She frowned, and picked up the boxes that sat on the passenger seat. "I'm here with some tea for Lucy and Mary Anne." She knew Lucy and Gary had moved in with Mary Anne for a little while, to help her get her house ready for sale so that the older woman could downsize and move to a place closer to town.

The sheriff grimaced. "Well, Lucy's in the back of an ambulance on her way to St. Michael's Hospital," he told her.

"Is she all right?" Sully asked, concerned, then realized what a stupid question that was. Of course the woman wasn't all right. She was on her way to the hospital.

Tyler nodded. "She will be."

"Uh, well, do you want me to stay with Mary Anne until she gets back home?" Sully offered. The poor woman had to be devastated by her son's murder, and probably just a little anxious with her daughter-in-law being rushed to hospital.

Tyler's face grew grim. "Mary Anne isn't going to be needing your tea anymore, Sully. She died earlier tonight."

Sully gaped, and sorrow pierced her from within. Mary Anne was a sweet lady. "Oh, no. That's so sad. Gary's death was too much for her, huh?"

Tyler shrugged. "We'll never know. She was murdered."

Sully blanched, stunned. "No."

"Well, we're still investigating, obviously, but from what I saw, I'm pretty sure it wasn't a suicide or an accident."

Sully tilted her head against the backrest. "How—how did it...?" she couldn't quite finish the sentence. How did Mary Anne die?

Tyler glanced back at the house. "I can't say. Not yet." He looked down at Sully. "But I will say this—go home and lock your doors. Stay safe."

He tapped the roof of her car, then turned back to

the Adler house. A deputy was unravelling yellow tape along the front veranda railing, and Sully's blood cooled in her veins at the sight, and what it meant.

The Adler house was a crime scene. Sweet little Mary Anne had been murdered in her home. That woman was so lovely, Sully couldn't imagine anyone having enough animosity, enough rage, to want to kill the older woman. And so soon after her son's murder. Were they connected? She couldn't quite believe that one murder had been committed in their sleepy little cove, let alone two. What were the odds that they were two separate, random acts? What were the odds they were connected? Poor Mary Anne. Sully shifted gears and reversed down the street until she could do a U-turn. It wasn't until she was pulling into her darkened yard, with only the moonlight and the stars to illuminate her garden, that Tyler's words really sank in.

Lock the doors. Stay safe.

What the hell kind of danger was out there? And why did he think it could visit her?

Chapter 5

Dave frowned at the Closed sign on the shop door. There was a lot of that going around Serenity Cove, today. He'd just tried to get some breakfast at the diner in town, only to find it was temporarily closed for business. He'd managed to find a burger joint down near Crescent Beach. He'd also found a bar, but it was too early to open.

He had not found a certain witch, though. He'd checked the beach he'd first seen her on, and then had taken the walk up the stairs to the top of the cliff. He'd found a cleared area at the top, and then a little road that led back to the highway. He'd found her home—her garden was very impressive, along with a little shed out the back. He hadn't been able to find her, though.

And he needed to find her. He needed to…seek forgiveness. Redemption, maybe. His gut tightened inside him, like a corkscrew twisting into a cork. What he did, killing witches, it was a crap job that someone had to do. He was there to stop witches from abusing power, abusing the vulnerable. It was an ordained vocation, and he was *supposed* to be doing *good*. He had a witch to hunt, but he'd found he couldn't concentrate until he made it right with the witch he'd wronged. His shoulders tensed. He didn't want to think about what he'd nearly done, but he didn't usually shy away from the difficult—that's why the Ancestors had picked him in the first place. Still, he felt like a heel for what he'd done, how close he'd come to really hurting her.

He glanced down at the flip-flop he gripped. He'd used it to perform a locator spell, and even now it was tugging away from him, toward the door that was closed to customers. He glanced about. Sullivan Timmerman's shop was on the edge of town. It was set back a little from the road, with a parking area in front. Just like the rest of the stores in the area, it had a sweet facade of Victorian wood trim, painted white, and a soft pastel blue on the clapboards. It gave an impression of welcome and charm, the kind of thing he'd associate with a sweet little grandmother—only the witch inside was no grandma, and after seeing her defense against him, he'd say sweet wasn't his first descriptor for her. Fiery, maybe. Sweet, not so much.

He was trying to ignore the towel, the sand pillow and the dressing that had soothed the pain in his chest.

He knocked on the door, then peered through the glass pane. For a moment all he could see was his reflection, his sunglasses glinting in the sunshine. He had to cup his hands around his eyes and press up against the window to see inside. The shop interior was dark. A little on the small side, and devoid of anyone, including the witch he sought. She was in here, somewhere, damn it. The flip-flop told him. He glanced carefully about in the gloom and finally noticed the flickering light through a transom window above a door that led from the shop room into an area behind.

He knew it. She was here. He shrugged out of his leather jacket and draped carefully, silently, over the glass-topped counter display. The garment was great on a bike, lousy in the summer, and creaky when he wanted to be quiet.

He muttered a quick yield spell, and the door unlocked, swinging inward. He shook his head. She hadn't bespelled her property at all, from the looks of it. He stepped inside and closed the door behind him. He hesitated, then flicked the lock. He had to apologize, and he'd prefer no interruptions, and no witnesses.

He stepped up to the door that led out back, and tested the doorknob. He shook his head when it twisted at his touch. Security was not a priority for this witch. He opened the door a little and peered through it. It opened into some sort of workshop. There was large machinery, grinding wheels, anvils and sharpening blocks. There was an artist's desk, with a number of sketches pinned to the corkboard above it. His eyes widened when he saw the wicked-looking blades lined up on a magnetic knife rack on one wall. Different lengths—hell, was that a *sword*?

He could hear a regular thump, thump, thump, accompanied with a faint grinding sound. It took a moment, but he finally narrowed down the source of the sounds. She sat at a machine, and every time she pressed her foot on the pedal, a weight would descend, making the thump, thump noise he could hear. He realized it was a press of some sort. She'd place a metal prong into the press, and the weight would descend, and then she'd remove and slide into another chute, and thump again. When she removed the prong, he could see tines had been cut into the metal end.

Forks. She was making...forks? He watched her for a moment. Her blond hair was tied back into a thick braid, and she wore a loose-fitting blouse over a long patterned skirt. She was so intent on her work, her head and shoulders dipped each time she set the prongs in the chutes. At one point she arched her back, and his gaze was drawn to the long line of her body as she tilted her head back and rubbed her neck. The flowing clothes made her look willowy and lithe, but he could see the strength in her arms as she placed the newly formed forks onto a tray next to her. Then she returned to her task, inserting the metal prongs into the chutes and cutting tines in the ends.

He stepped inside the room, and the floorboard creaked beneath his feet. She whirled, and he ducked, hearing the thud as the fork hit the timber door behind him. He glanced over his shoulder. The fork had impaled in the wood, quivering, at roughly the same position his head had been mere seconds before. Yeah, he guessed he deserved that reaction—and a whole lot more.

He turned, and she'd already picked up another fork and held it poised to throw again.

"Whoa, whoa," he said, hands up as he straightened. "I come in peace."

"Then go in peace—or pieces. Your choice."

Okay, so he could understand her...resistance to meeting with him. Fair enough. "Please," he said. He tried to send her some calming waves, only he could sense the block between them. Damn, she was good.

"Why are you here?" she asked, slowly rising from

her stool to face him properly, her movement fluid and graceful. She'd lowered her hand, but he noticed she still retained her throwing grip on the fork. She had dark circles beneath her eyes, as though she was tired. He couldn't blame her.

He held up her flip-flop. "I've come to return this. And to say thank you…" He took a cautious step toward her, offering her the footwear. He cleared his throat. "I also came to apologize," he said in a quiet voice.

She tilted her head, as though assessing him, then stepped forward, accepting her flip-flop. "That's okay." She dropped the fork into the tray.

Dave frowned. That's…okay? It was that easy? He was expecting shouting, ranting, at least a remonstrative finger waggle. "You're not—you're not angry?"

She nodded. "Oh, I'm angry, but I know you had good reasons, and you're already beating yourself up about it way more than I could."

He gaped for a moment, then his eyes narrowed. This didn't make sense. He'd expected her to react explosively—okay, and maybe the fork still buried in the door behind him went a little in that direction, but… "You're awfully Zen about this."

She stepped closer to him, her eyes dark with emotions he couldn't name. "It's not every day the Witch Hunter comes after me," she admitted. "And it's not every day the Witch Hunter admits to making a mistake."

He winced, then nodded. "It was a mistake. A big mistake. A mistake of epic proportions. What happened…shouldn't have."

She tilted her head, and her honey-blond braid slid over her shoulder. She gazed at him in open curiosity. "Who are you?"

"You know who I am."

"No, I know you're the Witch Hunter. What's your name, though?"

"Ah, that's right. We haven't been formally introduced." He inclined his head. "My name is Dave Carter."

Her brow dipped. "Oh."

"Oh?" She sounded…disappointed.

"I just thought your name would be more…exotic."

His eyebrows rose. "More exotic?"

She nodded. "Yeah. Not so plain."

"Plain."

"Uh, normal," she tried to clarify. Dave pursed his lips. Normal. His name was probably the only normal thing about him.

She looked at him carefully. "So, how does it work?"

He shifted. He'd never talked about it. He wasn't supposed to. The Witch Hunter was the blind justice of the Ancestors of witchcraft. His mother knew—he'd *had* to tell her. She'd been his elder, and needed to know why he wasn't going through the Degrees for their coven. He should have guessed his sister, Melissa, was eavesdropping at the time—or maybe he did and he'd still wanted her to overhear so that she would understand, and there was at least one person he could talk to. Some of the other covens in Irondell knew—the witch community wasn't as big as the werewolf or vampire tribes, so news got around. People were wary of him, though, and his occupation didn't inspire shared confidences. Most witches avoided him like the plague. But other than that, he mentioned it only when he was performing a hit, as he recited the ritualistic words that would send the witch beyond the veil.

"It's…complicated."

She arched an eyebrow. Well, he guess she at least deserved a little bit of an explanation.

"I receive the name when a crime is committed, and I go hunt." Simple, really.

She frowned as she glanced at his chest. "I saw... how." Her voice was soft, confused. "I haven't committed any of those crimes, though."

His eyes narrowed at her word selection. *Those* crimes. Did that mean there were other crimes she *had* committed? He was getting curious about those coins she'd mentioned on the beach.

"It's never happened before," he admitted.

She frowned. "How can you be certain?"

Cold horror washed over him at the prospect. "Because I wouldn't be able to continue," he said roughly. The thought he could have killed other innocents...it would crush him. Cripple him. He shook his head. No. If that had been the case, the Ancestors would have yanked his ass into the Other Realm. The punishment for a Witch Hunter to break the laws they've sworn to uphold would be extreme, to say the least.

She folded her arms and strolled over toward another door he only just noticed. "Soooo," she said slowly, "when a witch breaks one of the Three, they...brand you with that witch's name, and you go hunt? Like a guard dog? Sic 'em, Rex?"

He tilted his head. "Kind of..." he said slowly, hating the analogy, no matter how apt it seemed. She opened the door and entered what was a small kitchen, with a door leading to the backyard, and another that led to a small bathroom, and a door that led to what looked like an addition to the back of the house. Shop. Factory. Whatever the hell this place was. She crossed over to the stove and lit the stove, then placed a kettle on it.

"But how do you know you're going after a witch for something serious? I mean, what if the Ancestors want you to just warn someone?" She reached up to a cupboard, and Dave's gaze flicked down to where her loose blouse rose above the belt of her skirt. He wanted to focus on the gold skin of her back and side, but his eyes widened when he saw the decorative panel at the back of her belt, with two metal prongs that looked suspiciously like the hilts of the blades she'd used on him. How about that.

He forced himself to concentrate on the conversation, and he narrowed his eyes at her words. "Do you feel like you've needed to be warned about something, Sullivan?" *What* was this chick into?

"Sully," she corrected him, then shook her head, her expression forced into something that almost looked innocent. "Uh, no. Not really. I just—I guess I never thought I'd ever have the opportunity to talk with the Witch Hunter, and I want to understand…how do you know you're doing the right thing?"

Wow. She cut straight to the heart of his current doubts. He wanted to shrug it off with some sort of general comment, but Sullivan—no, *Sully*—deserved at least the truth from him, in all its unadorned, vicious glory.

"When a witch breaks one of the Three," he said, referring to the Three Immutable Laws of Witchcraft— never draw on nature's power to provoke another to an unlawful act—never seek power through the suffering of others, and never draw on nature's power for personal gain at the expense of another's well-being, "I am delivered their name, and I see their crime."

She frowned. "You *see* the crime?" Her face relaxed into something he could only call sympathy. "That's got to be hard." She turned as the kettle whistled, and lifted it off the stove. She pulled down a tin and spooned tea into two strainers and popped them into the ceramic mugs she'd pulled from the cupboard.

He was glad he was wearing his sunglasses, and could hide is surprise as she made the tea. He hadn't told anyone about that before, and it was difficult to broach such a personal subject. He'd never expected to feel sympathy directed toward him over it, but she was right. It *was* hard. There were some things you just couldn't unsee. Some crimes—especially the kids, damn it. He swallowed as he shut down that line of memory. He'd seen his own kind do terrible, horrible, heinous things. He'd seen them do great things, too, but when dealing with the dregs, you started to feel like you were covered in the muck, and it was all you generally got to see.

He cleared his throat. "I see the crimes, so I know what they've done, and generally where I can find them."

Her hands halted, and she slowly turned to face him, her face showing her confusion, and perhaps a hint of nervousness. "What did you see me do?"

He reached for one of the mugs—he couldn't quite believe the woman he'd tried to kill the day before was calmly making him tea in her kitchen.

His lips quirked. Sully Timmerman was proving to be an unexpected intrigue, on so many levels. "I didn't see you."

She frowned, confused. "Then why come after me?"

He sighed. "Usually, I see the crime through the killer's eyes, and can be with them for as long as it takes to identify them, or their whereabouts. This time I got neither."

Her frown deepened as her confusion did, and he

leaned against the doorjamb. "I saw what Sullivan Timmerman did. Not you, this…monster. I saw—" he hesitated. It was one thing for him to witness these horrendous acts, he didn't need to spread that taint to this woman.

Her brow eased. "It's okay. You can't surprise me."

His mouth tightened. "Oh, I think I can."

"I think I have a right to know what I was accused of, don't you?" Her tone was gentle, yet with a core of steel-like implacability. She wasn't about to be fobbed off with half-truths and generalizations. She wanted— and deserved—the facts.

"I see through the witch's eyes," he explained. "So I see what they do. I saw someone get stabbed, and some ritualistic markings, the drinking of blood…"

She shuddered. "Yeah, well, I didn't do any of that. What did this witch look like?"

Dave grimaced, then sipped his tea. "That's the problem. Usually I can stay with the witch until he or she looks in the mirror, or passes a window, and I can see their reflection. Usually I get to see the neighborhood, some more of the crime scene, enough to establish their location… This time I got bumped."

"Bumped?"

He took another sip, nodding. Once the dam broke, it felt easier to talk, easier to explain. There was something surprisingly relaxing about Sully Timmerman. "Bumped. He—or she—drank the blood, said a spell and bam, I was out of there."

"So you didn't get to see this witch's face, or where they were?"

"I saw an alley, I saw a sign on a building—Mack's Gym, by the way—and I had the name."

Sully's mouth pouted as she mulled over his words.

"Mack's Gym is in the next town..." Then she shook her head. "But I don't understand. My name?"

He nodded. "Yep. Sullivan Timmerman." He frowned, then glanced down at the tea. "What's in this?" He was finding it too easy to talk.

"Oh, it's just a little lavender, lemon balm, a tidge of nutmeg..."

His eyes narrowed. "Antianxiety?" Most of those ingredients were relaxants.

She shrugged. "A calmative. I thought you could use it."

He had to admit, it worked. He'd come here with his gut roiling, concerned about how she'd receive him, whether she'd hear him out...whether she'd forgive him. But...how did she know? Realization dawned, and he put the mug down.

"You're an empath." It wasn't a question. Everything added up. She'd made him a poultice to ease his pain and help him heal, had made him as comfortable as possible on his bed of sand and had displayed an unexpected insight to his turmoil—accepting he had a job to do.

She stepped back, her skirt moving around her legs as she did so, her movement was so sudden. "What—what makes you say that?" she asked cautiously. Warily.

He eyed the increased distance that now separated them. He'd spooked her, somehow. He shrugged, trying to keep it casual. "Oh, just putting the pieces together. I don't know how many witches would patch me up, hear me out and make me tea after I've tried to kill them." She was a sweetheart. She'd tried to ease his pain, and ease his guilt.

She frowned as she crossed to the sink—putting even

more distance between them. "That's quite a stretch. Maybe I'm just a sucker for a bad boy."

His lips quirked. As tempting as the suggestion was, he doubted it. He edged a little closer, and put his own mug in the sink, managing to hem her in at the same time. Sully paused, her gaze on the mug he still clasped. "Ah, now that's where you're wrong, Sully," he said in a low voice, leaning forward. "I can be very, very good."

Sully lifted her gaze from the large hand that made her mug look like a kid's tea party toy, up the corded forearm, over the bulging bicep, the edge of the dark tattoo peeking out from beneath the sleeve of his fresh black T-shirt, and across the broad shoulder and torso to the strong column of his throat. She swallowed, hesitating, before lifting it farther. The man had a great jaw. Strong, defined, with just the right dusting of hair that made you want to reach and stroke it. Was he—was the Witch Hunter *flirting* with her? His lips curled up at one end, a sexy little smile that made heat bloom tight and low in her stomach. She couldn't see his eyes behind the dark lenses of his sunglasses, couldn't see whether he was flirting, teasing, or just making an observation. And she desperately wanted to see his eyes.

The fact that she couldn't was frustrating, and just a little unnerving. She could relax her shields, get a sense of what he was feeling, but that method was fraught with risks. Risks she'd learned long ago weren't worth it, and she should have the sense to know better.

She stepped back, clearing her throat. "I'll take that under advisement," she said softly.

He tilted his head, and she tried to keep her expression impassive. Aloof. That's what she was going for, here. Distant. Cool. He was the Witch Hunter, tracking down a murderous wi—she frowned.

"I want to help," she blurted.

His eyebrows rose over his sunglasses. "What?"

"There is a witch out there murdering in my name. I want to help you catch him. Her. Whatever."

He shook his head, backing up a little. "Sorry, sweetness. No can do."

Funny. He didn't sound apologetic at all. She put her hands on her hips. "I insist. You said Mack's Gym. That's local. You'll need someone with local knowledge to help you. I can do that."

He shook his head. "I work alone."

"And look where it got you," she said, gesturing to herself.

"Hey, that was an honest mistake," he said in faint protest.

"One that you should avoid making again," she said primly. "Let me help."

"Not happening."

She stepped closer. "Someone is using my name—"

"It could be just as much his as it is yours," he pointed out.

"I can tell you now, there is no other person in the county with my name," she informed him. "But this person even has the Ancestors confused," she told him, her tone serious.

This time Dave stepped closer toward her, and she had to tilt her head back to meet his gaze through his sunglasses. "The term is Witch Hunter—not hunters," he told her roughly. "We don't buddy up on a job. This is something I've got to do on my own, Sully. You haven't seen what this person is capable of. I have. I don't want you anywhere near him."

"But this is *my* name, Dave," she protested.

"And I will get him," he assured her, "and you will stay far away from this matter, and be safe."

She opened her mouth to protest further, then halted when he stepped closer and cupped her cheek. Sensation. Heat. Desire. Protectiveness. Everything bombarded her, leaving her trying to catch her balance. Her shields. It was like he could pierce her shields with just a touch, invading both her personal and mental spaces. She tried to shore them up, but no matter how many times she tried erecting them, his presence kept swamping her.

"I owe you one, Sully," he told her seriously, his voice low. "What I did, I have to make it up to you. I'm granting you a favor."

A flare of forthrightness, a heavy dose of resolve, washed over her. "A favor," she repeated.

He nodded. "I happen to take debts very seriously. I owe you."

Well, she didn't think he owed her anything, but if this was important to him, she wasn't above using it. Warm promise. Integrity.

"Great. Let me—"

He placed a finger on her lips, and again, sensations rolled through her, her senses awakening to him, overriding her personal shields. She could feel his determination, his dedication—and his resistance. And something else. Something… Oh. Desire. She trembled, feeling a reciprocal flare of attraction.

"I have to find this witch," he murmured, "and I will not endanger you. This favor I grant you is for your use, at a time of your choosing, but I will never let you use it to put yourself in danger. Do you understand?"

His voice was so deep, so low. His expression was

grim, intent. She stared up at his sunglasses, stunned by the sincerity, the commitment behind his words. "Uh, yes." She whispered the words against his finger.

"You need anything, you call for me."

She nodded slowly.

"I'll come for you. This is my promise to you." He said the words like a vow, conveying a determination that was…well, knee-weakening.

He dipped his head once in acknowledgment. His finger trailed across her lips. It was as though every cell in her body awakened and paused in anticipation. He brushed his finger first over her top lip, then across the bottom, pressing it down gently. Her mouth parted, and he lowered his head, removing his finger as his lips pressed against hers.

Chapter 6

Oh. My. God. She closed her eyes as he kissed her. His kiss was sweet, tender, capturing her lips in a firm yet delicate kiss. She sighed against his mouth, and then his other hand rose until both of his hands cupped her cheeks, and he deepened the kiss.

Warmth, slow and seductive, curled inside her. She could taste him. Coffee and male, a sweet and savory concoction that had her tilting her head back, wanting more. He smelled magnificent, all woodsy—sage, juniper and neroli. His lips were soft, yet firm. Supple. His mouth moved over hers, dancing almost, with a grace and skill that stole her breath along with her caution.

He slowly raised his head, and he was so close she could see his eyes behind the dark lenses of his sunglasses. It was too dark to see any detail, but his gaze swept across her face, and then he stepped back.

"Uh, I'd best be going," he rasped, jerking his thumb in the direction of the door.

She nodded. She would have said something—anything, only her brain forgot to kick-start again from the sensory overload.

He backed toward the door. "I'll keep in touch," he said, his voice husky.

She nodded. Yep. She would have said it, too, but she got only as far as opening her mouth.

He walked back through her workroom, then paused at the door that led to her shop floor. He gestured beyond to the front door, his brow dipping. "You should beef up your security," he told her. "Maybe a perimeter spell."

She blinked. Uh, maybe…? Only it wouldn't be much use. Nulls. She half nodded, then shook her head as he departed. What?

She heard a motorbike start up outside, then sagged against her kitchen bench as she heard it roar away. She lifted her right hand and gently pressed her fingers against her lips.

The Witch Hunter had kissed her.

He'd kissed her.

Dave shifted on his bike as he rode through town. He was sitting just a mite uncomfortably. What the hell had possessed him to kiss her?

Well, she was attractive, in a fresh, girl-next-door kind of way. Sexy girl-next-door, though. And she was sweet. Too sweet for her own good, really. He shook his head. Tea. She'd given him a calmative tea because she'd sensed his turmoil at what he'd done to her. Who *does* that?

She was such a fascinating mix, though. Back on the

beach, she'd given as good as she'd got. She'd matched him with her powers, and had fought him with a skilled strength that was impressive. And she was armed. He'd seen her belt. She seemed so sweet, so trusting, yet she carried twin blades, and had made him concerned for his ability to bear children. Sweet, but spicy. A contradiction of lethal innocence.

And he'd granted her a favor. He *never* granted favors. He was the collector of debts, and had a bank of favors owed to him from a number of members of Reform society, from vampire or werewolf primes—to light warriors. And he'd granted this witch a debt.

Maybe it was because every time he touched her, he lost time, lost awareness of everything save her. The scent of her, all floral and summery, her warmth, her gentleness—when she wasn't trying to unman him—her…care. She'd minimized his effect on her, because she could see, feel, sense—however it worked with an empath—the effect of his job on him, and sympathized, putting his needs above her own.

That humbled him. He sensed her shields, though. They were impressive, almost tangible blocks to getting to know the woman inside—and he really wanted to get to know that woman. He could usually get a sense of people when he touched them…good, bad, past, present and future—he saw some of each. He was selective with his clients for that very reason. He didn't ink up anyone with one of his spells unless they deserved it, or desperately needed it, needed his special brand of protection. Sully, though, well she consumed his senses at a touch, but those messages, those visions he normally received about a person were missing with her. The protective walls she'd erected within herself were stunningly effective, and it made him wonder why she felt the need to close herself off so thoroughly from those around her. It had to be exhausting, maintaining those protections.

He glanced about the town square as he rode around it. The diner still hadn't opened, but there was a cluster of people at the bottom of the steps. Even when the place wasn't open, it seemed to be the hub for the town people to gather and gossip. He recognized the waitress, Cheryl, who lifted her hand at him as he rode by. He gave her a brief salute in return, then turned at the end of the block. There was a bar at the far end of the marina, he'd discovered. He glanced at the docks. Most of the boats were out. He'd learned Serenity Cove wasn't so much a vacation spot for cruisers, but a working fishing port. The salt and brine was distinctive, and he drove around the weighing station and the fishermen's co-op, to the small parking lot of the bar at the end.

He parked his bike and set his helmet on the dash, uttering his security spell as he did so. That was one more thing he didn't understand about Sully. Her store was poorly secured. One flimsy lock on the front door that a teenager with a penknife could pass. When he'd visited her home, he hadn't sensed any blocks or shields there, either. As though she couldn't be bothered. He didn't know a witch who didn't layer their security with any number of spells. Some were innocuous, some had painful elements invoked for trespassers. Personally, he preferred the painful variety. He didn't have any patience for those who tried to steal or damage his property.

He walked into the bar, pausing when he stepped into the dim interior. At this time of day a couple of patrons sat in a booth, a couple more at the bar. A game of college baseball was playing on the television above the bar, and the thickset, middle-aged bartender leaned his palm on the bar, watching it.

Dave walked up to the bar and sat on a stool two down from another patron. The bartender looked over at him, an eyebrow raised in query.

"Beer, please," Dave said.

The bartender lumbered over to the under-the-counter fridge and pulled out the first beer his hand grasped. He grabbed a bottle opener from the counter, then slapped a coaster down and thunked the beer onto it.

"Thanks," Dave muttered.

"Well, if it isn't Sully's friend," a tired voice muttered from the stool two down from his.

Dave turned, then frowned at the familiar man until he recognized him. The sheriff, out of uniform. No wonder he hadn't recognized him immediately. It was like seeing your elementary school principal sitting at your dinner table. Out of place and damn uncomfortable.

"Tyler, right?" That was what Cheryl, the waitress, had called him, wasn't it? He purposely didn't address him by his title. The man was out of uniform, and Dave hoped this was an opportunity to get the man to open up about the murders he'd seen.

He gestured to the sheriff's nearly empty bottle. "Another one for my friend," he told the bartender.

Tyler's eyebrows rose, but Dave noticed he didn't decline the beer.

"How'd it go with Sully?" Tyler asked idly, although Dave suspected the man wasn't as nonchalant as he appeared to be.

The bartender clunked the new bottle down on the bar. "You know Sully?" he asked, and Dave almost saw curiosity flare, but then the crowd roared on the TV, and he turned his attention back to the game.

"Didn't quite go the way I expected," Dave admitted to the sheriff.

"Oh? No more spark?"

"Oh, there were plenty of sparks," Dave said, thinking of their power struggle on the beach. "I had this meeting all thought out in my head, and it didn't go at all to plan."

Tyler chuckled. "Hell, been there. But you're still here?" His expression was friendly, but Dave could see the interest in his eyes at figuring out the new stranger in town.

Dave nodded. "Yeah. I thought I'd stay a couple of days. Hey, what's with the diner? I went for breakfast, but it's closed, even though the sign says it's usually open today."

Tyler moved his now-empty bottle aside and reached for the new one. "Yeah, well, Lucy, the owner, isn't well."

Dave's eyes narrowed. He sensed there was more to that than the sheriff was letting on. The game on the TV hit a lull, with the teams changing over, and a news broadcast filled the ad break. Dave watched as the announcer read about the murder of a local woman. His arms muscles tightened when he saw a photo of the deceased woman. It was the elderly woman from his vision.

The bartender sighed, then looked at the sheriff. "Mary Anne? What sick bastard would go after an elderly woman in her home?"

Tyler nodded, his gaze flitting to the screen momentarily before dropping back down to the bottle of beer he held. "Well, Tony, you got the sick bastard part right."

Dave frowned. "Isn't that the second murder in the area in what, a week?"

Tony, the bartender, nodded. "Yeah. First one was her son." He shook his head. "Seems like the family pissed off someone."

"So, the murders are related?" Dave asked casually.

Tyler tilted his head to stare at him for a moment. "Yeah, looks that way." He lifted his beer to his lips and drained the bottle, then stood. "Thanks for the beer."

Dave realized the sheriff was shutting down any further conversation on the topic. He smiled, masking his frustration. He knew the law weren't supposed to talk about open cases, but he'd hoped he could make the sheriff crack.

"Good luck with your investigation," he said.

Tyler hesitated, glancing over his shoulder. "We're going to get this sick bastard," he said quietly, his gaze meeting Dave's. Dave's eyes narrowed. Was that—was the sheriff warning him?

Tyler pulled at the door and disappeared into the daylight.

Dave turned back to the bar, his attention now on the bartender. "So, mother and son, huh?"

Tony tore his gaze away from the game that had now resumed on the TV. His gaze flitted to the door, then around the bar, and then he nodded, folding his arms on the bar.

"Yeah. Pretty sad. Gary was a great guy. Didn't come in here all that often, wasn't much of a drinker, but he was the kind of guy who'd always stop and say hi, or give you a hand if you needed one. He and Lucy were going to be married in June."

Dave winced. That woman was going to need some time to heal. He added her name to the list of folks affected by this witch's actions. "And the mom?"

Tony grimaced. "Well, I didn't have too much to deal with her. She was a great crocheter, though. She'd make beanies for all the newborns at the hospital. My sister got one when her daughter was born. Meant a lot, to her, that kindness from a woman she barely knew."

Dave frowned. "It doesn't sound like they were the kind of people to have any enemies."

Tony snorted as he straightened from the bar. "Nulls always have enemies."

Dave's eyebrows rose. "They were nulls?"

Tony looked at him, surprised. "Well, yeah. They're all over the north end. That's why we're so into fishing, here. Tourism blows."

"Huh." Dave drained his beer, than pulled some cash out of his wallet, placing it on the bar. "Thanks."

Tony nodded, picking up the cash and strolling over to the cashier. "Anytime."

Dave strolled to the door, then hesitated. "Say, do you know a Sullivan Timmerman?"

Tony frowned. "Sully? Sure. Everyone knows Sully. Sweet lady."

"Uh, no, I mean another Sullivan Timmerman," Dave clarified.

Tony shook his head. "Nope. That would be weird."

Dave nodded. "Yeah, I guess it would be."

He left the bar, and straddled his bike. He frowned as he gazed out at the tiny harbor. Nulls. Why the *hell* would a witch want to kill *nulls*? The very nature of a null meant that the witch's powers were nullified in their presence. No werewolf could shift in their presence, no vampire could get their fangs on, no witches could cast spells...

He kick-started his bike and eased open the throttle as he rode out of the parking lot. Maybe it had nothing to do with nulls, and everything to do with the victims?

He needed to find out more about Gary and Mary Anne Adler.

* * *

Sully stood next to Jenny as the preacher gave his graveyard sermon. She glanced across the open grave to Lucy. The woman leaned heavily on Cheryl, her face streaked with tears and pale with exhaustion. Even from this distance, Sully could see the deep bruise on her chin and along her cheek. Cheryl had told her the previous day that Lucy had been attacked from behind and had fallen heavily on the wooden floor. She hadn't seen her attacker, hadn't witnessed Mary Anne's murder, but had found the older woman's body when she'd regained consciousness.

Sully returned her gaze to the open grave, Gary Adler's coffin poised above it. His mother would be interred at the end of the week, as her body was still at the county coroner's, her autopsy only just recently completed.

"This is so sad," Jenny whispered. "A family wiped out."

Sully nodded. It was beyond sad, really. "It doesn't make any sense, does it?"

Jenny shrugged. "Depends which side of the fence you're sitting on. Some of the older folk remember the Reformation, and what happened with us. They say it's happening again."

Sully flicked a glance at her friend. "Seriously?"

Jenny nodded, just once.

Sully frowned as she watched Gary's coffin lowered into the grave. The late afternoon was fiercely hot, and bottles of water had been handed out among the small crowd. The funeral directors had erected a tent, and Sully wasn't sure whether it was better to stay under the tent and out of the sun, or to get some distance from all the hot, sweaty bodies and brave the furnace beyond the shade. And of course, everyone wore black.

She glanced at Jenny. Her friend had a point. Nulls had experienced a varied history. On the one hand they were reviled by the shadow breeds. Any shifter or vampire, or even witch, was reduced to being powerless and vulnerable in the presence of a null, which meant ordinary humans had seen the benefit in protecting them, and using them as a barrier against the breeds. They lived in the gray area between natural and supernatural. Not quite a shadow breed, but not an ordinary human, either. As a result, they were hunted by the shadow breeds in well-planned, ruthless skirmishes. During Reformation, they were given no territory, being classed as a subcategory of the human race. As such, they were often not treated as equal to any other race, shadow breed or not. Some of the crimes that had been committed against them were horrific, but with the recognition of a new hybrid breed just outside Irondell, there was renewed action to also recognize nulls as a race of their own.

In the meantime, no shadow breed would willingly go near a null community. That meant a lot of trade and tourism was restricted in the null-saturated areas. Humans walked the fine edge of losing business among the shadow breeds, and having protection from being prey to the breeds if nulls were about. To hear that the murder of two nulls—the first murders in the area since Sully had moved there—was possibly race-based was... disheartening.

Sully had gotten to know many of the nulls. They'd initially viewed her with mistrust. Why would she want to associate with them? She'd learned that apart from the block on her powers, there was something familiar about the nulls. They loved family. They had a tight-knit community, where each looked out for the other. They worked hard and partied harder, but they were just like any other human community—or witch, vampire or shifter, with one major difference. They just didn't get into power plays.

And that was probably one of the most attractive qualities, in her mind.

"Tyler will find whoever did this," she whispered to Jenny.

Jenny turned to her, her eyebrow raised. "We're not going to wait for the humans to help."

Her friend turned to walk over to Lucy, and Sully caught up with her. "What do you mean?" Sully whispered.

"Tyler's a good guy," Jenny whispered back, "but these crimes have targeted nulls. We have our own ways of dealing with this."

"Really?" Sully glanced around the mourners.

Jenny smiled. "I keep forgetting you're not a born null."

"Thanks." Sully frowned. "I think."

Jenny halted, scanning over Sully's shoulder. "Oh, hey, I see my brother. You go ahead, I need to go see him. Gary was one of his close friends."

Sully nodded. Lucy crossed over to the group of nulls that had stepped away from the grave to have a quiet talk. She turned back to approach Lucy, and it was as she was stepping up to hug her that she felt the little scratching at her shields. She was out of null range. But no, she should be able to manage.

She smiled sadly at Lucy and held out her arms.

Lucy stepped into them, sobbing softly, and Sully

held her. She smiled briefly at Cheryl over Lucy's shoulder. The waitress looked almost as miserable as Lucy.

"I'm so sorry," Sully whispered into the crying woman's ear.

"Thank you for being here," Lucy said softly, hiccupping into her shoulder. "I'm so sorry about the cutl—"

"Shh," Sully hushed her. "There's nothing to apologize for. This is more important."

Lucy squeezed her tight, and Sully could feel the woman trembling in her arms. She could sense the grief, the heartrending sorrow in her. It was muted, like an annoying pain knocking at her shields. Sully hesitated, then heard Lucy sob anew. She couldn't leave her like this. Nobody should have to go through this heartfelt agony. Lucy had lost two members of her family in quick succession in the most violent way. Sully could feel the woman fracturing in her arms. Her trembling increased, her breath grew ragged as her sobs grew harsher. Sully closed her eyes, then opened her shields a crack. She sucked in the pain, trying to absorb only some of Lucy's pain, but she could feel the grief of the fellow mourners clawing at her shields, peeling them back. She fought, trying to shed the talons that were shredding her walls. She slammed a barrier down, and Lucy's head lifted, surprise on her face. The woman hiccupped, then patted Sully on the shoulder as she turned to the next person lining up to offer their condolences, her composure once more slipping into place as she brushed away her tears.

Sully stepped back, and would have staggered if Jenny hadn't caught her arm. Her friend eyed her curiously. "Are you okay, Sully?"

Sully nodded, smiling tightly as the pain screamed inside her head like a banshee with her finger in an electrical socket. The nulls could stop her using her powers, but once she absorbed pain, they couldn't stop her from feeling what was already inside. And with them around, she couldn't dispel it.

Oh, God, so much pain. It was unbearable. Sully could feel it eating at her mental walls, coursing through her brain like a hot wash of acid. Even now, her vision was beginning to darken at the edges. She had to dispel the energy, but had to get away from the nulls to do it—and you never did a discharge of this magnitude where other humans might pick up some of the spill.

"I have to go," she rasped to her friend, and started to walk between the gravestones toward the parking lot. She had to get out of here. She was going to lose it. Even now, bile rose within her, burning her throat. She swallowed, trying to contain everything.

"Oh, hey, there's your boyfriend," Cheryl said.

It took Sully a moment to realize Cheryl was talking to her. She tightened her lips as she glanced about. Boyfriend? What? Sully saw Dave in the shaded corner of the parking lot, leaning against his bike.

He frowned, straightening from his bike as she hurried toward her car.

"Sully."

She braced her hand against the car, bending over as her stomach muscles clamped as though a vise was trying to squeeze her gut in half. Her hands shook as she delved into her satchel and finally found her keys. They jangled in her hand like a wind chime in a tornado.

Two hands clasped hers, removing the keys from her grasp, and then she felt a strong arm guiding her into the passenger seat.

"I'll drive."

Chapter 7

The voice sounded like it was echoing down a long tunnel. She blinked furiously, trying to see beyond the darkness that was now bleeding into her vision. Perspiration broke out on her upper lip and lower back, and she winced, bending low in her seat. She felt rather than saw Dave slide into the driver's seat, and within seconds the car was in motion, driving out of the cemetery and headed wherever the hell they were going—she couldn't see, and quite frankly didn't care.

She groaned, her jaw clenching as she rode another wave of intense pain. As though from a distance she could hear the scream of wheels as Dave sped along the coast road.

They'd been on the road for only a few minutes—maybe. She was beginning to lose track of time, but she thought—hoped—they were far enough away from the crowd.

"Pull over," she gasped. Oh, God, this was intense. The pain—she panted as she tried to ride the hot wash of agony.

"What? Are you sure?

"Pull over." Her voice emerged as something low and guttural and quite unnatural. The car jolted and bumped as he steered it onto the shoulder, slowing down.

She opened the door before he'd quite stopped.

"Sully!"

She tumbled out of the car, falling to her knees on the gravel. Her fingers clawed over, and she dug her nails into the earth, trying to ground herself.

"Sully—"

She held up her hand in warning. *Don't come near me.* She couldn't speak, couldn't communicate other than that one abrupt, urgent movement. She crawled a foot, her stomach muscles wrenching, and she screamed at the excruciating heat that rose up from within, as though a ball of fire was exploding inside her—inside her gut, inside her brain. It was blinding light and suffocating darkness, it was fiercely hot and blisteringly cold, it was nothing and it was everything, all at once. She released the pathetic hold she had on her mental barrier, opened her mouth and retched up all that heartache, all that crushing sadness and consuming sorrow.

Over and over, the hot tide of negative energy roiled through her, and her stomach heaved, her throat burned and her eyes watered as she expelled Lucy's and the other mourners' grief in a hot black sludge that splashed on the ground and ran to rivulets, steaming as it soaked into the ground.

When she had no more to expel, when the last drops had left her body, she wiped a shaky hand across her chin. She straightened on her knees and started to sag.

Strong arms caught her, and this time she was too weak to fight that coalescence of power, that collision of energies. His scent, sage, juniper and neroli, his warmth, and then an overwhelming tide of tenderness, concern and just a hint of awe. It embraced her.

"Come on, sweetness. Let's get you home."

Dave pulled into Sully's driveway and cut the engine. The sun was setting, streaking the sky with fiery pinks and tangerines as dusk crept in. He climbed out and walked around the back of Sully's car—a sky blue station wagon throwback that should have visited a wrecking yard years ago, from the looks of it. The gears had been a little clunky, too. He'd have to look at them for her. He opened the passenger door, and Sully's eyelids slowly rose.

She hadn't quite passed out, but she was close. Whatever the hell she'd done had clearly drained her. He didn't question the relief that she was still conscious, still breathing, after what he'd seen her do.

She grasped the upper frame of the door, as though getting ready to haul herself out. "Thanks for the ride—" her voice trailed off as he leaned in and scooped her up.

"Relax," he told her. She needed sleep. She felt so limp in his arms, so…spent.

"No, I can—" her head bumped against his shoulder "—walk."

He snorted. "Please. You can't even keep your head straight."

He cradled her as he strode up the steps and uttered a yield spell. The lock clicked and the door swung open. Dave walked into her house, glancing about. A hallway ran from the front door of the house and doglegged at

what he assumed was the kitchen. There was a room
on either side, neither of which looked like a suitable
place to set her down.

"Bedroom?"

Her head lolled forward, and she waved her arm
down the hall. "Back."

He walked down and around the corner. The hallway had a small bathroom at the very end, a doorway
that led to the kitchen on the right and a closed door on
his left. He muttered a few words, and the door swung
open as he approached.

Yeah, this looked exactly like what he'd imagine her
bedroom would look like—if he'd wondered about it.
There was a bay window that overlooked her garden,
and sheer, gauzy white curtains that blew in the breeze
coming in from the open sash windows. There was a
window seat beneath the bay window that looked well
cushioned, with pillows in what looked like delicate
blue flowers that matched the other cushions with blue
or green striped panels, and a navy knit blanket hap-
hazardly draped on the end.

Her bed was queen-size, with an ornate white iron
bedframe that surprisingly didn't look overwhelmingly
feminine. He flicked his fingers beneath her knees and
the powder blue coverlet pulled back enough that he
could lay her on the crisp white cotton sheets. She subsided against the pillows, and she struggled against the
heavy weight of her eyelids.

"Thank you," she whispered, as though she didn't
have the energy for her full voice.

He smiled as he drew the coverlet over her body. So
polite. "My pleasure."

She snuggled down, rolling over a little and sliding her hand beneath her cheek. She frowned, and he leaned closer.

"Sully, are you okay?" he asked softly, concerned by her expression. Was she in pain?

"Why are you my boyfriend?" she murmured drowsily. Her tone was breathy, but there was no mistaking the confusion.

"Uh…" Dave hesitated. Oops. He hadn't expected that rumor to still have legs. "Well—" His eyebrows rose at the faint snore. "Sully?" he said gently. Her eyelids didn't even flutter.

She gave another delicate snore. He tucked the coverlet in around her, knowing he'd dodged a conversational bullet, then leaned forward and kissed her forehead, a little surprised at the tenderness he felt. That was a first. "Sleep well, sweetness."

He stood over her for a moment, his brows pulled down in a frown. What the hell had she done? She'd hugged that woman, and then couldn't seem to walk or see straight. He reached out and lightly cupped her cheek. He couldn't see, damn it. No past, no future and certainly no clue as to what had happened to her at the funeral. She was like a vault, closed off to his visions. He removed his hand, his fingers trailing across her smooth skin in a gentle caress. He curled his fingers into a fist. He liked touching her.

He stared at her thoughtfully. He couldn't afford to like touching her. His hands—they'd hit. They'd hurt. They'd killed. Sully was—well, she was different. She was… His brow dipped in a slight frown. She was too interesting for his own good. She was sweet—when she wasn't throwing forks at his head—she was gentle and caring. He'd seen how she'd embraced that woman at the funeral. Just walked right on up and opened her arms to the woman. She'd supported her when the woman looked on the verge of collapsing. She'd seemed so strong, so calm—until she'd turned and walked away. And then he'd seen her face when her mask had slipped. He'd seen the pain, seen how her face had drained of color, and how her legs had seemed to wobble. But she'd kept that hidden from her friends. She was open and genuine, and yet impressively well guarded and cautious. So strong for her friends, and conversely, so vulnerable away from them. And yet, he didn't mistake this vulnerability for weakness. And that brought him back to where he'd started. She was too damn interesting for his own good.

He couldn't afford to explore the mystery that was Sully Timmerman. Not with what he did—and what he'd done... He was a ghost. Once he'd figured out what was going on here, and resolved it to the satisfaction of the Ancestors, he'd be going back to Irondell—until the next trip, the next hit. He had no business getting interested in Sully.

Dave crossed over to the window seat and toed off his boots. He made a nest among the pillows, and drew the throw blanket at the end over his legs. He leaned his head back against the inset wall, and gazed at the woman sleeping so soundly in the bed. It took a while, but eventually he fell asleep, too, watching over her.

"You told them we *dated*?"

Dave jolted awake, slightly disorientated. Coffee. Bacon. He hadn't had dinner. God, that smelled amazing. He straightened the sunglasses that had slipped a little in his sleep. He looked around, blinking when he saw Sully standing next to him, arms akimbo, a frown on her face as she glared down at him. His gaze swept over her. Her hair was unbound, falling in loose waves around her head and shoulders, all shiny honey and totally appealing. She wore an off-the-shoulder peasant-style white top. He couldn't see any bra straps. Was she wearing one? His gaze drifted down. That thought had him waking up fast, along with the realization that she was not in a happy mood. His gaze snapped back up to hers.

But she was obviously back to her usual spitfire setting, which was a good thing to see. A damn good thing to see, actually. His gaze started to drift south to her chest again, and he forced himself to blink, look away. *Don't perv, you perv.*

"What?" he asked, then yawned, mentally scrambling to think past the bra situation and the bacon in the next room.

"You told Cheryl we dated in high school. I've just got off the phone from Jenny."

Dave blinked as he rose from the window seat. Ouch. Apparently the window seat wasn't much better than the sand the night before.

"Jenny? Who's Jenny?" He needed coffee to jump-start this conversation properly.

"My friend, Jenny, who had an interesting chat with Cheryl yesterday at Gary's funeral."

He closed one eye as he looked at her. "Cheryl is the waitress at the diner, right?"

Sully nodded, her eyes narrowing.

He blinked again, then nodded. "Oh, yeah. She's nice. Got a thing for the sheriff, I see."

Sully pursed her lips. "Everybody knows that except for the sheriff." Then she went back to frowning. "You told them I was an old girlfriend."

He stretched, then smiled as he started to walk to the door. "Don't sell yourself short, you're not *that* old."

She thumped him in the arm. Ouch. Okay, so she wasn't in the mood to be teased. Sully strode across the hall and into the kitchen, and made a beeline for the kettle that was beginning to whisper on the stove. She was barefoot, and he caught a glimpse of tanned calves and pink polish on her toenails. Her skirt flowed with each movement, but he was pretty sure she didn't know how it skimmed her hips and butt in a way that couldn't help but draw a guy's attention. Damn, he had no idea domesticity could look so damn sexy in the morning.

He settled himself on a stool at her kitchen counter and watched as she moved through the kitchen. Her clothing might be loose, but it still draped over her limbs, and he could make out the shape of her thigh, the indent of her waist, the swell of her breast... And he shouldn't be noticing that. Not with this woman. And right now she was upset with him.

"I told her that so I could find out where you were," he told her truthfully. "Back when I thought you were murdering people."

"The whole town is talking about it," she hissed. She pulled out two mugs and started pouring the coffee.

He tilted his head. She sure was fired up about this. She was so Zen about him trying to kill her, but having her name connected with his seemed to really tick her off. "Shelving the fact I may have told a little fib to find you, what's so bad about people thinking we used to date?" he asked conversationally. The more he thought about it, the more the concept interested him. Heck, when was the last time he'd *dated* a woman? Not a hookup, not a one-night stand, or a spontaneous, fun-minded bed-buddy, but a *date*, with planning, and a full meal, real conversation, aftershave…

She slammed the mug down next to him on the counter. "Because I would never date someone like you," she snapped.

He blinked, surprised by the little flash of hurt at the words. He schooled his features into calm disinterest. "Someone…like me?" he asked conversationally. His gut tightened with tension as he waited for her response.

Her mouth tightened, then she nodded. "Yeah. Someone like you." She grabbed a plate at the side of the stove and started serving up some scrambled eggs and bacon.

"What is that supposed to mean?" He abandoned all attempts at remaining casual as she thunked the plate down in front of him, followed by the cutlery she pulled from a jar at the end of the counter.

She turned back to serve up her own plate. "You're physically dominating, and you'll do or say whatever you need to in order to get what you want."

She walked around the other side of the bench and sat on the stool next to him.

He stared down at his plate. *Uh, wow.* He slid some scrambled eggs on his fork and shoved it in his mouth, even though he'd lost his appetite.

It wasn't like he could argue with her. He did use his body to dominate others, particularly when doing a job. And after what had happened on the beach, Sully would know that better than anybody. Problem was, he had to. No witch he ever faced *wanted* to cross the veil to the Other Realm. These people were criminals, murderers…psychopaths. If he didn't dominate them, they'd kill him—and many others.

And yeah, he would say or do whatever he needed

to if it meant dispatching a witch in order to protect the vulnerable.

He swallowed his scrambled eggs, and reached for his mug. "Fair call." And he hated it.

She sighed. "It's just—I don't date, and now they think I do."

Dave frowned. "You don't date…ever?"

"Never."

"Why not?" She was attractive, sweet-natured, smart, strong—she'd held her own against him. Mostly. She had the body of a siren. His gaze drifted over the creamy skin revealed by her top, and again wondered about her underwear—or, hopefully, lack of it. She was gorgeous. Why didn't she date?

She shrugged. "It's a lifestyle choice. I have my work to concentrate on."

He cut up some bacon and chewed it thoughtfully. He could relate to that. Kind of. There was no way he, as a Witch Hunter, could have a significant other. He'd known that from the start, and had accepted that. But he couldn't deny it—every now and then he'd feel lonely, and would seek out company. Not as a *date*, though. But Sully—Sully wasn't a Witch Hunter. She didn't have to up and leave in the middle of the night, didn't have to fight to the death every time she went to "work", didn't have to try to give the impression of being normal instead of being all torn up inside, hating what had to be done. He didn't know why she didn't date, why she wasn't available for a relationship, why she wasn't looking for company, or just plain fun… and yes, he was very curious, but was in no position to be allowed to care. Either way, though, his story at the diner had unintended consequences, which is the last thing he wanted for her.

"I'm sorry. I'll clear it up with Cheryl when I see her." He looked at her briefly. Her cheeks were still a little pale, and there was the faintest of shadows under her eyes. "How are you?"

She met his gaze as she sipped her coffee. She placed her mug on the counter. "Better, thank you."

He turned to face her on the stool. "What happened?"

She averted her eyes. "Uh, not sure. Probably sunstroke." She nodded. "Yeah. It was really hot." She finished her breakfast quickly.

He frowned. "That's the first time I've seen someone with sunstroke throw up black gunk."

"Really? Oh, I've seen it happen," she murmured as she rose from the bench. He watched her as she walked around to the sink, concentrating fiercely on navigating her way through her kitchen. Sully Timmerman sucked at lying.

"Sully."

She halted at the sink, head down, then turned to face him. "Yes?"

"Is it because you're an empath?" he asked softly. He'd heard of them, but had never encountered one, before. Empaths were considered the witch version of truth seekers, those individuals occasionally born across the shadow breeds with the uncanny ability to sense emotion, and to gauge honesty and subterfuge. They were highly sought after in some cases—fantastic to use in civil litigation or high-value deals. In other cases, they were considered a threat, particularly by those who were trying to keep secrets or maintain lies. He knew one, Vassi Galen, but she'd always kept her truth-seeking talents a secret. Maybe that's what Sully did, to avoid the risk of folks wanting to shut down the walking lie detector. He held up a hand. "It's okay, you don't need—"

"Yes." She nodded slowly. "Yes, it's part of being an empath." She shrugged, palms up. "When you do your stuff, you get a name branded across your body. When I do my stuff, I draw in other people's pain, and it can sometimes make me...ill."

"Are you sure you're okay?" He couldn't help his concern. She'd coughed up a bucket-load of steaming black goop, and practically passed out.

"Yeah. Once I get rid of it, I'm generally fine. Yesterday was hard to control, though. There was so much grief and heartbreak."

"And you drew it all in?" Hell, no wonder it looked like she was barfing up toxic tar.

She shook her head. "No. Not all of it. Lucy lost the love of her life, as well as the woman who pretty much adopted her as her daughter. She will feel sorrow, and she'll feel grief, and I can't take that away from her, because that's based in the love she has for those people, and I'd have to take away that, too. I took away some of the pain of it, that's all." Sully grimaced. "Only I can't necessarily cherry-pick who I help in that kind of situation. Once I crack the wall, anything can come through."

"Crack the wall?" His eyebrows rose as he looked down at her. "Is that what it's like?"

She thought about it for a moment. "Yeah, I guess it is. When you open that gate, the emotions come in. In a situation like that, it's like a...flood. With claws." She shuddered, then waved her hand. "But that's gone now." She took a deep breath. "Thank you so much for driving me home." She frowned. "Why were you there?"

Dave looked at her for a moment. "Actually, that's

a really good question," he said slowly. "I wasn't expecting to see you there." Over the past few days he'd tried talking to the first victim's neighbors, his work colleagues, people at the gym, but they were all pretty noncommittal, and for the first time he couldn't just bespell these people to tell him what he wanted to know. Darn nulls.

"I knew Gary, and Lucy is a friend. Naturally I'd go to his funeral. What about you?"

Dave frowned. "You knew Gary Adler?"

Sully frowned back at him. "Yeah. How do you—?" Her eyes rounded. "Oh. Good. Grief. You saw Gary die."

Chapter 8

Sully leaned back against the counter and looked up at him in horror. "Mack's Gym. Gary was a member. I didn't know where he'd died—Tyler didn't tell me that, but that would make sense." She closed her eyes briefly. Another realization dawned.

"Oh, heck. On the beach—you saw Mary Anne die." She felt the itch of tears in her eyes. Whoever had killed that nice little lady had done it in a way to bring a Witch Hunter down on him. She blinked, then looked up at him. "When I went to visit her that night—"

Dave frowned. "You went to visit her?" His voice was low and harsh.

"Yes, I'd heard about Gary, and thought I'd take Mary Anne and Lucy some tea—"

"You could have walked in on the killer," Dave exclaimed.

"No, her body had already been discovered, the sheriff was there—and why are you angry with *me*? It's not like I went looking for a killer—like you," she said, glaring at him.

Dave took a deep breath, then nodded. "You're right. You weren't to know, I just—I just don't want you hurt."

She blinked. "Oh." He sounded so…protective. He was taller than she, and his shoulders…she eyed his shoulders. There was so much strength there, in his broad chest, his muscled arms. His short hair was rumpled, his T-shirt a little wrinkled and the sunglasses shielded his eyes, yet for once she had no trouble reading his expression. He looked rough and sexy and just a little dangerous, with the soft curve of his lips when he let his witchy protective side out.

But she'd seen how protectiveness could be used to disguise control, and she wasn't going to be sucked in again. "But I'm an empath," she told him firmly. "I constantly feel hurt, and I know how to handle it. You don't need to worry about me."

His lips firmed. "I can't let anything happen to you."

"Anything else," she said, giving him pointed look. Then she sighed at the obstinate lift to his chin. "Look, it's very sweet, but I don't need a protector. What I do need is to figure out what's going on, here."

"*I'll* figure it out," he growled.

"Dave, please," she said, clasping her hands together. "Whoever did this, did it in *my name*."

Dave walked back a little and leaned back against the fridge, shaking his head. He folded his arms, and his biceps bulged with the movement. He'd caught some of the fabric of T-shirt with the movement, and it pulled out from his jeans, exposing just a little bit of skin, that fascinating marking framing his navel—oh, good lord, she was staring at his navel. She snapped her gaze back to those sunglasses. He looked sexy and strong and more than a little stubborn.

"Nope."

"Lucy was one of the first people I met when I moved to Serenity Cove," Sully argued. "She introduced me to a lot of the folks here, including Gary, who introduced me to my best friend, Jenny. He and his mother were super sweet to me. They brought me into their community, and that's where I—" Sully shut her mouth. Uh. That's where she met more of the nulls, and learned how they were all battling poverty, and how she came upon the idea to use the offcuts of her cutlery and weaponry to produce counterfeit coins. Gary had even helped her build the coin press.

Dave arched an eyebrow at her hesitation. "That's where you...what?"

"Really got to know these people," she said, then cleared her throat. "Uh, these people, they gave me a safe place, Dave, and now someone is killing them in my name."

Dave frowned. "What do you mean by safe place, Sully?"

She'd said too much. She bit her lip. She never talked about...before. Dave straightened from the fridge, his face grim as he walked a little closer. He dipped his head so that he was on eye level with her. She saw her reflection in his sunglasses—did he ever take them off?

"What are you running from?" His voice was low, and she could hear the curiosity tinged with concern in his tone.

She frowned. "No. I don't run from anything." She didn't try to delude herself anymore, either. She'd worked damn hard over the last four years, and felt stronger than she ever had before. Hell, she'd been strong enough to hold off a Witch Hunter. No. She didn't run from anything, not anymore.

"When I said safe place, I mean for an empath. They shut everything down. With these people, I don't have to shield myself so much, I don't have to protect myself. *They* become my wall." She trailed her finger along the sink. "You have no idea what that is like, for someone like me. To not have to constantly watch for emotion, to always guard against everyone around you." Sully lifted her gaze to meet his. "So when someone starts killing these very special friends of mine, I want to help stop that. And you can't do this on your own."

Dave lifted his chin. "Of course I can."

Sully's eyebrow rose. "Really? How many nulls have talked to you about Gary? About his mother?"

Dave's lips pursed, and Sully's gaze was drawn to them. They looked…soft. Just a little plump—not stung-by-a-bee plump, but kissy-plump.

And here she was again, getting all woozy-doozy over the wrong kind of man. She cleared her throat. Focus. Think of Gary, and Mary Anne…

"Please, tell me what happened to them. Let me *help* you. What did you see?"

Dave sighed, his breath gusting over her bare shoulder. She trembled. She couldn't deny it, the sensation was…nice.

He held up a finger. "Fine. I'll tell you, but this is my gig. We're not partners, you're not doing any investigating, you're—" He hesitated, as though trying to find the right word. "You're a consultant."

A consultant? That wasn't going to work for her, but she knew when to pick her battles. She gave him a nod. Just one. Enough to make him think she actually agreed.

He reached past her and started to run some water

into the sink, then reached for the detergent on the windowsill. "I see a blade in the heart, which is the kill action that gets the Ancestors involved," he told her. He started washing the breakfast dishes, and she grabbed a tea towel from the oven handle, and started to dry as he handed her the cleaned dishes.

"Then he—or she," he added, "removes the knife from the chest, and carves some sort of symbol into their wrist, squeezes some of their blood out—"

Sully looked up at him when he stopped talking. His mouth was curled in distaste. "Go on," she urged him. "I'm no shrinking violet."

He turned his head to look at her. This close, she could see the light of his eyes behind the lenses, maybe even his eyelashes. She saw his gaze drift over her. "You're not, are you?" He was making a comment, more than asking a question. He washed the frying pan and set it on the drainer next to the sink, and pulled the plug.

"He squeezes some of their blood out and drinks it."

Sully scrunched up her face. "Ew, gross."

"He—or she—says a few words, and then I get bumped."

Sully wiped up the frying pan and bent down to put in her pot cupboard. "And that's not normal?"

"No."

She frowned in puzzlement. "I wonder if he—or she...?" She looked at Dave. "You really don't know whether it's a man or a woman?"

Dave shook his head. "I really don't, and I'm an equal opportunity hunter. The killer wears gloves and whispers the spell. Can't tell whether it's a guy or a chick, and I know chicks can be just as psycho-crazy as guys."

"Oh," Sully said faintly. "Good to know."

He turned to face her, and folded those big, beautiful arms of his again. She shook her head slightly. Stop staring at those arms. "Uh, so, we have a witch who has killed nulls. *Nulls*." She shook her head again. "I don't get it."

"Neither do I." Dave sighed.

"Maybe the witch didn't realize Gary and Mary Anne were nulls," she thought aloud. "Maybe the witch thought they were ordinary humans. I can't see what benefit he'd get out of killing a null—" She frowned, and tapped the sink. "Drinking null blood—that's going to reduce his powers. I don't get it. He must not have known."

"I need to find out more about the guy, and his mother. Who they came into contact with, who might have held a grudge—who stands to gain from their deaths…"

"We can talk to Jenny," Sully said, turning toward the door. Dave caught hold of her arm.

Fierce protectiveness, warm and snug, curled around her. Exasperation. Frustration. Curiosity. Damn it, he was doing it again, plowing through her shields as if they were made of tissue. Why couldn't she block this guy?

"Whoa, sweetness. *I'll* go talk to Jenny. I'll do it subtly. I don't want to go around announcing I'm a Witch Hunter, here to kill a witch. One—it would be around this town before I got out the door, and two—that's a conversation I really don't want to have with your sheriff."

Sully glanced down at his hand. "She won't talk to you," she told him.

Dave's lip's curled in a lazy smile. "I'll have you know some women find me charming."

She just bet they did. Smoking hot muscles, sexy

smile, a handsome face and an overall impression of…
experience.

"I told her we broke up because you cheated on me.
My best friend won't give you the time of day unless
I'm with you. And this *is* a small town. How many nulls
do you think know about you now?"

His grip slackened, but not before she felt the flash of
surprise. She continued on her way to the door. "You're
not the only one who can tell a fib."

Dave shoved his hands in his jeans' rear pockets and
tried to make himself comfortable against the wall. He
hadn't even bothered to try the tiny little seats attached
to the tiny little desks. Had he ever been that small as
a kid? The kids were outside on a short break, and it
was surprisingly relaxing, hearing the kids' chatter and
laughter outside, a little muted, while he stood in the
silence inside the room.

Okay, maybe not *that* relaxing. He lifted his gaze
from the students' desks to realize Sully's friend was
still staring at him. Coldly.

Well played, Sully. There was no way he'd be able
to get this woman, or any of the nulls they'd passed
on the way in who'd given him similar death stares, to
give him the time of day, let alone any solid information on the victims.

"So you want to find out more about Gary and Mary
Anne, huh? Why?" Jenny definitely wasn't sounding
cooperative. He pursed his lips as he looked over at his
new "partner".

Sully nodded, seemingly oblivious to the tension in
the room. "We want to find out who did this."

Jenny frowned. "Why?"

Sully frowned back at her. "Why not?"

Jenny's eyebrows rose. "We're not used to others being interested in what happens to us."

Dave watched as Sully folded her arms. "Jenny, this affects all of us. A murder is a murder, no matter who the victim is."

Jenny tilted her head. "Sully, you have no idea how many nulls have been murdered in the past where it's been treated as though they were dogs being put down. Heck, Reform doesn't even recognize us as a breed of our own. We are a *subset*."

Dave winced. Sully's friend had a valid and sobering point.

Sully's frown deepened. "Have you ever felt like I've treated you like a subset?"

Jenny's eyes widened. "Of course not," she said hurriedly. "No, you've been so generous and helpful with all of us, especially with—"

"Nothing," Sully interjected, and Dave's eyebrow rose.

"Uh, nothing that I wouldn't do again," Sully quickly supplied, her cheeks blooming with heat. Dave's eyes narrowed behind his sunglasses. What had she done for them? What had she done that she didn't want him to know about?

Jenny's gaze slid quickly between Dave and Sully, then back to Dave, and she nodded. "Exactly." She tried to mask the confusion and curiosity about them, but apparently Sully's friend was about as good as Sully when it came to lying.

So Sully's friend knew whatever it was his sweet little partner was into. He shelved that observation for later.

"When someone hurts you guys," Sully said quietly,

stepping up to Jenny's desk, "I hurt, because you guys are my friends. You're my family."

Dave found himself wondering what had happened with Sully's original family. She'd made comments about her First Degree classes, so she'd been brought up in a coven, but where were they now? And why had she left them?

Jenny smiled, although there was a tinge of sadness to it. "Thanks, Sully. That's so lovely to hear." The young woman turned to face him, and her eyes narrowed. "So why do *you* want to help?"

"Uh…" He wasn't quite sure what to say to that. Sully had shut down his one plausible excuse for being in town. He needed to set the record straight. "Look, about Sully and me—"

"He's trying to make it up to me." Sully's quick interruption made his mouth slack. What was she doing?

"Don't you think that's too little, too late?" Jenny commented.

Dave looked at Sully. What happened to setting folks straight? For right now, though, it would work for him. He could adapt. "I made a mistake," he said, and this time it wasn't so much a lie but a variation of the truth. "I need to make things right between us."

"So you're going to do that by…looking into a couple of null murders?"

"He's also got skills in this area," Sully added. "He's an investigator."

This time Jenny eyed him shrewdly, and he felt like he was being measured carefully.

"You mean, like a cop?"

Dave shuddered. "Not quite." Not at all.

"A private dick, or something?"

Hell, this was getting worse. He frowned. "Or something."

"Seems apt," Jenny muttered, and Dave noticed that Sully was trying not to smile and failing spectacularly.

Great. "Uh, Gary and Mary Anne—did they have any enemies? Did they owe money? Did Gary…cheat?"

Both women frowned at him. "No," they said in unison.

Jenny rose from her seat. "Gary loved Lucy. There was nobody else for him. Mary Anne—she was well respected in our community. Loved, even. Gary really tried to help with these kids, and everyone could see that. He was a nice guy, and didn't deserve what he got."

She glanced out toward the kids lining up in the schoolyard. "Look, I can't talk now, I have to go." She smiled at Sully. "Come over to Mom and Dad's for dinner. A few of us are getting together to remember the Adlers. We can talk, then." Her gaze slid to Dave. "You may as well come, too."

He nodded. "Fine." He would have loved to have talked more, but maybe this way he'd get a chance to talk with more of the nulls, and get a better sense of what these Adler folk were really like—and how they became the target of a murderous witch. He followed Jenny out to the door, but halted when she paused.

"If you hurt Sully again, I'm going to pulverize your nuts," she said in a low voice, then smiled brightly at the kids lining up outside the door. "Hey, guys!"

Dave's eyebrows rose as the fierce woman of less than a second ago morphed into a sweet kindergarten teacher as she walked out to the students. Sully stepped up behind him, and he turned to glance briefly at her. What was it with the women in this area? So nice, so…he kept coming back to the word, but he couldn't find one that fit better than *sweet*. So damn sweet. And so dangerous you had to guard your life, your gonads and your heart.

Sully raised her eyebrows when she saw him looking at her. "Is everything all right?"

He nodded as they stepped down toward the parking lot. Sully turned and waved as her name was called, and then stopped to catch a little red-haired boy who literally threw himself at her. She laughed as she set him down.

"Hey, Noah. How are you doing?"

"Good! Are you still coming to the festival?"

"I sure am! Don't want to miss those donkeys. Hey, how are your mom and dad?"

"Dad says he's going to catch you a big tuna!"

"And what does your mom say?" Sully asked with a knowing glint in her eye.

"Mom says we're having mac and cheese, then."

Dave's eyebrows rose at the comment, and Sully grinned. "Well, you tell your dad that if he does catch that tuna, I'll have to make you all my tuna and rice bake."

"Noah! Come on, we have to get back to work," Jenny called from hallway.

Noah sighed. "I have to go," he said, and Sully nodded.

"Yeah, but I'm pretty sure Miss Forsyth has some art planned."

Noah's face brightened, and he waved as he ran back to his class.

Dave watched the pupils wave at Sully as they walked back into the building. There was no hiding from the fact that these kids adored her. Her friend, Jenny, seemed decent, once you got past her frosty defenses and painful threats, and she was protective of Sully—like any good, loyal friend. The nulls respected Sully. That was…unusual.

He slid into the passenger seat of her beat-up car, and glanced over as she climbed into the driver's seat. "How did you get so cozy with the nulls?" he asked, curious.

She frowned as she started her car. "What do you mean? They're people. They're nice people."

"Yeah, but they're also a fairly closed community. They don't like outsiders."

"I guess they don't see me as an outsider then," she said simply as she drove away from the school.

"Hmm." He leaned back in his seat and watched the scenery flash by. How was it that a witch was able to be accepted by a null community? They normally avoided everyone with supernatural abilities, and the practitioners of magic did the same. He frowned.

"They don't know you're a witch, do they?"

She kept her gaze on the road. "I can't be a witch around them, so it doesn't really come into the conversation. I can't do spells, I can't do rituals, I can't practice magic near them, so when I'm with them, I'm not really a witch, am I?"

His eyebrows rose. "Wow. That's an interesting defense."

She frowned. "Defense? Defense for what?"

"You're lying to them."

She shook her head, flashing him a brief but pointed glare. "No. I'm not. I've never said I'm not a witch. In their presence, I'm just plain old me. Normal." She held up a finger as he opened his mouth to argue. "And that's me without any shields or artifice, so in reality, I'm more me when I'm with them, than when I'm not. Totally authentic."

He pinched the bridge of his nose, raising his sunglasses just a little. "Your logic is giving me a headache." He positioned his shades and stared out the window. She'd mentioned something similar before, about how she didn't have to block herself when she was with the nulls. And yet, she kept this one important, innate detail about herself from the community she said she trusted. But if she couldn't be a witch around them, like she said—was she really lying to them? Or just omitting a detail about herself that had no impact on them?

"Where to now?" Sully asked, interrupting his thoughts.

"The graveyard, please," he said. "I need to pick up my bike."

Sully nodded, then flicked him a quick glance. "Then what are we doing?"

"Well, I have to find a place to sleep," he told her. "I wasn't expecting to stay in town this long." He shifted in his seat. No, he'd fully expected to roll into town, kill Sullivan Timmerman and then roll on out again. "Can you recommend any places to stay?"

Sully frowned. "There's a motel down south, about thirty minutes' drive. Nothing much up north. We're not really a tourist mecca."

He frowned. Thirty minutes away. That was a little too far from the action. "Nothing closer?"

Sully drove carefully around the bends of the coastal road, then looked at him briefly. "I have a foldout couch," she offered.

His eyebrows rose. Staying with Sully…he could feel his body throb at the prospect, and tried to hose it down with rational thought. Sully was nice. And she didn't date—she wasn't the love-'em-and-leave-'em type of woman. She was a lady, and deserved so much more than the frolic-in-the-bedsheets that he was limited to offering.

But…she could give him access to the nulls, provide some local information in the tracking down of this killer.

And it would be pure hell living in the same house and not touching her. He eyed her hands on the steering wheel. Her skin was covered in small marks, a legacy of the craft she worked. They weren't the soft hands of a woman who did office work. They revealed a delicate strength, and a capacity for pain and perseverance. Almost like the dainty hands of a warrior, if that was possible. He wondered what it would feel like to have her hands on his body. He could feel himself growing hard at the prospect.

And that was exactly why he should stay the hell away from Sully, and her foldout couch. He couldn't afford to be distracted from his duty.

"Thanks, that would be great," he said, then glanced back out the passenger window. *Hell, here I come.* He tried to distract himself, and thought about what they'd learned from Jenny—pretty much nothing. He frowned.

"Why didn't you let me set Jenny straight about us?"

Sully's lips pursed as she focused on the road. "You heard her. There is a real us and them attitude there. If you don't want people to know who you really are, tell them something they'll believe. I couldn't think of another way for us to get them to talk."

He looked at her carefully. *If you don't want people to know who you really are, tell them something they'll believe.* That had just rolled off her tongue, as though she was talking from experience. She was talking about convincing people, not about telling them the truth. What other "omissions" was she guilty of? The difference between what he knew about his new "consultant", and what he didn't know, just got greater.

Sully Timmerman just got a whole lot more interesting.

Chapter 9

"A toast to Gary."

Sully sipped from the cup of ale she'd been handed. She was leaning against the wall near the living room door inside Jenny's parents' home, and the house was packed. People were still arriving, mainly men who'd just come in off the boats, and had done a quick shower and change before heading over. Food was set out on the kitchen table, and people were helping themselves, piling up plates before they sat or leaned against any available surface.

Sully peered around the doorjamb. Dave was just outside the back door, talking to some of the younger fishermen as they smoked cigarettes outside. They'd been wary of him, at first, but she could see they were beginning to relax around him. Even if he still wore his sunglasses at night.

She turned back to those gathered in the living room.

Sully was content to listen to the stories the gathered folks wanted to share. Some were funny, some were poignant, but all showed the deep respect and love this community had for the murdered victims.

"So, you have a boyfriend, huh?"

The deep voice whispering in her ear made her jump, and she turned.

"Jacob," she said, half laughing in relief when she recognized Jenny's older brother.

He grinned. "Sorry, didn't mean to startle you."

He stepped back into the hallway, and she followed him, so that they could talk without intruding on the memories being shared within the room.

"How are you, Sully?" The tall fisherman tilted his head to the side as he looked down at her. "I didn't get a chance to talk to you at the funeral."

She waved a casual hand. "I think it was something I ate, combined with being in the hot sun. I'm fine now." And she was. She'd tried to bolster her shields before coming, but the null effect made her work unnecessary. Surrounded by nulls, none of her empath powers worked, and she didn't have to worry too much about shielding herself, even if she could. "How are you?"

"Dealing with the fact you've got a boyfriend," Jacob teased, although there was a slightly serious light to his eyes.

"It was quite the surprise to see him," she said truthfully, although she felt a little discomfort at perpetrating an untruth. "How's the fish?" she asked in an effort to distract.

Jacob shrugged, his blond hair glinting in the light. "Biting, but not busy."

Sully winced. The community were doing it tough, and were hoping the fishing loads would increase.

They'd implemented a sustainable fishing program, but that didn't seem to be paying off just yet. "Sorry to hear that."

Jacob glanced around, then leaned down toward her. "Hey, I hear Leo Campi is doing it tough. Dislocated his shoulder in a netting accident and can't work for several weeks. We're passing the boot around tonight," he said, pointing to the leather boot that Jacob's father, Jack, just passed to the person next to him, after stuffing some paper money into it.

Sully nodded. "I'll see what I can do," she said quietly. She had some silver that had been delivered the day before at the shop, and had some cheaper metals she could melt and press into coins. "They'll have to travel into Irondell to spend it, though. Too many coins circulating here will draw attention."

Jacob nodded, patting her on the shoulder. "Thanks, Sully. You're all right, you know?"

"She is, isn't she?"

Sully turned at the sound of Dave's voice. He stood just behind them in the hallway. The Witch Hunter smiled at her friend, and stuck his hand out. He hadn't removed his leather gloves. Sully's brow dipped. Huh. Funny, she'd only just noticed that. This man always wore his sunglasses, and with the exception of eating, he pretty much always wore his gloves.

"Hey, I'm Dave, the ex."

Jacob eyed the gloved hand for a moment, then shook it. He smiled grimly. "I'm Jacob, the current…friend."

Sully looked at both men who seemed to be engaged in some sort of staring contest. Both men were tall, with broad shoulders and an impressive physical presence, yet they looked as different as night and day. Dave, with his neat beard and dusty blond hair, and Jacob with his dark hair and hazel brown eyes. And both looked like they were sizing each other up.

"Hey, Jacob, I wanted to ask you—this is the first time I've been invited to this sort of thing," she said, trying to distract them both. "It's really powerful. Is this how you normally handle someone's passing?"

Jacob finally relinquished Dave's hand. "No, but Gary and Mary Anne were PBs, so it's a special night. For both of them to go…" He shook his head, his expression a mixture of sadness and concern. Then he frowned. "Jenny mentioned you two were wanting to help, somehow…?"

"Uh, Dave has some experience with this sort of thing," Sully explained.

Jacob's eyebrow rose. "With null murders?"

Dave shrugged. "Murder is blind," he said. "Shouldn't matter what breed, it should just matter."

Laughter rose from inside the living room. Another story had been shared about the Adlers. Sully could hear the clink of glasses and mugs as people toasted their departed.

Jacob looked at him thoughtfully, then folded his arms. He dipped his chin in the direction of Dave's sunglasses. "Do you have a vision problem?"

Dave smiled. "I think I see pretty good. Hey, you said the Adlers were PBs—what does that mean?"

Jacob glanced at Sully, and she shrugged. She hadn't heard of the term, either.

"PBs are purebloods," Jacob informed them. "They can trace their lineage back to before The Troubles." The man shrugged. "Shape-shifters have their alphas, vampires have their primes, covens have their regents and everyone has elders—we have our purebloods. Their lineage hasn't been tainted with shadow breed blood, or diluted by ordinary humans."

Sully blinked. It was interesting. The shadow breeds took a similar view of null blood tainting their bloodline, and muting their supernatural abilities...but there were many mixed-bloods throughout all communities. Still, this was a surprise. What else did she not know about these people she'd just spent the last four years with? "Huh. I never knew there was a hierarchy within the null community."

Jacob grimaced. "Meh. We respect them, and the purebloods definitely get a voice at the council, but we like to think it's your actions that define you as a person, not your ancestors."

"Interesting," Dave said grimly. Sully realized he was thinking about his own actions, and how closely linked it was to the Ancestors. For Dave, it really was a case of ancestors defining him as a Witch Hunter.

"Are there a lot of purebloods around?" Sully asked, curious about this new facet of the community she'd adopted.

"Some. There's more over on Stoke Island—it has the highest population of purebloods in the country."

"How is it that the rest of the breeds don't know about this?" Dave asked.

"In case you haven't noticed, the rest of the breeds don't give two hoots about us," Jacob said. "Besides, it doesn't really mean much. PBs are still normal like the rest of us. There's no added strength or ability. Just inherited blood."

Sully met Dave's gaze. "Interesting," they said in unison.

Dave followed Sully into her home. He'd driven his bike out to the null area, and Sully had taken her car, so they hadn't had a chance to talk on the way home.

Now her expression was thoughtful as she turned on the lights in her living room. He glanced inside the room. There was an impressive bookcase on one wall with— he squinted—gardening books? Mathematical theory? Reform politics? Yeesh. He definitely wouldn't be borrowing a book from her. He looked away from the bookcase. She'd already pulled out the sofa and covered it in sheets and a blanket. She must have done it in the afternoon when he'd been out at the library, looking up any stories he could find that mentioned the Adlers. All the articles he'd located had been complimentary. His lips quirked as he stared at the made-up sofa. There was even a neatly folded towel on the pillow.

He looked over at Sully. "So, are you and Jacob an item?"

He could see his question surprised her. He didn't know why it did—he'd seen the way Forsyth looked at Sully, and the almost protective, possessive glare he'd sent in Dave's direction. You didn't need any magical powers to see the guy had feelings for her.

"No, just friends," she told him. She scratched her temple. "Did you think Gary's and Mary Anne's murders have something to do with the fact they're PBs?"

He looked away as he set his backpack down on the floor. Her answer had pleased him, and he didn't want to think too much on the why. He focused on what they'd learned. "I don't know. Why would a witch want pure null blood? It's not like they can do anything with it." *Ugh*. He'd just spent the last two hours with a bunch of nulls, and the knowing, the awareness, the darkness that surrounded his natural ability like a cloak… Well, it was enough to give a witch the heebie-jeebies.

Except for Sully. She seemed to enjoy it. Go figure.

"But it could explain why you get bumped out of your visions…?"

He thought about it for a moment, then nodded slowly. "Possibly." He frowned. "But it's *null* blood. Why consume it? What possible benefit would that have for a witch?" Just the thought made him want to gag.

Sully crossed over to the small end table that held her phone and a notepad and pen. "Can you remember what the witch drew on their wrists?"

"Yes," he said slowly, watching as she brought the notepad and pen over to him. "Why?"

"Can you draw it?"

He nodded. In two strokes of the pen he'd drawn the symbol he'd seen carved into Gary's and Mary Anne Adler's wrists. *X*. He showed it to Sully, who frowned when she glanced down at it.

"It's from the Old Language?"

Dave's eyebrows rose. "I'm impressed. You're familiar with the Old Language."

Sully gestured toward his chest, her cheeks heating. "I saw my name…"

"And you were able to translate it?" Okay, he was more than impressed. For all intents and purposes, the original language of the witches was dead. Learning it, deciphering it, was usually down to Witch Hunters and bored scholars wanting to challenge themselves. But the language was one thing. Learning the symbols, the ancient runes—that was another thing entirely. "How did you learn it?"

Her shrug was noncommittal. "Oh, it was just something I was interested in at one time."

A general interest didn't explain being able to decipher without a key, or instantly recognizing a rune for what it was. His sweet little cutler seemed to hide some pretty big secrets.

"Do you know what this rune means?" he asked her. She frowned, her attention caught by the symbol on the notepad.

"No, I don't. I might be able to look it up, though."

Dave's eyes rounded. "Look it up? How?" There were no computer databases for this sort of thing. No text books to consult. No dial-a-friend service. She would have to have—

Sully walked over to the bookcase, arms out. She closed her eyes, murmuring something so softly he couldn't hear it. The books on the shelves began to glow and shimmer, the defined edges blurring as they transformed into an entirely different library. Damn, she'd hidden it behind a camouflage spell—a damn good one if it fooled another witch. He'd had no intention of going anywhere near her books.

She held out her palm, and again murmured something. This time, though, he recognized the ancient language. She was asking for information on runes. His brow quirked. Who was she asking? He could feel the crackle in the air, the weight of power in the room.

A tome flew from a shelf, and she caught it, staggering back under the force. Her eyebrows rose. "Uh, thanks," she muttered.

"Who are you talking to?" He gazed around the room, then looked back at the bookcase.

She glanced up at him as she walked over to the end table. "The books, of course."

He nodded. "Of course." He looked down at the book she held in her arms. It looked remarkably like—his heart thudded in his chest.

"Is that what I think it is?" he asked hoarsely, stepping closer.

"What do you think it is?" she asked as she set the tome down on the table. He looked down at it. No. It couldn't be.

"A coven grimoire."

Sully glanced at him for a moment. "Yes, it is." She tilted her head, her brows drawing together. "You act like you've never seen one before."

"I haven't. I'm not allied with a coven." Only those in the third level of a coven could even view their coven spellbooks. As a Witch Hunter, he had heard of them, but never seen one. Until now. Dave felt like his eyes were going to pop from his head.

"You have your coven's spellbook?" He had to ask again. It was incredible. These things were passed down from generation to generation, added to through the years... They were the living resource of a coven's history, their power, their alliances and enemies, the spells they'd devised and recorded.

"Not the current one. This is an old version," she said. "We had to make a copy to allow for new spellwork."

"And you have your coven's original? I thought these were protected, that a coven never let any of them go?"

She frowned. "This *is* protected," she told him. "It's with me."

"This is your coven's archive?" he asked in disbelief. A coven's archive was sacrosanct. It held the history, the good and the bad, the strengths and weaknesses, of a coven. The coven protected those references, and they were always honored as deeply private and confidential material. If you accessed a coven's archive, you could access and then exploit those weaknesses, or sabotage their strengths, or worse, steal from them. A coven protected their archive just like a werewolf pack or vampire colony protected their territory. Accessing a coven's archive without permission or supervision was a serious crime among the witches.

And only the most loyal and powerful witch within a coven was entrusted with the security and care of an archive.

Mind. Blown.

He looked down at the volume she held in her hands. "How old is it?"

Sully blew her cheeks out. "Well, that's a good question. This one's been handed down for several generations, it's hard to date it."

His jaw dropped. No. It—it couldn't be. The pages were made of vellum and what looked like—Dave clutched his chest. Honest-to-God papyrus. He pulled his leather gloves off and reached for the codex. Halted. Then took a deep breath and touched it.

Images swam through his mind, of a man painstakingly writing in the book, of passing it to his son, of a ritual within a ring of monolithic stones, of a woman clutching the tome to her chest as the howls of werewolves echoed through the forest, along with the screams of her coven. A young man stumbling along a riverbed, ducking and weaving as vampires chased him, while hundreds fought in the fields behind him. The Troubles.

That same man handing it to a pregnant woman, his face twisted in pain and anguish, an arrow sticking out of his gut. The woman sobbing as she bent to kiss him. "Gabriel…" she cried as he died.

Holy fu—. Dave whipped his hand away. He swallowed, then wagged his finger at the ancient book.

"That—that's not possible," he said, despite the visions he'd seen that proved it was, indeed, possible. "That is not supposed to exist." Gabriel. Gabriel, a legend of The Troubles, who'd saved so many lives with his magic, who'd unlocked many of the secrets of the shadow breeds during the wars, and had helped devise spells and weapons to fight against them. This—this was Gabriel's grimoire.

"You're right. It's not supposed to exist."

Dave lifted his gaze to Sully. She looked remarkably calm for having the oldest book of witchcraft in modern times here in her living room. "Who *are* you?"

She frowned at him, perplexed. "You know who I am. My name is branded onto your chest, for crying out loud."

He tried to think. He really did, but the ramifications of this, of the very existence of this book long thought destroyed before the dust had settled on a new world order...

"Gabriel's grimoire. It was believed to have died, along with his line, during The Troubles."

"He had a family."

Dave held up a hand as he subsided onto the sofa bed. "Whoa. Stop. My brain is exploding. Are you telling me that his wife managed to pass it on to someone?"

Sully shook her head. "No, I'm saying that young woman passed it on down the line."

Dave took a deep breath. *Okay. Settle. This* will *make sense.* "What coven are you from?" he asked quietly.

Sully hesitated, then dropped her gaze to the codex on the table. "I'm from the Alder Coven." Her voice was so low, he barely heard the words.

"The Alder—" Dave closed his mouth. The Alder Coven. Conspiracy theories abound about the infamous coven. It died out in the Roman invasion. They all perished with Atlantis. Pompeii. Or the Minoans, with the first reported shape-shifter. Hell, there was even the story of them being swallowed by flames in a city that burned after an earthquake. Then of course, came The Troubles. He didn't think anyone had connected Gabriel to the Adler Coven, though. Wow. He would have thought she was crazy. Crazy beautiful, but definitely a few sandwiches short of a picnic. Now, though, with the evidence right in front of him, he couldn't deny it.

"Man, you guys are good." He moved from stunned amazement to full acceptance and realization in the blink of an eye.

He rose, picked up the grimoire and gently but hurriedly placed on the shelf. "What the *hell*? You can't just whip something like this out whenever you like," he whispered furiously.

"Dave, this book is so protected—"

"You brought this book into a null area," he whispered harshly. "You bring a null into the house, and all of your protections don't mean diddly."

"No, this is different," she whispered, then frowned. "Why are we whispering?"

"Because you have Gabriel's grimoire in your living room," he whispered back as he turned to face her.

"Dave, relax."

"You can't tell me to relax," he exclaimed softly. "You have a mammoth book of ancient spells, Sully. Do you know how many people would *kill* for this?"

She frowned at him, then straightened her shoulders as she glared at him. "I am a member of the Alder Coven. I have sworn to protect this book with my life. Of *course* I know how many people would kill for this," she said, her voice low and fierce.

"Then why show me this?" he asked, gesturing at the shelves. Now he would have to keep this secret to his dying day, and if his sister ever found out he knew and hadn't told her, well, she'd make sure his death was slow and painful. Hell, his mother—God, she'd have a field day with this. And then would plot until she held the tome in her own hands. Every witch he knew would want to get their hands on this, and every shadow breed in existence would want to destroy it.

This book was the source of modern-day spells, but covens only worked from bits of it. Nobody had the full resource.

Until now.

"How can you just pull this out, like it's so damn ordinary and mundane?" he asked, and had to shove his hands in his jacket, otherwise he'd act exactly like his coven elder mother on a rant at his rebellious sister, and gesture wildly.

"Because I trust you, Dave," Sully said.

He thought a blood vessel popped in his brain. "You *trust* me?" Okay, he hadn't meant to yell that at her, or make her flinch, but her words had surprised him. Stunned him. "You *can't* trust me. I tried to kill you, remember?"

"You apologized for that."

He clutched his temples. "You have to stop defending that," he told her. "You—you're so—so—" his brain scrambled for the right word.

Sully lifted her chin. "So what, Dave?" She arched an eyebrow.

He flung his arms out. "I'm trying to think up the right word, but all I'm getting is gullible."

Her blue eyes widened in surprise, then darkened with anger. "Gullible? You think I'm *gullible*?"

"No, but I can't think of the right—ah!" he snapped his fingers. "Naive. You're naive."

Sully blinked, as though trying to marshal her thoughts into a logical sequence. Good, because he'd hate to think he was the only one losing his mind over this.

"You trust too easily. I came up to you on the sand—a stranger, and you stopped and talked to me," he said, his thumbs pressing against his chest. "You were going to let me kill you, you've invited me into your home and you barely know me—" his eyes widened as a thought occurred to him. "What would have happened to the grimoire if I'd killed you?" he breathed, as the slow chill of horror crept over him.

"The grimoire would have gone to its new owner," she stated calmly. "There is a built-in hereditary spell."

For a moment he was distracted by all the protections and wards this book must have on it, but then brought his gaze back to the woman in front of him—the woman who could get herself into serious trouble for trusting too easily.

"You have to protect yourself better," he told her. God, the more he learned about this woman, the more he wanted to shield her. And that totally wasn't what he was used to. He was used to annihilating witches, not protecting them.

"Dave, you're the Witch Hunter. Our own version of law enforcement. Why shouldn't I trust you?"

"I kill people, Sully," he rasped, pain burning his throat. "I kill witches. Like you."

She shook her head. "No, not like me. You kill the evil among us, Dave."

He shook his head at the blind faith, the respect in her voice. He deserved neither. And that hurt. It hurt how much he wanted it to be true, and how far away from the truth it was.

"You don't get it. The Ancestors picked me because I can kill my kin and walk way," he told her. "I've had to, in the past." He shrugged out of his jacket, and then pulled his black T-shirt over his head. "Look at me, Sully."

He held his arms out, and then slowly turned around. "Every single one of these names belongs to a witch I've killed." His back was covered in the black tattoos. His biceps. And now the spot over his heart. It was getting so that he barely recognized himself in the mirror anymore. He sometimes had to force himself to stare at his reflection. Those names…each kill was burned into his memory. Those who had begged for mercy… those who had resisted and fought to live, or tried to kill him instead. He lifted his gaze to hers, and it was one of the hardest things he'd had to do. "You can't trust a monster like me, Sully," he rasped.

Her eyes were bright and luminous, as though she was fighting back tears. She took a tentative step forward, her hand out. She paused, then laid her hand on his chest.

There it was again, that clash of energy, that tidal wave of sensation, and then there was her touch. He closed his eyes at the contact, so light, so gentle and warm. He hadn't realized how much he'd craved a woman's touch—*her* touch. It was soothing, it was arousing, it was the very essence of a complex and complicated woman, and he wanted more—and hated himself for it.

"You may be a Witch Hunter," she whispered, and took a deep breath. "But I know you're not all bad."

He slowly opened his eyes. She stood so close, her honey-blond hair loose and luxurious around her shoulders, her blue eyes so full of sympathy, of tenderness. He felt like a brute next to her.

"I'm not all good, either."

She bit her lip, then moved her hand to cup his cheek. "You're good enough."

Her gaze dropped down to his lips, and his breath froze in his chest for a moment. She nodded. "You're good enough," she whispered. She rose up on her toes and pressed her lips against his.

He stood there for a moment, stunned.

Hell, if he wasn't a monster, he sure as hell wasn't a saint. He wrapped his arms around her waist, and slanted his lips across hers.

Chapter 10

She slid her arms around his neck as he gathered her close. So many messages, it made her dizzy trying to make sense of them all. Desire, so hot, so sharp, it took her breath away. Frustration. Loneliness. Self-recrimination. Arousal.

She'd meant to comfort him. She'd sensed his guilt and remorse, so heavy it was nearly suffocating. His gaze was hidden behind his sunglasses, but those lips, the set of his jaw… She'd wanted to reach out.

Now, though, there was no thought for comfort, for reassurance. Sully opened her lips to him, her breath hitching as his tongue slid against hers. His hands tightened on her hips, pulling her against him, and she could feel the hard ridge of his arousal pressing against her stomach.

Her hands trailed over his shoulders, his arms—oh, heavens, his arms. The man was magnificent. So strong and broad, so warm, so—

Dave flexed his hips against hers, and Sully thought she was going to combust. She slanted her head first one way, then the other, their tongues dueling, their breaths coming in shared, staccato pants.

His large hands slid beneath her loose top, and goose bumps rose on her ribs. She arched her back as his hands trailed up her back. She moaned. Heat, so much heat. Her heart thudded in her ears, and she could feel herself getting damp between her thighs. Her breasts swelled, and she pressed herself against him firmly. God, his chest was amazing. She ran her hands over the defined musculature of his torso. His skin was smooth, so sleek, so not what she expected. She could see some marks that weren't tattoos. Scars. But, astonishingly, the evidence of his strength, of his skill, just felt sexy against her fingertips as she caressed him.

Dave made a surprised sound against her lips when his fingers encountered the clasp of her strapless bra. She raised her eyebrows as she drew back, and he gave her a wicked smile. "I've been fantasizing about your underwear," he murmured, then took her lips again as his clever fingers undid the clasp.

He drew the garment away from her, and she shivered in his arms at the caress against her skin.

And then his hands covered her breasts beneath her top. She moaned, tearing her lips from his, her head tilting back as she surrendered to the sensation. He cupped the weight of her breasts in his hands, his thumbs strumming over her nipples.

So hot. Liquid heat slicked her thighs, and she pulled his head down, capturing his lips in a kiss that conveyed her own hunger. For him. For the Witch Hunter.

He growled softly into her mouth, then his hands glided down to her butt. He caressed her there, clasping the fabric of her skirt and inching it up her legs. She slid her tongue against his, her breath coming in pants. She could feel the heat of his body, the cool against her legs, her nipples tight with want. Dave bent his knees. His grip tightened, and he lifted her up. Sully swung her legs around his hips as he walked her back to rest her butt on a shelf of the bookcase. She ignored the clatter, the tumble of magical texts falling to the floor.

She lifted her head to take a quick breath, then closed her eyes as she tilted her head back. He was hard against her. Everywhere. Hard. Hot. His hips rolled against hers, and she shuddered. Her thighs tightened around his hips, and he moaned, low and sexy, as he trailed his lips down the line of her neck.

So much heat. She heard him hiss in her ear, felt him shudder. Heat. Like, burning. She pulled back, and his neck arched, the veins in stark relief against his skin. He leaned back, his hips holding her in place on the shelf.

The mark on his chest glowed. Her name.

Realization hit. *Oh, God, no.*

"Dave," she gasped.

The mark brightened, and Dave clasped the shelf on either side of her, gritting his teeth as he sucked in a breath. His biceps bulged, his knuckles whitened and his thighs tensed beneath hers.

He was in pain. She could feel it. Intense, burning. Consuming.

"Sullivan Timmerman," Dave gasped, tugging off his sunglasses.

Sully gaped as his light gray eyes turned silver, and his expression went slack as he stared sightlessly at the shelves above her head, entranced.

Instinctively, she reached out to give him comfort, to offer him support.

Red. Fire. Scalding. Darkness. Running. Panting. Determination. *A woman, scrambling down the side drive of a house. She pauses at the chain-link fence, fumbling with the gate's latch.* Satisfaction. Gotcha. *The woman turns to face her, her eyes wide with terror.*

"No! Please, no!" She holds up her arms to ward off blows, but the knife strikes fast. Not to kill, just to stop her from running. Triumph. *The woman clutches her stomach, her face twists in pain. She gasps as she falls to her knees, and she collapses, cradling her stomach as the stain blooms across her blouse.* Cold intent. End it. *The knife flashes again, plunging into her chest. The confusion, the shock, the terror, gently wanes as the light leaves her eyes.*

Dave lowered her to the floor and stumbled back, breaking their contact. Sully's vision snapped into focus once more. She was back in her living room, leaning back against her bookshelf, her skirt gently draping down to her calves as Dave grimaced. He shook his head once, still caught in the violence of his vision.

His lips tightened. Then his lips turned down, and for a brief moment sadness crossed his features, before it was removed by determination and that same ruthlessness she'd seen on the beach. He blinked, and the light in his eyes flickered down to a light silver.

"Are you okay?" she asked. His chest didn't glow anymore, and she could see him in his eyes again, not some vacant glaze.

His chest, though, looked painful. The mark that had healed a little was now rebranded onto his skin. Her name.

Sullivan Timmerman had killed again.

"I have to go," Dave muttered, wincing as he reached for his T-shirt.

Sully raised a shaky hand to her lips, trying to fight back the tears.

"Aman—Amanda Sinclair," she said, then clutched her stomach. Oh, God. Her family...

"What?"

"Amanda Sinclair. The woman he just killed. That's her name," she said, then covered her mouth. Deep breaths.

Dave frowned. "You—you saw?" he asked, his tone baffled as he took a step toward her.

She nodded. "Touch, we were touching. Oh, my God, Amanda," The tears fell, hot on her cheeks. Her gut clenched, and she could feel the bile rising in her throat.

Dave's eyes widened in shock, then his features showed his dismay. "Oh, Sully. I didn't know—I'd never want you to see—"

"He hunted her," she cried, her hands twisting in the cotton of her blouse.

Dave stilled. "What?"

"He—he was hunting her. I could—I could feel it."

Dave looked from her to the door, and back to her. He reached for her arm, gently pulling her away from the bookshelf, and then turned and guided her to sit on the foldout sofa.

"I'm sorry, I have to go, I have to find him—we'll talk later," he promised, his face filled with regret. "Where does Amanda live?"

"Lived," she corrected automatically, shock putting her into a numb autopilot. The woman was now dead. Oh, hell.

He nodded. "Yes. Lived. Sully, where did Amanda Sinclair live?" he asked gently.

"Two streets down from where we were tonight. Number 6." Her response was automatic, the words falling from her lips as she replayed what she'd seen in her mind. Amanda had been so terrified. Another tear fell on her cheek. She'd never felt so helpless, so useless, watching the woman's murder.

He cupped her cheek, and tilted his forehead against hers. "I'm so sorry, Sully." Intense guilt. Remorse. Grief. He was full of it. For Amanda—and for her.

"No, this isn't on you," she told him, blinking back her tears. "I'll come with you," she said, and braced herself to rise off the sofa. The Sinclairs…she had to go to them.

Dave's hand on her shoulder prevented her from moving. "No," he told her firmly. "You're staying right here."

"Dave, I know the family," she told him urgently.

He nodded. "I understand. But I'm going to the scene of a murder, Sully. This guy—he might still be there. I don't want you anywhere near this."

Her eyes narrowed. "I can take care of myself, Dave." She'd spent the last four years making sure that was true.

His lips firmed. "You're strong, I'll give you that. But this guy has now murdered three people. I'm not willing to take the chance that you could be the fourth."

She opened her mouth to protest, and he cut off her words with a quick kiss. "Please, Sully. I have to do this, and you being there—it will be a distraction. I'll be wanting to make sure you're safe, and not focusing on the job." Dave straightened. "I have to go. But we'll talk when I get back. I promise."

"Your chest," she said in protest. Dave was pulling his T-shirt on over his as head as he walked toward the door.

"I've got a first aid kit on my bike," he said brusquely, and then left.

Sully sagged back on the sofa, and stared around the room. Dave's suggestion was definitely the safest course. His job was to hunt the null killer. The witch killing the people she knew and loved in her name.

"Screw it," she muttered. Dave expected her to sit quietly at home. She hadn't let a man make her decisions for her for four years. She wasn't about to let that happen again. Her friends needed her. She trotted out to the shed in the back garden to gather some supplies.

Dave drove up to the makeshift barricade on the street and surveyed the scene. A crowd had gathered along the designated perimeter, and deputies were out to direct traffic and enforce the boundary. Red-and-blue lights flashed down the street, casting colored flickers into the darkness. The sheriff stood near the driveway gate and was talking to a man who Dave could only guess was Amanda Sinclair's husband, judging from his devastated, grief-stricken expression.

Darn. With the sheriff and his deputies traipsing all over the area, he couldn't get any closer to the scene. Couldn't witch his way past, couldn't bespell people to tell him what he needed to know, couldn't become invisible or forgettable—not in null territory, anyway. This was a novel experience, not being able to use his powers to get what he wanted. Which was exactly what Sully had said before, wasn't it? She wouldn't date him because he was the kind of guy who did and said whatever was needed to get what he wanted.

And yet, they'd kissed. So maybe dating was off the table, but other stuff wasn't...? He frowned. The burn in his chest had subsided, but was still an aching reminder of what he was in Serenity Cove for—and it wasn't to get up close and all kinds of personal with an empath witch who seemed to know him way too well for his liking.

He kicked out the stand for his bike and swung his leg over. He removed his helmet, wincing at the pull on his chest. He'd slapped a nonstick dressing over the wound and used tape to hold it in place, but it ached, and his skin was pinched by the tape with each movement. He hung the strap of his helmet over the handlebars, then strode a little farther along the edge of the perimeter. He eyed the front of the house. The door was closed. His lips tightened. No sign of forced entry. He glanced over toward the gate. A sheet was draped over the figure on the ground. He backed up a little. The drive had a five-foot-high wooden fence down one side. She wouldn't have been able to scale it, not with her killer right on her heels. House on one side, fence on the other, her only option would have been to run down the drive toward the street. He wondered if that had been the killer's plan, or whether he'd just been lucky.

"Excuse me, sir."

Dave turned as the deputy stepped around the roadblock, gesturing beyond him. Dave realized he was standing in the man's way and stepped aside, giving a casual wave of apology as the deputy passed him.

He turned back to the scene. Sully was right. Amanda Sinclair had been hunted down and killed. He glanced up at the night sky. The moon was a chunk of silver. A waxing gibbous moon. Enough light to stop you from tripping off the curb, but still kind of gloomy, especially in this neighborhood with no streetlights, he noticed, eyeing up and down the street.

A warm breeze ruffled his hair. He would have liked

to remove his jacket, but with the law already here, he didn't think he'd be sticking around for long. A hand thudded down on his shoulder, and he turned, hiding the wince at the resulting pull of muscle and scorched skin.

Jacob Forsyth. Sully's wannabe-boyfriend nodded grimly at him. "I thought you left?"

"I turned back when I saw all the police cars on the highway," he lied. He couldn't very well say he'd received a magical vision from the Ancestors. That wasn't something folks readily understood or accepted—except for Sully, it seemed.

Jacob nodded, accepting his excuse at face value. He looked over toward the cordoned-off house, his expression dark and grim. "This sucks. Ronald found her when he came home from the Adler farewell."

Dave looked over at him. "She wasn't at the farewell?"

Jacob shook his head. "Nope. She was home with the kids."

"Kids were in the house?" Dave looked back at the house in horror. He hadn't seen the kids in the vision.

Jacob nodded, his lips tight. "Yeah. They slept through the whole thing." His answer was short. Abrupt. The man was visibly upset—no, maybe angry was a better word—at what had happened.

"But they're safe?" Dave's gut clenched with apprehension at the risk to the kids.

"Yeah, they're safe."

"Thank God," Dave muttered in relief. Jacob watched him closely for a moment, then glanced back up the street.

"When did you say you arrived in Serenity?" Jacob's tone was conversational, but the words cut like hot steel.

Dave met his gaze. "I didn't." He should have expected this. "I arrived the morning of Mary Anne Adler's death." Which meant he wasn't in the area for Gary Adler's death, and he hoped that was enough to eliminate him from Jacob's obvious suspicions.

"Murder," Jacob corrected.

Dave inclined his head. "Murder."

"Where's Sully?"

"She's back home," Dave said.

Jacob nodded. "Good. She doesn't need to see this."

Dave turned back toward where the sheriff was talking quietly with the husband. Jacob sounded protective. Proprietary.

Not that he should care. He was here to hunt his witch. If the witch moved on, he moved on. If he managed to kill the witch, he moved on. If another witch committed a crime, he moved on. He couldn't see a scenario where he didn't move on. It shouldn't matter to him what Jacob and Sully did. He wasn't here to interfere with Sully's life—after what he'd done to her on the beach, he'd be ensuring that Sully's life was a long and happy one. If that meant a life with—*ugh*—Jacob, so be it.

Only, that idea was more irritating than the recurring brand on his chest, and just as painful, if he let himself follow that thought down the rabbit hole. He tried to tell himself he had no business feeling annoyed at this man trying to stake his claim on Sully.

But he was, especially when he still had the taste of her on his lips.

He tilted his head as he eyed the sheet-covered body. "Was Amanda Sinclair a pureblood?" he asked, curious.

Jacob stilled. He seemed to be considering his response. Then he leaned closer, and Dave lifted his chin to meet the null's gaze directly. "I know you're a friend of Sully's and all, and I know the noise you've made about helping us, but my bullshit radar is going full alert around you. You may have Sully convinced that you're here to help, but I don't know you, and I don't trust you. If you're wanting to get into Sully's good graces, figure out a different way, because this," the man said, gesturing between Dave and the Sinclair house, "is a pretty crap way of doing it."

Jacob turned and walked farther down the street, and Dave saw Jenny running up to her brother, her face distressed as she took in the scene.

Dave shoved his hands in his pockets, and turned to look at the few people nearby. Each time he made eye contact, they turned away. Jacob wasn't the only one who didn't seem to trust him. He wasn't going to get any answers from this crowd.

He sighed as he strode back to his bike. Tracking down this killer witch was getting more complicated by the day.

Sully quenched the blade in the tub of oil, watching as steam curled up from the surface. She withdrew it slightly, then dipped, repeating the process gently, moving her head out of the way of the small billowing flare-up when the vapors burned. When the blade had cooled, she placed it on the stone bench where the others lay, then raised her protective visor.

She surveyed her handiwork. Four blades. As soon as the metal blades were thoroughly cool, she'd do a hollow grind them on them, sharpen them and polish them, and then she'd cut out and fix the tangs inside the handles. She'd have four more close-combat weapons. When finished, these blades would have a forty-five-degree angle to the blade from the hilt that made it easy to draw them from whatever holster or sheath they occupied. She picked up one of the blades. The steel she'd used was composed of a greater iron alloy than usual, and then she'd give them decorative silver engraving along the blade. A kind of catchall against the shadow breeds. While the null's presence voided a shadow breed's supernatural abilities, it didn't stop the effect of injuries. With iron as the base metal, the blade had not only the physical aspects of creating damage, but any race sensitive to silver, or to iron, would still feel the effects of the metal. It was like a double-pronged attack by the wielder. Shadow breeds naturally had a greater muscle mass that put them at a slight advantage over ordinary human beings, whether they were nulls or not. This kind of blade did a little toward evening out the playing field.

Once the blades had cooled sufficiently and she didn't run the risk of shattering them, she'd engrave on them some simple spellwork, and bleed some molten silver into the designs. The spells would be voided if being wielded by a null, but if it was, say, a witch against a werewolf, or a human against a vampire, or even witch against witch, the spells would still engage—and cause significant damage. Her lips firmed. She wanted to get this witch, but if she couldn't, then she'd damn well protect her friends—protect them in a way she'd wished someone had protected her, all those years ago.

She rolled her shoulders, shaking off the tension, the dark memories. She'd worked through the night, and her neck and shoulder muscles were tired, her feet were sore and she'd definitely be feeling her biceps tomorrow. She reached over and turned off the burners for her forge. She'd added an extension to the back of her factory shop, creating a blacksmithing Shangri-la. It had taken her a few years, but she finally had a number of forges using different fuels, and anything she could think of in the creation of her cutlery…and weapons and coins. She could have made these blades at home. She eyed the other daggers, dirks and swords she'd also stockpiled that now were lined up neatly on one wall, weapons that she could create only here, in the bigger forge. In the past few days she'd made a whole bunch of arrowheads, and this time, she'd used her own unique broadhead style, with three blades angling out from the tip of the arrowhead. Excellent penetration, minimal deflection, maximum damage.

She removed her protective glasses, apron and gloves and started to clean up. She wrinkled her nose as she hung her leather apron up on a hook. Man, she was rank. She'd have to go home and shower before she did anything.

She put all her tools away, and then placed her new blades and their handles on a shelf running along the wall. She then pulled the sliding wall along its track until it settled into its position. She stood back and eyed the wall, then nodded, satisfied. It looked like a normal wall, and not the entry to her secret armory.

Once everything was cleared away, and the floor swept, she switched off the lights and locked the doors. She smiled as she turned to her car. Dave expected her to bespell her factory and shop. The problem was, in null territory, it didn't matter how many wards she layered over the access points, they were rendered useless here.

She yawned as she drove out of town and along the coast road toward her home. The ocean was on her right, and the sky was already lightening, the sun just beginning to edge its way over the horizon. It was early. Too early to call Jenny. She'd go home, have a quick shower and some breakfast and then—she yawned again. Okay, so it had been a while since she'd pulled an all-nighter in the forge.

She braked gently, eyeing the turnoff that would take her to the null neighborhood. She clenched the wheel. Poor Ronald. He and Amanda had just celebrated their four-year anniversary. She'd babysat their little darlings, Becky and Lily. She took the turn, and moments later was driving quietly down the main street. She stopped at the corner and looked down the street. Yellow crime scene ribbon fluttered in the warm morning breeze. Two deputies stood by their car, and another was using one of those wheely measure things as he walked along the driveway. The sheriff rose from where he'd squatted near the gate, camera in one hand as he rubbed his other over his face.

Sully eyed that gate. That's where it had happened. A flash of memory, Amanda's terror-filled eyes, her trembling hands. Sully blinked rapidly to dispel the vision.

A long night for the local law, too, by the looks of things. She eyed the house. Now was not the time to visit Ronald and express her condolences. She drove on down the street and took the next right, and then another right and then a left to head back out to toward the coastal road. A little while later she was pulling into her driveway and avoiding the motorcycle that was parked up near the side of the house.

She climbed out of the car, closing the door quietly, then climbed the stairs to her porch. She turned and gazed out over the headland. The sun was higher now, the sky bathed in fiery pinks, burning away the horrors of the night. Sully bit her lip as she again remembered seeing Amanda run down the driveway, only this time the memory morphed into her running, her stumbling along, trying to get away.

Of being caught.

Sully sniffed and turned her back on the beautiful view of a stunning sunrise over the ocean. She had stuff to do. Shower. Breakfast. Call Jenny.

She let herself inside the house, wincing as she tried to close the door silently, then cringing at the soft snick of the latch. Darn it. She hesitated. The house was quiet, save for a sonorous snore emanating from her living room. So Dave had returned. Her lips tightened as she remembered him commanding her to stay. That chafed. And she hadn't rebelled, either. She'd stayed away from the Sinclair home, from the null neighborhood. Damn it. She'd have to watch for that. She wasn't some guy's doormat anymore.

She slipped her flip-flops off and started to tiptoe across the foyer toward the hall. She peeked into the living room as she passed. Well, peeked and then stopped.

Dave lay sprawled out on her sofa, his feet dangling over the sofa arm at the end, one arm draped toward the floor. He made her lounge look like furniture from a dollhouse. The blanket laid pooled on the floor—it had been a warm night—and he lay there, with just the sheet covering him. Almost. His sunglasses were folded and placed on the end table by his head.

Her mouth grew slack. Holy mother of smoking hot men. His chest was bare, and she could see again all the Old Language lettering inked across his biceps, and down his rib cage and across his abdomen. A white square dressing was taped across his left pec, but it didn't quite cover his nipple. It was almost as if the Ancestors had used his musculature as a writing guide, and the markings enhanced the dips and bulges of his body. His sheet was—she swallowed—*just* covering his groin, and she could see his bare hip, and the curve of his butt cheek… She curled her fingers into a fist. *No touching.*

Warmth bloomed inside her. Damn, Dave Carter was one crazy hot Witch Hunter. She tried to look down the hall. She really did. Her lip caught between her teeth as she eyed his smooth skin, his broad chest with the—she frowned. Good grief. Had he used *duct tape* to stick his bandage down?

She shook her head. Men. She let her gaze travel down his body. The one leg outside the sheet revealed a strong thigh and muscular calf. Her heart thumped a little faster in her chest. She was perving on a guy who was sleeping, a guest in her home.

And she was not sorry at all. She eyed the sheet. It really was draped precariously. She tilted her head to the side. She wasn't sure if that was just a large rumple of the sheet or whether that was him…

She blinked. No. She should march herself down to the bathroom and jump into a nice cold shower. She nodded. Yep. That's exactly what she should do. She took a step back, and the floorboard creaked.

Her eyes widened.

Dave's eyes opened to slits, his silver-gray gaze meeting hers.

Chapter 11

Dave's lips quirked. Sully looked like she'd been caught with her hand in the cookie jar.

"Hey, good morning," he said, his voice husky as he started to sit up.

"No!" Sully said, her hand flashing up in that universal stop signal.

He froze. "What?" He glanced about, narrowing his eyes against the soft morning light. He couldn't see any threat. He looked back at her, bewildered. "What's wrong?"

"Uh, you might want to cover up," she whispered, gesturing in the general direction of his groin while keeping her gaze on the ceiling. Except for when she peeked at him. Twice.

His lips curved into a smile as he sat up. He didn't touch the sheet. Not that he was in any danger of losing it. His body had apparently recognized Sully before his brain kicked in, and his hard-on had hooked the sheet.

And then he realized she was wearing the same clothes he'd kissed her in. That loose billowy top with the strapless bra underneath. His eyebrows rose. "Are you just getting in?" He'd tiptoed in last night, thinking she was asleep down the hall in her bedroom.

Sully nodded as she glanced toward the end of the hall, then back at him. "Yeah. I couldn't just sit here, last night, so I went into the factory."

"The factory," he repeated, then frowned. "Your factory near town? With the lousy locks?"

She nodded. "Yep, that would be the one." Her gaze dropped to the sheet, and her cheeks grew rosy.

The room was gradually getting lighter, as the sun climbed higher, glinting through the bay windows, and he had to narrow his eyes against the glare.

"Sully, that could have been dangerous," he told her as he reached for his sunglasses.

She folded her arms, her flip-flops dangling from one hand. "You can't have it both ways, Dave. If it was too dangerous for me to go with you to Amanda's house because the killer may have been there, it should have been fine for me at my factory."

His lips tightened at her logic as he slid his glasses on. The dimming of the room gave him some relief, but he could still see Sully clearly. Too clearly. She was annoyed. Well, so was he. He'd slept here, knowing that he'd hear anyone entering through the house and could protect her. It was galling to realize he'd been protecting an empty bed.

"Sully, until I catch this guy, anywhere you go—"

She shook her head. "No, let's put this into perspective. So far, this witch has gone after nulls. I am not a null. There is no link between me and the victims, other than I know them, and in a town this size, so does pretty much everyone else. I'm going to go wherever I want, whenever I want—starting with visiting Jenny after breakfast."

"The guy kills in your name, Sully. The Ancestors gave me *your name*." He rose from the couch, frustration eating at him. He pulled the sheet with him to save embarrassment—not his, hers. Her eyes widened, but to her credit she kept her gaze fastened on his. "You say you only have a minor connection to these people, but we both know that's not right."

"You're right. My connection to these people is not minor. These people…" She gestured toward her front door, to the community beyond, "These people have become my family, my *home*." She turned to face him, and her expression was so sad, so frustrated, he took a step toward her before he realized what he was doing. He halted, clutching the sheet to his groin.

"I will do what I can to help them, to protect them," she said, her shoulders straightening. "So for the record, I will do everything within my power to stop this witch. Don't even think you can sideline me on this."

Her gaze had turned fierce, her blue eyes practically snapping fire at him.

This time he took that step, bringing him closer to her, and her gaze dropped to his chest. "Don't even think I'm going to let you risk your life here doing *my* job," he said, his voice low and rough. His job sucked. She had no idea the toll it took on a person, especially a witch, to kill another. It was that one little loophole— and every spell and rule had one. Witches were supposed to honor and protect nature and her creatures. Witches weren't supposed to harm another, but when they did, his ordained job was to harm them. And it sucked a little at his soul, each and every time.

She had to drag her gaze up from his chest, and he saw the moment his words sank in. Her eyes narrowed, and his chin jutted forward as he waited for her response, a response he could just see was going to be fiery.

"I am not about to let another man dictate what I can and can't do," she said, her voice sounding like it was pulled tight over sandpaper, all husky and coarse. "If you ever again tell me to sit and stay like a good dog, I will show you just how much of a bitch I can be."

He blinked. There was so much to unpack from those remarks, he was trying to figure out what to address first. Okay, the dog comment definitely had to be straightened out. He was horrified that's how she'd perceived his remarks, that he'd made a woman feel like that. "I'm sorry, Sully, I never meant to treat you, or make you feel like a—"

She smiled tightly. "I know you didn't, but when you command a strong, capable witch to stay at home and out of trouble, how do you expect it to sound?" She folded her arms, and he saw her breasts swell against the material of her top. He adjusted the sheet in front of him. They were having a serious conversation, for Pete's sake. He wasn't supposed to be distracted by her body.

Her gaze dropped to track his movement with the sheet, and a blush crept over her cheeks. So, he wasn't the only one battling distraction. Good to know.

She cleared her throat. "Would you have said it to me, if I was male?"

"Yes," he answered immediately. "Gender has nothing to do with this. If you were male or female, and I thought you were in danger from this witch, I would say the same thing—which is, let me handle this," he emphasized, leaning forward to meet her gaze. "If you're a witch, or a vamp or a shifter, this witch is capable of performing magic of some sort around a null. I've never seen that before—I didn't even know it was possible. We have no idea what this witch is capable of. We do know that he's killed two women as well as a strong, physically fit and capable man, so yes, guy or chick, I'm saying steer clear for your own safety."

He raised his hand to tuck a tendril behind her ear—and *pift*, there was that zing, that little clap of power that always happened between them, that awakened his senses on a cellular level, that heightened his awareness and made him feel like he was surrounded by a field of electricity with her. "Your safety is very, very important to me," he told her in a low voice.

Her gaze dropped from his eyes to his mouth, and her own mouth opened. She pressed her lips together. Swallowed. "It's just as well you're being sincere. A bit of a douche, but a sincere douche."

He smiled. "I've been called worse."

Sully nodded, then her gaze drifted down. He was tempted to lose the sheet, to sweep her up in his arms, step back to that damn sofa and make these sparks between them fly.

Sully gaped at him, then snapped her mouth shut. She jerked her thumb over her shoulder. "Shower. Me." She was looking at him. All of him. And there was a desire, a hunger in her eyes that was so naked, so blatant, he so damn wanted to reach for her then and there and finish what they'd started the night before.

He raised an eyebrow. "Is that an invitation?"

Her cheeks got rosier, and she shook her head. Just

a little nervous shake. "I mean, I'm going to take a shower." She hurried down the hall, and Dave smiled.

"Pity."

Sully pulled up in front of Jenny's drive, and glanced over at Dave. He'd opted to travel with her this time, instead of riding his motorbike. She wasn't sure if it was for the sake of convenience—they were both going to the same place, so it made sense—or whether it was to keep an eye on her.

Protect her.

She swallowed. She'd spent way too much time in the shower this morning, thinking about Dave and that sheet. Or rather, Dave without the sheet. Even now her cheeks heated with the images that had flashed through her mind as she'd washed away the sweat and grime from her night in the factory. His golden skin, those markings that followed the line of his sculpted muscles, those amazing silver-gray eyes.

The man was gorgeous. He oozed a dangerous sensuality that seemed to bypass any of her personal controls and call to something deep inside her, something she thought she'd gained control over.

She'd wanted him to join her in the shower. Heck, she'd wanted to join him on that sofa, just like she sensed he wanted. She couldn't remember ever having such an intense physical reaction to a man. Sure, things with Marty had been physical—way too physical, especially toward the end. She thought she was past all that, or at least wary of it, with a logical desire to steer clear of that kind of allure. Dave, though, was…more. More man. More muscle. More presence. More power. She should be running in the opposite direction, especially when he got his alpha witch on and demanded she stand down.

When he'd touched her, she'd sensed him—again. She couldn't mistake his need to protect her, and it was so genuine, so sincere, it touched her. He was frustrated, and he was worried—for her. She couldn't sense any darkness to his need to protect her. It was pure, it was light and it was so damn seductive, she'd wanted to jump into his arms and give him what they both wanted. Whatever that may be.

Which, in turn, annoyed her. She'd spent the past four years proving to herself she didn't need to be with a man… She didn't need permission, she didn't need approval, or assistance, or support, or any little tie that would anchor her to a guy. No. She'd learned she was more than capable of standing on her own two feet, of paying her own bills, of developing her own business, honing her craft—establishing her own damn identity.

She didn't need to be told where she could and couldn't go, who she could and couldn't see, what she could and couldn't wear, and what she could and couldn't think, feel, say, do.

There was something about Dave, though, something that snagged at her, drew her in. She had to shut that crap down right now. Before she got sucked into another nightmare.

Sully turned her head to eye him. He looked deep in thought, staring through the windshield. He'd showered after she had—which involved more fantasizing on her part about his naked body under the stream of hot water. Steam. Soap suds. Muscles.

She cleared her throat, and he turned to look at her, his eyes shielded by the dark lenses of his sunglasses. He was wearing a navy T-shirt, and she could see one of his markings peeking out from beneath the edge of his sleeve. Name, not marking, she corrected herself. The name of a witch he'd killed.

See, just that thought should give her chills. She'd been on the receiving end of his murderous intent, after all. Yet, it didn't. She'd seen him in action, seen his ruthlessness, his power turned on another—her—along with a physical dominance that should have her ducking for cover. But...it didn't. Why was that? What was it about this guy that made her ignore all her safeguards, all those red flags she'd warned herself to watch out for and steer away from?

"You might want to let me do the talking," she said to him. He'd told her the conversation he'd had with Jacob. She was mildly surprised the nice, friendly guy she knew had so abruptly shut Dave down, but she was beginning to find out a lot of mild surprises from the people she thought she'd gotten to know so well.

Dave's lips tightened, but he nodded. He didn't like it, she could tell, but, well, what could he do about it? Nulls didn't like outsiders. It was only because she'd been able to make teas and ointments that made them feel better that they had welcomed her in, initially. And Dave—well, Dave didn't look like the tea-drinking type, let alone the tea-making type.

They got out of the car, and Sully squinted against the bright sunlight as she closed her car door. She wore a loose cotton top with thin straps, and the sun beat down on her bare shoulders. Today was going to be a hot one.

She slid the strap of her tote up her arm to her shoulder as she waited for Dave to walk around the car, and they crossed the street together. They were walking up the garden path to Jenny's cottage front door when they heard the scream.

Chapter 12

Dave bolted up the steps and across the porch, hand out to thrust open the door. Heart hammering, he could feel the skin over his pec muscle beginning to warm. More screams.

No. God, no. Not again, not here. "Jenny!"

He heard a clatter in the kitchen. His arms pumped as he ran down the hall, scanning the rooms through the open doorways until he raced around the bend in the hall.

"Jenny!" He heard Sully's cry, the sound of her flip-flops smacking the floorboards as she raced along behind him.

The door to the kitchen was closed. Dave didn't slow down, just bent his right arm in front of him and shoulder-charged the door.

The door gave way, whipping open as he barreled through. Jenny was on the floor, screaming, legs kicking. A guy straddled her, but froze when he heard the door. Dave roared. Instinctively he summoned his powers, only to feel…nothing.

Damn it. Nulls. The guy didn't even turn to face him, but rose and raced through the back door. Dave's skin stopped itching.

His gaze met Jenny's wide-eyed fearful stare. She was crap-scared, but physically all right. He didn't stop, but darted through the back door. He hesitated briefly, scanning the yard. There. The back gate hung agape, as though it had been slammed closed but not latched, and was slowly swinging back open again.

Arms and legs pumping, he ran through the gate, and caught sight of a dark leg and shoe as his quarry raced down the narrow lane between rows of houses, and then around the corner. Dave took off again, hands straight, his stride lengthening. So close. Finally. So. Damn. Close.

He skidded around the corner. Damn it. Another lane. There. Farther up, the guy was hitting the gravel pretty damn hard. He wanted to send a blast toward him, level the bastard with a powerful shove of magic, yet being in the heart of the null neighborhood, it didn't matter how much he tried to draw on his powers, nothing would come forth. Dave sprinted after him. The man turned and jumped over a low fence, and Dave followed, bracing his hands on the horizontal rail as he swung his legs over in a smooth movement, and then took off running across someone's back lawn. Well, dirt patch.

He ducked under the low-hanging branch of a magnolia, and ignored the cry of an older woman peering through her kitchen window.

The witch pounded along the driveway, then took a gradual curve across the front lawn, jumping over the fence like an athlete in a hurdle race. Dave sprinted, then inhaled as he leaped over the fence. He didn't break stride as he hit the ground running.

The witch raced along the street. *Look at me.* Dave's jaw clenched. The guy wasn't looking in any direction except straight ahead. Wasn't even checking if Dave was still in pursuit. All Dave could see was the back of the man's head. The witch hit an intersection and turned right, his hand raised to shield his face.

Dave pumped his legs harder, faster. Damn him. He was hiding his face. The witch ducked behind a tall fence, and it took Dave a couple of seconds to reach the spot. Dave skidded to a stop, glancing about wildly.

What? Where the hell had he gone? An old woman, stooped over so much that she could barely make eye contact with him, gave him a friendly smile and wave as she started to cross the street.

Dave went up to the fence, grabbed the top and pulled himself up to peer over it. He scanned the backyard. A dog lifted its head, then rose when he saw Dave. He barked.

There was no sign of the witch he'd been pursuing, and the dog would have sounded the alarm had someone tried to scale the fence and run through the yard.

Dave dropped to the ground, then glanced up and down the street. What the hell? He jogged from one driveway to the other, glancing down and around. Nothing. Nobody. He tried to summon his powers again, and frustration licked at him like a hot flame at the silence, the cool…the void.

He hurried in the direction of the old woman.

"Excuse me, ma'am?"

The woman slowed, and it took seconds for her to scan the street.

"Ma'am," Dave said again as he jogged up to her. It seemed to take a moment for her to realize he was behind her, and she shifted. Slowly. Little shuffling steps.

"Excuse me, ma'am, but did you see where that man went?"

She was hunched over, her gaze on his shoes, and it took her a moment to try to lift her head enough to meet his gaze. Dave leaned forward to save her the effort.

"What?" she asked, her white brows dipping. She raised her hand to cup her ear.

"The man," Dave repeated loudly. "Did you see where he went?"

"Man? What man?" Her rheumy eyes showed her confusion. She blinked at him, as though trying to understand him. Or remember him. Or…maybe just focus on him.

"Uh, the man—I was following a man round here," he said, gesturing toward the corner.

She shifted. Slowly. Little shuffling steps so that she could see where he was pointing. She blinked, squinting. "Where is he?" she asked him.

He took a breath. "I don't know. Did you see where he went?"

"Where who went?" she asked curiously, angling her head this way and that to peer up and down the street. She reminded him of a bird, with her hooked nose, small eyes and the tilt of her head, first one way, then another.

He sighed. She was nearly deaf and blind, and obviously hadn't seen anything. "Never mind. Thank you," he added. He looked around. The witch had disappeared. Somehow. "Here, let me help you," he said, offering her his arm. She smiled up at him.

"Why, thank you."

They shuffled across the street together, and he cupped her elbow as she stepped up onto the curb.

She nodded at him, then shuffled on her way. Dave turned back to the street, his hands on his hips as he tried to figure out how he'd managed to lose the guy. Lips pressed tight, he started to walk back the way he'd come, then started to jog. He wanted to get back to Sully—and to Jenny.

Sully's friend was going to have to talk with him, now—whether she liked to or not. He wasn't going to take no for an answer.

Sully looked up from Jenny as Dave thumped up the back steps and through the back door. Jenny startled, her tea sloshing in her mug, and Sully covered her friend's hands as they cupped the ceramic mug on the table.

Dave's large frame seemed to darken the kitchen, until he stepped farther into the room. His navy T-shirt sported a damp V-patch on the front, and perspiration dripped down the sides of his face and neck. He'd run hard.

He walked over to her friend and put his hand on her shoulder, bending low to meet her gaze.

"Are you okay?" he asked Jenny quietly. If it had been appropriate, Sully would have stood and hugged him. His tone was low, so gentle, with just the right amount of concern that was heartwarming, but still strong enough that Jenny wouldn't break down into tears—which seemed likely. Sully could feel her friend trembling, and she so wanted to take some of that fear, that residual terror from her. For the first time, she wished she could still use her powers with the nulls.

Jenny nodded, her eyes wide. "Yeah," she said, her voice hoarse.

Dave reached for a high-backed chair at the end of the table, swung it around on a leg and straddled it, his muscled forearms folded across the top as he looked directly at Jenny.

"Mind telling me what happened?" he asked in a mild voice.

Jenny nodded. She opened her mouth, then blinked. She frowned. "I don't—I don't know," she said, then looked uncertainly at Dave, then at Sully.

Sully reached for her shoulder. "It's okay, Jen. Take your time."

Jenny shook her head, her expression becoming distraught. "I—I don't know," she said, her voice rising in pitch. "I remember..." Her gaze drifted to Dave. "You," she breathed. "You, breaking through my door..."

Sully glanced over at the kitchen door. The section of the door where the doorknob was located was rough and splintered, and there was a long crack down the middle panel. From the moment they'd heard Jenny's scream from the front door, Dave had become a force of energy, barreling through the house, and not slowing down for something as trivial as a door. She had entered the kitchen only to see him race through the back door.

For a big guy, he could move like lightning.

And Jenny had been on the floor, shaken and trembling. Sully had made a quick call to Tyler Clinton, and then to Jacob, and then had tended to her friend.

Now, with a cup of tea in her hands, Jenny was beginning to calm, although her cheeks were tear-streaked, and her knuckles were white as she clasped the ceramic mug.

Dave nodded. "Yes, we heard you screaming," he told her. "What can you tell us about the man, Jenny?"

Jenny's hand went to her neck. "My throat is sore."

Sully nodded, smoothing her hand across her friend's back. "You were screaming, Jen."

"The man?" Dave prompted.

Jenny frowned, her gaze caught by a bruise on her wrist, and she turned her hand over to see how far it extended. "The man..." she repeated. She blinked, then looked at Sully. "I don't remember him," she whispered, tears forming in her eyes. "Why don't I remember him?" Her voice held a hint of panic.

"Shh, it's okay," Sully said, knowing it was anything but. "Take your time." Her gaze flicked to Dave, but his face was composed. Neutral. She smiled gently at Jenny. "What were you doing earlier?"

Jenny frowned, looking around the kitchen. "I—I'm not quite sure."

"Why aren't you at school?" Sully tried a different tact.

"Uh, the principal has to do a day each month or so in a class, and today she's teaching my class. She says it keeps her fresh, gives her a chance to see the syllabus in action. She's done it for the past six years." Jenny nodded. "It's a good thing—she can foresee some of the issues when the curriculum changes. So I'm home preparing lessons for next semester."

"Where were you preparing the lessons?" Dave asked.

Jenny blinked. "In—in my living room," she murmured. He rose from his seat and indicated the doorway.

"Would you mind showing us?"

Jenny nodded, and rose, leaving her tea on the table. She led them to her small living room. The coffee table in the center of the room was strewn with papers, and her large diary was opened up to a couple of months away.

Dave nodded, then glanced around the room. "Okay. Can you remember what happened after that?"

Jenny touched her hand to her mouth, then turned to the hallway. "There was a knock at the door…" Her hands trembled, and she pressed her fingers to her temple. "It's so murky. Why can't I remember?"

Dave reached for her hand, and cupped it in both of his. "It's okay, Jenny. We'll figure this out," he reassured her.

Sully watched as her friend seem to draw comfort from Dave's words. He pulled her gently into the hallway. "So, there was a knock at the door…you went to answer it?"

Jenny nodded, and Dave guided her closer to the door. "Can you remember what happened? You would have reached for the doorknob…"

He raised her hand, and Jenny whipped it out of his reach. She stepped closer to Sully, her face pale. "No."

Sully glanced at her. "No? Do you remember something, Jen?"

Jenny shook her head, folding her arms as she looked at her front door with trepidation. "No."

"It's okay, Jenny. He's not here anymore. He can't hurt you."

"Can you remember anything about him, Jen? His hair, his eyes…?"

Jenny caught her lip between her teeth. Sully watched the movement, dismayed. Her friend was so…timid, so afraid. On one level, she could understand—the guy had tried to kill her. But—this was *Jenny*. Her friend was normally so feisty and vivacious, and here she was, too scared to open her own front door.

Memories surfaced, of a similar time when her own heart would stutter at the slightest sound inside her city apartment... She reached for her friend's arm, trying to imbue support and comfort, and feeling nothing rise inside.

Jenny shook her head and took a step back, her gaze fixed on the door.

"Okay, Jenny," Dave said, and Sully was momentarily distracted by the smooth, soothing tone he used. He stepped between Jenny and the door.

"You can remember the knock at the door, you can remember going to answer it. Once you opened the door, what—"

The pounding at the door made them all jump. "Jenny! Jenny, are you okay?"

Sully's shoulders sagged when she recognized Jacob's voice. The doorknob turned, and the door swung inward.

Jenny screamed, collapsing to the floor sobbing, holding her arms up in front of her. "No, please, no," she cried.

Jacob stared down at his sister in stunned shock, and stepped toward her. Jenny screamed again, scrambling back on her hands and feet.

"No! Stop, get out!"

Jacob halted, his mouth agape. Sully glanced between Jenny and the brother her friend adored. Why was she reacting like this?

"Jenny—" Jacob breathed in dismay as flashing red-and-blue lights flickered into the hallway, and Tyler Clinton bounded up the stairs in his sheriff's uniform.

"No!" Jenny screamed, almost hysterical as she backed away.

Dave held out his arms between the siblings, inserting himself between them. "Jenny, it's okay," he said, soothing.

"It was him," she cried, stopping when she backed up against a wall. Her head tilted, and she drew her knees up as though trying to back her way through the wall.

Sully frowned, looking over at Jacob. He looked so shocked, so hurt, so worried. She looked back at Jenny. Her friend was trembling, pale and teary as she tried to curl up and disappear.

Tyler frowned as he stepped inside the house, and looked between Jenny and Jacob. Sully knelt next to her friend, holding her arms out, and Jenny collapsed against her, sobbing. She lifted her gaze to meet Dave's. His expression was grim as he looked between the Forsyth siblings.

"What happened" Tyler asked curtly, surveying those gathered in the hallway.

Dave shifted his gaze from Sully to Jenny. "Good question."

Chapter 13

Dave followed Sully into her home and watched as she rubbed her neck. He closed the door behind them, locked it, then put a magical ward over it, just for the sake of it. Relief swelled through him as he saw the brief bloom of color, the intricate markings of his spell take hold of the door and its frame before disappearing from view. It had felt damn weird not being able to call on his powers when he was chasing the witch.

She turned to look at him. "Nightcap?"

"Hell, yeah."

She turned on the light to the living room, and he narrowed his eyes. She must have seen his reaction, because she turned off the lights, then waved her hand casually. The candles that were placed around the room sputtered to life, and he smiled his appreciation. She crossed to the white timber cabinet, and his eyebrows rose when she pulled out a bottle of Irish whiskey and two glasses. She poured a measure of the amber liquid into each and handed him a glass. She took a seat in the armchair, and he subsided on the folded out sofa.

"What an awful day," Sully muttered as she took a sip of her drink.

Dave nodded. It had been interesting, explaining to Sheriff Clinton about an intruder the victim believed had been her brother. But he'd chased that bastard, and it wasn't Jacob. Wrong height, wrong weight, wrong hair color—just wrong, wrong and wrong. Jacob had been removed from his sister's home to give her a chance to calm down, but with Jenny being a null, Dave had been unable to do any body or brain scans to figure out what the hell had happened.

"He blurred her memory," Sully murmured, incredulous. "She's a null, and he tricked her." Her lips tightened. "And to make her think it was Jacob—that's just plain low."

"While I think Jacob Forsyth is more than capable of being a dick, you're right, he wasn't the man I chased out of Jenny's kitchen."

He took a sip of his whiskey, enjoying the mild burn as it slid down his throat. "I just wish I'd gotten the bastard."

Sully tilted her head. "So, he just…disappeared?"

Dave nodded, and finished his drink. He didn't like failing—hated it, but he just couldn't figure out how the witch had done his vanishing act.

In null territory.

When he couldn't so much as muster a powerpuff punch.

Sully rose and crossed to her library, waving a hand across the front of the bookcase. Dave watched as the camouflage spell glimmered at the movement to reveal the tomes of magical spells and history.

Sully dragged her finger gently across the spines, and for a moment he was distracted by the graceful movement.

"What are you looking for?" he asked, and rose from the sofa. He placed his empty glass on the end table and crossed to her. She pulled out a book and passed to him, then scanned again, pulling two more volumes from the shelf.

"Something isn't adding up here," she said, as she crossed to the liquor cabinet and snagged up the whiskey bottle. "This guy has used my name—I don't understand that part, or why the Ancestors sent you after me. That's number one," she said, holding up the bottle. She poured another measure in his glass, and one in her own, then placed the bottle on the table.

"Number two, he's able to use magic. Around nulls. That doesn't compute. Nulls void any natural magic. Wolves can't shift, vampires can't fang out, witches can't cast spells."

Dave nodded as he sat down on the sofa again. "I know, that's something that's confusing the crap out of me, too," he admitted.

She nodded, then started to flick through one of the books she held as she sank into her armchair. "So, how is he doing it? There has to be something in these books that can help us figure this out."

He eyed her for a moment. He didn't need to ask her why she was doing this. He'd seen her with her friend. She'd been worried. Jenny had been distraught, clutching on to Sully as she'd given her statement to the sheriff. He and Sully had spent hours with the nulls, and he had even walked the neighborhood again, with some of the deputies, in case they could find some trace of the man who'd managed to enter Jenny's home through her front door, mess with her memory and almost kill her.

When Sully had been sitting with Jenny, he'd been trying to soothe Jacob. The one thing he and Sully had agreed on was not to mention the witch aspect. It didn't make sense—yet. They couldn't explain it, and Dave didn't want the sheriff looking at them as potential suspects and distract the man from pursuing the relevant clues—or interfere with his own objective of finding the witch and sending the bastard to the Other Realm.

Jacob, though, had had a difficult time accepting that his sister believed he'd tried to kill her, and was looking for answers—and Sully had wanted to give them to him, and Dave knew how hard it was for her to bite her tongue.

"They're PBs, obviously," Sully muttered absently as she scanned the pages in front of her.

Dave's eyebrows rose. "Really?"

She nodded, her honey-blond braid sliding across her shoulder. "Yeah. Jacob confirmed it. He told me the Adlers, Forsyths, Sinclairs, Drummonds, Maxwells and Tarringtons are the PB families in their community. A member from each family sits on the council."

Dave blinked. "When did he tell you that?"

"When you helped Jenny up, and I had to tell her brother she wasn't really losing her marbles," Sully said calmly. She winced. "Those were Jacob's words, not mine."

Dave's lips tightened. "So when Jacob told us about the PBs, he just happened to forget to mention he was one of them?" That was damn annoying.

Sully shrugged. "They'll tell us stuff when they trust us. We just need to work harder to earn their trust."

Dave frowned as he glanced down at the old and weathered book he held. "And in the meantime, more of them are in danger." It didn't escape his notice that Jacob Forsyth trusted Sully enough to divulge this information, after pretty much telling him to get lost the night before.

Sully played with her braid, and Dave found himself watching her more than reading from the book in his lap. She turned a page, and he forced himself to look down at the book he held. Yet in a moment, he found his gaze lifting to surreptitiously peek at her again. Her slightly crooked mouth was quirked, and a faint line had appeared between her eyebrows as she read through the spells and histories. For some, it took only a momentary scan. For others, she seemed to catch her lip, as though hopeful she'd found the answer, and then she'd press those sexy lips into a disappointed pout and turn the page.

She glanced up at him, distracted, and he glanced back down at his book.

"What about the Ancestors?"

He blinked at the question that seemed to come out of left field. "What?"

"The Ancestors," she repeated, then rose from her seat. She disappeared into her kitchen, and he heard the tap run in the sink, and then she came back into the living room carrying a bowl of water.

"Can you ask them?"

He put the book off to the side, frowning as she set the bowl down on the floor between them. She slipped her flip-flops off to the side, then sat cross-legged on the floor.

"Ask them what?" He leaned forward, bracing his

elbows on his knees as he tried to figure out where she was going with this.

She met his gaze. "The Ancestors directed you to me. They were wrong. Can you ask them for help?"

Dave shook his head briefly, confused as he tried to work through her suggestion until it made sense. He eyed the bowl.

"It's the Ancestors, Sully. They've only ever given me the name, and I take it from there. There's no conversation. It's not like a phone call, where I can chat with them over it."

"Have you ever tried?"

He frowned as he lowered himself to the floor, eyeing the bowl. "You want to scry the Ancestors?" He crossed his legs. He'd never heard of that being done, so he had no idea whether it would work or not—or whether it would just piss off the Ancestors.

Sully shrugged. "It can't hurt to ask, right? This guy is doing stuff that we've never seen before. Surely they can give us a clue."

He gave her a doubtful look, and she responded with an expression full of exasperation. "This guy managed to give you the slip—and I've seen you in action. I even went invisible, and you still caught me. Aren't you interested to see how he managed to evade you?"

He shifted uncomfortably. Admitting to failure yet again was like running a cheese grater over his skin. Damn it, she had a point. He nodded, then settled himself comfortably. Sully did the same, and he closed his eyes, centering his awareness. Once he felt the peace, the warmth of relaxation, he slid his eyes open. He tried to extend his awareness, his senses, to encompass the witch in front of him, but her shields were in place yet again, blocking him off. His brow dipped briefly. It wasn't unusual for witches to combine powers in something like this, but Sully was completely closed off to him. He'd have to do this on his own.

Sully met his gaze, then dipped her finger in the bowl and swirled her finger to create a gentle whirlpool. She murmured a chant in the Old Language, and he shoved aside his surprise at her knowledge and skill, focusing on the water in the bowl that was beginning to cloud over as steam rose from the surface.

Sully kept chanting, and once he could decipher the words, he joined her. The water thickened, and Sully nodded at him. Dave closed his eyes, and using the Old Language, summoned the Ancestors, and asked his question—who was this witch, and where could they find him?

He removed his sunglasses, then opened his eyes. He could feel a coolness sweep over him, the gentle but dizzying sensation as his perception of Sully's living room, of Sully herself, slipped from view, and instead the steam enveloped him. At first it was gentle, its touch against his face whisper-soft, but the pressure increased, and the color faded from white to red. Murky shadows, dark and indistinct, danced around him, weaving and ducking, fading and reappearing. Flashes of light snapped and crackled around him, so bright it hurt his eyes, but he remained steadfast, eyes open, until the light dimmed into that X symbol he'd seen carved into flesh. Over and over, the symbol flashed around him, and then he saw a face emerge from the red mist. The features were fuzzy, and he squinted, but no matter how much he tried to focus, the features wouldn't sharpen, but would twist and morph as it got closer, bigger, growing larger the nearer it drew.

"Dave," Sully gasped, and Dave blinked.

The red mist dispersed with a soft hiss, and he had to blink again to snap Sully into focus. She was staring down at the bowl, her expression perturbed.

He glanced down. The clear water they'd started with was now thick and red, and the metallic scent was nearly overpowering.

Blood.

It was expanding in the bowl, creeping up to the lip. "There's so much of it," Sully whispered.

He reached for the bowl, sweeping it up as he rose to his feet and strode into the kitchen. He tipped the blood down the sink and ran the tap to get rid of the liquid that had splattered the sides of the basin.

Sully followed him, and he turned to face her. "Well?" she asked him, curious. "Did it work? What did you see?"

He frowned. "I'm not sure. Red cloud. That symbol, flashing over and over," he told her, his fingers spreading out like mini fireworks. "Then there was this face, but I couldn't see it, the features kept twisting and moving." He gestured to the now clean bowl sitting in the sink. "Then the blood."

She shuddered, and rubbed her hands over her arms. "There was so much of it," she whispered. "What do you think they meant?"

He shrugged. "No idea. I've never tried to contact them before, so..." He winced. "I don't understand their code."

Sully gestured to his chest. "So the Ancestors can freakin' spell stuff out, but use cryptic picture codes for the important stuff. Nice going," she muttered, glaring up at the ceiling, as though talking with them directly.

"That symbol is obviously important," he murmured,

and headed back to the books in the living room, then halted. He turned to her.

"You use your safeguards, even when you're at home?" Why was she so guarded? She certainly had the right—every witch could decline a sharing of powers, it was their prerogative, but it had still been a surprise. He'd felt a companionship with her, a camaraderie, a shared intimacy as they worked together to figure out what the hell was going on. Admittedly, the magical block had made him realize he'd taken that for granted, and now was uncertain just how much they could or would share.

Her expression was surprised for a moment, then understanding crossed her features. "Yes. I guess it's just reflex." She scratched her head. "I'm sorry, I didn't even think to try to link for the scry." She indicated the bowl. "It's been so long, I just instinctively do it by myself."

He turned to face her fully. "How long has it been, Sully?" Witches were funny creatures. Mostly, they gathered in covens, but there were plenty of outliers, and one could certainly reserve their right not to link. Sully, though, seemed too sociable, too connected with the well-being of others to be so isolated. He'd seen her with Jenny, the amount of times she'd reached out to touch her friend, and the frustration on her face when whatever she'd wanted to do to help her was blocked. He'd seen her comfort her friend, hold her, reassure her... She genuinely cared for others, and that kind of witch seemed conducive to sharing, to linking and bonding. It was almost as though she was fighting her own instinctive nature.

Sully shrugged as she stepped toward the living room. "Four, maybe five years."

He reached out and clasped her arm, halting her.

His ears popped, and the hairs rose on his arms and the back of his neck as their magical fields collided once again, awakening and enhancing his senses. He blinked, then swallowed, trying to ignore the physical sensations bombarding his body. He wanted to understand—no, needed to understand why a witch, why Sully, would bury herself in a place where she couldn't use her powers.

"Why?" he asked hoarsely.

She hesitated, and he wasn't sure if she realized her slow shift toward him. "I needed to," she said to him. "I needed…space."

It was that line. *I need space. It's not you, it's me…* he'd heard it a dozen times, and used it himself at least a dozen more. Realization, swift and unavoidable, hit him. "Who was he?" he asked. He slid his hand down her arm and loosely grasped her hand. It was meant to be comforting. Friendly. But her smooth skin beneath his touch was distracting.

She lifted her shoulders in a casual, dismissive gesture. "He was nobody important."

"He must have been, for you to hide yourself here for four, five years," he pointed out. He slid his thumb back and forth over the back of her hand, enjoying the feel of her silken skin.

She frowned up at him, her blue eyes darkening. "I'm not hiding, Dave." She gave a slight shake of her head in denial. Her gaze drifted to his chest, then down to where their hands joined.

His eyebrows rose, and he shifted toward her. "Oh, really? From what I can tell, you're the only witch in this area—"

"You can't know that for sure. This is null territory," she interrupted. "You could have a whole coven here, and they wouldn't be able to practice or reveal their talents. We wouldn't even know."

"Is that why you're here? To conceal your talents?"

"I—" her gaze dropped to his lips, and then she met his gaze again. "I'm not concealing my talents," she said in a near whisper. Her breath hitched, then released in the sexiest sigh, the sound curling down deep inside him, flooding him with a molten desire that had him hardening in his jeans.

How could she make that sound so damn suggestive? So hot? He tried to focus on the conversation, but felt he was losing that battle fast. "Are you sure?" He stepped closer, and brought her hand up to rest against his chest.

She swallowed, and he smiled when he heard the audible gulp. He slid his other hand beneath her braid, cupping the back of her neck. He could see her nipples tighten against the cotton of her camisole, knew he wasn't the only one affected by this attraction, this fascination between them.

"Show me," he whispered, leaning down to kiss the side of her jaw. He inhaled, and her scent, roses, vanilla and sunshine, hit him like a drug.

She rested her hand on his waist for a moment, her eyes dark with confusion. "Show you what?"

"Show me you, Sully," he whispered, his lips trailing down her neck. She angled her head to the side, exposing more of her neck.

"What—what you see is what you get," she murmured, then moaned when his lips found that delicious indent between her neck and collarbone.

His hand slid from where it cupped her head down her back, and he halted when he found her belt with the concealed sheaths, and the blades they contained. His lips curved against her skin. "Oh, I think there is more to you than meets the eye," he murmured, then raked his teeth gently against her shoulder.

She trembled, a slight quivering that set off an answering throb deep inside him, hardening his cock. She slid her arms up over his chest to twine around his neck, her nails raking through his short hair. Her fingers clenched in his hair, pulling his head back up.

"I'll show you me if you show me you," she whispered, then stood on tiptoe to kiss him.

Chapter 14

Sully parted her lips against his, and was rewarded when his tongue slid inside to tangle with hers. His arms enveloped hers, pressing her against his body. She could feel the strength of those arms, those muscles, against the sides of her breasts, could feel the hardness of his chest and hips against her, and could feel the throbbing hard length of him against her stomach.

She could sense his curiosity, his tenderness, as well as the tidal wave of desire and arousal. He'd asked her about her shields. Suggested she was hiding. With Dave, though, there was no hiding. There was no defense against his overwhelming presence, with *feeling*, and there was no way she could fight the burning attraction she felt for this man. It was hot, it was immediate and it was undeniable. And she didn't want to hide anymore.

Her hands trailed down the column of his neck, tracing the breadth of those massive shoulders, and trailing over the soft fabric of his T-shirt. She angled her head, and he deepened the kiss, sucking and nipping with a skill that had her desire pooling in her panties as she arched against him.

"Oh, sweetness," he moaned, kissing his way to her jaw and down her neck. Her head leaned back, and he pulled her tighter against him, leaning forward so that her world tilted. His hands slid down and cupped her butt, and he picked her up, turning to seat her on the kitchen counter.

Her legs wound around his hips, pulling him into the cradle of her groin, and she moaned when she felt him, hot and hard, against her. She tugged at the hem of his T-shirt, and he leaned back, hips still pressed to hers, and helped her pull the garment over his head. Her eyes widened at having his chest so close, and for a moment she was content to place her palms against his warm skin. The mark over his heart looked almost healed, and she traced it very gently.

"So much pain," she murmured.

He winked, grinning as he ducked his head. "Nah, just a tickle." He took her lips in a hard kiss. His hands played briefly over her shoulders before hooking the thin straps of her cami and tugging them slowly down her arms.

She shrugged out of the straps, sighing when he dragged her against him, her breasts mashed against him, and they both moaned. He kissed her shoulder, nipping at her gently, and she shuddered, her breasts swelling at the sharp but seductive sensation. She dragged her nails down his back as he kissed and licked his way across her chest while he slid his hand under her long skirt, dragging the fabric up her legs. She trembled as his hand skimmed over her knee, gliding up her thigh.

Liquid heat pooled between her legs, and her pulse thudded in her ears.

He got to midthigh, then halted. He lifted his head, eyebrows raised. "You're full of surprises, aren't you?" he gasped, before taking her lips again. He fumbled with the leather strap of the sheath she'd strapped to her leg, and she laughed breathlessly.

"Sorry, I forgot that one."

He undid the tie, and she shuddered at the caress of leather against her sensitive skin when he tugged it away from her. He placed the sheath, with her custom-made push-dagger on the bench beside them. He chuckled.

"You are so dangerous," he murmured, gazing into her eyes, his hands rising to cradle her jaw. There was a humor, but there was also warmth, admiration and a little concern, all bombarding her with his touch.

She looked up at him, feeling the answering smile on her lips. "You have no idea," she whispered, then took his lips.

He sighed against her mouth, their tongues tangling. He lowered a hand to her chest, and she gasped, arching her back when he covered her breast with his warm palm. He pressed back, their hips rubbing against each other, and she could feel his hardness, separated by the folds of her skirt and the denim of his jeans.

Heat. Desire. Tight arousal. It hit her, and she wasn't sure if it was him, or her, or that they were just so perfectly in sync.

Panting, she reached for his belt, and within seconds she'd undone it, as well as his button fly. His hands gripped her body as she reached inside his jeans, and her lips curved against his when her fingers slid beneath his boxer briefs and found him.

He growled softly, and she gasped when he pinched

her nipple, just enough to make her tremble with delight. It was as though the floodgates opened. She pushed at his jeans. He tugged at her skirt, and she felt his fingers slide under her panties, felt the brief tug of the cotton as the fabric gave, and then she moaned when she felt those fingers against her, then inside her.

He groaned, then took her lips in a kiss so carnal it stole her breath. He played with her, strummed her, and she shook as she used her feet to shove his jeans down his legs. She gasped when she felt the tension coil inside her. Her nipples tightened, as his tongue slid against hers, his fingers moving with ease inside her, and then his thumb found that secret little pleasure nub, and everything tightened, tightened, tightened, until she exploded. Sensations, so sharp, so crystalized, cascaded over her. He positioned himself between her legs and entered her smoothly.

She tore her lips away from his, crying out with the pleasure as he thrust. Over and over, the waves of intense bliss crashed. Swirls of colors, sparks, everything was exploding—around her, inside her, until he finally groaned his release, his head back, the cords of his neck standing out as he found his own pleasure inside her.

He slid his arm around her waist, pulling her up tight against him, chest to chest, heart to heart, as their panting subsided. He hugged her, and she could feel him. Inside her, around her, it was all warmth and tenderness, an intimate gentleness with the steel edge of determined protectiveness.

She'd never felt safer.

Dave blinked. Hair. Honey-gold hair. All over his face. He brushed it away, blinking some more, then shifted, drawing his thigh up against the warm curves enfolded in his arms.

Sully.

His eyes opened.

Sully. They'd made fireworks last night. He'd seen them. Lots of pops of colors, sparks… While he wasn't shy with women, and thought he could hold his own in the sack, he'd never quite experienced fireworks before with a woman.

He lifted his head slightly, shaking away the last of the tendrils that seemed to want to cling to him. She was asleep in his arms, her back to his chest, her butt resting—he sucked in a breath. Damn, she felt good in his arms.

They were on the foldout sofa, and sunlight streamed in through the bay windows. They'd tried to make it to her bed, but somehow got distracted.

Very distracted. Twice.

His lips curved, and he dipped his head to press a kiss to her neck. She sighed and smiled as she scooted closer. Her stomach growled, and Dave chuckled as he caressed the curve of her hip.

She turned in his arms, her eyes opening, and he pressed a kiss to her lips. "Good morning," he murmured.

She smiled. "Good mor—" she yawned, then blinked "—morning."

"Feel like pancakes?" He was ravenous, and her stomach was making all sorts of hungry noises.

She grinned. "Are you cooking?"

"Yep," he said, and gave her another long kiss. When he drew back she sighed and stretched, then nodded.

"Sure, pancakes sound wonderful."

Dave reached for his sunglasses and slid them on,

then rolled off the foldout sofa and snagged up his boxer briefs, hopping into them as he walked through to the kitchen. Within minutes he had a pancake mix going— they were his specialty—and started to set up the counter for breakfast.

Sully walked in. She was wearing his T-shirt, the navy blue bringing out the blue of her eyes. Her hair was a tussled tangle, her features soft and relaxed. The shirt hit her midthigh, and he paused for a moment, taking his fill of her. She had the longest, sexiest legs he could ever remember seeing in a woman.

He watched as she crossed to the fridge and leaned in to grab the juice, the T-shirt riding up a little to expose a hint of butt cheek. He swallowed. She was a beautiful woman. He glanced back down at his pancakes. They were bubbling. He flipped them, his gaze briefly diverting back to the domestic, disheveled goddess behind him, and was pleasantly surprised when the pancakes landed back in the pan.

He smiled as he got the plates ready for serving. They didn't converse as she got glasses and poured the juice. They worked alongside each other in companionable silence, and he smiled when she caressed his back as she passed. He pulled her back for a kiss, enjoying the feel of her against him, so scantily clad in his T-shirt. The pancake batter in the pan popped and fizzed, and he drew back, winking at Sully's grin as she backed away toward the pantry. This felt...nice. Normal. But a normal he'd never had before. A cozy kitchen, a sexy woman with a heart of gold and a body built for sin. He could get used to this.

He halted midscoop of the pancake. What?

He could not get used to this. He had a job that translated to here today, gone tomorrow. He had a home and business in Irondell, and a task that meant the Ancestors would always take priority in his life. There was no room for a woman, for a relationship, no matter how tempting playing house could be.

He flipped the pancake onto a plate and poured a ladleful of batter into the pan. Sully started to hum as she moved around the kitchen, and he saw her place a bottle of maple syrup on the kitchen counter, along with a basket of strawberries. She even did a cute little dance move when she thought he wasn't watching.

He focused on the pan, watching as the air bubbles popped on the mix. He liked this. He *really* liked this. It was so tempting, just to reach out and kiss her again, feed her strawberries in an indulgent, dreamy little episode of domestic codependency.

And that scared the ever-lovin' crap out of him.

He quickly served up the last of the pancakes. His job—his calling—wasn't something he could just walk away from. He figured once a Witch Hunter, always a Witch Hunter. Everyone assumed his tattoo parlor in Irondell was his main focus, but they were wrong. It was the sideline, the business that bubbled along when he wasn't hunting witches. Eventually, though, his luck would run out. Somewhere along the line, he'd face a witch who was faster, stronger, more powerful...and it would be he crossing to the Other Realm. And another Witch Hunter would be assigned the hit and carry on the duties.

This moment, this side trip down fantasy lane, was exactly that—a fantasy. And he didn't do fantasy. He didn't drift away on daydreams, wishing for what couldn't possibly be. What he did—well, it was a special low, dealing with the excrement of the witch world, but damn it, it was necessary, and he believed in it, believed in the necessity, and that the bad was done for the greater good. He shouldn't be here, cooking breakfast and stealing kisses. This fantasy, this illusion of a different life, was a recipe for a whole world of hurt—at his hands.

"Wow, they look great," Sully said, eyes widening when she saw the stack of pancakes. She smiled as she sat on the stool. "I'm famished."

He gave her a small smile as he sat down next to her. He picked up his cutlery, but sat for a moment, eyeing the food on his plate. He'd lost his appetite.

Sully frowned. "What's wrong?" She eyed the pancakes suspiciously. "What did you to them?"

His lips quirked. "They're fine. Tuck in." He cut out a bit of pancake and popped it into his mouth, his gaze resting briefly on the woman next to him. Sully deserved to be someone's priority. Not someone's booty call, not someone's "between jobs", but someone's first, last and always. He'd eventually hurt her. He'd let her down when he'd have to pursue another witch over spending time with her. Or worse, what he did for the Ancestors could wind up hurting *her*.

He stabbed more pancake onto his fork and shoved it in his mouth. Damn. This sucked. Domestic bliss was obviously some sort of weird mind-meld crap designed to make you assess your life decisions and cry.

Sully eyed him closely as she chewed, then swallowed. "Is everything all right, Dave?"

"It's fine," he said, then put his cutlery down on the plate. "No. No, it's not fine." He turned to look at her. "You and I—we shouldn't have…done. What we did. That." He gestured to the kitchen counter, and then the living room.

Sully's cheeks heated, and she glanced down at her

plate. "Oh." She frowned. "You didn't…enjoy it?" She blinked, then waved her hand. "Don't answer that."

His eyes widened. "We did it three times. Yeah. I enjoyed it. A *lot*." Too much. "We just…shouldn't have."

Sully kept her gaze steadfastly on the glass of juice as she reached for it. "I see," she said. Her voice was low. Calm. Like, dead calm. He glanced at her. Her lips were pursed. Just a little, but that cute crooked little pout of hers was just a little more pronounced.

"No, I don't think you do, Sully. I have—"

"A job to do," she interrupted. She nodded. "I get it." She rose from her stool and placed her plate on the bench with just a little too much force.

"This—" he gestured to the kitchen, to her. "I can't do this. And I shouldn't have done that."

"Because of your job," she said, and folded her arms as she leaned against the doorjamb. "How does sex with me interfere with your job, exactly?" She tilted her head, and although her expression was curious, he could see the darkening anger in her eyes.

Sex. She'd called it sex. They'd made fireworks. It had been more than just sex. Hadn't it? Dave forced himself to focus on the question, and not the quiver of uncertainty that perhaps he was the only one who'd felt the impact of what they'd done, the magical coalescence of their power…

"I need to track down a killer," he told her solemnly. "I'm here having breakfast with you, when I should be out hunting that witch." He rose from his stool and leaned his palms on the counter—the counter where they'd first made incredible, firework-inducing love.

"That other night, when Amanda Sinclair was killed—I should have been out there, hunting, not in here, kissing you."

She gaped at him for a moment. "Are you saying it's my fault Amanda Sinclair was murdered?" Her voice emerged as a hoarse rasp. She folded her arms.

He gaped. "No! God, no! No, not your fault—*my* fault. I should have been out there. I should have been looking. My fault, Sully, not yours." He pressed his thumb to his chest. "None of this has anything to do with you. It's all on me."

Her eyes narrowed. "Ri-ight," she said slowly, although her tone didn't quite suggest agreement. "So this," she said, unfolding one arm to encompass her kitchen, "this was all what? An *oops*?" her voice rose on that last word, and he winced.

O-kay. He'd screwed this up. Monumentally. And he'd managed to minimize the first real emotional connection he'd had with a woman in years. Ever. "No. Yes. Hell, sort of."

She gaped at him. Then she held up a finger. "Okay, first, the correct answer to that was supposed to be a hell, no."

"What we shared meant something to me," he said through gritted teeth. "And that is the problem. I'm not supposed to feel this—" he held up his palms, shrugging. "I don't even know what *this* is, that's how foreign it is," he exclaimed. "I'm supposed to up and go when the Ancestors call, and if we keep going down this—" and again he gestured, palms up "—then I won't want to answer the Ancestors' call."

She stared at him for a moment, and that cute little crooked pout of hers got more crooked, the tighter she pursed her lips. "I see."

His eyes narrowed. "See, I get worried when you say that," he said. "I think you see something that I don't mean."

"Okay, well, let me break it down for you," Sully said, her hands dropping to her waist. The position hiked up his shirt, exposing more of her tanned, toned thighs. "You are hiding from this," she said, and gestured between them. "You feel something, so you are running. You're using your vocation as an excuse to avoid a personal relationship. With…me. You don't trust. You don't trust me, you don't trust us."

His eyes rounded. "Trust?" He placed his hands on hips. "Really? Me? Trust issues?" He found he could only repeat the hot words, so surprised was he by her comments. He was sure he'd get around to forming some rational response.

"Yes. You. Trust issues. You didn't want to tell Sheriff Clinton about the killer witch. Reform law recognizes your authority as a Witch Hunter, Dave—just like they would a guardian enforcer hunting down a werewolf, or a vampire guardian hunting a rogue vampire. Tyler's not going to arrest you for enforcing tribal law on one of your own kind. But you don't want his help—because you don't trust him?"

Dave frowned and opened his mouth to argue, but she was already talking.

"You don't tell the nulls there's a null-killing witch coming after them, you don't want to trust them with the information and still allow you to hunt that witch down. And if I hadn't enhanced that white lie you told about us dating with the breakup factor, you wouldn't have allowed me to tag along in your investigation— because you don't trust me. I'm a witch who wants to help, and you don't trust me to do that. Now, you're starting to feel something, and you don't trust *us*. You want me to believe that all I am to you is some quick screw that you can't get involved with."

"Hey, there was nothing quick about us," he told her, and she shot him an exasperated glare. "And you're not completely wrong," he allowed, holding his hands up. "You're right. I don't trust the sheriff. Nice guy," he said quickly, "but once I approach him, I have to follow Reform rules, and they don't work, not for us. He'd want us to arrest the witch, and have him stand trial with Reform peers—who may or may not be witches, when we already have a higher authority who have made a decision. I trust Tyler—to do exactly what his job tells him he has to do, which doesn't align with what I have to do."

He sighed. "The nulls—I'm not sure about them. Someone is walking among them. Both Amanda Sinclair and Jenny opened their front door to this guy and let him walk right in. He's somehow been accepted by that community, and is able to walk freely among them, so yeah, you're right, I don't trust them. But you…"

He stepped around the counter. "I have never met anyone who is so damn trusting, and that scares me."

Her frown deepened, and he paused, searching for the right words. "You…you're amazing. You're so… big-hearted," he said, shrugging. It was the only word he could think for her. "You can't help yourself, you need to help others. You try to ease people's pain—I saw you with Jenny. You were so frustrated that you couldn't use your empath powers on her and ease her suffering—yeah, I saw that." He nodded at her shift in position, her disconcerted expression. "You tended to my wound, when I'd done everything that should have made you run in the opposite direction. You're wanting to hunt down this killer—to prevent him from hurting others. You're helping me, because I need it. I saw you at the funeral, Sully. When you take on the pain of others, you put yourself at risk. When I visited your shop, you made me tea."

"After I tried to skewer you with a fork," she argued.

He nodded. "Okay, granted. But that's my point. It's so easy to get past your defenses. You sense, therefore you trust, regardless of whether I'm worthy of that trust. You don't really know me," he told her, and he had to force the words out of his throat. "You don't know what I've done. You're right—I don't trust easily, but in my line of work, that's a survival skill, not a flaw." He ran his hand through his short hair. "Which is why I have to leave. The longer I stick around, the more danger I put us both in."

Her blue gaze was dark and solemn, and she sighed. "I would never, ever, beg or force someone to stay with me against their will," she said quietly. "You want to leave, leave." She levered herself away from the wall, and dragged his shirt over her head, and tossed it to him.

He caught it to his chest, still warm from her body. He looked at her, standing naked and proud, her shoulders back, her chin up. And no, he damn well didn't *want* to leave.

"I hope you find your witch," she told him sincerely. "Be safe."

She turned, walked across the short hall to her bedroom and closed the door behind her.

He turned in her kitchen, holding the warm garment to his chest, and stared at the abandoned plates on the counter, the sullied remnants of a glimpse of heaven.

He'd blown it. He blinked, then turned and walked down the hallway to the living room. He scooped up his gear and was dressed in minutes. He looked around for his jacket, and realized he'd left it in the back of Sully's car the night before.

He glanced down the hallway, toward the bend that led to Sully's bedroom. This was lousy. He didn't want to leave her like this, thinking...thinking what? That he thought she was just a brief dalliance? Or that he didn't trust her?

His lips tightened. Maybe that was for the best. If she knew how he felt, that he wanted nothing more than to walk down that hall and crawl into bed with her and never, ever leave—would that change the situation? Would it make her feel better, or worse?

He closed his eyes, letting his senses drift down to that bedroom at the end of the hall. He could sense the peace and tranquility of her room, and he tried to sense her, to comfort her. He gently searched for her essence—a spark exploded in front of him, and he flew across the room, flipping back over the sofa.

Ouch. He looked up from his position on the floor. Okay. She was pissed. He could respect that. He'd knocked, and she'd sent him flying. He got the message. Go away.

He rolled to his feet, pulling up his backpack as he did, and strode out of the house. He shoved his backpack into one of the panniers on his bike, then crossed to the trunk of Sully's car for his jacket. He shook his head. Sully had left the rear window down. The woman had no regard for securing herself or her possessions. He reached in for his jacket and tugged at the sleeve. It caught on the lid of a long metal box in her trunk. He tugged harder, and the jacket pulled free. The lid clanged open, and Dave froze when he saw the contents.

What the—? He reached in and pulled the box closer, frowning at the weight of the darn thing. He peered inside, his jaw dropping.

A supply of swords, axes, knives and arrows—along

with a heap of deadly looking blades, gleamed in the light of day. A cloth bag sat in one corner of the box, and when he pulled at the fabric, he heard a clink, then saw the treasure of Reform dollars winking up at him. A lot of them.

He heard the soft slap of flip-flops on the veranda, and looked up at the woman, that sweet, naive, gullible woman, standing on the top step, hands on hips, as she glared down at him. He glanced back down at the mobile armory and cash stash in the trunk of her car, then back up at her.

"Who *are* you?" he exclaimed.

Chapter 15

Sully padded down the steps and across the yard. "I'm a cutler," she responded shortly, and reached for the lid of the box. First he'd dumped her—although they'd only had a one-night stand, so she didn't think that was the technical term for the one-night-wonder-lover walking out on her. Skunk, maybe. Now he was snooping through her stuff. Dave's large hand flashed out to catch the lid, preventing it from closing.

"This is not cutlery," he exclaimed, pulling out a stiletto blade.

"It's a knife," she pointed out.

"That's one hell of a knife," he remarked. He replaced the stiletto and removed one of her short swords. "Why do you have these in your car, Sully?"

She shrugged. "I made them."

"All of them?" he asked in disbelief, scanning the weapons. She tried to close the lid again, and he braced his hand against the lid, then delved his hand into the cloth bag and pulled out a fistful of coins.

"Where did you get this money?" he rasped.

"Weren't you leaving?"

"Where, Sully?" His voice was low, grim. Determined.

She considered lying, but decided against it. "I made that, too."

He dropped the coins, and closed his eyes as he pinched the bridge of his nose. "Oh. My. God."

She rolled her eyes. "It's not a big deal, Dave."

He removed his sunglasses, and his eyes opened to slits as he peered closely at her. "It's not?"

His voice was quiet, almost conversational. Reasonable. Receptive. And he'd removed the dark lenses that hid his eyes. He seemed open. Approachable. "No, it's not."

He lifted his chin in the direction of the box. "So, that's not really what it looks like?"

She paused, looking at him, then the box. "What does it look like?"

"Well, it looks like you're selling counterfeit cash and weapons," he said.

"No," she said. "I give the money away, not sell it, and I'm not an arms dealer." She thought about it for a moment. She did make weapons on commission, though. "Uh, technically, I might be an arms dealer, but only a little bit." She pinched her thumb and forefinger together to show just how little an arms dealer she was. The thought almost brought a smile to her face, but Dave's expression was so serious she didn't think he'd see the humor in it.

His mouth gaped open for a moment. "Only a *little* bit?" his voice emerged as a high-pitched whisper.

"Well, if I'm being completely honest—"

"Please—"

"I do make weapons for a price, but it's only on a commission basis."

"—don't tell me."

Sully blinked as his words sank in. "Oh."

Dave's shoulders sagged. "You told me."

"You did ask."

"I wanted deniability."

Dave slung his jacket over the rim of the trunk and braced both hands against the car.

"You're not a cutler," he said, shaking his head.

"I am a cutler," she told him, then shrugged. "I also make…other stuff." She leaned back against the car and folded her arms. She'd quickly changed into a cotton camisole and a skirt, and had come outside to make sure he left—or so she told herself. It wasn't because she'd wanted one last glimpse of the man who'd given her fireworks and made her feel safe.

Four years.

"Ah," he said slowly as comprehension spread across his face. "These are the coins you were talking about, when we first met."

She frowned. "What?"

"You mentioned coins on the beach, as though you were surprised the Ancestors had sent me after you for that."

"Oh." She vaguely remembered asking him about it, and feeling confused and hurt that the Ancestors would sic a Witch Hunter on her for such a trivial matter. "Yeah." She eyed the way his biceps flexed as he gripped the edge of her trunk window. She wasn't going to stare. She wasn't going to think about them wrapped around her, or the way she felt when she was in those arms…the passion, the sense of protection. She had to remind herself he was on his way out. Leaving. Adios, amigo.

And she was going to be just fine. This was not a— she pressed her palm to her chest. God, she hurt. No, damn it. This was no big deal.

"Why?"

She blinked, his question bringing her back to the matter at hand. The serious matter at hand. She hadn't expected him to find her...stuff. Only a few people knew about her sideline business, and it was weird, having to explain it to the man she'd shared a bed with. Well, sofa. Kitchen counter. Whatever. This wasn't a conversation she'd expected to have. Especially not when she really wanted to go curl up in bed and cry.

"Why?" She eyed the drive. "I really thought you were leaving," she grumbled.

He turned to face her. "Sully."

She narrowed her eyes against the glint of morning light. "You want me to tell you?"

He nodded.

"Really?"

He nodded again.

"But Dave, I'd have to trust you with some sensitive information," she said, "and I'd hate for you to think I'm too naive and gullible." She glared at him meaningfully, and his lips tightened as he recognized his words thrown back him.

"Sully."

She levered herself away from the car. "No, Dave. You can't have it both ways. You accuse me of being too trusting, while you won't trust anyone, and then you demand me tell you what you want to know." She leaned forward. "Well, guess what? Trust works both ways, buddy."

She turned to walk away, but stopped when his hand

gripped her arm. Not enough to hurt, but enough to turn her to face him. Worry. Genuine concern, flooded her. Damn it, he was doing it again, without even realizing it.

"Are you in trouble, Sully?" he asked earnestly.

"Not if you don't tell the sheriff," she answered honestly.

His exasperation, tinged with frustration, pricked at her, but she could still feel his very real worry. For her. No. He didn't get to do that. He didn't get to worry about her, or feel that warm concern for her, because that made this whole walking out thing really, really suck. But obviously, he wasn't walking out, not until he had some answers.

She sighed. "Look, you've probably noticed the nulls here are really struggling. The fishing season hasn't really hit the high mark, and we have families who are struggling to put food on the table. This," she said, jerking her chin in direction of the coin bag, "is just to get them by until the fish stock picks up. That's all. That's all it's ever been." She wasn't some criminal mastermind, for crying out loud.

His mild relief warmed her, and she pulled her arm from his grip. She didn't want to feel his emotions, didn't want to understand. She wanted to hold on to her anger from earlier. Because if she held on to that anger, the hurt couldn't touch her.

"The weapons?" he asked.

She paused as she considered her answer. "I like weapons," she answered in a low voice. They made her feel…safe. "And I think Jenny and others can use them, right about now."

Dave sighed, his lips firm. "I don't like this."

"You don't have to," she said, stepping away from the car. "You're leaving, remember?"

"Sully, I don't want to leave, I *have* to leave. Every minute I spend with you, everyone else is in danger from this witch, including you."

Damn it. She glanced down at her flip-flops. Buried beneath his need to flee she could see his annoying, frustrating, bloody-minded logic. It didn't mean she had to like it.

Four years.

The words kept repeating themselves over and over in her head. Four years since she'd been with a man, and when she finally surrendered, when she shared something of herself, he ran.

Rode a motorcycle. Whatever.

"Well, don't let me stop you," she whispered. She cleared her throat, then looked out past her front yard toward the headland. "I have things to do, too."

She could see him out of the corner of her eye. His expression was somber, his gaze an almost brilliant silver against his tanned skin and close-cropped beard. She wasn't going to meet his gaze, though. She didn't want him to see how shredded up she was inside.

Silly, silly girl. She'd gone and gotten hooked on a Witch Hunter.

"I'll, uh, get going, then." He stood there for a moment, waiting for her response.

She nodded. Her pose was casual, arms folded, but she could feel the tiny little arcs pressing into her skin as her fingernails dug into her biceps. She wasn't going to cry.

At least, not until after he'd left.

He turned and walked toward his bike, slipping his leather jacket on as he went. He got to his bike, then paused, his hand resting on the handlebar. Then he abruptly turned and stalked over to her. She straightened, frowning, and her eyes widened when his arms slid around her waist, pulling her in for a hot kiss.

Frustration. Anger. Lust. Sorrow. All bombarded her at his touch, his tongue tangling with hers. It was quick, but it was a whirlwind of emotion and passion that left her breathless when he lifted his head. He tilted his forehead against hers.

"I'm sorry," he whispered. He stepped away, and this time he didn't look back when he reached his bike. He slid his helmet on over his head, straddled his bike, and within too few seconds he was riding out of her driveway.

Sully stood where she was, shoulders sagging, by the trunk of her station wagon. She listened as the sound of his bike slowly diminished, to be taken over by seagulls, crashing waves and the sound of cicadas looking for their mates.

Tears blurred her vision. She had done so well. She'd avoided guys—especially the strong, dominant kind of guy. She'd managed to secure her heart, her safety, her *sanity*... She straightened her shoulders. No. She wasn't going to fall apart again. She wasn't going to surrender her peace of mind, her independence, her identity, to a man. Never again.

She turned back to the house. She hadn't been lying to Dave. She did have things to do, and a delivery to make. He was going to pursue this witch on his own. He'd made that clear.

Well, she hadn't said anything about stopping her own search for this bastard. This guy was hurting her friends, and she had every intention of stopping him—with or without Dave's help.

Dave smiled at the librarian who brought forth another old book from the archives and placed it with the others on the table at which he sat. "This is the last one, and contains the first census records since Reformation," she told him in a hushed tone. He glanced about. It must be a reflex for the woman, as he was the only person in the records section of the library.

"Thanks." He summoned forth a slight wisp of power. She was human, and there were no nulls in the library that he could sense. "If there is anything else you can think of that will show me the family trees of the nulls, let me know."

She smiled at him sweetly as she nodded. "If I think of anything else on null families in the area, I'll let you know." He watched as she walked away, her low heels making a slight clack-clack as she lowered her reading glasses. She tucked a strand of gray hair behind her ear as she crossed to the catalogs.

Dave opened the large-paged book. The pages were divided in columns, with neat, meticulous script detailing the names, ages and connections of the residents of Serenity Cove since the town was recognized as part of Reformation society.

He placed one hand on the pieces of paper the librarian had given him to make notes on, and another on the book. There were lots of pages, and more volumes to sift through. It would take him hours, if not days, to sift through all of this on his own.

A little voice whispered that he didn't have to do it on his own, that Sully wanted to help, and that she could get the nulls to reveal the names he was looking for.

He lifted his chin. Well, that would dangerous. For everyone. He'd never had to rely on anyone else to do his job. Witch Hunters worked alone. He'd never had a partner work a hit with him before. Nor had that partner wanted to bring in a whole damn community to help, either.

No. He was on his own. It was better this way. Less… danger. To Sully, anyway.

He closed his eyes, summoning his powers. He murmured a reveal and transfer spell, and could feel the pages warm beneath his hand. He raised his hands from the surface, slowly opening his eyes.

Names on the page started to glow, and he watched as the glow drifted out of the book and onto the piece of paper. Names, dates and connections—they all imprinted on the paper, giving him a list of the purebloods in the area since the town's formation. The pages started to flip, faster and faster, as the names were pulled forth. More books opened, more glowing references. He sat back and waited until the last name landed on the paper, and then he murmured a genealogy spell. He watched as the names reconfigured on the page. Some names faded—individuals who had already passed away.

It took a while, and it was probably early afternoon by the time he had a list of purebloods currently residing in the Serenity Cove area.

He rose from the desk, then waved a hand at the books at the table, sending them back to their homes among the shelves, to save the little old lady at the desk some work. He walked up to thank her, but kept his mouth shut when he heard her snore. He walked out to his bike, opened up his pannier and removed his map of the area. He spread it out on the seat of his bike, then bent down and scooped up some dirt from the ground. Holding his clenched fist over the map, he glanced at the first name on the list, murmured a quick location spell, and let the dirt fall out of his hand in a measured funnel. Within seconds he had the address, and within a minute he was riding out of the Serenity Cove library parking lot.

Chapter 16

"**A**gain," Sully instructed, then brought the wooden blade down toward Jenny's chest in a low-handed grip. Jenny blocked with her arm, pushed Sully's arm outward and stepped in close. Jenny hesitated, then frowned.

"I can't remember the next step," she admitted.

Sully reached for Jenny's other arm. "Your hand. Bring it up and into my armpit—" she stopped talking when her friend followed through with the movements, and was able to bring the practice knife in under her outstretched arm, just beneath the armpit. "Good."

She glanced down at the row of ten or so adults who'd accompanied Jenny over, and were now lined up in her front yard. Kids, including Noah and his sister, were sitting up on the steps of the front veranda watching, or else had taken their cue from the adults and were play wrestling. "Okay, let's do it again."

"So this is supposed to help us, huh?" Jenny said,

as she faced off and started to go through the steps. From what Sully had seen, when she'd piggybacked on Dave's vision of Amanda Sinclair's murder, and from what she'd seen when she and Dave had interrupted Jenny's attack, the killer got his victim on their back on the ground, then delivered the death blow. She was giving the group of purebloods that Jenny had managed to convince to come over for defensive training some choreographed moves to fend off a similar attack that would get them into that kill position.

"Yep." She'd shown them a couple of moves, and was getting them to practice, over and over again. She could hear the clang of metal against metal out in the backyard. Jacob was showing some of the men how to use some of their fishing gear in defensive movements. Jenny was still wary around her brother, and so Sully and Jacob had decided it was best if he was out of sight, out of mind for this.

Jenny looked up at the sound of the mock fighting coming from around the back. "I wish I could remember," she said quietly as Sully slowly made her go through the defensive motions again.

Sully nodded. "We'll figure it out. But you do know that Jacob would never hurt you, right?"

Jenny hesitated, then nodded. "I know. On a rational level, I know. But there's something up here," she said, tapping her temple, "some glitch, and I keep—I keep having these flashes."

Sully narrowed her eyes. "What kind of flashes?"

Jenny performed the block, and a smooth shift to bring the knife up to mock stab her under the arm. Sully smiled and stepped back, assuming the attack position again.

"His face, but—not his eyes. It's…it's so weird." Jenny's lips tightened as she met Sully's gaze. "I'm a null.

This crap has never happened to me before. It's not supposed to happen." She shook her head. "If I didn't know better, I'd say it's...magic." Jenny shuddered. "But then, never having experienced it, I wouldn't know. It's just wrong as all crap."

Sully blinked, then averted her gaze. "We'll figure it out, Jen." After how close her friend had come be being viciously murdered, Sully was even more determined to track down this damn killer witch.

"How the hell do you know this stuff?" Jenny panted as Sully repeated the attack, gradually getting faster and faster.

"I learned it a few years ago," Sully said, then held up a hand. "Okay, let's try something else."

She lay on the ground as the adults gathered to watch. "If you find yourself in this position, and your attacker is kneeling over you, this is what you do."

She gestured to one of the men, Sam Drummond, who tentatively straddled her. She handed him the wooden practice knife. "If he's bringing the knife down at you, he's got the advantage," she told the group. "Grab the wrist with the knife—you want to control that. Use your other hand to strike, preferably punch the throat," she said, showing them slowly a strike to the throat. "Wrap your hand around his neck, and bring him in close—"

"Close?" Jenny exclaimed. "Don't we want to get away?"

"Yeah, but he's got a knife, and close quarters are good. If you try to push him away, that's giving him more room to attack," Sully said, and showed them by gently pushing Sam back to arm's length. "See, here he can stab, strike, etc." She grabbed the back of his neck and pulled him down to her. "Here, he can't, he's too close." She pushed him back so that he straddled her once more.

"So, he's got a knife, and is bringing it down to you.

Grab the wrist with the knife," she told them, wrapping her fingers around the thick wrist. "At the same time, strike at his throat." She demonstrated slowly and gently. "Then pull him forward, wrap your opposite arm over the back of his shoulder, like this, then under his wrist so that you can grab your wrist in a lock." She did the move slowly. "Then, turn his wrist up."

Sam grunted, and tapped the ground as he released his grip on the practice knife. The kids on the veranda cheered, and the adults made noises of surprise and appreciation.

"Then you can control the wrist like this," Sully said, levering Sam's wrist up, and she heard him hiss softly, and his tapping on the ground became fiercer. "You can wrench the shoulder, snap the wrist, move him off you," she said, demonstrating by using the vise-hold to direct Sam's gentle momentum off her body. "You can do various strikes, and run—or pick up that knife and finish him."

The gathered adults gasped, and Sully looked up at their shocked faces. Two of the women shared a look, horrified at the suggestion. Sully rose to her feet. "Guys, this person has killed three of your neighbors. Friends. In some cases, family," she said, eyeing Ronald Sinclair. "If he's coming for you, he wants you dead. Take him out before he takes you out."

Jenny gaped at her, then exhaled. "Well, uh, thanks, Sully." She brightened as she looked around at the others. "Hey, who's hungry?"

The adults nodded, and the kids on the veranda cheered. Sully glanced back at them. Oops. She'd forgotten the kids were there. Not really a conversation you wanted to have in front of the littlies...

She forced a smile on her face. "I have some salad fixings. We could have a cookout. We just need some meat."

The children squealed, then jumped up and down. Which led to a little bit of pushing, and then quickly deteriorated into a game of tag around the house.

"I've got some meat back home," Ronald said.

Sam rolled to his feet. "So do I."

"I've got some bread rolls," one of the women offered.

"I've got more salad—you'll need some more," Mrs. Forsyth suggested. "We could pop home and be back within the hour."

Sully smiled. "Uh, great. That would be great." She blinked, looking at the group as they discussed what to get for the spontaneous potluck meal. It seemed so... big and hearty and wonderful, to have all these people get ready for a large, communal meal. At her place. Like...family.

"Okay, I'll stay here with Sully," Jenny stated as Jacob led more of the adults around to the front. They were all sweaty from their exertions, and most of the men were shirtless, Jacob included.

"I'll help with the kids," sixteen-year-old Rhonda Maxwell offered, winking at her younger cousin, Noah.

"Me, too," Susanne Maxwell, Noah's mother, stated, and Noah pouted, then ran off with his sister, with Rhonda jogging close behind.

"Hey, did we hear something about a barbecue?" Jacob grinned as he rested his foot on the bottom step of the veranda and braced his hand against the railing. Sully watched as Jenny forced a smile to her face, but her knuckles were white as she hugged herself. Jacob's smile faltered when he saw his sister's awkwardness.

"You can come help me pack the car," his mother told him, patting him on the shoulder as she walked toward the street. Some of the purebloods had carpooled, but there were still too many vehicles to fit in Sully's drive. The overflow were parked on the grassy verges on the road beyond.

"I'll start cleaning the grill," Jack Forsyth stated, turning toward the barbecue pit Sully had built shortly after arriving in Serenity Cove. It included a basic grill and metal plate set on a low ring of cinder blocks, and was set in a sheltered corner of her yard that still allowed for a one-hundred-and-eighty-degree view of the ocean.

"I'll take the kids down to the beach," Rhonda sang out as the children ran out of the yard in the direction of the path and stairs that led to the beach below.

The group split up, and Sully led Jenny and Susanne through to her kitchen.

"Do you mind, Sully?" Jenny asked. "I mean, we've all just invited—"

"I love it," Sully interrupted, beaming. "This is great. I miss having family gatherings…"

"Where's your family now?" Susanne asked as she started opening Sully's cabinets. She made a triumphant sound when she located the wooden chopping boards.

Sully smiled, but it took a little effort. "We're all kind of spread out." She crossed to the fridge and started to pull out lettuce and tomatoes and anything else she could use to feed the hoard that was about to descend.

"So, what happened to your family?" Jenny inquired, her brow dipping in curiosity as she reached for a knife in the knife block. "I don't think you've ever told me."

Sully shrugged. "Nothing happened to them. I just… left."

"Why?" Susanne asked as she started to pull off leaves from the head of lettuce. "Wow, that sounded nosy, didn't it?" the woman said, chuckling.

"It's fine," Sully said. "I needed to move away, find my own feet. They're still around, but I don't generally see them unless there's a special event." She'd missed so many birthdays, so many weddings and baby blessings, coven gatherings... She forced a smile on her face. She hadn't let herself think about that, but now, with these people who were being so lovely and warm, so inclusive, she found herself thinking about her family, her coven. Thinking about them...missing them.

But she couldn't go back—she couldn't risk it, for their sake. Something clanged outside, and Jenny smiled. "Sounds like Dad's decided to give your grill a good going-over." She leaned forward. "So tell me, what happened with Dave?"

"Is this the boyfriend Noah was telling me about?" Susanne inquired, and Sully could feel her cheeks heat.

"Uh, he left me this morning." Sully focused on washing the tomatoes.

Jenny slapped the knife down on the board. "What did that son of a bitch do? Where is he? How badly do we need to hurt him? Bruise him up, or make it impossible for him to father children ever again?"

"No, no, it's—it's not his fault," Sully said hurriedly, although she was touched by Jenny's fierce loyalty. "He—he really wants to find the person behind all this," she said, waving her hand around carelessly. "So, he's off—"

"He's dicking around, isn't he?" Jenny muttered, then glanced at Susanne. "He's a private dick."

"Investigator," Sully corrected, then sighed. She could see his point about working without interference, but she still felt like she was not being completely honest with her friends, and hated it.

"Oh, no," Jenny said as she reached for one of the washed tomatoes.

"What?" Sully glanced at the tomato. Was there something wrong with it?

"You have that look," Susanne said, running the lettuce leaves under the tap.

"What look?" Sully frowned, looking between the two women.

"That look that says you've totally fallen all over again for the guy you dated in high school," Jenny said. She brought the knife down sharply on the cucumber, chopping off the end.

"No, I haven't."

"Well, you've done something," Jenny said. Sully's cheeks heated, and she turned away to open a cupboard door, ostensibly to find a bowl. Yeah, and that something had been wicked fun.

"Oh, my God, you did," Jenny exclaimed, and Susanne gasped.

"Whatever it was, from the look of that blush it had to have been good," Susanne said, grinning. "Or very, very bad."

"Guys," Sully pleaded.

"Oh, my God, you did, too!" Jenny squealed.

"Shush," Sully said, looking out the window. She couldn't see Jack Forsyth, but she certainly didn't want Jenny's father to hear the details of her sex life. "It's... over." She pulled the bowl out of the cupboard and placed it on the kitchen counter.

Susanne frowned. "Why, was it bad?"

"No! No, it wasn't bad."

"So it was good, then?" Jenny said, resting the base of her palms on the wooden chopping board.

Sully covered her face. "This is so embarrassing."

"That means it was very good," Susanne explained in a knowing voice to Jenny.

"And he left you?" Jenny asked, a slight frown of confusion on her forehead. She firmed her lips, then nodded. "Fine. Castration it is, then."

"Jen, it's not that simple."

"Yes it is. You can hold him down, and I'll show you how simple it can be."

Sully laughed. "Jen, calm down." She sobered. "We're just—he doesn't trust me as much as I want him to," she admitted quietly.

Jenny hesitated, then placed the knife down on the board. "So *he's* the one with the trust issues…?"

Susanne winced, then leaned her hip against the counter. "Ouch."

"What do you mean?" Sully glanced between her two friends.

"I mean," Jenny said, leaning forward, "you have enough weapons here to arm every man, woman and child in the greater Serenity Cove area, and you showed us some pretty lethal moves out there. That doesn't just come out of a vacuum, Sully. You've been holding out on us."

"What the hell happened to you?" Susanne asked quietly, and for once, her face was dead-set serious.

Sully opened her mouth, then closed it. How did she respond? There was so much she hadn't told her closest friends…

"Hmm, I'm thinking your Dave may not be the only one with trust issues," Jenny stated, then started to resume chopping the cucumber.

There was a knock at the door, and Sully held up a hand. "I'll get it," she said, hurrying toward the hall.

"This conversation isn't over," Jenny called after her.

"I'm already pouring the wine," Susanne sang out.

Sully sighed as she walked down the hallway. Her friends had a point. She'd hidden so much from them—but was she ready to let them in? Was she ready to tell them anything? Everything? And did Jenny have a point? Did her own lack of trust affect her relationship—such as it was—with Dave?

She opened the front door, and raised her eyebrows when she saw the deputy standing on her veranda. He clasped his hat in his gloved hands, and smiled at her.

"Hi, ma'am. I'm looking for Jennifer Forsyth, and I was told she was here…? The sheriff has asked me to stop by with some follow-up questions about her attack yesterday."

Sully's eyebrows rose. "Oh, uh, okay." She stepped aside, gesturing down the hallway. "Come in, she's in the kitchen."

She turned toward the hallway. "I'm surprised Tyler didn't just call," she said.

She heard an agonized cry and turned back. The deputy had stopped just inside her home, and had ducked his head as he clutched his face in pain. She hurried toward him. "What—" she reached for him, but jerked her hand back when he lifted his head.

His features twisted, his skin bubbled and then his eyes flashed rage at her. Her body processed the danger before her mind could quite grasp it. She turned to run, but he grabbed her hair and spun her around. His fist flashed out, catching her in the jaw, and her head smacked against the hall wall. Anger, fury and an evil that was suffocating, slammed into her. Dizzy, she brought her arms up, but his fist struck her again, and darkness crashed over her.

Chapter 17

Dave peered in through the front window. The house really was empty. He stepped back from the front door, and glanced down at his list. Susanne and George Maxwell, not home.

Just like the other purebloods he'd called on. Nobody was home. Anywhere. He glanced down the street. None of the Forsyths—and he'd tried Jenny first—were home. Neither were the Drummonds, or the Sinclairs. Maxwells, and a bunch of others… It was as if they'd all suddenly gone to ground.

He strode down the garden path and had almost reached his bike when his tattoo started to heat. He halted, and pressed his hand to his chest. *No. Please, no.*

"Sullivan Timmerman," he whispered, removing his glasses and staring blindly down the street.

His vision blurred, and then cleared. He was walking up behind a man. The man was stooped over, and using a wire brush on something he held, the grating noise masking the sound of his steps. He reached for the man at the same time he swept his leg out.

The man cried out in surprise as he was grasped, then tripped backward onto the ground, the grill he was cleaning clattering against cinder blocks.

Like lightning, he straddled the man, and Dave grimaced in horror when he recognized the shocked face staring up at him. Jack Forsyth. Bracing one hand against the older man's shoulder, the killer brought down his blade in a smooth arc.

"No," Dave rasped, bracing his hands on his bike. *Damn it.*

Jack's eyes rounded as the blade pierced him, and Dave's hands clenched into fists as he saw the life drain out of the older man's gaze. The killer reached for his wrist, and moved quickly, carving that *X* symbol into his wrist, draining the blood into that damn horn. The killer rose, turning away from the thicket surrounding them, and faced a house.

Dave's breath caught. He knew that house. The killer raised his horn in a silent toast, then drank its contents. He started to walk toward the house—Sully's house— and murmured those words that blackened Dave's vision.

Dave blinked and shook his head. Oh, God. *Sully.*

Heart pounding, he started his bike and roared down the street, his helmet still dangling from its strap over his handlebars.

Sully was in danger.

The tattoo over his heart began to heat again, and Dave gasped, leaning forward, accelerating out of the null neighborhood and onto the coast road. He blinked furiously, trying to dislodge the vision that was slowly creeping in over the road ahead. "Sull—Sullivan Tim—Timmerman," he gasped.

Sully lay still on the floor of the hallway, her face bruised. "No!" Dave roared, taking the curve of the road at a dangerous speed. The killer walked down the hall, and Jenny turned from the kitchen bench. Another woman was closer, one Dave didn't recognize, and she turned from peering into the fridge.

"Who was at the door?" Jenny asked, and turned back to sliding salad ingredients with a knife along a wooden chopping board and into a bowl.

The other woman smiled. "Sauvignon blanc or—"

The blade flashed, catching the woman in the chest, the smile slowly slipping from her face.

Jenny screamed, and the board she held fell to the floor. The killer worked quickly, laying the woman on the ground and carving the mark into her flesh, then draining her blood. Jenny darted past him, running for the front door. The witch sipped from the horn as he raced after Jenny.

"No," bellowed Dave, his muscles tensing, and he leaned forward, ignoring the high-pitched wail of his bike as it hit maximum speed.

The witch caught up with Jenny in the hall, tackling her to the floor next to Sully's still body.

Jenny screamed and lashed out with the kitchen knife she still held. The witch clasped her wrist, forcing it above her head as he brought his own blade down, and Jenny's scream ended in a gasp.

Within moments, the witch had performed his gruesome ritual with the mark, and was drinking from the horn. His gaze turned to Sully as he murmured those damn words, and Dave's vision again darkened, and he found himself staring at the asphalt of the road unfolding ahead of him.

Sully.

Hands gripping the handlebars tightly, his gut clenching, Dave focused his gaze on the road. He overtook a series of cars all heading in the same direction. One of the cars started honking its horn at him, but he ignored the sound.

He prayed. Prayed for Sully, making all kinds of promises to the Ancestors. He'd never look at a woman again, never get distracted. Keep her safe. He'd walk away, he'd never see her again, just make her safe. Alive.

He heard the squeal of rubber behind him, but didn't turn around to look. The turn for Sully's street was ahead, and he leaned into the turn early, taking it like a motorbike racer on a circuit, before screaming down the road to Sully's house. He turned into her drive and jumped off the bike, not even slowing down to stop it properly. He could hear the bike clatter as it fell, the screech of tires on gravel behind him, and ignored it when someone called his name.

He ran across the yard and up the stairs to the veranda. He shouldered the door open, then raced inside. He skidded on the floor to reach Sully.

"Please, Jenny." Sully was sobbing, clutching her friend's hand. She placed her other hand over the wound in Jenny's chest. Sully's shoulders where shaking, her face tear-streaked as she cried. She started murmuring, and Dave felt his own eyes burn with tears at the grief, the heartbreak in Sully's voice as she tried a healing spell.

A spell that would have no effect on a null.

Dave placed his hand on Sully's arm. "Sully," he

murmured, trying to get the sound past the razor blades in his throat.

She shook her head, the tears streaming down her face. "No, let me help her," she cried, and crawled a little closer. Footsteps pounded on the veranda outside, and Dave looked up as Jacob halted at the front door. The big man had to clutch the doorjamb as he swayed, his face torn with grief and shock as he looked down at his dead sister inside.

"Jenny, please," Sully sobbed, and Dave grasped her shoulder.

"Sully, she's gone," he said softly.

"No, no, she can't be," Sully cried.

A scream, heartrending, full of grief and rage, echoed through the front yard, and Dave looked up at Jacob. The man had turned, and his eyes widened in disbelief. He took a step forward, and more screams, more wails were heard. Jacob took another step, then collapsed to his knees, his face twisted in anguish. He leaned forward, rocking on the veranda, a howl of pain erupting from deep inside him.

"Jenny, come on," Sully gasped, and squeezed her friend's hand in hers. "Let me take it, let me take it," she wailed. She stopped, squeezing her eyes shut, but no matter how much she concentrated, Dave knew she wouldn't be able to take on any of this pain. Not now. Not for Jenny.

"Sully," he whispered, pulling her toward him. "She's gone, love. You can't help her."

"No, no, no," Sully sobbed, and dropped Jenny's hand. Sully's hands clawed over, and she lifted her head and screamed. Her pain, her anguish, her frustration pierced his heart. Dave felt the hot lick of tears trailing down his own cheeks in the face of her despair, and rocked her in his arms.

* * *

Sully poured the steaming water into the mug, and blankly watched the chopped-up leaves and twigs swirl as though caught in a mini hurricane.

A storm in a teacup.

Sully placed the kettle back on the warmer, and took a seat at the table. The tea had to steep. Not for long, but she needed this tea to be potent. A trickle of perspiration ran down the side of her face. She glanced around the tiny little motel room. She'd turned off the air conditioner. It had made an annoying crank-crank-crank noise, and she'd shut it off before she'd screamed.

Her eyes skimmed over the ugliest coverlet she'd seen, its geometric pattern looking like a witch's vision quest on acid. The carpet may have been orange and cream at one point, but now looked brown. Gray. No, baby-crap brown and dead-fish gray.

Her home was a crime scene. She blinked at the tears that welled in her eyes. Correction. Three crime scenes. The tears fell slowly as she stared at the mug, steam curling up from its surface. She watched the steam as it rose, and sucked in her breath as the tendrils roiled, and she saw his face again, the bones moving underneath the skin, his flesh blistering as he stepped inside her home. She blinked. No. She wasn't going to think about that anymore.

She plucked at a loose thread of the long skirt she'd changed into. She'd had to change at her house. Tyler had folded her clothes, covered in Jenny's blood, and placed them separately into evidence bags. She'd given all the information she could to the sheriff. She'd sat through hours of grueling interviews, had flicked through photos…but she'd known it would be a pointless exercise.

Still, Tyler needed to feel like he was doing something, that he was taking action at tracking down this killer. She could understand that. She could give him that, at least.

An image of Jen lying bloodied and still on her hall floor filled her mind. Sully blinked slowly. She didn't want to see that anymore. Didn't want to feel that pathetic uselessness ever again. She'd reached for her friend, but couldn't feel her, couldn't sense her, no matter how much she opened her walls. She couldn't take away any of that pain, that fear and horror that must have preyed upon her best friend in the last moments of her life.

Her gut clenched, and her shoulders shook off a dry retch. Oh, God. *Jenny.*

Hot tears welled in her eyes, before trailing down her cheeks. Jenny. Jack. Susanne. They were all gone.

And it was her fault.

She reached for the mug, her fingers trembling. A knock sounded at the door.

"Sully."

She closed her eyes briefly at the familiar sound of that voice. Dave. She didn't want to see him. Didn't want to speak with him. Didn't want to look him in the eye and see the disappointment, the blame.

"Sully." The voice was louder, as was the pounding on her door.

She pulled the mug closer, but opened her eyes when she heard the lock disengage, the handle turn and the door open.

"Sully." He filled the doorway. So big, so strong. He wore his leather jacket, despite the heat outside. His sunglasses shielded his eyes, but she could guess at the accusation, the recrimination. She deserved it. Hell, she deserved so much more than looks of censure. From everyone. Dave. Jacob… She winced. Mrs. Forsyth.

"Go away," she said, her voice hoarse from screaming.

He stepped inside and closed the door behind him. "I'm not going away."

She cupped her cold hands around the warm mug but couldn't seem to absorb any of the heat. His words sank in, but slowly, like sharp little barbs hitting rubber walls. Some stuck, some didn't, but not quite penetrating the numbness surrounding her. For once, she could feel…nothing.

"You were going away," she said, her gaze fixed on the mug. "Jenny wanted to castrate you." She almost smiled, remembering the conversation, only she couldn't quite get her facial muscles to work. Nothing worked anymore.

Dave paused, then bowed his head. "Yeah, well, I would have deserved it," he said in a low voice.

He crossed over and lowered himself into the seat opposite her at the table.

"I don't want you here," she said in a low voice.

"Well, from what Jacob and Tyler have told me, you don't want anyone here."

She drew the mug closer to her. "I want to be alone."

"You shouldn't be alone, Sully. Not now."

She slowly lifted her gaze to meet his, and decided to ignore the pain and grief she saw etched into his face. "Yeah, I should."

"Sully—it wasn't your fault," he said roughly, leaning forward to rest his arms on the table between them.

This time her mouth did move into a smile, a bitter, self-hating smile that bore no joy or warmth. "But it was, Dave," she whispered. "I let him in."

Dave frowned, and looked down at the table. "Every-one let him in, Sully. Gary let him in close. Mary Anne let him into her home, so did Amanda... Jenny." He clasped his hands together. "I don't know how he does it—"

"He's a skinshifter," she said, and tried to hug the mug closer to her chest. Dave's gaze met hers.

"What?"

"He's a skinshifter," she said, and she moistened her lips.

Dave's eyebrows rose, and he leaned forward some more. "A skinshifter? How do you know?"

"When he—when he came inside, I don't know why, but his facade started to drop." She shuddered. "Literally." She could see it happening again, the way his bones seemed to dissolve, the skin bubbling... She flinched. "He couldn't keep up the disguise." She glanced down at the tea.

Dave sat back for a moment, stunned. "A skin-shifter."

She nodded. Skinshifters were a special breed of witch. They could rearrange their features, their phy-sique, to look like anyone they'd physically come in contact with. They couldn't shift into a different spe-cies, though, like a bird or a cat, only people. They were the chameleons of witchcraft, and not very well liked. The only time you disguised yourself was when you had something to hide, and these witches had a ques-tionable moral compass. They passed themselves off as others. Sometimes it was a harmless form of mis-chief, but most of the time it was a form of betrayal and deceit. As such, those witches born with skinshifting abilities were generally outcast—the witch equivalent to a werewolf stray or a vampire vagabond. Tricksters. Imposters. Charlatans.

And in this case, a murderer.

"So that's how he got close to them," Dave murmured.

"Yes." She stirred the tea. "He looked like a deputy. I guess he couldn't pretend to be me with me."

Dave's eyes narrowed. "You say his disguise faltered when he stepped inside your home?"

She shuddered. "If by faltered it looked like his face was melting off his skull, then yes."

Dave rubbed his hand over his mouth. "I, uh—I put a ward on your door," he said quietly.

Sully lifted her gaze to meet his. "What?"

"Uh, the night before, when we got home. I put a ward on your door. A protection spell. You only have a very basic lock on your door, and I wanted to make sure you were safe."

Her lips twisted. "Those spells don't work when the source of dark intent is invited in," she told him.

"No, but they reveal dark intent," Dave told her. He winced. "I, uh, I'm so sorry. About Jenny. And…the others."

She shrugged. "You were right. I should never have gotten involved. I'm just an amateur hack when it comes to catching bad guys."

Dave shook his head. "No, you're not, Sully. This guy is strong, and he's smart." He rose from the table, crossed to the tiny kitchenette counter and picked up a mug. "Mind if I have some tea?"

"Yes," she said sharply, then realized how snappy she'd sounded. "I mean, there's none left."

"Oh." He turned back to the board she'd used to chop her ingredients, and she raised the mug to her lips.

He whirled back to face her, his arm flashing out, and an arc of power zapped from his fingers, blasting the mug from her fingers.

"What are you doing?" she asked shrilly, jumping to her feet.

He stepped up to her, his expression fierce. "Water hemlock? Oleander? What are *you* doing, Sully?"

"Go away, Dave," she cried, stepping away from him.

He grabbed her arm, and for the first time, she sensed nothing from him. He glared at her.

"Why? So you can try to kill yourself again?"

Chapter 18

Sully tried to pull her arm out of his grip, but Dave wouldn't let her go.

"What do you think you're doing, Sully?"

"Let me go," she said, her curled-up fist thumping him on the chest.

He shook his head. "I'm not letting you go, Sully." No. He wasn't going anywhere, he wasn't about to leave her alone, not like this. Maybe not ever.

"Jenny's dead," she hissed, and for the first time he saw a spark in her otherwise dead eyes. She thumped him again on the chest, and he met her gaze squarely. His lack of response seemed to anger her. She thumped him again. "Jack's dead." He remained silent. She thumped him. "Susa—Susanne's dead," she cried, then hit him again. And again. He stood there and let her hit him, again and again, relieved at her anger compared to the blank numbness he'd seen from her since she'd accepted that her best friend was dead.

"They're all dead," she cried eventually, sagging against him. He enfolded her in his arms, felt her shuddering against him as she sobbed. "It's my fault. I shouldn't have let him in," she said.

"Shh, it's not your fault," he murmured against her tangled hair.

"I let him in," she said, and kept repeating it as she leaned her forehead against his chest. "You shouldn't have destroyed my tea." Her knees bent, and he caught her.

"Come on, sweetness," he said, scooping her up and carrying her over to the double bed. He flicked his fingers and the coverlet folded back. He lay her down, then climbed over her to lie down next to her.

"You should have left me alone," she cried softly.

"I'm not going anywhere," he told her gruffly as he pulled her back against his chest. "Hate me all you like, but I'm not leaving you. Never again."

"They died because I invited that evil in," she whispered, and he levered himself up on his elbow so that he could see her face. He smoothed her mussed hair away from her face.

"They died because a witch killed them," he told her. "He's killed before, Sully. Odds are, he would have gone after them, sooner or later. They just happened to be at your home when he did."

"I brought them there," she wailed. "I brought them all there. I may as well have sent up a damn Bat Signal to the universe that the purebloods were at my home, come and get them."

He closed his eyes briefly at the devastation, the regret he heard in her voice, emotions that he was all too familiar with. "You aren't responsible for the bad deeds of another," he murmured, gently caressing the hair at her temple. "You were trying to help."

"You don't believe that," she said into the darkening room.

He frowned. "Why do you think that?" He didn't believe for one minute that she was responsible for her friends' deaths, and he needed to make her see it, before the guilt ate its way through her.

"You feel guilt," she said in a low voice. "I've felt it. You feel responsible for those witches you kill, and you feel responsible for those they killed. You carry that guilt with you."

His lips parted, stunned at her insight. "Uh…"

"You think you can take this from me?" Sully glanced at him over her shoulder, her eyes dark and solemn. "You think you can carry this weight for me? Make me feel better?" She shook her head. "You can't take this away from me. This is mine to bear. I did this. This is my darkness to carry, not yours."

He leaned forward so that his head touched hers. "This darkness, Sully…it will weigh you down. With me, it's different—"

"Why? Because the Ancestors gave it to you?" She shook her head. "That's a cop-out."

He sighed, stroking her arms. "You can't carry someone else's sins. It doesn't work like that."

"It works that way for you."

"But it doesn't have to work that way for you," he whispered into her hair.

"They were my friends," she whispered. "My family."

"And you loved them," he said, and hugged her just a little tighter. "I understand. Believe me, Sully, I understand. But you have to let it go. The blame is not yours to hold on to."

There was silence for a moment, and then her body jerked, and he realized she was crying silently.

"Sully."

"I can't," she wailed. "I can't let it go. If I let it go, I let *them* go, and I can't do that to them. I can't dishonor them. I can't forget. *I* should be dead, not them. This is so. Not. Fair." She whispered her words harshly, forcefully.

He closed his eyes, drawing her even closer, feeling each shuddering breath. She was so devastated, he couldn't bear it, couldn't bear the guilt that made her want to cross over to the Other Realm. He tried to reach out to her, to draw in some of that pain, to exchange it for some comfort...

He surrounded them with a light cover of warmth, of well-being, tucking the essence around her like a cloak. He took care, making sure he left no gaps, and was surprised when he found it. The slight crack in her shield. He gently pushed the warmth inside her. He heard her gasp, felt her stiffen in his arms and saw the splintering of those walls.

He scooped her up close as she started to cry anew, drawing on the pain and grief. His eyes itched, and he sucked in his breath as the darkness creeped out. Into him.

"What are you—"

"Shh," he whispered, concentrating on rolling the darkness into ball, feeding the light into it and gradually dispersing it. He had no clue what he was doing, but whatever it was, it felt right.

He sensed her relaxing in his arms, and her breathing deepened. He inhaled, slowly, relaxing against her as the warmth spread over them both. He could feel her walls loosen, become more fluid, more flexible, allowing more light inside. She became still against him, so relaxed. He listened as she breathed, deep and regular.

He smiled as he, too, allowed himself to drift off to sleep, and for what seemed his first time in years, he experienced a true sense of peace.

She ran down the hall, her heart thumping in her chest. It was her hall—but…not. No. Familiar, but wrong. Where…? Wait. This was her apartment in Irondell. *No, not again.* She glanced over her shoulder, eyes wide with fear. He was behind her, the deputy with the melting face. She ran faster, but the hall kept getting longer and longer. She looked behind her once more, and stumbled when she saw his face blend into Jack Forsyth. The older man reached for her, and his features twisted, then slid into Susanne. Susanne stared back at her, saddened and disappointed, before morphing into Jenny.

Sully stumbled onto her knees, hands smacking against the tiled floor. She'd fallen in front of the mirror next to the door. She tried to look away, tried to turn back, to face Jenny, to tell her how sorry she was, but her reflection caught her gaze, held it.

Her mouth opened when she saw her own features start to swim, to slide down her face, and she would have screamed, only her jaw felt boneless, loose. She watched in horror as her face melded into masculine features, features she recognized and had prayed to never see again.

Marty.

Sully jolted awake, gasping.

"Hey, it's okay," Dave said, blinking as he reached for her. "It's just a bad dream," he said, caressing her arm in an attempt to soothe her.

She shook her head and sat up. "No, no, I don't think it was," she panted, pushing her hair back off her face. She turned to look at him. "I think I know who's doing this."

Dave frowned. "What?" He sat up in bed, his biceps

flexing as he braced his hands against the mattress and shifted his hips. His silver eyes still bore the shadows of sleep, and a little confusion. Adorable confusion. It took her a moment to get past the fact she'd been snuggled up against this man. And he'd kept his word. He'd stayed.

She didn't quite know why that was so important, but it was a fact that kept reverberating around her skull. He'd stayed.

And he'd...shared her pain. How—? What—? So many things were swirling around in her head, but she plucked the most pressing, the most urgent, out of the maelstrom.

"I think—I think I know who's doing this," she repeated, and threw off the coverlet. She rose from the bed—whoa, headspin—and then lurched for her tote bag, her skirt slowly untangling from around her legs.

"Sully, hold up," Dave said.

Sully shook her head, certainty filling her with determination. "No. I need my books. Now." A sense of urgency sparked inside her.

Sully made her way to the motel room door, but Dave beat her to it. His silver eyes—it took her a moment to really look at him—showed his concern, his bewilderment. "Sully, talk to me."

She met his gaze, still grappling with the shock. "Marty—Martin Steedbeck," she said.

"Who is Martin Steedbeck?" Dave asked, and opened the door for her. He stood aside to let her pass, then followed her out to the parking lot.

"My ex."

"Whoa. What?"

Dave scooted around in front of her, his hands up. "Come again?"

"Marty Steedbeck, my ex-fiancé," she said, and then

fumbled in her bag for her keys. Dave shook his head and guided her toward his bike. "But I need my books."

"I'll drive," he said, and removed a helmet from a pannier. He placed it on her head and connected her strap when her fingers fumbled with it.

They made it to her place in about fifteen minutes. It possibly would have been sooner, but Dave parked the bike near the turn and they ran down the street toward her home. It was past midnight, the darkest part of the night, and the stars were hidden behind clouds, disbursing a dull illumination, full of murky shadows and patches of gloom.

Dave held up his hand, and she halted behind him as they sheltered behind the hedge. A deputy stood by her gate, smoking a cigarette, and she could see Tyler through her living room window. Her front yard was lit up like a football field on a Friday night, and a technician walked out of the front door carrying a number of brown paper evidence bags.

"Can we go in?" Sully asked, and Dave shook his head, his fingers on his lips.

"No, it's a crime scene. It looks like they're about to finish up for the night," he murmured, eyeing the technician who placed the bags in a container in the trunk of a four-wheel drive vehicle, and then started to tug off his gloves. Dave guided her gently behind a bush, squatting down beside her. "We'll wait until they go."

"I feel bad about this," Sully said, eyeing Tyler as he nodded at another deputy, and then they started to walk toward the door. "Can't I just go and ask Tyler to let me go grab my stuff?"

Dave looked at her. "Do you remember talking with him yesterday afternoon?"

Sully glanced at him. "Sort of." A lot of yesterday afternoon was a blur. Evening, too.

Although she did clearly remember Dave blowing the bejeebus out of her tea.

"Your house is a murder scene, Sully. You're not allowed in for several days. You can't remove any-thing—and they still want an explanation for all those weapons."

"But it's my stuff," she protested in a low voice.

Dave shook his head. "No, at the moment it's evi-dence. So we wait." He patted the ground next to him. "You may as well get comfy."

He sat down, bringing his knees up and resting his arms across his knees. She followed suit.

He leaned closer, and she caught a whiff of his scent. That neroli did things to her, strange, wicked things. She eyed him. For once, he'd ventured out without wearing his sunglasses. His lips looked soft and relaxed, and his beard had gotten just a little longer, a little scruffier. His leather jacket was open, and his T-shirt was navy. Her brow dipped. Maybe dark gray. Perhaps black. Ei-ther way, his shoulders looked broader, and he looked tougher. His short hair and scruffy short beard made him look dangerous. Dangerously sexy.

She looked down at her flip-flops. She shouldn't be thinking about how sexy he looked in the dim light of the stars. Jenny flashed in her mind, sprawled on her hallway floor. She blinked. She was such a horrible person, noticing how good-looking her witch-hunting companion was the day three people had been mur-dered on her property.

"Mind telling me about this ex?" Dave inquired, his tone low but casual.

She winced. She'd hoped never to have to utter his name again, let alone discuss him in depth.

"It wasn't a healthy relationship," she murmured.

Dave looked at her. "Is he the reason you're hiding in Serenity Cove?"

"I'm not hiding," she argued, her voice low.

"Sully, these people you live among don't know you're a witch. You purposely stay where your powers are restricted, where no other witch will come near you because they'd be powerless...if that's not hiding, it's a damn interesting lifestyle choice that I just don't understand."

"It—it may have started out that way," she admitted, "but I stayed because I wanted to."

"Why?" Dave said, scooting around to face her. "What did he do to you?" His whisper was fierce.

She shook her head. "It was more what I let him do," she said, her eyes on her toes. She sighed. "Marty had...issues." God, just putting into words what had happened, what a monumental failure that relationship had been and how blind, or ignorant, or self-delusional she'd been, was so damn difficult—and humiliating.

Dave's eyebrows rose. "Why do I get the feeling that's an understatement of epic proportions?"

She nodded. "A little. Marty's father was a coven elder. His mother, though, was human. Marty's powers weren't very strong." She rested her chin on her knees. "And his father never let him forget it. The only thing he could really do was skinshift, and even that he wasn't very good at."

Dave leaned back to look up the street, and she followed his gaze. Tyler was now by the drive entrance, talking with the deputies. Dave turned back, and lifted his chin in a silent "go on" signal.

"So Marty started to drink. And when the buzz was dying there, he'd do drugs." She shook her head. She'd been engaged to a drug addict. She couldn't remember when she first noticed the little white lies...and then chose to ignore them. "At first, I didn't realize how much he was drinking when I wasn't there. He was very good at playing sober." She winced. "But the drugs made him...different." She hugged her knees tighter as the memories surfaced. "He'd wait for me to come home, and he'd get angry over the slightest thing."

She hugged herself a little tighter. Maybe it was sitting behind a bush, whispering in the dark while light blazed just a short distance away, reassuring but still hidden. Maybe it was Dave, and this sense of intimacy, of familiarity and friendship on a level that she couldn't remember experiencing before, or the fact that her best friend had died without knowing any of this about her, but for the first time in the longest time, Sully wanted to talk. It was like getting rid of some emotional dregs she'd held in way too long. She'd carried so much darkness with her, but whatever Dave had done earlier that night, it had shone a light on that darkness...illuminated it. Shared it. For the first time since she'd been hiding the reality of her and Marty's relationship from her family and coven, she felt ready to reveal.

"He was in so much pain," she said, shaking her head. "And I'm an empath. I could help him. Like, *really* help him," she said, her hand moving in a smooth roll to emphasize each word. "I could take away his pain." Her chin dipped. "And I'll admit, in some sick way, I felt good about being able to help him." She paused. "But then he'd have more pain, and he needed me to take that, too. I almost think that among his other addictions, my taking away that pain from him, making him feel good, became an addiction in and of itself.

"He'd show me that he was trying, that he was doing some small measures to get better, like taking a different way home to avoid that bar, or showing me where he'd hide his stash so that I could check at any time…" The apologies, the promises…

She shrugged. "But then, he'd stumble again, fall prey to those insecurities, and I'd have to fix him—because the last time didn't work as good as it should have, or my fix didn't last as long as it should have, or I should have known that this would flare up and stopped it from happening… He had me convinced that it was actually my fault. I—I started to feel…useless. He would demand more of me, and would be upset and angry about it." She turned her head so she could look at Dave. "This sounds so pathetic, but he made me feel like I couldn't do anything right, and that—that just wrecks me."

"What do you mean?" Dave asked softly.

"I mean that I know now that he doesn't make me feel anything, I do. So I let him do that to me. That was on me," she said, and squeezed her eyes shut. That haunted her. That she'd fallen so low, and yes, Marty may have pushed her that far, but only because she allowed it. Which only made her feel worse.

"He'd get angry, and we'd argue." Her lips twisted in an ironic smile. "I used to get hurt a lot by accident," she said. "He'd push, and I'd fall into that table, or smack into that door…you know, by accident. He didn't mean for me to end up smashing into the table and knocking myself out…it was an accident."

She swallowed, and Dave moved closer. "How did you get out of there?" he asked quietly.

She blinked back the burn in her eyes. She was not going to cry. Not over Marty. Hell, no. She'd wasted enough tears on that bastard.

"I don't quite know what set it off in my mind, but

I finally figured out the reason he'd call me stupid, or useless, or powerless, or ugly...wasn't because I was actually those things, but because he was afraid of losing me." She held up a finger. "Oh, and when he threw me against a mirror. That may have had something to do with it, too." She still remembered the earsplitting crash, the pain as her head smacked the wall, her back broke the glass, the cuts as she fell to the floor amid the shattered pieces, all showing a warped reflection of her.

Dave sat there for a moment, and she didn't know if he was stunned, or disgusted, or trying to think up an excuse to run down the road, hop on his bike and ride as far away as he could get.

"I left—I ran out the door, with my shoes in my hand, and I ran."

Dave tilted his head. "That's why you make weapons." It wasn't a question, but a statement. A realization.

She nodded. She'd made a promise to herself, all those years ago, that she would never be in a position of weakness with a man—or a witch—ever again. "Yeah. I spent two years learning how to defend myself, how to protect myself... How to shore up my mental shields so that nobody could ever drain me dry again, and then I found Serenity Cove."

"With a null community," Dave finished for her. Sully nodded.

"Yep. You can't scry yourself up a witch if she's surrounded by nulls."

"But—" Dave indicated with his thumb over his shoulder in the direction of her cottage "—you brought your coven's books with you. That means your coven can't access their knowledge base. Why?"

Sully grimaced at the memory. "Marty was so damaged by his father, and was always wanting to prove him wrong—constantly. But he just wasn't that strong a witch. So he used his skinshifting abilities to pass himself off as me, and access our archive."

Dave gaped. "No," he said in horror.

She nodded. "Yes."

"What happened?"

"I found him before he could find the spell he was looking for. There was a fight—and like I said, his talents as a witch weren't as strong as others."

She'd kicked his ass, and protected her coven in the process.

Dave reached for her, his movement slow, as though giving her time to withdraw, or rebuff his touch. She did neither. He cupped her cheek.

"You are amazing, you know that?" he whispered. She closed her eyes, letting herself sense his emotions. The warmth of wonder and admiration. Sorrow and sadness. Anger—but not at her. No. It was tinged with a strong sense of protection. He pulled her closer. "You are the strongest person I know," he whispered against her lips, and kissed her.

She leaned into him, giving herself up to the kiss. His lips were gentle, tender and exactly what she needed from him right now.

The sound of car engines starting interrupted them, and they hunkered low as the sheriff and his deputies drove slowly down the street. Sully looked back at her house. Yellow crime scene tape was draped across her veranda and across her door.

Dave looked at her over her shoulder. "Let's go get you your books. Then you can tell me why you think your ex is killing nulls."

Chapter 19

Dave looked at the array of books strewn across the bed in Sully's motel room. She'd been very methodical in her approach at the house, and had selected volumes quickly. Then she'd performed a transfer spell that had removed the archive from her shelves to a place he didn't know where, and wasn't about to ask.

At which time she'd grabbed some personal items, including a change of clothes and weapons that the deputies hadn't found in their search. Getting the load home on the bike had been a minor miracle. They'd spent the hours since combing through the books. His stomach grumbled. He glanced at his watch. They'd missed lunch. And breakfast. Oh, and dinner the night before.

"I think we need a break." He reached for one of the books. So much...age. He wrinkled his nose at the slightly musty smell. Sort of like old people's stink.

"I think we've been approaching this from the

wrong angle," Sully said as she quickly flicked through some pages. "We know that nulls void any of the natural elements of a shadow breed—werewolves can't shift, vamps can't fang out, witches can't perform their spells..." she said, her hand rolling as she went through the litany. "But this witch has been able to work magic—when no witch working with the natural order can do so."

He nodded. He knew the limitations around nulls, had experienced it personally since arriving in Serenity Cove. That void made him feel almost naked. "I admit, it's one thing that's been driving me crazy, trying to figure out how he's been able to do the spells, bump me out of the visions, etc. I mean, how can a skinshifter even keep his facade around nulls?"

"Especially a skinshifter with limited natural ability," Sully stated. "I think he's drawn on unnatural elements."

Dave frowned. He'd seen the skinshifter carve into flesh and consume blood. "Do you mean blood magic?" Blood magic was a slightly more potent form of magic, and a witch had to be very careful—if their blood supply was killed in the process, it drew the wrath of the Ancestors, and a quick and painful trip to the Other Realm, courtesy of yours truly.

Sully shook her head. "No. From what I saw, he kills his victim, and *then* consumes their blood. I think he's using death magic."

Dave stilled. Oh. Hell. No wonder the Ancestors had called on him.

"The dark arts." It was so obvious, and yet, so damn reckless. Only those on a power thirst used death magic, better known as black magic, and it always—*always*—ended badly. Did this witch not realize that he would eventually pay for his sins? Either in this world or the next... Black magic had a kick to it. As long as you served the dark arts, it served you. One wrong step, though, and it could consume you. Hell into perpetuity. He'd prefer facing down the Ancestors in the Other Realm, thank you very much.

"I don't know why I didn't see it," she murmured, then chewed her lip—*look away from her lips*—before finally lifting her gaze to meet his. He whipped his gaze from her pretty, pouty mouth to her eyes. "Marty used to say that he wanted to find his happy place. When I asked him where that was, he said it was any place where he was the strongest witch—especially stronger than his father."

She shrugged. "I used to think this was a hypothetical what-if kind of conversation, and I'd say to him that even the strongest witch is vulnerable to nulls. He wanted to find a way to be powerful, despite the nulls." She held her hands up in a helpless gesture. "I never thought there was a way to counteract that."

Dave frowned as he flicked through the pages of the book. "You think he found a way to void the null effect." The idea was so extreme, so ludicrous, it was chilling that it might be true. The kind of "sure thing" you bet with a drunk at the bar and then laugh yourself silly as he tried to count out the logic on his fingers. Dave shook his head as he turned the page. He might need a beer or six for this. He glanced down at the page, then froze.

The X symbol was drawn on the side of the page, along with a spell written in the Old Language. Right there, in plain Ancestors-speak.

"Sully."

She looked up at the tone in his voice, then leaned over to look at the page.

"Oh, my God. You found it."

"I need to translate this," he muttered, reaching for the notepad and pen on the table by the bed.

She shuffled around next to him, her head close as he hastily scribbled. Her scent, rose, clove and vanilla, teased at him.

"No, wait," she said, placing her hand on his arm. "That's not liberation," she said, gesturing to the symbol. "That's sacrifice." He frowned, then realized she was right. He hastily crossed out the word and corrected, and then went through the rest of the spell, forcing himself to ignore that teasing, tempting scent.

It took a few minutes, but he finally finished the translation. He showed her the notepad. "Do you agree?"

She scanned the spellbook, and then the translation, line for line, then finally nodded. "Yep."

They both sat there for a moment, staring at the translated spell. "Holy crap," Dave finally murmured in awe. It was—it was—hell, he wasn't quite sure what it was. His brain was having trouble computing it.

"Yep," Sully breathed.

"The Gift," Dave said, his lips tightening. The marking the witch carved on the inner wrist of his victims— the pulse point—was a symbol used by the Ancients, the ones who predated the Ancestors. The symbol, directly translated, meant gift. This spell, though, added some further meaning. A transformative gift, a connection, with the addition of unification.

"He's tying the elements of the null blood—pure-blood—to his through the unification spell," Sully said.

Dave nodded. "He's not fighting the null effect, he's accepting it. That enables him to control the effect."

"Like when he bumps you out of the vision," Sully

said, and Dave nodded. This was—this was incredible. Son of a bitch.

"So he uses their sacrifice under the guise of a gift, receiving the qualities and transforming it to become a part of a new...him." Dave met Sully's troubled gaze. "This means that he's warping his magic with a null effect. When others come near him, he nullifies their power and uses it to boost his own." His brow dipped. "An alpha elder." Like elders needed an extra creep-factor. His own mother would love this.

Sully shook her head slowly. "It's...it's ingenious."

"It's dangerous," Dave said. "He can effectively rob supernaturals of their power and convert it to his own, thus becoming the most powerful creature on earth." He frowned as he glanced down at some markings at the bottom of the page. What...what was that?

"But it's only temporary," Sully surmised, reading through the spell. Dave leaned closer to eye the markings, then counted them. Nine. Ni—ine. Three groups of—realization hit him.

"Holy crap."

"What?"

"If I'm correct, the effects can become permanent under certain conditions..." The blood chilled in his veins as he absorbed the meaning of the text.

"What conditions?" Sully frowned as she eyed the page, trying to find the clause.

"Sacrifices," he said, tapping his finger on the markings.

Sully nodded. "Yeah, well, we kind of figured that. He kills for the blood."

Dave shook his head. "No, he has killed six people so far. There are nine markings here."

"The law of three," she whispered, her eyes widening in realization. "Three groups of three—a threefold blood sacrifice."

He then pointed to the circle at the top of the page. "And a celestial event."

He glanced at his watch. When was the next celest—

"The harvest moon," Sully gasped.

Dave closed his eyes briefly. The witch was going after three more purebloods.

This year the harvest moon coincided with the fall equinox. With the day and night being of equal hours, the full moon would rise the closest after sunset, effectively the longest moonshine of the year. A natural phenomenon on steroids. Sheesh.

"So if he completes the blood harvest by harvest moon, he keeps his powers forever." Sully bit her lip.

"Son of a bitch."

"This is massive. We have to do something," she said hastily reaching for the book. "Does this mention anything about a counterspell? There has to be a counterspell—right?" She eyed him hopefully.

Dave shrugged, incredulous. "I didn't even know this spell was possible until two minutes ago. I have no idea about a counterspell."

"We have to do something. This means he's got to kill three more nulls, by moonrise in two days' time."

She started flicking through the book, her movements gaining speed. He tugged over another book and started scanning the pages. "Maybe we should—"

Her murmurs interrupted him, and he glanced over at her. Her eyes were closed, fingers splayed as she tried to encompass all of the books on the bed in her...discovery spell. Damn, she was good.

She growled in frustration, her fingers clenching when her spell turned up nothing.

Okay, so *mostly* good. Nobody was perfect, and you could only discover something if there was something to discover.

Her eyes opened, and he was struck by the panic he saw there.

"What are we going to do? I can't find a reversal."

He smiled. "We do what I do best."

"What's that?"

"Improvise."

"Please, we need to talk," Sully implored. Jacob stared down at her, his brown eyes dark with devastation. His gaze flicked to Dave standing behind her, then back to her.

"Sully, now's not a good—"

"I know." She swallowed. "God, I know. If it wasn't absolutely necessary, I would never come near you and your family ever again." Tears filled her eyes as that treacherous guilt ate at her like a gutful of chilies.

His expression gentled. "Sully, it's not your fault." He lifted his gaze to meet Dave's over her head. "It's not her fault."

Dave nodded, and she felt him place his hand on her bare shoulder. "I know. But you need to hear us out."

Jacob glanced over his shoulder, then stepped out onto the veranda of his parents' home. "I can give you five minutes," he said in a low voice. He shoved his hands in the back pockets of his jeans and leaned against the front wall of the house.

Sully nodded. She'd take whatever she could get, and be super appreciative of it. She turned to Dave, who pulled a scrap of paper from his jacket pocket and handed it to her. She caught her bottom lip between her teeth, and he gave her a reassuring nod. She turned back to Jacob, unfolding the piece of paper. Okay. Deep breath. She could admit that she'd lied, that she'd pretended to be someone she wasn't, that she was, in fact, a dreaded witch implanting herself secretly into the null community to hide her own ass from a psychotic ex. She hated what she was about to do, and was dreading Jacob's reaction. And his mother's. And everyone else she knew. Deep breath.

"We think we know why someone is killing nu—" she halted, "your family and friends." *Nulls* was a generic word, a catchall for the individuals she loved and mourned, and whom Jacob loved even more fiercely. But this was now very, very personal. For everyone.

Jacob watched her. "I'm listening."

She held out the piece of paper to him, and it fluttered in her trembling fingers. She could do this. She wasn't going to hide anymore. These people deserved more. They deserved better. And they'd lost far more than her peace of mind and comfort zone.

"He's carving this into them," she whispered.

Jacob glanced down at the symbol Dave had drawn on the paper. His lips tightened when he recognized the graphic. "I know. I saw it on my sister, on my father," he said roughly.

"He's carving this on them to steal the null restraint for the supernatural."

Jacob's gaze flicked up to meet hers. "Say what?"

"The man doing this—" she took a deep breath "—he's a witch. This symbol allows him to—"

She halted when she realized she'd be going into horrifically gory detail to him about Jenny's and his father's deaths.

"It allows him to use the null effect to cancel out any supernaturals around him," she said the words in a rush.

Jacob frowned. "I don't understand. If he's a witch, it doesn't help him."

"He's figured out a bypass," Dave said from behind her.

"How?"

Sully hesitated.

"He draws on the blood of his victims," Dave stated, and Sully sucked in a breath. His words gave an adequate description without sharing too much more. "He's figured out a spell that can help him absorb the effect without being affected by it."

Jacob frowned, shaking his head faintly. "How do you know this?"

Sully swallowed, then lifted her chin. "Be—because I'm a witch," she said in a whisper.

Jacob stilled. His gaze flicked between her and Dave, and back again. "Say what?"

"I'm a...witch," she finished in a hushed voice.

"A witch."

"Yes, a witch."

Jacob shook his head. "I don't believe it. You've been here for years, and you never—"

"I make remedies," she interrupted. "I know how to do that because I'm a witch, and I'm a student of nature."

"You make teas," Jacob argued. "Ointments. Like a doctor. Or a naturopath. That doesn't mean you're a witch."

Sully's mouth opened. She'd hidden the truth for so long, and it had taken much effort to come clean. She had expected yelling. Rebukes. Anger, betrayal. She hadn't expected not to be believed.

"Uh..." She glanced over at Dave. He shrugged his broad shoulders, a don't-ask-me look on his face.

"I am a witch," she said earnestly.

Jacob shook his head. She wasn't sure if it was in denial, disbelief or disappointment.

"I just didn't tell anyone," she said lamely.

"I don't believe you," he said, and looked at Dave.

"Oh, believe her." Dave smiled, but there was no humor in it. "For the record, so am I."

Jacob closed his eyes briefly, and when he opened them again, Sully saw the betrayal, the desolation in his eyes. And felt yay-high to a slug.

"You lied," he said in a harsh whisper.

She blinked back the tears his tone, his words, brought forth. "Yes," she admitted.

"You pretended you were normal," he accused her.

She opened her mouth. Paused. "When I'm with you guys, I am," she told him truthfully.

Jacob straightened and brought his arms forward to fold them across his broad chest. "You've lived among us for four years, Sully," he said, his voice low and harsh. "And that whole time you never hinted at what you really were." His lips pressed tightly together, and he looked out at the shadows lengthening down the street. "Did Jenny know?" He didn't look at her directly, but kept his gaze fixed on the middle distance.

This time she couldn't blink fast enough to stop the hot tears that spilled down her cheeks. "No," she whispered, ashamed.

Jacob's gaze slid to her, and her lips trembled when she saw the accusation in his eyes. "Liar," he rasped.

She flinched, then looked away. "I know. I'm so sorr—"

"Jenny's dead," he hissed. "My father. Susanne—we all welcomed you. We *trusted* you."

Sully squeezed her eyes shut, her heart clamping at the pain, the grief she heard in her friend's voice.

"There's more," she said, her voice catching. She glanced up at him. She had to tell him. She had to—oh, this was hell.

Dave's hand squeezed her shoulder, and she felt the comfort, the reassurance, the strength.

"The man doing this…is my—" her stomach clenched, and the muscles tightened in her jaw. "He's my ex."

Jacob's eyes rounded, and he stepped forward.

Dave drew her back behind him, shifting forward to stand toe-to-toe to Jacob, meeting his gaze directly. "Calm down."

Jacob's gaze narrowed. "Don't tell me to calm down," he said through gritted teeth. He glared at Sully over Dave's shoulder. "Is this guy here because of you?"

"I—I think so," she whispered.

Jacob swore and closed his eyes in pain.

"I'm so sorry, Jacob," she cried.

"Go." Jacob turned back toward the front door.

"But—"

"Sully, just…go."

Dave glanced over his shoulder at her, and his brows dipped. He turned back to Jacob.

"You need to hear her out."

Jacob turned on the witch, his expression fierce as he grasped the lapels of Dave's jacket. "I said g—"

Dave moved fast. Grasping the other man's wrist, he twisted his body—and Jacob's arms, and shoved Jacob's chest against the wall, the man's arm twisted behind his back. Sully gasped.

"This guy is not a friend of Sully's," he whispered harshly. "She left him for good reason, and she never believed he'd come anywhere near her. She risked her life to work with you guys, to help you guys, and from the moment I've met her, she's only wanted to keep you all safe. I know you're hurting, and I know you're angry. Calm down, and hear her out."

Jacob tried to struggle, but Dave shoved him back against the wall until the man stopped resisting. He looked over at Sully. "Go on." He nodded encouragement.

Sully took a deep breath. "He's coming after more nulls. He needs to kill three more purebloods to complete his spell."

Jacob stilled. She had his attention. "We believe we can stop him," she said, "but we'll need your help."

Chapter 20

Dave dabbed at the pinpricks on the wrist, then smiled at the tear-streaked face of the six-year-old red-haired pureblood. "All done, Noah. And you have a badass tatt to impress the girls when you're older," he said, and winked. He glanced briefly at the boy's father, and he smiled hesitantly back as he rubbed his son's back. Before tonight, he'd never tattooed a kid. Now he'd worked on four. Inflicting pain on kids was now on his "never do again" list.

The boy sniffed, and gave a tremulous smile as he glanced down at the white-inked tattoo. Dave reached for the antiseptic soap and gave the markings a gentle wash. Within minutes he'd taped the adhesive bandages to the boy's wrist. The tattoo was an ancient rune quaternary design, a protective shield. Simple, but effective.

"Does this mean I won't die?" the boy inquired tentatively.

Dave looked up at him, then raised his sunglasses to the top of his head. This was the son of one of the victims—a woman who'd been killed at Sully's house. No wonder the kid was concerned. His mother had been murdered by this sick prick. "This means that you will forever have the witches protecting you," he told the boy in a low voice, his tone sincere. "This guy won't be able to come near you."

"Are you going after him?"

Dave nodded. "Yeah."

The boy frowned, worried. "Aren't you scared?"

Dave tilted his head, assessing the kid. He could appreciate that, living in such a tight-knit community as this null one, the boy had heard about the recent murders, and was scared—as well he should be.

But Dave had discovered he didn't like kids to be scared.

Dave lifted his chin in the direction of the boy's wrist. "That tattoo makes you pretty badass," he said, and lifted up his T-shirt to reveal his own markings. "These make me the king of badass."

The boy's eyes rounded, and he nodded. Dave dropped the garment, then grinned. "Get going." He gestured to the door, and turned back to clean up and put away his portable tattoo kit.

The bathroom door opened, and the kid ran out. His father followed, mouthing "thank you" to him as she went.

Sully peered around the doorjamb. "That was the last one. Can I get you anything?"

"Nah, I'm good." Dave answered as he gently placed the needles onto a little tray, and poured some bleach over them. He snapped the lid on the tray. He'd have to clean and sterilize them properly back at the motel room.

He carefully loaded the kit into his backpack and turned. Sully was waiting patiently, but it was the older woman behind her that drew his gaze. His eyebrows rose. "Mrs. Forsyth."

Jacob's mother smiled tremulously. "I just wanted to say thank you," she told him. He could feel heat fill his cheeks, and he cleared his throat.

"I wanted to say I'm so sorry about your husband, and Jenny," he said in a low voice. If he'd managed to catch him the day he'd first attacked Jenny, or any of the other times before, he would have been able to prevent the deaths of half of her family. Sully had it all wrong. It wasn't her fault her friends were dead. It was his.

He ducked his head as he walked past, but halted when Mrs. Forsyth touched his arm. He looked down at her. Her wrist also bore the adhesive bandages of one of his recent white-ink tattoos. She was so tiny, so frail. How the hell could such a petite woman spawn a giant douche like Jacob?

She smiled sadly as she lifted her hand to cup his cheek. "You're a good man," she told him in a low voice. Her smile broadened, although it was slightly shaky. "Even if you are a witch."

His lips curved briefly. She patted his cheek. "I know you had nothing to do with Jenny's and Jack's deaths. Neither did Sully." She reached her other hand out and grasped Sully's hand. "You both need to believe that."

Sully closed her eyes, her face pained. Mrs. Forsyth pulled them both in for a group hug. "It's not necessary, but if you need it, you have my forgiveness." She took a deep breath, then stepped back from them. "Now, you hunt that bastard down."

She patted Dave once more, hard enough to make him blink, then turned and shuffled down the hall.

He took a deep breath. That tiny little null had just given him more tenderness than his coven elder mother ever had. He frowned. It made him feel…weird. He shuddered. God, he was getting as sooky over these folks as Sully was. Yeesh.

He stretched his neck, then eyed the woman next to him. She wore the same weary expression he suspected he did. "Come on," he said. "Let's go."

They'd been at the Forsyth home for hours. Jacob had rounded up as many purebloods as he could find, but they knew there were still some who hadn't been inked—and that ink would mean the difference between life and death.

He'd been a little wary when suggesting this option for the purebloods. Tattooing involved injecting ink beneath the skin—resulting in a minor contamination of the blood. Most of the shadow breeds would have balked at tainting their bloodlines, but the nulls didn't seem to have an issue with it. And Jacob had been the first to accept the offer, showing his mother it didn't hurt "that much". Dave winced. He'd developed a basic design—something that could be done quickly so that more nulls could be protected in a short time, but also to try to limit the level of discomfort, especially for the kids.

Sully slid her arm around his and gave him a gentle smile. "That looks like it was tiring."

Dave shrugged. "Meh. I think that was a record for me." He'd worked quickly and consistently, and had managed to imprint the warded tattoo onto almost all of the purebloods in this area. He'd be coming back in the morning to work on anyone else who came forward. It was the Harvest Festival, with streets blocked off and stalls already being assembled. The nulls were determined to go ahead with the celebration. Which meant there'd be lots of purebloods walking the street fair, among many others. A skinshifter would be next to damn near impossible to locate in such a large crowd. All the witch would have to do is come into physical contact with a person, and he'd be able to take on their facade. It would be like having a haystack and looking for the needle—no, the ax—no, now the nail...

At least, if Dave was a skinshifter, that's how he'd do it. But with this protection ward tattooed onto the purebloods, they'd both tainted the blood supply with ink, which meant technically the purebloods were no longer pure of blood, but they also had a blocking ward to prevent attacks.

Take that, skinshifter.

They just needed to make sure they found all of the purebloods. If there were three left untattooed, this witch could still complete his spell. And that would make it incredibly hard for Dave to send him to the Other Realm. Sully claimed Mental Marty—his name for the witch, not hers—wasn't a skilled witch. He wasn't so sure he'd agree. He'd managed to come up with a really twisted plan, find an ancient spell and become almost undetectable in the process. It was like hunting and fighting a shadow—a shadow that had proven time and time again just how lethal he could be. Sully was so damn lucky she'd escaped him when she did.

He eyed her. Sully had dark circles under her eyes, and that crooked pout was just a little more pronounced, the lines a little more drawn, her complexion just a little more pale.

"You look tired."

"Gee, thanks."

He winced. Oops. "Sorry. But it's understandable."

She'd had very little sleep since Jenny's murder, and had startled awake with nightmares. "Do you need to recharge?"

Witches used nature to feed their energy. Finding a place to sit with exposure to the elements…sun, wind, rain, earth. Even moonlight helped. It was a chance to be still, to meditate and to become a little more present. After his inking marathon, he could do with a recharge, too.

She nodded. "That sounds great. I usually go the headland at the end of my street, but…" She shrugged, wincing.

He nodded. Her home was still classed as a crime scene, and she wasn't technically permitted access to it. If you followed the rules.

He didn't really follow the rules.

"Sounds great. Let's go."

Sully led him downstairs, but she halted when she saw Jacob coming out of the living room. The tall man paused when he saw them, his eyes on Sully. Dave stiffened. If this guy was going to threaten Sully—

The fisherman shoved his hands in his jeans pockets as he took a step toward Sully. He gazed sheepishly at her for a moment, then sighed. "Sully, I'm so sorry—"

"Shh," Sully said, shaking her head. "You've got nothing to apologize for."

"No, I do. You were Jen's friend, you're my friend. I shouldn't have said the things I did."

"You had every right to—" Sully's words were cut off when the big man swept her up in a bear hug.

"No, I didn't. I was being a royal dick."

Dave's eyebrows rose. Well, he wasn't about to argue with a royal dick.

Sully hugged Jacob back. "You've lost your sister

and your father," she whispered. "And you're my friend. You can always speak freely with me, especially when I deserve it."

"But you didn't."

Jacob lifted his gaze, and met Dave's over Sully's head. Dave arched an eyebrow. He sure as hell wasn't going to give the guy a hall pass for being a royal dick. Sully had been so worried, so heartsick about telling the nulls the truth. And the big jerk had hurt her feelings when she was already feeling so much pain and guilt over the recent deaths.

But the big jerk had just lost his sister and family. He guessed if Sully could cut Jacob some slack, he could, too. He relaxed his features when he met Jacob's gaze. And then realized the man's hands were smoothing down Sully's back. Dave narrowed his gaze. Well, there went that warm and fuzzy moment. He narrowed his eyes as he met Jacob's, and this time it was Jacob's eyebrows who rose.

He gave Sully one more squeeze, then set her back. "Thank you," he whispered. "For everything."

Sully ducked her head and nodded as she stepped past.

Dave made to follow her, but stopped when Jacob stuck out his hand. "Thank you," the fisherman said sincerely. Dave eyed the extended hand. Aw, darn. The royal dick was being halfway decent. He grasped the man's hand and shook it, giving him a nod, then he followed Sully out into the night.

He handed her a helmet, and within minutes they were back on the coast road. The motel was on the other side of town, so passing Sully's home and pulling in at the headland was virtually on the way.

He slowly drove past the house. It sat, dark and silent,

at the end of the street, the crime scene tape blocking off the drive fluttering in the night's breeze.

He pulled over onto the grassy verge, and waited for Sully to dismount before doing so himself. He removed his sunglasses and gazed out over the water. Light gray clouds drifted slowly across the sky. Stars glittered, and the moon cast a silver swathe across the water. The breeze was soft and still bearing the final warmth of a summer on the wane.

He sucked in a deep breath. Held it. Slowly exhaled. Salt and sweet blossoms. He glanced about. Yep. Sully's garden backed up to the fence.

"What do you think?" Sully asked as she sat cross-legged on the grass. He joined her. He could feel the night dew soaking through his jeans.

He looked out over the water. "It's beautiful," he said quietly. Even if he did have a wet seat.

They sat there for a while, soaking in the serenity. Dave's lips curved. No wonder this area was called Serenity Cove.

He tilted his head back, enjoying the feel of the breeze ruffling his short hair and the stretch of his neck muscles after the long day of bending over to ink up nulls. He watched the stars for a moment, then closed his eyes. He put aside his thoughts on Mental Marty, his very grave concerns that Sully's ex would find an unprotected pureblood—or worse, get desperate when he couldn't, and strike out in a much more dangerous and lethal way. He put aside his thoughts on Jacob, of the teeniest spark of jealousy that had awoken when the man wrapped his arms around Sully... He put aside the torment of fulfilling another task for the Ancestors, and the self-doubt and guilt over the six people already killed by the target he had yet to dispatch.

He let nature have its way, let the calm and peace soak in, let the delight in a breeze against his skin take hold. He opened himself up, dissolving his mental wards, letting the energy gently roll in to fill his reserves.

He sensed a lightness, a warmth that was sweet and pure, with the cooling edges of worry and anxiety.

Sully.

Instinctively, he touched those cooler, darker edges with his own energy, feeding her reassurance as he drew in her worries to make them his own—and then realized what he was doing.

He snapped his eyes open and sat bolt upright. "I'm sorry," he blurted. After what she'd told her relationship with Marty, he could well understand her resistance to link with another witch, to have that witch consume anything from her, especially without her permission. They hadn't fully linked, but he'd forged a connection, one that hadn't been invited.

Sully sucked in a breath, her gaze fixed on the sea that glittered with silver diamonds under the moonlight.

"It's—it's okay," she said in a small voice.

"No, no it's not. You've never invited me in, and after hearing about Marty, I understand that. I—I didn't intend for that to happen."

She nodded, and her bottom lip disappeared between her teeth again. She tilted her head, and it was almost as though she was wanting to look at him, but trying to avoid him at the same time.

"You—last night you—" She sucked in a breath, and he watched as her breasts quivered beneath her cotton camisole top.

He whipped his gaze back to the sea. First he intruded on her mentally, and when she's trying to talk to him he's ogling her. *Bad form, Dave.*

"I don't know what happened last night," Dave admitted in a low voice, and this time it was him averting his gaze. "I just know that you were dealing with so much pain, more pain than I'd ever felt in a person, and…and I wanted to help ease it." He grimaced. He'd intruded on her then, too. Had no idea how he'd done it—he'd never done it before.

She remained silent, and he didn't know if she was mentally screaming "I hate you" and trying to map out her escape route. What she'd endured with her prick of an ex was on his mind, her vulnerability, the abuse of not only her generosity, but her body, her mind and her powers…and for a witch, that was a painful violation.

He raised his knee and rested his forearm on it. "I know—I know there's a protocol with power bonding," he said in a low voice. "I've bonded with other witches, like my sister, when it was necessary—and agreed to, but I haven't lived in a coven." He shook his head. "That's not an excuse, it's—it's that sometimes I'm ignorant of the process, and for some folks, I take shortcuts that can be…confronting."

It was a constant source of frustration for his coven elder mother—something he'd rather enjoyed doing, up until now—when someone he was beginning to really care about was affected.

Sully turned, and reached put her hand on his arm—and there it was. That little pfft of a power meld that he still couldn't get his mind around, but that awoke every single one of his senses and focused them on her.

"It's okay, Dave," she said, and gave him a tremulous but reassuring smile, and gave his arm a gentle squeeze. He felt an answering throb in his groin. Felt the want, the need for her, and battled it. He met her gaze, saw the tenderness, the interest. He raised his hand to cup her cheek. Her skin was so soft, so smooth, her eyes so dark, full of wariness, full of curiosity, and yet showing him a hunger he wasn't sure she intended for him to see.

But he did. He leaned forward a little, then halted.

He wanted her—desperately, but thoughts of Mental Marty, of what he'd done to her, bubbled up. He never wanted her to feel forced around him—for anything.

As though reading his mind, Sully moved. Tilting her chin up, she closed the distance, her lips pressing against his as she slid her hand up his arm and over his shoulder.

Dave closed his eyes, content to let her lead, let her set the pace, the level of intim—

Her tongue slid past his lips, and heat flooded him, tightening inside him, flooding his body with an arousal that was so damn gripping, so tight, it had him panting as he angled his head.

Without breaking contact, Sully rose up on her knees, her arms sliding around him, under his jacket. He shrugged it off to give her access—*oh, please, access*—and dropped it to the ground behind him. He raised his hands to her hips, guiding her as she straddled his hips. He wrapped his arms around her, crossing them over her back as he pulled her against him. Sully sighed, her breath drifting across his lips as she tilted her head first in one direction, then the other, as though trying to find the best position.

He groaned at the teasing contact, and slid one hand up into her hair. He could feel the damp heat of her pressed against his groin and his cock stiffened. She moaned, her hips writhing against his, and he shifted beneath her, trying to get even closer, despite their clothes.

She drew back, tugging at his T-shirt. He brought

her lips back to his, impatient at the loss of contact, and ripped his shirt from neck to hem, shrugging out of the scraps. She laughed huskily, and the sound had to be the sexiest he'd ever heard, that playful rasp against his neck.

She pushed him back, and he lay down across his discarded clothing. She made that sexy, crooked pout with her lips, and he raised a finger to trace her mouth. She captured his fingertip with her mouth, sucking on him in a way that almost made him delirious with need.

She pulled back for a moment, scanning his chest, running her hands over his body. He closed his eyes, enjoying the feel of her caressing her skin, until he felt her lips against his nipple.

Oh, wow. He bucked beneath her, and she chuckled throatily as she kissed her way down his torso. Her fingers fumbled with his belt and fly, and then suddenly she had him, all of him. He gave himself up to the intense pleasure as she took him into her mouth.

She tugged at his control, teased at his restraint, until he could feel himself swelling in her mouth. He reached for her and found the straps of her camisole instead. He pulled gently at the garment; she helped him draw it up over her head. He grasped her head, tugging her up to him. He skimmed his hands over her back, dispensing with the clasp of her bra, and the bra itself. Her skin was so warm, so smooth, and he ran his fingers down her back. His lips curved as he felt her shudder.

He pulled up her skirt, dragging at the lacy band of her briefs until they skimmed over her bottom.

Sully moaned, shifting so that they could pull her panties off, and then she straddled him again.

He looked up at her. Bathed in the silver glow of the moonlight, her skin looked pearlescent, and he reached out to touch his midnight goddess. She gasped when he caught her breasts with his hands, and he fondled them. She quivered, head tilting back, and her hair cascaded down her back. She writhed against him, and this time he could feel the molten core of her pressed against his cock. God, he wanted her.

She caught her lip between her teeth as she quivered above him. Looking up at her, seeing her body, the way she undulated against him, was setting off a fire in him that he needed to control, before he exploded. He grasped her hips, rolling over so that she lay beneath him, and she panted, surprised but smiling at the move. He gazed down at her for a moment, and they both paused, catching their breaths.

He stared at her face, the gentle arch of her eyebrows, those beautiful blue eyes, the straight nose and that crooked, sexy smile. She was magnificent.

"God, you're beautiful," he whispered, and she smiled, almost shyly.

"You're pretty gorgeous yourself," she whispered, her gaze skimming his body, before her eyes once again met his. In that moment, in that infinitesimal connection, something shifted inside him, something he couldn't name, but seemed to rock him to his core.

Slowly, he dipped his head and pressed his lips to hers.

Chapter 21

Sully closed her eyes, her arms twining around his neck. The kiss was tender, hot, slick and carnal, but yet she felt something, a weight, an impact that seemed to set her senses to overload and her emotions into a headspin. It was the perfect kind of kiss, full of emotion, passion and sensuality. Meaningful.

And so not what she was expecting.

She sucked in a breath as he pulled away from her, and kissed his way down her body. He carefully undid her skirt and belt—avoiding the daggers—and pulled the garment down her body, following it with his lips and tongue. She shuddered as the fabric slid down her legs, and then off her body. He shoved at his jeans, discarding them, and then was kissing his way back up her body until—

Her eyes widened as his lips kissed her. There. His hands stroked her, drawing out her reactions, making her tremble as the heat, the tension, coiled inside her. Oh. My. G—her neck arched when his tongue slid inside her, and she groaned, long and loud into the darkness. The stars above them were swimming as he laved her, over and over, until she was a hot, wet mess in his arms. He used his hands and mouth to wring extreme pleasure from her, and her back arched when that tension suddenly snapped, sending her spiraling into a cloud of bliss.

He didn't give her a chance to catch her breath. He crawled up her body, stroking her breasts, then biting and sucking on her breasts, until his hips found hers. He braced his arms on either side of her, his silver eyes meeting hers, and she gasped as he slid inside her. She brought her thighs up to his waist, and they both moaned at the change in angle, the deeper penetration. She reached for him, her breath hitching each time he withdrew, then slid back to the hilt. He covered her body with his, his hips thrusting, and she cried out as the passion once again swept over her, pulling her body taut with need.

He held her in position, hands grasping her shoulders as he slid home, and the heat exploded. She cried out, a sound snatched away by the breeze. Her nipples, her core, her very mind seemed to overload on sensation. She heard him groan as he thrust once more, his body hard and tight against hers, and then he, too, found release. Lightning crackled above them, and the air practically snapped with energy.

Heart thudding in her chest, she embraced him, trembling, as she tried to catch her breath, her reason, some modicum of control. She gazed up at the stars, and realized even her toes were clenched, and it took conscious effort to get her muscles, everywhere, to unclench.

"Oh, my," she panted, and he chuckled, setting off little rockets of sensation as he kissed her softly.

"Oh, my," he said, nodding.

He rolled onto his back and pulled her into his side, and they lay like that for a while, letting the wind play over their naked bodies. Dave stroked his hand down her arm, and she stretched against him, enjoying the contact.

"Well, that's one way to recharge," he commented, and Sully started to laugh. She definitely felt…renewed.

He pulled his T-shirt on over his head, then looked across at Sully. They'd arrived at the motel room in the wee hours of the morning, and had managed to catch a couple of hours' sleep. Which was hard when curled up to a soft, warm, luscious body like Sully's. Now, though, there was nothing warm, or remotely soft about the woman. Still plenty of lush, but as she strapped her weapons to that luscious body, he wasn't about to mention it.

She slid a dagger into her boot, and she was carefully drawing a long-sleeved blouse on over the interesting-looking contraptions strapped to her arms. He also noticed she wore her tricky little belt with the twin blades. The woman was a damn walking armory.

"Do you really think all that's necessary?" he gently asked her.

She eyed him, her expression set in an implacable expression. This woman before him was so far removed from the moaning siren in his arms from just hours before. She'd been like this, so grim, so focused, since she woke.

"Today—tonight—Marty will either finish off his spell and become the most powerful creature walking among us, or we will have killed that nutter."

He frowned, and stepped around the bed. "*We* are

not killing him, Sully. I'm the Witch Hunter, remember. If you see him, you tell me. Don't go after him."

She tilted her head as she returned is gaze. "I don't want to see him. Just the idea that I will see him again makes me…nervous," she admitted. Then her chin dipped, and her stare became intent. "But I will do whatever I can to protect these people from him."

He didn't know whether to kiss her or criticize her. Sometime overnight, his sweet little Sully morphed into a fierce warrior woman. He eyed the leather pants, the boots, the black singlet with the gray overshirt. Her hair was pulled up into a braided bun on top of her head, and the severe style highlighted her cheekbones and drew attention to her bright eyes and that gorgeously crooked mouth.

He couldn't deny this whole badass vibe he was getting from her worked. He was a confident guy, he could admit when a woman turned him on, and right now Sully was ticking all the boxes. And that secretly worried him. He didn't want her anywhere near her psycho ex.

"This is why I'm here," he told her. "If you see him, let me know, and then let me do my job." He gestured to her outfit. "I don't want you to hurt yourself."

Sully's eyes narrowed. "Excuse me?"

He walked up to her. "These weapons—they're not toys. You could be in more danger from yourself with all these sharp blades than from anyone attacking you."

Her jaw slackened, as though she was lost a little for words. He sighed, and gestured to the guards strapped to her forearms. "Do you even know how to use these things?"

Her eyebrows rose. She thought about his words, then gave him a small smile. "If you can take them off me, I'll leave them."

Dave cocked his head to the side, both annoyed and pleased with her challenge. "Really?"

She nodded. "Really."

He moved quickly, reaching for her right forearm. She moved so damn fast, her movements almost a blur as she flexed her wrists, and the pronged swords slid from their sheaths. She caught the handles, the blades moving in a wicked twirl as she easily evaded his grasp. He stepped after her, then hissed when he felt the flat of the blade smack his arm away. The blades twirled, and suddenly the tip of one was against the indent of his collarbone. He halted.

She eyed him coolly. "Yield?"

His eyes narrowed. "Never."

He dodged the tip, bringing his arm up to hit hers away from him. She turned, the blades flashing. He raised his arm to block her strike, and she hit him again with the flat of the blade. And then smacked him in the thigh with the second blade. He grimaced, and caught her wrist.

The world tilted, and he had a vague impression of the room flipping upside down, and then he landed on the floor, with a blade at his neck and one over his heart.

She arched an eyebrow. "Yield?"

He pursed his lips. That was...impressive. "Only if you show me that move," he said, and she grinned as she straightened.

"Let's get through today, first." She slid the pronged swords back into their sheaths, then extended her hand to him.

He grasped it, moving smoothly to his feet. "Fine. You...wear those." He gestured to the weapons she'd now hidden behind her long sleeves. He got the impression that she'd taken it extremely easy on him.

She nodded. "I'm glad we sorted that out."

She turned for the door, but he stopped her. "It's going to be okay," he told her. She smiled and nodded, but he knew neither of them were fully convinced. They were going up against a guy who could easily neutralize their powers, if the surrounding nulls didn't do it already. He grabbed his mobile ink kit and followed her out, his eyes on the leather-clad hips swinging in front of him.

Damn, but this look worked on her.

Sully stared at the street scene. The road had been closed to traffic, and people milled about, strolling from stall to stall. There was a fish market section down the end, and local farmers had brought produce. There was apple-bobbing, pumpkin-carving, clowns, wood-chopping, animals, bake stalls, food stalls…the scents and sights were like a colorful burst to the senses.

"I don't like this," Sully said, lifting her gaze from the crowd to the darkening clouds skidding across the sky. Talk about portent. The clouds had started to skid across the sky after lunch. A storm was coming.

Which was surprising, as the forecast called for a faux summer day.

She turned to Dave. He wore leather pants and a black T-shirt beneath his leather jacket, his dark sunglasses shielding his eyes. Tall, muscular…dangerous.

Badass sexy.

She ran her gaze over his body. Last night had been… wow. She had to admit, sex with Dave was…cosmic. Fireworks, lightning…she'd never experienced anything like that before with a lover. But there was something else, something more…like the buildup of a spell before the effect was visible. Full of magic, full of meaning and fraught with just as much danger. When this was over, though, she didn't know what was to come next, and that scared her. She'd lived her life quietly, safely, since leaving Irondell and Martin. Well, except for the two years she spent on the West Coast learning how to defend herself. But the four years since arriving in Serenity Cove had passed in idyllic peace and, well, serenity.

Dave had turned that all on its head. He'd threatened her—physically. And then had vowed to protect her. He challenged her, with every word, with every touch…he was able to get to the heart of her, the heart she'd successfully shielded from everyone. Until now. She was in very real danger of losing her heart to the Witch Hunter. She gazed around the crowd. And that was the problem. Marty had figured out a way to close down the Witch Hunter's vision. He'd figured out a way to nullify the null effect—which was pretty damned clever. He'd killed six people. He'd avoided the law, Dave and any number of nulls out searching for him. If they didn't find the other nulls before he did, they could be looking at a new world order by sunrise.

"There's Jacob," Dave said, raising his chin. Sully looked. Jacob was standing beside a chair and table set up, with a Free Tattoos sign. Dave grimaced. "Free?"

"They needed something to use as a cover," Sully said. Jacob had called them earlier that morning at the motel. He and his mother had convinced the mayor to let them set up another booth on the street so that Dave could tattoo the last of the purebloods under the guise of a market stall.

"But free?"

She smiled at the mock whine in his voice. "You're being very generous, whether you like it or not."

He turned to face her, his smile dropping a little.

"I'm going to be at that stall pretty much for the rest of the day."

She nodded. "I'll be helping Jacob and his mom round up the rest of the purebloods."

Dave pursed his lips. "Don't stray too far. Stay with the crowd, no wandering off by yourself. This guy is using your guise to get close to these nulls, and I don't think that's by accident."

Her smile faltered. Dave was right. Marty had tracked her down, had tricked her friends to get close enough to kill him. Apparently her departure must have been a sore point for him. She nodded. "I understand."

"Good." Dave leaned forward and pressed a quick kiss against her lips.

"Dave!"

Dave startled at the call and drew back. They both turned. Noah was hurtling down the street, weaving his wave through the crowd.

"Hey, Noa—oh." Dave grunted when the kid ran into him full tilt. Noah clung to his legs, and Dave stooped down to hug him back.

"How's my little badass going?"

Sully winced at the language, but Noah laughed. "Great. How is the king of badass?"

Oh, my God. Now the kids were repeating it. She watched as Noah's father—George, Susanne's husband—shook his head as he approached, overhearing his son.

"The king is good," Dave remarked, then dropped Noah to his feet. He shook hands with George. "Hey, how you doing?"

George nodded. "We're…getting by." Sully could see the haunted look in his eyes, the dark circles and deep grooves. His wife's death had hit him hard. She ruffled Noah's red hair.

Dave looked down at the little boy. "Hey, do you want to come help me at the booth? Folks might be a little braver if they know you've got one of my tattoos…?" He raised his brow at George, who nodded in relief. "Thanks. I've got to go watch his sister in the pumpkin fairy production."

Sully blinked away a tear. Susanne was usually one of the stagehands for these things, working behind the scenes to get all the kids into costumes, soothe fluttery tummies and offer all sorts of encouragement. Noah's sister, Cherie, would be facing her first concert without her mom.

"Take your time, Dave and I can watch Noah," she told him.

George patted her on the arm. "Thanks," he said hoarsely, his eyes red, and hurried away before his son noticed.

Dave stretched his hand out to Noah. "Come on, LB, let's go get our ink on."

Noah scrunched up his nose. "LB?"

"Little Badass." Dave put a hand up over his mouth and mock whispered, "It'll be our secret."

Noah nodded. "Okay, KB."

Dave tilted his head. "KB?"

"King of Badass," Noah explained, his tone suggesting it was obvious.

Dave chuckled. "Yeah, that'll definitely be our secret."

Sully watched as the tall, leather-clad man led the little boy over to the booth. Noah was practically skipping. Jacob greeted both of them, then went and got a stool for Noah to sit on as Dave set up his kit.

It was sweet, in a weird, testosterone-laden way.

She pulled a piece of paper out of her pocket and glanced at the list of twelve names. Mrs. Forsyth was already trying to locate the older purebloods, and as soon as Dave was ready for clients, Jacob would be out combing the crowd.

For now, it was her turn. She was on the hunt for purebloods.

Dave taped the adhesive bandage over the new tattoo and smiled at the twentysomething-year-old woman. She flicked her hair over her shoulder and eyed him.

"I'm thinking about getting a tattoo…here," she said. His gaze dropped to where she indicated. She was drawing her denim skirt higher up her thigh.

His eyebrows rose, and he gently grasped her wrist, stopping her from baring any more leg. "Uh, another time. It's best to let the body recover a little before going for the next tatt."

She pouted. He was sure she was trying to be flirtatious, but all he noticed was that her mouth didn't have that cute little quirk in it like Sully's did.

The woman sighed. "Fine. Maybe later, then?"

He gave her a noncommittal nod. "Maybe."

He turned away to clean and sterilize the needles, and looked up when Jacob joined him.

"How many is that?"

"Seven," Dave said, washing the needles in a solution before placing them in the pot on top of the camping stove Jacob had provided. It was rough, it was rudimentary, but the end result was sterilized needles ready to be used on the next pureblood null to make it to his booth.

Mrs. Forsyth had managed to locate the older purebloods, and Sully had tracked down three. Jacob had found two.

Dave leaned back to look behind Jacob. "Where's Noah?"

"Oh, he's right—" Jacob jerked his thumb over his shoulder as he turned. He frowned. "He was right behind me."

Dave closed his kit with a snap and rose. He lifted the cloth on the booth to look under. No Noah. He straightened to scan the crowd. "Well, he's not there, now."

Jacob paled. "I swear, he was right behind me."

Dave nodded, holding up a hand. "Okay. He's a kid. There could be lots of explanations, from deciding to go watch his sister in her concert to being distracted by a funny-shaped bird poop. Let's look."

Jacob nodded. "I'll go look around the stage," he commented, and strode off in the direction of the area designated for performances.

Dave sighed. "Great. I'll take the bird poop." He walked around the booth, scanning the crowd. He wasn't going to panic. Sure, the kid was cute. Pretty cool, actually. And tatted up with his own special ward. Noah was also full of curiosity, if his gazillion and one questions about tattooing, motorbikes, sunglasses, laser eyes, magic powers, leather underpants—how the hell that had come up, he still didn't know—and needles maybe turning into ninja spears for grasshoppers were anything to go by.

"Noah!" he called out the boy's name as he made his way through the crowd. The colors of the booths started to darken, and he looked up. Storm clouds were skidding across the sky.

Dave glanced about, his pace quickening. He didn't like this. He didn't like this, at all.

"Noah!"

Chapter 22

Sully glanced down at her paper. She, along with Mrs. Forsyth and Jacob, had managed to find eight out of the twelve remaining purebloods. Four were still outstanding. Marty needed only three. The paper in her hand darkened, and she looked up. Dark clouds, thick and voluminous, skittered across the sky, as though the Ancestors were angry and frowning down at everyone. She frowned. That cloud action was too fast to be natural. The night would arrive early.

Marty.

Damn him. She started to walk back toward Dave's booth. She waved to Cheryl, who was manning the Brewhaus Diner coffee stand. She noticed Tyler, in his sheriff uniform, standing beside it. She almost went up to him to ask him when she might be able to get into her home, but he was frowning as he tried to catch Cheryl's attention, and Cheryl was steadfastly ignoring him as she chatted to a young man who'd received his coffee but didn't seem in any hurry to move along.

Sully turned away. She'd have to catch Cheryl later for an update, but it looked like something had definitely changed between those two. She took two steps and halted. Was that Noah?

The red-haired boy was being led away from the crowd, toward the head of the walking trail that led down to Crescent Beach. He was being led by a woman wearing a long flowing skirt and a billowy top. A woman who looked a lot like Sully.

Sully blinked. No…

Noah tripped, and the woman turned to tug on his hand. Sully's heart seized in her chest, then started hammering.

"Noah!" She started to run after the pair, and stumbled a little when the woman looked casually over her shoulder. It was like looking into a mirror, or at a long-lost twin. The face staring back at her was her own.

Except for the eyes. Where Sully's eyes were blue, this woman's eyes were jet black. The woman spotted Sully, and her lips lifted in a smile. Then her features started to waver, and the boneless mass morphed into masculine features she knew all too well, and Marty scooped up a surprised Noah and started running.

"Noah," Sully screamed and bolted after them.

Dave stared around the petting zoo in frustration. Noah wasn't here, either. He moved his arm away from a donkey whose attention was becoming way too personal. Jacob hurried over to him, with George, Noah's father, close on his heels, his face pale with worry.

"I take he's not watching his sister's concert?" Dave commented.

Jacob shook his head, and George ran his hands through his dark hair. "Where is he?" The man's tone was panicked, his eyes wide with consternation. The man had lost his wife in a violent crime—Dave couldn't begin to imagine how he was processing the disappearance of his son.

"Is everything okay?"

Dave turned at the query. Tyler Clinton, in full sheriff's uniform, was eyeing George with concern. His normal reticence to involve the police, to involve others, disappeared. A little boy was missing.

"Sheriff, we need your help." Dave quickly informed him of Noah's disappearance, along with the fact that he may have been taken by a man who can change his appearance, by taking on the facade of anyone he came into physical contact with, and who was responsible for the recent murders in Serenity Cove.

To his credit, the sheriff took it well.

"You son of a bitch," Tyler hissed, eyes flashing with anger, his fists clenched. "You've known all this time—" he bit the words off, his gaze taking in George and Jacob. The sheriff pulled the radio from its holster on his hip and called for all available deputies to attend the festival in search of a missing six-year-old, believed to have been abducted. Then he pointed a finger at Dave. "You're with me. You withheld vital information to an ongoing murder investigation. That's obstruction."

The sheriff turned to George. "Do you have a recent photo of Noah? I'll need to distribute to the guys when they get here. We'll also make announcements from the staging area, and see if we can get everyone to help." He placed his hands on his hips, then looked at Dave. "Can this guy really play swapsies with his face?"

Dave nodded. "Yep."

Tyler sighed, then turned in the direction of the stage. "Let's get to it, then."

It wasn't long before most of the activities at the Festival were shut down—not because Tyler called for it, but because pretty much all of those attending the street fair wanted to help in the search of the boy. Tyler split the crowd into groups and assigned the groups areas to search.

Tyler beckoned him, and Dave followed him down the length of the street.

"You should have told me." Tyler's voice was low, and full of controlled anger.

Dave shot him a look. "Yeah, I can totally see how that conversation would have gone. 'Hey, Sheriff, your killer is a witch—I don't know who he is, or what he looks like, or why he's doing it, but I'll take it from here.'" Dave shook his head.

Tyler peered through the glass windows of a store. "You still should have told me."

"You were already suspicious of me," Dave reminded him.

"No, I wasn't."

"How many tourists do you ask when they're leaving?"

Tyler's lips curved as he looked back at him, eyeing the bike leathers. "You were never a tourist."

"But you see where I'm going with this. I have a job to do, too."

"You could have just told me."

"We witches don't air our dirty laundry." Dave looked inside the window of the next store. Most of them were closed for the festival holiday. "Just like the wolves, the vampires, the bears…"

"So you were really going to kill your witch and leave me with an unsolved murder?"

"I'm a Witch Hunter."

Tyler grimaced. "No wonder people don't trust witches," he muttered.

"Hey, people trust witches," Dave protested. Tyler arched his eyebrow. "Mostly," Dave added, trying to be as truthful as he could.

Dave held up both hands. "Witch Hunter." He didn't like playing that card, would prefer to just drift in and out of a mission without pissing off the local law enforcement, but the reality is that he had a duty that, while focused on witches, had the recognition and enforcement from Reform authorities.

"The path of least resistance," Dave told him as they crossed the street. There was a break in the buildings, with what looked like a trail down toward the beach.

"So keeping this from me was to avoid an uncomfortable conversation," Tyler said, his tone dry.

Dave nodded. "Like this one? Hell, yeah." He squinted as he scanned the beach briefly. The wind was picking up, the temperature had dropped several degrees and the waves were crashing against the shore as though being hurled at the beach. He was about to move on when a figure running in the distance. Black pants, gray shirt.

Sully.

And she was bolting after something.

"Sully!" he cried out, taking the trail. His words were snatched away by the wind.

"What is it?" Tyler asked as he reached the top of the trail.

"Sully. Something's wrong."

Sully wasn't jogging leisurely along the beach. She

was running at full pelt and was almost at the end of the beach where the headland started to rear out of the water. Dave took off after.

Sully clambered over the rocks. She heard Noah cry out, heard the fear in the little boy's voice. She hurried, her feet scrabbling over the wet stones slick with seaweed. The waves rolled in, smashing against the rocks, and she ducked under the spray.

She had to wait for a wave to recede before she climbed around a larger rock formation and stumbled when she landed on wet sand. A hole loomed in front of her, the entrance to a cave. The sand was drier up near the mouth of the cave, and she ran, plowing through the sand until she reached the cave and entered.

"Mar—"

An invisible force pushed at her, sending her flying against the rock wall of the cave. She landed heavily on the sandy floor, coughing as she tried to catch her breath.

Wicked laughter echoed through the cave, and she raised her head. The cave was huge, with various rock formations that created bridges and ramps within the space, so it was almost like a multilevel labyrinth, resident monster included.

She eyed Marty who was presently carrying a struggling Noah up a ramp. Had he—had Marty just magically blindsided her while carrying a null? His powers were getting stronger. Her shaking hands clenched fistfuls of sand. This was Marty. The guy who'd almost drained her dry, who had scared her so much, had hurt her so much, that she'd run from him. Not walked out. Not left. *Run.* All those years of training on the West Coast, all those hours of practicing with the weapons she created, all of that fled her in the face of the man she'd once trusted, and who had abused her so much. Memories, of him screaming in her face, of him pushing her, of her falling over furniture, against walls and doors, of glass breaking, cutting…they all surfaced, along with her sense of powerlessness, of the very real danger she faced with this witch.

"Let him go, Marty," she called out to him, and rose to her feet. She quickly bolstered her shields as she ran over to the base of the rocky ramp. The closer she got to Noah, though, the harder it was to maintain the protection.

Marty turned to face her. "I'm afraid I can't do that, Sully." He looked different. His skin was almost radiant, his eyes flashing. As though power itself was coursing through his veins, bringing with it a confidence and brashness she could never feed him. "I need him. He's the last."

Did that mean he'd killed already? She didn't think so. Each time she'd delivered a null to Dave at the stand, he'd seemed in good health and not reeling from the wound on his chest. Did that mean he'd captured the nulls? Is that why nobody could find the remaining purebloods?

"No, you don't." She started to jog up the ramp, and Marty whirled, his hand out.

"Stop right there," he told her. He reached behind him and pulled something out from the waistband of his jeans. Sully swallowed when she recognized the ceremonial knife she'd seen used in the vision to kill Amanda Sinclair. "Admittedly, I don't like using kids, but I'm working with a short time frame, here."

"You have to see this is crazy," Sully said, panting as she slowly advanced, arms up, palms out in a nonthreatening pose. Even she could see how much her hands were shaking.

Marty's eyebrows rose. "Crazy, huh? Crazy like a fox, maybe."

Noah squirmed, and Marty shook the boy. Sully took a couple of extra steps forward.

"I know what you have planned," she told him. "And it's clever, I have to admit—but it's so wrong, Marty."

Marty smiled grimly. "Only those in a weaker position would say that. To me, this feels very right—and long overdue."

Sully stepped closer again, and she had to lock her knees to stop from collapsing. Everything felt so unstable, so...shaken. "Why, Marty? Why are you doing this?"

Marty's smile turned into an unattractive twist. "Do you remember what you called me, Sully? Remember that day you ran out like a rat scurrying in a sewer...?"

Sully glanced at Noah. The boy was looking between them, his face pale, but his eyes—so like his mother's—showed a spurt of rebellion. She held out her palm in his direction, trying to make her warning to the boy to hold still look casual in the eyes of his captor. She'd learned that if you didn't move, didn't make eye contact, just burrowed down and let him vent, the storm would eventually pass.

"I remember begging you to stop," she told him quietly. "I remember you throwing me against that mirror."

Marty huffed. "Well, that was an accident," he told her. "You got me so mad."

She pursed her lips. So him throwing her up against a wall mirror was her fault? She shook her head. "You hurt me."

"When my father found out the Alder Keeper of the

Books had cast me aside, he banished me from my coven," he rasped, and Noah cried out as the grip on the back of his neck tightened. "You called me pathetic."

Sully took a deep, quivering breath. "I realize that must have sounded harsh," she allowed. She couldn't agree with him, but she didn't want to outright challenge him, not knowing how he'd react.

His comment, though, brought a lot of things into sharp relief. He'd been cast out. For a witch whose powers were limited, he needed the safety of a coven to ward off threats. He would have been vulnerable. Alone. Although she thought that was a fitting outcome for this guy, she wouldn't have actually wished it on anyone. After living so long without her own coven, she knew how lonely, and how scary, it could be on your own.

Marty sneered. "You called me a pathetic vessel of puerile misery."

"I'd have to agree," a deep voice called out from behind her.

Relief flooded her when she recognized Dave's voice. She didn't turn, though, didn't take her eyes off Marty and little Noah.

Marty's eyes widened, and his hand moved. A fireball burst from his palm, and Sully ducked. She heard a grunt, a hiss and then a thud. She glanced over her shoulder. Dave was on the sandy floor of the cave below, and steam was rising from his jacket. Dave shot Marty an exasperated glare.

"Hey, watch it. This is my favorite jacket."

"Stand back," Marty shouted, and Sully turned in time to see him angle the knife toward Noah's throat.

She met Noah's eyes and saw a familiar terror, one she recognized from her own experience with this man. That day he'd pushed her down the hallway, and she'd fallen in front of the mirror… She'd seen her expression, seen the fear, the desperation…the depths she'd allowed herself to sink to. She saw that same fear, that same desperation in her friend's son. Something snapped inside her. Rage—but not fiery and unpredictable. No, this anger filled her like a cold, calm curtain of control.

She stepped closer. "You can't hurt him," she told Marty, her eyes on his.

"Oh, and who's going to stop me? You?"

She shook her head. "No." She lifted her chin in Noah's direction. "He is."

"He's a little badass," Dave called as he grasped the lip of the ramp and pulled himself up and over. He rose to his feet and winked at Noah. "Aren't you, buddy?"

Noah looked at Dave, then nodded faintly.

Marty smirked, then brought the knife down.

The blade halted about half a foot away from his body. Marty frowned and tried again. Again, he faltered, as though the knife encountered an invisible barrier.

Marty looked up at her and Dave, his eyes wide. "What have you done?" he rasped.

"You're not the only one who can draw symbols," Dave responded as he came up to Sully's side. "Only I'm better at it."

"He's protected," Sully told Marty. "It's over. You can't make your quota."

Marty shook his head. "No," he bellowed, his face blooming with the heat of his rage. He shoved Noah, who screamed as he stumbled and fell over the edge of the ramp. Dave launched himself over the edge, diving for the boy. He caught Noah midfall and twisted so that his body bore the full brunt of the landing on the cave floor about twelve feet below.

Sully screamed, racing to the edge of the ramp to look down. Dave wheezed, but he gave her a thumbs-up signal. She turned around to see Marty running farther up the ramp. The witch leaped across a divide to a rock ledge. He scurried along to a tunnel opening and disappeared.

She hesitated, then Dave groaned.

"No," he gasped, his hand to his chest. He lifted his gaze to Sully. "I'm warming up. He's got someone back there."

She turned and ran, heart in her throat as she jumped over the gap between ramp and rock ledge. She hissed as her hands slammed into the rock wall, and she almost bounced back. She clasped a rock bulge to prevent herself from plummeting backward into the cave. Taking a deep breath, she scurried along the ledge, hugging the wall until she reached the tunnel, and then started to run.

It was so dark. Sully braced her hands outward, using her contact with the wall of the tunnel as a guide. A strangled scream echoed down the tunnel, and she sped up, stumbling along until the tunnel opened up into another smaller cavern. She skidded to a halt. A shaft of light came through an opening in the roof of the cavern, almost like a natural skylight. The light was weak, though, and growing dimmer.

A man lay cowering on the floor, Marty straddled his body. His hands and feet were tied, and his yells were muffled by his gag as he shook his head rapidly at Marty. A woman lay on the ground nearby, her wrists and ankles bound, tears streaking her face. Marty raised his hand and the blade gleamed in the weak light.

Sully reacted. She ran toward him, her hand pulling out one of her belt blades as she did. She raised her hand behind her ear and flung the blade.

Chapter 23

The woman screamed. Marty cried out in pain as the blade sliced across the back of his clenched fist, and he dropped his knife.

Sully leaped, her legs out in front, and caught Marty in the back with her foot. He tumbled off the man, and Sully landed heavily on the rocky ground, rolling with her momentum to gain her feet and spin around.

The null on the floor rolled rapidly away from Marty and kept rolling until he hit a boulder.

Marty reached for his knife as he rose to his knees, then his feet. His face was grim and full of anger as he faced Sully.

"You bitch," he said through gritted teeth. Sully put both her hands out, knees bent, waiting for his move. Marty started to laugh. "You think you can fight me?" He tossed the blade, letting it turn in his hand. Sully flinched at the nonchalance of his movement. "These are nulls, Sully. You have no power here."

Sully licked her lips, her gaze darting to the couple on the ground to the left. The man stretched his hand out and grasped the hilt of the blade she'd thrown at Marty. She brought her gaze back to the maddened witch in front of her. As long as she had his attention, he wouldn't realize the purebloods were cutting through their restraints.

She just had to keep him occupied long enough for them to escape…her, against the only witch to ever be able to use the null effect to his advantage. She swallowed.

"See, this is your problem, Marty," she told him, shaking her head as she sidestepped to the right. His gaze followed her—away from the bound couple on the ground. "You never got it."

He smirked, and she had to wonder what on earth she'd ever seen in this man who was becoming even more unattractive to her. "What's that, Sully?"

"You were always thirsty for magic, you always craved it and you never realized that magic isn't the only form of power," she said softly. She flexed her wrists, and her sai swords ejected from their sheaths, sliding along her arms until she grasped their hilts.

He grinned and his left eyebrow rose at the move. "You think you can take me on?" he asked silkily. "Do you forget all those times, Sully, when you were cowering on our living room floor, or beside the bed, quivering?" He spread his arms out. "That—that was power. And you always gave it to me."

Her eyes narrowed. "Well, I guess I'm taking it back."

She launched herself at him, and he brought his blade

up. The clink and clank of blades striking each other filled the cave, little sparks coming off as the metals collided. Sully moved rapidly, spinning and ducking. A movement caught her eye. The couple had freed themselves, and were running toward the tunnel.

Her distraction cost her. She hissed when she felt the hot slice against her forearm. Marty had cut her.

He gave her a triumphant grin—until he saw the couple dart down the tunnel behind her. He shifted his gaze back to hers. "You bitch."

This time she smirked at him. "You have no idea."

She flicked her wrists, drawing her blades along her forearms in a defensive yet elegant move. His eyes narrowed and he came at her again, his blade flashing. Over and over, she blocked his strikes, the clash of metal ringing through the cave. He was forcing her back, his eyes wide with fury, his teeth bared.

She stepped back and halted. Her back was to the wall. Marty smiled.

Sully flicked the sai swords around to an offensive position, then started twirling them. She got faster and faster as she stepped forward, and Marty was forced to step back, unable to penetrate her wall of whirling blades.

"Martin Steedbeck," a familiar voice bellowed from within the tunnel. Dave.

She waggled her eyebrows at Marty. "Ooh, you're in trouble now."

"In accordance with Nature's Law, passed down by the Ancients, you have been found guilty, and for your dark crimes, the Ancestors call upon your return to the Other Realm, to a place of execution—"

Marty roared, lashing out with his feet and kicking Sully's knee out from under her. She fell to the floor, her knee landing hard on the rock surface. Marty smacked one sword out of her grasp, and grabbed hold of her other wrist as he stepped behind her, his knife at her neck. "Drop it."

He squeezed her wrist, and she could feel her fingers tingle. Her grasp relaxed on the blade, and it clanged as it fell to the stone floor.

Dave emerged from the tunnel. He stopped talking when he saw Sully on her knees, Mental Marty's knife to her throat.

"I don't recognize Nature's Law," Marty rasped, panting.

"It recognizes you," Dave said in a low, dangerous voice. He removed his sunglasses, sliding them casually into the inside breast pocket of his jacket. Son. Of. A. Bitch. He had to fight the natural instinct to go berserk all over the witch's ass.

The tip of the blade pressed under Sully's chin, and she had to tilt her head back to avoid it piercing her skin.

"Get up," Marty hissed to her. She rose to her feet, very carefully. One stumble, one awkward lean, and she could end up with a knife in her skull.

Dave's heart was in his throat. His fists clenched. He could still sense the nulls in the cave system, although their effect was weakening. Tyler was guiding Noah and the couple he'd almost cannoned into on the rock ledge outside. He'd told the sheriff to clear the area of nulls. If there were any nearby, they'd mute his capacity to fight this witch, and Marty would have the advantage.

"You're going to be fine, Sully," Dave said, trying to keep his voice calm and warm for her benefit, when he really wanted to bellow with rage at this witch putting the woman he loved at risk. He tried to convey all the hell he was going to visit on this witch with his eyes. "Don't even think about hurting her."

A clap of thunder reverberated throughout the cave. Sully glanced upward. The sky that she could glimpse at the end of the shaft was dark gray, and a flash of lightning jolted across the diameter of the shaft.

"Can you feel the power in the air, Witch Hunter?" Marty asked as he started to back toward the shaft. "That's *my* power. I created that."

Dave advanced, his shoulders moving in a way that made him look like a big cat stalking prey. Sully shuffled along with Marty, the knife at her neck silently urging her movement.

"But you can't complete the spell," Dave told him. Noah was protected. The other two nulls had escaped.

Marty shrugged. "Then I simply complete it between now and the summer solstice. I only need two more." He stepped up on a rock, and Sully hissed at the painful little prick under her chin. "Up."

"Sully," Dave's voice was low.

She gave him a shaky smile. "Trust me," she said in a tremulous voice. "It's going to be all right."

Marty laughed. "I don't think you're going to be able to make this feel better, Sully."

Dave frowned, his silver gaze full of concern. Sully was…calm. Alarmingly so. She slowly slid her hand to her belt. *Trust me,* she mouthed at him.

His mouth opened and his gaze flicked between hers and Marty's. Aw, hell. She could get herself killed.

He'd heard their fight through the tunnel, and he'd seen her display back at the motel. He'd been fairly confident she could protect herself—until she wound up with a knife at her throat. He wanted to blast Mental

Marty. He wanted to annihilate the bastard. That was his job. He did this alone.

His gaze met Sully's. She was pleading with him with her eyes. It wasn't like he didn't *want* to trust her, but…she was in a vulnerable position.

And she's armed to the teeth and knows more about personal safeguarding than he may ever learn. Damn it. He hated this. It was anathema to him, letting a woman—a woman in a vulnerable position—call the shots. But it was Sully. He had no idea what she was thinking, but she knew *something*…this was the woman who'd managed to hold her own against him, who could block an invasive threat to her mind and magic as easily as swatting a fly.

His frown deepened, but then he nodded. Just once. He kept his gaze on Marty. He could distract the witch, at least. "The Ancestors call upon your return to the Other Realm, to a place of execution, until you are dead. May the Ancestors—"

Sully's movement was graceful as she slid her blade from her belt and caught Marty's knife-wielding hand. She jerked it back, and Marty roared—and Dave winced—at the audible snap of bone. The knife fell to the ground, and she held his hand close to her body as she twisted and knelt. Marty flipped over her head, his feet flying through the air, as she used that same move on the man she'd used on Dave in the motel room. Marty yelled, his head tilting back as he cried out in pain. Dave ran forward, but the witch sat up, hands outstretched, and a wave of power rolled through the cavern. Dave was knocked backward, as was Sully. By the time he rolled over onto his back, Marty was hastily climbing the shaft toward the darkened sky above.

Dave bolted across the floor to Sully, who was just sitting up. "Are you all right?" he asked.

She nodded, then pointed at the shaft. "Go. I'm fine."

Dave sprinted across the cavern floor, leaping up over a boulder to grasp a bulge in the wall, and he started hauling himself up after the witch.

Sully stumbled to the bottom of the shaft. She wasn't anywhere near as fast as Dave, or that skunk, Marty. Her heart was pounding. Dave. All she could think about was Dave. Marty was strong. She could sense it in him. She would have tried to draw some of that power out of him, when he held her, but he would have sensed it immediately, and she couldn't get her magic on with a knife in the brain.

Her foot slipped and she gasped, clinging to the rock face. A ladder. A ladder would be really good about now. She kept climbing. The light was almost nonexistent now, and she was feeling her way up the rock wall.

Her arms were shaking by the time she got to the top and could feel the grass around the edge of the hole. She raised her leg, using it to lever herself out awkwardly. Panting, she looked around.

Oh. My. God. Clouds were swirling as though caught in a twister. Lightning flashed among the fiercely spinning clouds, illuminating the dark strands of a lethal magic. The sea at the bottom of the cliff showed white peaks as the waves roiled and rolled, as though caught in Mother Nature's washing machine. The wind was biting, and she had to bend forward to avoid being pushed back by its gale force.

Marty had tried to blast Dave with a ball of power, and Dave was currently holding it off. Streams of dark red fire were swirling toward him, but she could see they were slowly getting closer to him. She forced one leg in front of the other, her arms up to protect her face from the wind whipping at her. Her shirt cracked like a sail caught in a thunderstorm, and she could feel the fabric tear.

She had to help Dave.

As though sensing her, Dave turned his head, his silver eyes bright in the darkness. "Go away," he called to her.

She shook her head. She summoned her power, raising her hands toward Marty. He noticed her, and braced one hand in her direction. She reeled back under the impact of the blast, but managed to stop the dark fire from consuming her.

"Leave, Sully," Dave roared, his focus now on the witch.

Sully slowly crept forward, gritting her teeth as she tried to find her wedge through the wall of power Marty had thrown up. Marty was able to keep them both at bay, and his eyes brightened when he realized this. He was strong...too strong. Tears filled Sully's eyes at the realization.

She couldn't fight him off, not in a power struggle. His death magic was too powerful for her, and for Dave. A dark flame danced across her arm, and she screamed at the burn. Marty was going to kill them.

Dave shifted toward her, protective to the last. An idea hit her. She dropped her shields and mentally reached out for Dave. She felt his surprise, his confusion and then his acceptance. He reached back for her, and she grasped his hand. Marty started to fade in her vision as shards of light transferred between her and Dave. Blues, pinks, purples, the spears of light brightened. She sent Dave a mental image, and he squeezed her hand. Together they started to recite a spell, the Old Language glowing across her vision, like a magical teleprompter.

Marty frowned, wincing as his right hand started to glow. The force coming from him stuttered a little, then flicked on to high wattage, before stuttering again. Marty glanced down at his hand, turning it over. Sully and Dave continued to chant, but then spread their arms out, calling on the tempest around them, drawing in the elements—the wind buffeting them, the water crashing below them, the spark of lightning fire and the solid ground beneath them.

Marty's eyes widened when he saw the mark Sully had carved onto his hand when she'd thrown him in the cavern below. His gaze flicked to hers, and full comprehension dawned on him.

"No," he cried, trying to blast them away. Harnessing the power of the tempest, they rebuffed his attempt to incinerate them.

The mark on his hand glowed, and his skin began to blister. His face roiled, and he screamed in pain as his bones melted into another's features. First Jenny, then Susanne… Jack, Amanda, Mary Anne and Gary. Each time his face twisted, Marty screamed. He clutched at his skull, but the fire from within consumed him, his flesh melting as his bones turned to ash, plucked away in all directions by the wind.

Sully weaved on her feet, her hand gripping Dave's until they both fell to their knees. Sully dropped his hand, catching herself before she face-planted in the wet grass. Thunder roared, and lightning cracked, the blade of light spearing downward from the spinning clouds above.

The lightning hit Dave square in the chest, and he

arched under the shock, his silver eyes glowing as the energy coursed through his body. Sully screamed as his lips pulled back, and for a brief moment his teeth glowed, his veins glowed, even his bones seemed to glow. And then the charge was gone, and Dave sagged to the ground.

"Oh, my God, Dave. Dave!" Sully hurried over to him, reaching for him carefully. She pressed her hand to his neck, her eyes closing when she felt his racing pulse, but even as she held her fingers against his skin, she could feel it start slow down.

"Dave, please be okay," she whispered as she cupped his cheeks. His eyelids fluttered, and it took a few attempts before he was able to force his eyes open. His silver-gray gaze met hers, and he gave her an exhausted smile.

"Well, that was shocking."

She laughed, her hands trembling, and she had to blink away tears of relief. "You are such a dick."

He lifted his shoulders.

"No, no, lie—"

He brushed aside her attempts to make him lie down, and she helped him sit up. She glanced up. The lightning was no more, and the clouds were no longer a whirling mess. They drifted slowly across the sky, revealing the night stars and the harvest moon.

"What was that?" she asked. Where had that lightning come from? Marty was dead. Incinerated. She didn't think it had been his hand that had called forth the spear of lightning.

Dave hissed, pulling at the neckline of his T-shirt and ripping it down the front.

Sully gaped. All of the markings on his body glowed on his skin, and then slowly faded, disappearing into smoke. All save one.

In the Old Language, emblazoned across his heart, was one name.

Sullivan Timmerman.

Dave gaped at his chest, then slowly raised his eyes to hers. "I—I think I just retired."

"What?" Sully gasped. She stared at his bare chest. His glorious, smooth, muscled bare chest, adorned with just her name. She smiled. All of those names, the proof of the Ancestors' hold over him, had disappeared.

Dave touched himself, then shrugged out of his jacket and the remnants of his T-shirt. He twisted about, turning his arms over. "They're gone," he breathed, stunned.

He looked up at her, and she smiled. "They're gone," he shouted, then clasped her head and brought her in for a kiss. She laughed against his lips, and collapsed against his magnificent chest. She smoothed her hands over him, testing for herself. The names were definitely gone.

Dave ended the kiss and rested his forehead against hers. His chest rose and fell with his pants, and she felt him shake his head gently against hers.

"You linked with me," he breathed.

She nodded. "I wanted to help you."

He closed his eyes in relief, in gratitude. "Thank you," he whispered, and kissed her sweetly.

Shouts drifted across the cliff top, and they both turned to the source. Flashlights were cutting swathes in the darkness, and Sully smiled when she saw the familiar faces of Tyler and Jacob, and Noah being carried by his father.

"Oh, look. LB." Dave slung his arm around her shoulders, and leaned in close to her ear. "I might be the king of badass, but you're the queen of whoop ass."

Chapter 24

Dave watched as the tall, dark-haired men emerged from the null council meeting. Both men had dark hair, both men had blue eyes, but both men were as different as night and day.

"Who are they?" Sully asked, curious. Dave slung his arm over her shoulders as the men approached, lazily inhaling her entrancing sent of rose, vanilla and… sunshine. She was wearing a pretty red summer dress, with buttons all the way from the V neckline to the hem. She looked so beautiful, so…feminine. He still marveled at the way she'd fought Mental Marty, and just how damn lethal she could be. She was smoking hot and fought like a ninja. He was in love.

"Friends," he said, finally answering her question.

One of the men shuddered, shaking out his shoulders. "I want out of here. It's weird," he muttered.

Dave's smile broadened. "Sully Timmerman, allow me to introduce Lucien Marchetta."

The lean vampire nodded at her, his smile quick and almost nonexistent. "Sully."

Dave gestured to the other man strolling toward him. He had a slightly more muscular build, particularly across his shoulders and in his arms. "And this is Ryder Galen. Ryder, this is Sully."

Ryder smiled and held out his hand. "Hi, Sully."

Sully shook his hand out of politeness. Cheers erupted inside the town hall, and her eyebrows rose. "Does someone want to tell me what's going on?"

A blond-haired woman skipped out of the hall, a wide smile on her face, and she caught up with the men, sliding her hand into Lucien's.

"And this lovely lady is Natalie Segova," Dave said, gesturing at the woman by Lucien's side.

"Marchetta," Lucien corrected, frowning. He glanced down at the woman by his side, and his frown disappeared, replaced by a genuine smile. "Her name's Natalie Marchetta, now."

"Hi," Natalie said, extending her hand. Dave's smile broadened. Natalie was a sweetheart, and her warm smile was contagious.

Sully shook the woman's hand, smiling back at her. "Hi, I'm Sully." His gaze stayed on Sully. She looked so relaxed, so…happy. He couldn't stop looking at her, and he could see out of the corner of his eye that Ryder was smirking at him. He would have frowned at the guy, but that would mean looking away from Sully, and well…he preferred this view.

There were more cheers inside, and Sully's brow dipped in confusion. "Okay, now I'm really curious. What's going on?"

Lucien shuddered again. "I'm paying my debt." He arched an eyebrow at Dave. "We're even."

Dave nodded. "Yes, we are."

Lucien strolled over to a dark car and opened the passenger door for his wife. Natalie slid inside, and waved at them as Lucien climbed in, started the engine and drove off.

"Wait—did you say Marchetta?" Sully gasped as she finally recognized the name. "The vampires?"

"Well, technically Lucien and Natalie are hybrids. Ryder here is a light warrior."

"But, why are they all here? I would have thought vampires—sorry, hybrids—and light warriors would want to avoid Serenity Cove."

Dave shrugged. "I think Lucien Marchetta was overcome by a sudden desire to contribute to the community. The Marchetta Corporation has just established an investment program with the fishing co-op here."

Sully gaped. "Why?"

He grinned. "Because Lucien Marchetta owes me one, as does his wife."

"What did Natalie do?" Ryder queried calmly.

"She's researched the requirements for a request of recognition of the nulls as a breed on their own, and will oversee the submission process."

He enjoyed Sully's stunned expression. "Seriously?"

He nodded. "Seriously."

Sully turned to Ryder. "So…why are you here, if you don't mind me asking?"

Ryder smiled. "I'm also paying my debt. Dave mentioned that your closest medical clinic is over an hour away. My brother and I will help set up a clinic here for the nulls, and run the training programs for staff."

Sully turned and gaped at him. "You did this?"

Dave frowned. She was looking at him weirdly. "Not by myself—I had help."

"Dave, this will help them so much," Sully exclaimed softly.

He shifted uncomfortably. This is why he'd preferred to stay outside while the hybrids and the light warrior made their announcements. He didn't need the thanks, he preferred just quietly getting on with things and then disappearing.

The town hall doors were flung open, and Mrs. Forsyth scanned the street. She squealed when she saw them standing across the road. Darn. Was it too late to disappear?

"I'm out of here," Ryder said, and quickly jogged to his car.

Dave glanced about. His bike was down the block, and him running away would look fairly obvious to the little lady who was now hurrying across to them. He eyed Ryder's car enviously as his friend drove away. Darn, he could move fast.

"David, thank you."

He tried not to cringe outwardly as Mrs. Forsyth hurried up to him, her arms open wide. Only his mother called him Dav—

"David, you are so lovely," she said softly as she hugged him, and he had to lean down, she was so short. He patted her shoulder awkwardly. This was sooo uncomfortable. But nice, in its weird little way.

"It's nothing, Mrs. Forsyth," he said, embarrassed as Jacob walked out of the town hall, arms folded. The fisherman grinned when he saw Dave's discomfort. Dave shot a pleading look at Sully, who shrugged, grinning.

Traitor, he mouthed.

"You have to come over for dinner," Mrs. Forsyth exclaimed as she stepped back. Dave straightened and tried to make his disappointment look sincere.

"Oh, I wish we could, but Sully and I are on our way out today," he told her.

Mrs. Forsyth blinked. "You're leaving?"

He nodded, then grunted when Noah threw himself against Dave's legs.

"Don't leave, KB!" Noah cried, hugging him fiercely.

Damn it. He hadn't bargained on the kid. Something warm flared in his heart, and he smiled tightly. He wasn't going to get sucked in. He was the rolling stone that gathered no moss. The tattoo artist that could up and leave at the drop of a hat, the retired Witch Hunter who could disintegrate another, how could—

Noah looked up at him. "Please?" the boy begged. Those green eyes, that quivering bottom lip...those freckles. That warm spot turned into goop. Mushy, fluffy goop. Dave was touched, so touched that these people were welcoming him so warmly. He could understand how Sully viewed these people as family. He'd had more physical contact, more interaction with this community than he had any of the covens back in Irondell—including his mother's.

"We'll come back," Dave promised.

"You swear?" Noah demanded.

Dave grinned. "I swear."

A shadow fell over him, and he looked up. Aw, darn. The royal dick.

Jacob held out his hand. "Thanks," the fisherman said. Dave accepted his shake, and winced as Jacob also thumped him on the shoulder. "For everything." Jacob's gaze slid to Sully, who was now talking to Mrs. Forsyth. "Take good care of her."

Dave nodded. "I will."

Then there was George, and Noah's sister, the sheriff and a whole bunch of others who wanted to come shake his—oh, wow, a hug. He nodded at Cheryl, the waitress, then stepped back toward Sully. He didn't miss the sheriff's gaze narrowing as he eyed the farewell.

"We should get going," Dave whispered in Sully's ear.

"Where are you going?" Jacob asked, squinting against the sun.

"Holiday," Dave informed them without giving too much information away, then waved as he and Sully managed to step away from the group. He handed her the helmet from his pannier, but hung on to it until she met his gaze.

"Are you sure you want to do this?" he asked, solemnly. It was a big move, for Sully. They'd decided to take a break—his first. Ever. Wherever they wanted to go, whatever they wanted to do...together.

She glanced down the street toward the small crowd gathered outside the town hall. She sighed. "You were right. I was hiding here. I love it here, but...you're right. This was my bolt-hole. I think I'm ready to travel, see some sights. Maybe even visit my coven." She nodded. "I want to do this."

He leaned forward and kissed her tenderly. "I'm looking forward to meeting your coven," he murmured. Then he grinned. "I'm also looking forward to introducing you to my family." He tilted his head. "Just don't mention your books."

She laughed as she slid the helmet on over her head. "I won't."

Her coven's archives were in a very safe place, and she'd pointed out to him that she could set up her factory…anywhere. They were going to keep things casual, see which way the wind blew.

He grinned. "Come on, sweetness. Let's go."

Sully stretched as Dave drove onto the grassy shoulder. He kicked down the bike stand and she slid off the bike as he cut the engine. She removed her helmet.

"Wow," she breathed, taking in the view. Chains of islands could be seen in the distance. "This is beautiful."

Dave made a sound of agreement as he removed his own helmet and straightened, his legs still straddling the bike. He crossed his arms over the helmet and lifted his face to the sky.

She took the time to appreciate the view—of him. His short hair ruffled in the light breeze. His sunglasses hid his eyes, but his face—it was probably the most relaxed she'd ever seen him.

"How are you?" she asked him as she walked toward him.

He looked at her. "I'm feeling great."

She gestured to his chest. "How do you feel about… the names?" They hadn't really spoken about anything in great detail. Nothing concrete about the future. Nothing concrete about a commitment—although this was the first time she'd up and left with a man. She wasn't quite sure how he felt about his change in circumstance, or what he wanted to do about his future…about them.

He shrugged out of his jacket, and then drew his T-shirt over his head. She looked about. They'd left the main highway about forty minutes ago, and hadn't seen a car since. Nor were there any buildings within view. This place, watching out over the ocean, seeing land in the distance…it felt like they were the only two people left in the world.

Dave glanced down at his chest. "It's…weird," he admitted.

"Weird, how? Like you've lost an arm, or something?" She couldn't begin to imagine what it would be like, having something that was such a part of you, that defined you, to a certain extent, suddenly disappear.

Dave shook his head. "No, not quite. More like an ache that you noticed you had, but only when it's gone."

She stepped close and ran her hand over his shoulder. "What do you think you'll do, now that you're not a Witch Hunter?"

His arm slid around her waist, and he tugged her close so that she was pressed along his side. Emotions fluttered at her. Attraction. Desire. Contentment. And something warmer, something deeper she was too afraid to identify. He removed his sunglasses, and his silver eyes stared at her intently. "I think I want to live a little, remind myself that life's not all about death." He leaned forward and kissed the corner of her mouth.

She sucked in a breath. "Oh?"

He nuzzled her ear. "Yeah. You taught me that." His voice was so deep, it practically vibrated in his chest.

She swallowed. "I did?"

"Yeah. You taught me…not to piss off a chick with a knife," he said, kissing along her jaw. Her nipples tightened in her bra, and she forced herself to focus on his kiss. *No! Words. Focus on his words.*

"Oh?"

"Yeah. You also taught me…that nulls are kind of nice. Even the ones called Jacob." He ran his lips down her neck, and she trembled.

"Uh, okay…"

"But mostly you taught me that I don't have to do this alone. Any of it." He lifted her over the bike, so that she straddled it, facing him. The skirt of her dress hiked up with the movement, baring her thighs. He pulled her close, and she wrapped her legs around his hips. He cupped her cheek.

"Sully, I don't care what I do, or where I go—as long as it's with you." His stare was so solemn, so full of promise. "Whatever my life holds, I want to share it with you."

She blinked, overcome with the weight of his words... A weight that, if uttered by another man, at another time, would have felt crushing, but here, with this man, right now, it felt...right.

"You've taught me a few things, too," she murmured shyly.

His eyebrow arched, and he gave her a wicked look that heated her from the inside out. "Oh, I'm listening."

"You taught me that not all men in sunglasses are douchebags," she said, and his lips curved. Amusement, light and teasing, tapped at her. He leaned forward and kissed her, long and slow. He pressed her back, and she found herself lying back against the bike. "Uh-huh," he said, a soft, husky sound of encouragement.

"You taught me that leather can look good on, but much better off," she said, trailing her hand over his bare chest.

Desire. Hot. Hard. Gripping. It flooded him, and it flooded her. Her fingers trailed over the tattoo above his heart, her nails lightly scraping his nipple. She smiled when he swallowed, and then closed her eyes as he kissed his way across her collarbone.

His fingers slid beneath the neckline of her dress, and she felt the top button pop out of its loop.

She opened her eyes, staring up at the blue, cloud-less sky. "But mostly, you taught me that I had closed myself off, that I didn't have anyone to truly share myself with, to talk with, to laugh with…"

He raised his head, his gaze meeting hers.

"You taught me that it was okay to trust again, Dave," she told him earnestly. "You taught me that a man could be safe." She smiled. "You taught me something that I hadn't even realized about myself…that I'd become a shadow, closing myself off to everyone. You taught me to open up, again."

He kissed her hungrily. "I love you," he whispered, kissing her over and over again. She arched her back, pressing her breasts against his chest, feeling his cock harden in his jeans. His fingers slid to the next button, and the next, and he peeled her dress open.

"I love you, too. So much," she said. She pulled back her mental walls, letting in his light, letting in the warmth of his love and feeding it back to him, firmly establishing their link. He groaned, caressing her, kissing his way across her chest. His hands slid under her, unclipping her bra and pulling it down her arms and off. She fumbled with the zipper of his jeans, sighing when she could feel the heavy, hard weight of him in her hand.

He drew back, just a little, his expression raw. "I will always be there for you, Sully. You're my everything."

"And you're the light to my darkness," she whispered against his lips, then kissed him, her tongue sliding in to tangle with his. The lace of her panties pulled taut across her hips until the fabric gave, the soft tear causing her to shudder as her desire turned her core into a slick channel.

She guided him inside her, and she moaned with pleasure as his length slid inside. When he was buried to the hilt, paused, then withdrew. His thrusts were long and slow, gradually quickening. She held on to his arms, and he grasped the handlebars. She moaned, the delicious friction of his body against hers, inside hers, sent her tingling. His eyes met hers, and they moved against each other, panting, linked physically, magically, emotionally, until it was too much, the pleasure, the sensations and sparks exploded around them. Sully cried out as she orgasmed, and Dave shouted his pleasure, out there in the middle of nowhere, bare to each other.

Dave swallowed, and Sully laughed with delight, experiencing a freedom, and a lightness of heart she'd never felt before.

Dave grinned and pressed his forehead against hers. "I give you my heart, sweetness."

She grinned back as she stroked her hand over the one tattoo that still marked his body. "You'd better. It's got my name on it."

He put his hand over hers, holding it there. "This is permanent, you know."

She wasn't sure if he meant the tattoo, or if he meant their commitment. Either way, she agreed. She nodded. "I know."

He leaned down, and they kissed, under a clear blue sky—with not a storm cloud in sight.

* * * * *